ALSO BY JAMES NOLL

Tales of the Weird
A Knife in the Back
You Will Be Safe Here
Burn All The Bodies
Mad Tales (Compendium)
Don't Turn Around (Illustrated Compendium)
Thirteen Tales (Short Story Compilation)

The Bonesaw Trilogy
The Rabbit, The Jaguar, & The Snake

The Topher Trilogy (Novels):
Raleigh's Prep
Tracker's Travail
Topher's Ton
The Topher Trilogy (Omnibus)

The Hive (Serialized Novel):
Seasons 1-4

Audio Books
A Knife in the Back
Thirteen Tales

The Hive: Seasons 1-4
The Wounded, The Sick, & The Dead

The Wounded, the Sick, & the Dead

JAMES NOLL

PULP!

Horror, Post-Apocalyptic, and Science Fiction

THE WOUNDED, THE SICK, & THE DEAD.
Copyright © 2019 by James Noll
All rights reserved. Printed in the United States of America.

Book Design by James Noll

Author Photo by Haley Noll

ISBN: 978-1-7337443-2-4

For Amber Johnson, who reads all my stuff and encourages me to mock Kevvie.

This is also for Kevvie, who is a massive tool.

CONTENTS

THE CATALYST

Milo should have paid better attention in school. It was a common lament, one usually remedied by marriage and children, but he felt it more acutely than most and much, much earlier. If he had read more books, solved more equations, written more papers, completed more labs, worked on more projects, memorized more facts, studied more languages, run for student government, tried out for the tennis team, joined more clubs, perhaps his life would have ended up differently.

But he didn't do those things.

He was what many educationists referred to as a "non-traditional" student, one who demonstrated proficiency in subjects not necessarily part of the standard curriculum: Desk-Sleeping, Plagiarism, Math Homework Transcription, Lap-Texting, Small-Screen Video Games, Social Media Shit Posting, Music Listening (with hand gestures and occasional lyric recitation), Off-Campus Dining Sprints, Back of School Spliffing, and other such specialties. The only thing he really wanted to do, the only thing he felt he was good at, the only thing he felt the need to perfect time and time again, despite setbacks, failure, catastrophe, disaster, debacle, loss, dud, flop, and defeat, was draw.

Comics.

Superheroes, specifically.

He'd even created a series: The Adventures of Holly Huntress, Warrior Woman of the Galaxy, who he modeled after Jennifer Reed, the most beautiful girl in school. Smart and funny, with a GPA in, as far as he knew, the upper twelve hundreds, Jennifer Reed was completely out of Milo's league; drawing her was as close as he'd ever get to actual communication, which was why he did it. His book featured a scantily clad Holly running around in space losing items of clothing, sometimes one piece at a time, sometimes all at once, while fighting aliens. He was currently on volume three.

Milo's favorite thing to do was skip school and work on his book, and his favorite to place to skip school and work on his book was what everybody called The Outdoor Classroom, which was really a little clearing in the woods behind the school with a few rustic benches made out of plywood and two by fours surrounded by tree stumps. Though the student handbook expressly forbade the creation of any kind of flame, be it by lighter, bomb, or tinder, a fire pit squatted in the middle for some reason. He liked to sit on one of the stumps and smoke weed and draw his comics.

One morning in the middle of March, Milo skipped Biology to sit in the outdoor classroom and smoke and try to get Jennif— Holly's—breasts just right. He had posed her so that, while escaping the clutches of the termite men of planet Petrifaction, one of them ripped off her shirt while she was spinning in the air, and since he'd never seen live breasts, let alone live breasts subjected to that kind of g-force, it was difficult for him to achieve the perfect balance, given their weight and size. He imagined there would be a certain warble and lift, and though he was sure it wasn't totally necessary, he wanted to make the bumps on each areola anatomically correct. After a long stretch of drawing and erasing and shading and erasing again, he had just put his sketchbook down to take a break and stand and stretch his back when a yellow tabby appeared at his feet and meowed at him.

"Hey, kitty," he said.

He reached out to pet it and it nosed his fingers and meowed again. Milo scratched it behind its ears and it purred and purred and, taken with its cuteness, he picked it up and held it to his chest. It purred some more and even licked the back of his hand.

"Such a cute little guy," he said, smiling.

As every feline owner knew, there was a switch in cats that turned them from coy and doting to ferocious and savage. One could be scratching a cat behind its ears, and the cat could be purring and pressing itself into the pet, really digging it, when all of the sudden the switch would be flicked, and the cat pounced, aggressive and merciless, and attempt to dismember the fool who dared show it affection.

This was what happened to Milo. One second the cat was purring in his arms, cradled and content, and then the next it lost its mind and bit him on the hand, puncturing the skin, and he found himself standing on a lonesome stretch of broken highway in the middle of the desert.

Milo dropped it, yelling "Ow!", and brought his hand to his lips to suck on the wound. The cat sprinted off into the desert brush, a little trail of dust in its wake.

It was then that he realized that he was no longer in the outdoor classroom, no longer in his dimension or world at all. The sky was strange. The air was strange. His clothes were strange. A leather duster. Cowboy boots. Salmon colored western shirt tucked into black jeans. A backpack seemingly filled with encyclopedias or hunks of iron.

At the sound of his voice, the shuffling dead thing behind him turned around and grabbed him by the shoulder. He spun to see what it was and it fell on him and chomped into his neck and—

Milo appeared on the highway again. Strange sky. Strange air. Strange clothes. Did that just happen? His hand flew up to his neck but it was fine. The cat wiggled in his grasp and scratched him and he cried "Ow!" but the second he did, his eyes went wide and he spun around and the zombie was on him, it's teeth chomping into his—

Milo appeared on the highway again. Stiff wind. Sulphur. Duster. Jeans. Cat. He tossed it away before it could scratch him and spun around, already backing away. There wasn't just one zombie on the road but a horde of them. Horde. Was that the right word?

According to his video games, a horde was . . . a horde? Big? Bigger than what he was looking at. This was more like a group, but 'group' sounded too harmless. So did 'bunch' and 'clump'. 'Assortment' sounded like flowers or candy. Maybe it was a knot. Or a cluster. Assemblage didn't work. He snorted. Who used that word, anyway? Screw it. This was a . . . a . . . a pack! Yes! A pack! A pack of zombies!

As he was determining this, his foot got stuck in a deep crack in the highway, and he fell backwards and broke his ankle. The pack of the dead heard his cries and turned for him as one . . .

Wind. Duster. Jeans. Throw the cat away and run. Run as far and as fast as you can. The road is cracked there. Watch out for that pothole. When you've made it far enough, when your pot-saturated lungs can take no more (how far did you run? A mile? Less?), toss a panicked look over your shoulder and take a step out into thin air where the bridge that crossed the canyon below used to be. The momentary joy of flying will be wiped out by the terror of the spiked concrete pylons toward which you're rapidly falling.

Wind. Duster. Jeans. Cat. Run forward five steps and stop. Immediately. Take special care to avoid the cracks in the road and the clumps of erupted asphalt. Turn.

The zombies were still there, but they hadn't heard or seen him yet. He could breathe. He could finally breathe. He knew that he shouldn't move too quickly or rashly. He knew he should try to stay as quiet as possible. He needed a weapon. The backpack! Of course! The backpack! It must have something he could use.

It clinked as he lowered it to the pavement, and he froze and looked hard at the creatures down the road. They swayed dumbly in the breeze, but they didn't turn. He forced himself to count to sixty before moving again. The bag had a leather flap fastened to the canvas with buckles and buttons, and he carefully undid them and opened it up to have a look. One by one, he withdrew the objects inside: three wires with looped ends, a roll of duct tape, oven mitts, and . . . what was that? He carefully slid a contraption out. It rang metallically as he did so.

Pause.

The zombie nearest to him jerked its head to the right and seemed to sniff the air, listening. Count to sixty. Count to sixty again.

Okay. Back to the backpack. The thing he pulled out looked like a braced crutch, the kind people with cerebral palsy used, only shorter and with a machete substituted for a cane. He put it on his forearm. Perfect.

Something to his left caught his attention. It was the cat, scrambling around in the bush. That didn't seem odd. Cats scrambled. Often for no reason. But this one seemed to be trying to get away from something. It leaped and yowled, finally backing up against a boulder and flattening its ears and hissing. Milo gripped the forearm machete, tense, waiting, and as he watched, a little girl with an enormous head popped out of a hole in the ground and snatched the cat up, giggling.

"Hey!" Milo yelled.

The zombies turned as one and lurched for him, but he was already off the road, running toward the mutant molesting the cat. He didn't particularly care for it (it had bitten him after all. And scratched him), but it was the only thing that connected him to his world, and he felt an odd kinship with it. The mutant shot him an irritated look, her smile fading. She was the most disgusting thing he'd ever seen, with tumors and growths pulsing out of her head, and large, misshapen teeth. She clutched the hissing cat to her chest, tight, too tight, making sure to clamp a knotted hand over its face, and jumped back down into the hole from which she came.

Milo had just started to run when another mutant jumped out of a different hole to his left. It was decidedly larger than the one that stole the cat, with larger tumors deforming its face, neck, and torso. Its muscles bulged with tense sinew as it wound up and sent a devastating blow to his neck, cracking his skull and severing his head from his body.

This time, Milo ducked when the second mutant appeared, feeling the whoosh as the beast's massive paw parted the air above him. He was so ecstatic (and surprised) at his success that he didn't see the thing's other fist until a microsecond before it caved his entire face in.

Count the steps. Duck at twenty-seven. Spin at twenty-eight. There's a pit of bone spikes at thirty-three. Another mutie shoots a poisoned dart at forty-one (that's the toughest). Roll under the decapitator at forty-seven. And then . . . nothing. He'd reached the end of the mutie warren. He'd never done it before. In front of him was a bleak desert. Behind him, a family of psychopathic murder mutants. And behind them, a pack of zombies. What now?

A little creature stuck its head out of a hole a few feet away, and Milo prepared for the worst. First, he saw its whiskers, then its nose, then its beady little eyes and floppy ears and . . . a rabbit? A rabbit. What was a rabbit doing out there? While he was watching, something crawled up under his pants toward his crotch. Screaming, he slapped at it, felt a sting in his thigh, a painful sting that radiated up into his belly. His leg began to swell.

Milo was sitting on the ground sealing both pant legs with the duct tape when he heard the voice crying out.

"Yoo-hoo!"

A figure in the brush on the side of the road opposite the mutie warren waved at him. When he didn't respond, it whistled.

"Hi! Hey! You! Come on! Come here!"

Milo's eyes shifted toward the zombies. They heard the call, too, and they moaned and turned and stumbled off the road, heading toward the sound.

"Hurry! They're coming!"

Milo looked at the mutie warren. He turned around and looked at where the road ended at the canyon.

"I have food! And water!"

Sighing, he ripped the tape and patted it down on his ankle, making sure the seal was as tight as possible. Then he picked up the backpack and ran toward the figure on the horizon.

It was a woman, though he couldn't tell at first. She was covered in dust and dirt, and she was wearing so many layers—dark green cargo pants, brown bomber's jacket, darkly tinted goggles, and a leather helmet and chin strap. It reminded Milo of something he saw on a documentary on WWI, one of the few times he paid attention in class. And her teeth, oh my, her teeth, they were . . . disgusting.

"Come on! Come on!" she urged. "They're coming. Follow me!"

She led him through the desert, sometimes jogging, sometimes speed-walking, a never-ending stream of chatter flowing from her mouth, alternating from gushing over his presence to warnings about the landscape.

"I'm Suzy. What's your handle?"

"What?"

"Your handle! Your honorific, title, tag, moniker, appellation! Your handle!"

"My . . . what?"

"Your name, you idiot! What's your name!"

"Oh, I'm Milo."

"Milo, Milo, rhymes with Fido, dogs are good food, good meat, good God, let's eat!"

"Um—"

"Haha! Haha! Don't mind me. I'm just a crazy old hag. I've been out here for too long, too long. Ever since that damn cat disappeared."

"Cat? Was it a yellow tabby?"

"So nice to get visitors. So nice. And one so accomplished! I've been watching you, I have —watch that spot there—you've learned so fast! So fast! So much faster than—mind that nest. That's a stinger! So much faster than— oh, gotta turn here, that's a bone spike. And it's so nice to—don't ever eat the flowers off of those bushes. They're poison—so nice to have company!"

Suzy led him to a butte, a sheer wall of colorfully striped rock, a natural fortress standing tall and sure in the middle of the inhospitable desert. A rope ladder with steps made out of thick branches hung from a ledge fifty feet above.

"You first, you first," she said. She reached for his pack and he struck her hands away. The woman's face fell from fawning to flat.

"Don't touch me," he said.

She stared at him, or he thought she did; he couldn't see what her eyes were doing behind the dark goggles. For a moment, a very short moment, he felt as though that was the real creature. Then, as if she sensed his realization, a smile flinched across her face, meek and brief, and she said, "Of course, sir. Of course." She performed an elaborate bow. "After you."

The ladder led to a ledge, and in front of the ledge was the opening to a cave. Suzy scrambled up after him, swinging her fat legs over the edge and rolling over once to lie on her back, spreading her limbs as if making an angel in the dirt.

"Home at last! Milo, Milo! Home at last!"

She popped up and trotted past him into the cave, and Milo followed, gripping the handle of this forearm machete. The first oven mitt he duct-taped to it was starting to wear, and he reminded himself to wrap the other one around it when he was done with . . . . whatever this was.

It was dark at first, but soon his eyes adjusted, and he saw that the cave was deeper than he first thought, that the opening served as a kind of vestibule that ended with a natural bend. Suzy had hung torches on the walls which flickered in the darkness, lighting the way back.

"He's here! He's here!" she cried. "Milo, Milo rhymes with Fido!"

The air grew cold and sharp, though he felt moisture. He rounded the bend and stepped into a larger chamber. A fire burned in the middle. Huge metal stakes formed a scaffold around it, something to hold up the wood and tinder, he supposed. Suzy ran around the edge of the cave, lighting torches, singing "He's here! He's here! Milo's here!" She stopped now and then to pat various white busts she had stored in little recessions carved out of the stone.

"Oh yes, Millicent, he is a big one!"

Milo took another step into the room, wondering what the bust named Millicent looked like, and stopped short. Suzy had stored piles and piles of roots at one end. Potatoes. Shallots. Carrots. Ginger. Turnips. Yams.

"Joseph! How dare you imply . . . why, no I don't think he's infected. Are you, Milo"

"Who, me? No."

"See, there, Joseph. Don't you feel foolish?"

Milo leaned over to inspect the pile of food, and his stomach growled involuntarily.

"Hungry, hungry, hungry! Milo's very hungry!"

The roots were piled high enough to cover another bust. Milo was curious to see what kind of face his host chose to immortalize. He started to clear a path, potatoes and yams fell away, and then he saw it. And he gasped.

The bust wasn't made out of marble. It wasn't a bust at all. It was a skull. A human skull. A noise from behind him, the edge of a whisper, and he turned just in time to see Suzy rushing him, wielding a pickaxe.

"Tut, tut, your time is up," she said.

"He's here! He's here! Milo's here!"

Milo gripped his forearm machete as Suzy scuttled around the room, talking to the skulls of her victims.

"Oh yes, Millicent, he is a big one!"

Wander over to the roots. Pretend to look.

"Joseph! How dare you imply . . ."

Out of the corner of his eye, he saw her pick up the pickaxe.

"No, of course not," he said.

"Tut-tut—"

Milo turned and swept his arm back like a pitcher winding up for a fastball. He saw Suzy's axe swinging through the air, the gems in the ceiling of the cave glinting in the fire. He'd never killed a woman before. He'd never killed anybody before. He wondered what it would feel like, to watch her eyes as his weapon sank deep into her body, to see the life drain from them. He flexed his bicep and shoulder, twisted his torso, putting every last ounce of effort and energy into the blow that he meant to deliver. Then his machete chocked into the stone wall behind him and wedged into a tight crevice. It stuck only for a second, but a second was all Suzy needed to finish her own arc and bury her axe in his brain.

This time, Milo extended his arm to make sure there was enough space between the tip of his machete and the wall.

"He's here! He's here! Milo's here!"

"No," Milo replied. "Of course not."

"What?"

Milo paused. Crap. Had she even asked yet?

"You asked me if I was infected, right?"

He peeked at her from the corner of his eye. Nope. She wasn't even close to Joseph. She clasped her hands behind her back and skipped along the row of skulls, whistling. Then she started to sing.

"Millicent, my dear, what do you hear? I hear a mouse a'scrabbling! It sneaks and it snakes and our precious food takes, but we won't allow it will we?"

Milo kept his back to her. He tapped his foot in time with her song. Eight beats per line.

"Joseph my sonny, will he try a'running? Will he try a'running away?"

Twenty-four.

"I'm sure he won't like it his skull when I spike it, and then we'll have meat and potatoes for lunch!"

Forty.

He turned around. Suzy was standing there, the pickaxe over her head.

"Tut tut—"

Milo turned and sliced her across the belly, making sure to cut as deep as possible. Suzy grunted. Her entrails splattered on the ground.

In all of the fight scenes in all of the movies Milo had ever seen, when the hero disemboweled an enemy, said enemy was usually rendered immobile, and, after a grunt and a groan, keeled over and died. Then the hero would recite some ironic catchphrase and swagger away. Perhaps a fetching young lady would appear out of nowhere and assail him with an aggressive kiss.

But that was not the way it happened in real life. In real life, Suzy, while momentarily stunned, followed through with her attack, and the pickaxe, rather than burying itself in his head, thunked into his neck and severed his carotid artery. They both fell to the ground, Milo on his side, hands trying to stop the spurting blood, Suzy to her knees, arms covering her eviscerated middle.

"Ahh! Ahh! Milly! Joseph! I'm killed! He's killed me!"

Milo's sight grew dim and gray, and he found it impossible to keep his eyes open. He was vaguely aware of something wet gathering beneath him.

"Joseph my sonny, will he try a'running? Will he try a'running away?"

Twenty-four.

He adjusted his grip and tensed for action.

"I'm sure he won't like it his skull when I spike it, and then we'll have meat and potatoes for lunch!"

Forty.

Spin, strike, roll. That was the plan, and he executed it perfectly. Suzy went down to her knees, just as before, her guts splattering on the cave's stone floor. But Milo didn't account for the speed with which he threw himself into his roll, and when he jumped out of it, the momentum carried him one step too far, and he tripped backward into the fire and impaled himself on one of the metal stakes.

How many variations of death by zombie could he accrue? The best was a throat tear. The worst, dismemberment. How many different stinging creatures existed? He studied the effects of their poison. This one acted fast. His body swelled, his throat swelled, and he died clawing at his neck. That one took its time, and he could watch the toxins creep through his body, red and purple stripes extending out from the mortifying wound, leaving him first weak and feverish, then writing in pain, then paralyzed.

Then there were the muties. He got to know them very well. Boil Lips and Ooze, Mushroom Head and Pedo, Big Daddy and Mama Squidface. They clobbered and pummeled and decapitated. More than once, they knocked him unconscious and dragged him by the foot back to their underground lair and performed unspeakable acts upon his body before his heart finally gave out.

He jumped off the bridge. Repeatedly. He loved the feeling of flying, however brief. He swaned. He cannonballed. He triple flipped. He triple flipped with a twist. He triple flipped with a twist and a backward inverse pike tuck.

It was after just such a dive that, rather than regenerate on the highway, he found himself unconscious and floating in a void. Voices glided through the ether, familiar and unfamiliar. The void turned into a lecture hall with a lectern at the front and a projector screen hanging in the back. Faceless shadows occupied the seats all around him, their voices rustling. A figure walked out onto the stage and cleared his throat, eyeing the crowd as if they were children who had been caught doing something nasty.

"There is no grounds or intent! There is no cause, no effect! It is what it is! Now, some of my opponents may object to this line of reasoning, but what they lack is proper context; what they own is a tendency toward Gordian thinking. The reason for this kind of work is simple: to redeem the narrator. Without the cycle, he would continue his abysmal existence, incurious, insouciant, and ultimately indifferent to himself and all those around him who, either by choice or happenstance, are sucked into his gravitational pull."

Milo was then sucked in a different direction, tumbling end over end, finally landing in a movie theater watching a series of images flash in an endless loop across a screen:

- A beautiful girl being slaughtered again and again.
- A woman with red hair sprinting down a city street.
- A middle-aged man shoving pastries in his mouth.
- A muscular criminal covered in homemade tattoos, words, addresses, memories misguided and muddy.
- A pair of aristocrats pouncing on a sheep that had wandered into a private library.
- A child in a tuxedo chopping a water pipe in half with an axe.

The lecturer continued his notes, his voice thundering over the speakers:

". . . conditions deteriorate. Trapped and resentful, he has a choice: grow violent and vengeful, revel in his worst tendencies, or find the path to inner peace. A choice that is reflected in the discomfort of charity."

And then Milo was jerked away again, falling through space and time. He witnessed his birth, the triumph of first steps and first words. Elementary school. Sports. Middle school. The death of his grandmother, his grandfather. A first kiss. And finally Jennifer Reed, her hair lush and full, flying toward him in one of the outfits he'd drawn for her, and she was smiling at him, beckoning to him. She was five feet away, then two, then one, their lips were inches apart. Then she was yanked backwards, and all of his milestones reversed, and he wasn't speaking, wasn't walking, simply wasn't until . . .

. . . he became aware again on the cracked pavement of the long, desert highway. A pack of zombies milled about behind him. The cat in his arms hissed and bit his hand and he dropped it and it scurried out into the desert, a trail of dust in its wake.

He jogged forward with mechanical precision, stopping after a few feet to stare out at the bleak landscape, seemingly preoccupied, like a lonely man contemplating failure at the edge of the ocean. He thought about the zombies. He thought about the muties. He thought about the cat. He thought about the rabbit. He thought about Suzy. He thought about Jennifer, her face, her body, her voice, her laugh. He made a pedestal of his palm and held her in it, examining her in every light and from every angle. He thought and thought and thought. The backpack was heavy, the items inside weighing him down, and he shifted his shoulders to alleviate the pain.

Then it hit him.

The images from the movies.

". . . the discomfort of charity."

The wire with the looped ends. The rabbits. The machete. The zombies. And the cat. The cat. Something was happening to him. Connections in the long-unused part of his mind. He felt the synapses fire.

A stiff wind blew in from the desert, sending up grains of sand that stung his face, and he automatically turned his back to it. The cat jumped atop a rock and sat there, staring at him like an Egyptian goddess, blinking its green eyes. He saw the trap door in the desert floor shift as Mushroom Head pushed it open to peek out at her prey.

As if reading his thoughts, a rabbit hopped out of its hole and right up to the edge of the road where, suddenly seeing him, it stopped.

"Yoo-hoo!" Suzy called.

The zombie closest to him turned its head.

"Yoo-hoo! Over here!"

Wire, rabbit, machete, zombie.

"Yoo-hoo! Over here! Hurry!"

Wire, rabbit, machete, zombie.

"Yoo-hoo! Over here!"

Wire, rabbit, machete, zombie.

"Yoo—"

A zombie fell into him and took a chunk out of his neck.

Milo got to work as soon as he materialized. He threw the cat. He ran through the mutie compound—count the steps, duck, count the steps, stab. The rabbit warren started where the compound ended. He duct-taped his pants. He stomped on the stingers. He found three different rabbit holes, outside of which he placed the snares. Then he fell back twenty paces and sat down, cross-legged, the machete resting on his knees. When one of the strange-looking scorpions came near, he spiked its stinger.

It didn't take long before the first rabbit poked its head out. Milo sat up. His entire life, anytime he wanted to eat, he went to the refrigerator and took something out that his mother had bought at the supermarket. Processed meat from an animal slaughtered in Montana. Apples shipped from an orchard in Maine. Chicken breasts culled from a farm in Virginia. He'd never snared a rabbit before. He'd never hunted for food before. Never fished. Never farmed. And, barring a field trip once when he was in fourth grade, and one time after Thanksgiving dinner when he and his sisters picked wild blackberries in a patch behind his Great Uncle's vacation home in the Poconos, he'd never gathered.

The rabbit sniffed the air, wiggled its cute little whiskers. Seeing and smelling nothing that could possibly harm it, it hopped out of the hole and snared itself in the wire.

"Yes!" Milo cried.

He hopped to his feet and scrambled over. It was a big one, fully as large as a small dog, and he chopped off its head and put the body in his backpack.

"Yoo-hoo!"

Suzy was waving to him from the other side of the desert, and Milo ran to her.

"Here!" he cried. "I have it! I have it!"

"Hurry! Hurry! They're coming!"

Still running, he threw a look over his shoulder. The zombies had indeed begun to shuffle in his direction, but they were hardly near. Then his foot got caught in one of the snares he set up and he fell and hit the ground hard, smacking his head on a rock so hard that his neck broke.

"Here!" he cried, picking his way carefully through the rabbit holes. "Here!"

"Come on! Come on!" Suzy cried as he approached. "They're coming. Follow me!"

"No. Stop."

"What?"

"I'm not coming with you. I'm not doing that again."

"Again?"

"Look. I know you're trying to kill and eat me—"

"Oh, sir, I—"

". . . but that's not going to happen." He held up the rabbit. "Here. I brought you this."

Suzy opened and closed her mouth. Her eyes shuddered over to the zombies.

"But . . . they're—"

"They're not coming. They're barely able to move. Look."

The lead zombie tripped over a rock and broke its leg in half. Several others fell over its prone body.

"See?" He held up the rabbit. "This is so much better to eat. No tricks. No murder. Just meat."

She reached for it, but he pulled it back.

"Uh uh uh. I need your help first."

It proceeded very quickly after that. The two of them sliced through the pack of zombies with relative ease. The muties were next. They cut down Boil Lips, Ooze, Mushroom Head, Pedo, and Big Daddy and all their sister/cousins, reaching the cat moments before Mama Squidface was about to slit its throat. It bit him when he snatched it off the butcher's block, and an electric zing buzzed throughout his body, from the center of his belly, then emanating in circles into his chest and his head, and then he was no longer in the desert, he was standing in the woods outside his school, and the cat was in his arms and it bit his hand again and he said, "Ow!" and he dropped it and it ran off, sending up dead leaves in its wake.

Milo fell to his knees, weeping with relief. He did it. He made it back.

"Where did you come from?"

He whipped his head around.

It was her. The goddess. Jennifer Reed. What was she doing out here in the middle of the day? Girls like Jennifer Reed didn't skip class. They arrived two minutes early, already had their notebooks out before the teacher started to teach. She pointed at his sketchbook, the one in which he'd drawn a very detailed picture of her, topless and fighting off squads of frog-faced aliens.

"Is that me?"

Milo snatched the book up, hugging it to his chest.

"No. No. Just a comic I draw."

"Of me."

"It wasn't you."

"It looked like me."

"No, it's . . . Holly Huntress."

He winced. She stared at him.

"Holly Huntress."

"Warrior Woman of the Galaxy."

"Oh, I see. And does Holly Huntress always fight topless?"

"She was escaping from the frog-men of planet Swamp and they ripped off her . . . Hey, what are you doing out here, anyway? Shouldn't you be in AP Brain Surgery?"

"Haha."

"Seriously, though. Aren't you worried about getting caught?"

"It's lunchtime, dork."

"What?"

"Lunch. Time."

She mimed eating.

"You know, eat?"

Lunchtime?

"What day is it?"

"What?"

"What day is it?"

Jennifer sighed.

"The Ides of March."

"What's the Ides of March?"

She sighed again.

"March 15th."

March 15th? Only two days had passed. He'd spent months trying to get out of that hell hole. He stared at the trees, trying to comprehend everything that had befallen him. Then Jennifer said, "Oh, look at the cute little kitty!"

The yellow tabby meowed as it stepped into the clearing. Milo turned, horrified at the sound. Jennifer was already leaning over, arm outstretched.

"Don't!" he cried, and he grabbed her hand right as the cat bit it.

THE WOUNDED, THE SICK, & THE DEAD

It was noon when Chavez saw the man standing on the roof of the run-down little ranch style house that stood on the corner of the street. He appeared to be surveying the area, a rifle anchored on his hip. According to the mailbox, his name was Grossman. Chavez looked at the mess of bodies on the lawn, the corpses strung up in tangled barbed wire, the tiger pits buzzing with flies, and thought the name appropriate. Grossman opened the trap door he was using to access the roof and disappeared inside.

Well. Time to get moving.

Chavez made easy work of the dead milling around in front, partially to clear a path, partially to prove that he could take care of himself. He knew Grossman was watching.

When he was done, he sheathed his knife and tucked it into his back pocket. He hadn't even needed to take his gun out, which was a good thing. There were only two bullets left.

Grossman's house remained still and silent as he walked toward it, hands up.

"Hello? I don't want any trouble. I just need help."

He counted to sixty, and when he didn't get a response, he counted to sixty again before saying, "I just need some supplies. A little food. Some water. Whatever you can spare. Then I'll be on my way."

A voice, nasal and reedy, came from out of nowhere.

"You cleared up them dead pretty good on your own!"

"Yeah."

"You armed?"

Chavez didn't want to answer that question. No need to show his hand yet.

"Maybe we can make a deal?"

"Deal?"

"Yeah. I can get you anything you want."

There was another long pause. Then Grossman said, "You got a gun on your hip. What else you got?"

"Nothing else."

"What about that knife in your back pocket?"

Shit.

"Take off your jacket. Let me see."

Chavez swallowed. This wasn't going the way he planned. He needed an exit plan. There were no trees in the yard, but the driveway was choked with vehicles: a white van, a gutted Honda, an old Lincoln. He could duck behind them if he needed to. He took a deep breath and let it out. Fine. I'll give you what you want. He unzipped his jacket. Showed the right side, showed the left side. Grossman was unimpressed.

"Nah, nah, nah. Take it all the way off and turn around."

"Not until we make a deal."

"You think you hold any of the cards here?"

"I have what I have. You have what you have."

"Okay. Take off your coat and pants and maybe we'll deal."

"No way."

"Gotta make sure you're not going to ambush me."

"Not interested."

"Then neither am I."

Dammit.

"Wait!" Chavez yelled. "Please. Don't go. Here. Look."

He shrugged his jacket off his shoulders, let it drop to the asphalt, leaving him standing in his jeans and a Dr. Who T-shirt. He kicked the jacket toward the van.

"Now the pants."

Muttering, Chavez unbuckled his belt and took them off, kicked them on top of his jacket. Then he stood there shivering in the cold.

"You ready to deal or not?"

Grossman appeared on his roof again, aiming the rifle at him.

"Well, I dunno. How can I be sure you ain't got anybody else out there with you?"

"I don't. Not anymore."

A gust of wind whooshed down the street, blowing leaves and dead weeds, bits of trash. Chavez turned his face away, gritting his teeth against the cold. Grossman smirked, seeming to take pleasure in his discomfort.

"I still ain't too sure."

"I'm starving. I just need some food."

"I seen the way you handled yourself. You're pretty good with a knife."

"Have to be."

"Uh-huh."

The curtains in the front window of the house pulled aside, drawing Chavez's attention. A pit formed in his stomach. He couldn't believe what he was looking at. It was too terrible, too sick. All of the sudden he wanted to run, to get away from Grossman and his dirty house.

He tried not to stare, forced himself to tear his eyes away, make it look like he was thinking, like he hadn't actually seen anything. But he was frazzled, and before he could properly plan his next thought he said, "Come on, Grossman. Let's do this. All you have to do is let me in your trap door and—"

Grossman shouldered his rifle faster than Chavez would have guessed possible for such a skinny guy.

"You been spying on me?"

"No! I—"

"How'd you know about my door?"

"I didn't! I mean, I just—"

"Well did you or didn't you?"

"I didn't. It was a guess!"

A few infected stumbled out into an intersection a block away, three in all. They saw Chavez standing there and turned toward him, moaning. One by one they raised their arms. Grossman smiled.

"All full-up here," he said. "Find your own place."

Chavez tried to jump behind the van in the driveway, but he couldn't beat a bullet. He heard the crack of the rifle and his thigh exploded in pain. He landed hard, bit back a scream. Then, without even thinking, he grabbed his belt and jacket and scrambled up the driveway, leg ablaze, wedging himself under the spikes sticking out of the van's grill.

"I know you ain't dead yet!" Grossman yelled. "But you will be soon!" He fired four more shots into the air. "Here they come! Whoo boy! We got ourselves an honest-to-goodness hoard! You got a job of work to do, boy."

Chavez had to act fast. He grabbed his belt and tied it tight around his upper thigh, making sure that the holster was on the outside. Then he snatched his jacket and lay down, forcing his wounded leg to bend until his foot was flat. The pain was excruciating, and he saw stars. Finally, he folded up his jacket and compressed the wound, trying to get the bleeding to stop.

The infected were coming. He had to get out of there, but when he sat up again he grew dizzy and sick. Had the bullet struck an artery? If so, he had nothing to worry about. He checked his thigh, looking for . . . ah, there it was. An exit wound. He breathed a sigh of relief.

He needed to get up and run for one of the houses, but he was just too woozy.

Maybe I can close my eyes and recharge, he thought. *Just for a second.*

It felt so good, so peaceful to nod off. A pleasant buzz settled in his mind, and his limbs relaxed. It would be nice to see Jenice just one more time, to talk to her, kiss her. An image came to him, a memory of their time back at the camp. She was talking to another woman and tying her long hair up in a ponytail. The woman said something and Jenice laughed and looked at him, smiling.

He missed her so much.

Then he heard a scraping sound and snapped awake with a jolt.

One of the infected was in the driveway, reaching for him from the other side of the wall of cars.

"No!" Chavez yelled, falling back.

The monster leaned all the way forward, but it couldn't push past the spikes. It strove for him, reaching, reaching, pressing its stomach into the metal. Something ripped, and it began to slide forward. On the ground, Chavez could see under the van. Hundreds of pairs of shuffling legs and ragged shoes were heading in his direction. Grossman hadn't been kidding; it really was a hoard. The beast in the driveway planted its hands on the hood of the van and trunk of the car and pulled itself forward. The spikes disappeared into its midsection.

Chavez pushed himself away with his good leg. He was so focused on the creature in front of him that he didn't notice a second one dragging up the driveway until it was too late. He turned and it was on him. He caught it by the chest and fell back, barely able to keep its teeth from ripping into his face. It moaned, heavy and hollow, its breath cold and putrid. Chavez turned his head to the side to avoid its snapping teeth.

It would be so easy, wouldn't it, just to give up? Let it tear into his cheek, his neck, his face? He was so tired, and his leg hurt so bad. But then he remembered what he'd seen in the window, and he knew what Jenice would have done. She wouldn't give up. She wouldn't let Grossman get away with it. He couldn't let her down.

With a desperate push, he shoved the monster up and off of him, screaming in anger and pain, hurling it backward. It landed on the spikes sticking out of the van's rims, the metal thudding through its chest. At the same time, the one wedged between the van and the car pushed all the way through, severing itself in two. It tipped over onto its head and performed a single, perfect somersault across the driveway, then lay there, waving its hands in the air like a turtle on its back.

Chavez barked out a laugh. What else could he do? The whole thing—the dead rising to life, getting shot by a crazy redneck—was ridiculous. The thing on the ground gasped at him and that made him laugh more. It was good, a catharsis, and he let it roll. Still laughing, he pushed himself off the ground, putting all his weight on his left leg. Once he got going, he found he could put a little weight on his right leg, and he half-limped, half-ran out into the street. The hoard followed his arc, turning as one as he aimed for the house on the hill across from Grossman's place.

Three tiers of sloping grass separated him from the front door, three flights of stairs. Hopping up was difficult, and he pushed himself until he saw stars, going up and up and up. The dead behind him flooded into the yard, slipping on the grass, unable to advance past the first tier. They reached for him, moaning, those in the lead crushed or trampled as more pressed in from behind.

When he reached the door he prepared to ram it down, but something told him to try the knob first, just in case. He grabbed it and closed his eyes, whispering "please please please."

He wondered if Grossman was watching, if he had his rifle trained on him that very moment. And he wouldn't put him out of his misery, either. No. He'd take out a knee or a shoulder, make him lie there and wait for the dead to swarm and tear him to shreds.

He tried the knob.

It turned.

It actually turned.

He threw open the door and fell inside

Chavez awoke to the crack of Grossman's rifle. He was still in the hallway, face down on a rug. The light through the window in the parlor to his right was pale and gray. He'd slept through the night. Another gunshot echoed outside, and he pulled himself to the window and peeked out. One of the dead, what used to be an old woman, lay in the street, a bullet hole in its forehead. Grossman was standing on his roof again, holding a rifle.

"Stay the hell off my property!" he cried.

He seemed to take pleasure in taunting them. He shot the legs out from another one, then pumped round after round into it, purposefully not aiming for its head.

Chavez backed away from the window on his belly and inspected his wound. The bleeding had stopped, so he took his belt off. It hurt like hell, but that wasn't what he was worried about. He was worried about infection. And starvation. He needed water, food, bandages.

He nearly sang when he found the tub in the upstairs master bedroom half-filled with water. It was clean and clear, so he dropped to his knees and scooped a handful up to his nose, inhaling. It smelled fine. He plunged his face in and drank deeply, then used more to clean his wound.

There was anti-bacterial ointment in the cabinet, and the closet was filled with pants, belts, and dry-cleaned shirts. He ripped the shirts into bandages and tied them around his thigh. He found a small stash of canned food in one of the children's rooms.

He was halfway through a tin of tuna fish when a huge explosion rocked the house. He limped downstairs and peeked out the front window. Grossman's yard looked liked it had been bombed. A huge gulch had been cut out of the earth twenty yards from his front door, and the infected were falling into it, the earth swallowing them one by one.

He had to admit that it was a brilliant plan. Grossman had, in one fell swoop, decimated almost the entire herd.

But now his defenses were down.

Chavez stood up and tested his leg, stomping it two or three times on the carpet. It hurt, but he could push through the pain. He picked up his knife and put it in his back pocket. Checked his gun. Still had two bullets.

Ariel tried not to flinch when the yard exploded. She didn't want to show any emotion. He didn't like that. He beat them if they cried. He beat them if they complained. He beat them. The girl next to her wasn't as good at swallowing her feelings. She was barely speaking when Grossman first brought her in; now she didn't do anything but cry. Ariel hugged her tight and lied to her.

"It'll be okay. You'll be okay."

Nancy glared at them from the other end of the couch.

"Stop telling her that."

"Shut up, Nancy."

"It's not going to be okay."

"I said shut up!"

"Both of you shut up!"

Grossman. He peacocked into the room, pumping his fist. He grabbed a half-empty bottle from the mantle and took a big swig. Then he pointed at the girl.

"You. Your turn."

"No," Ariel said.

Grossman took two steps over and backhanded her.

"Get her back there!"

"No. Leave her alone. I'll do it."

That stopped him. He took another swig.

"Fine," he said. When she didn't jump up, he screamed. "Well, what are you waiting for!"

Ariel took her time getting to the back room. She sat on the bed and tried to calm herself down. She knew better than to try the windows. They were all nailed shut. Even if she managed to get them out, Grossman had installed bars on the outside. The closets were empty, there was nothing under the bed, nothing in the dressers, no lamps no—

A hand clamped down over her mouth and she screamed.

"Shh!" someone hissed in her ear. "Quiet. I'm here to help."

Ariel stopped struggling.

"If I take my hand off, you can't make a sound or he'll know. Nod if you understand."

She nodded. The stranger took his hand away, and she stood up and backed into the corner.

The man was dirty, his beard thick and unkempt, his hair greasy and long. But he was wearing clean clothes, a fresh, button-up Oxford and a nice pair of jeans. It was an odd juxtaposition to his otherwise disheveled state. Grossman yelled from the living room.

"What's going on back there?"

Ariel raised her eyebrows. What do you want me to do? The stranger motioned for her to answer.

"Nothing! Just a minute."

He held up a gun and pointed it at the hall. Ariel nodded and he limped over behind the door.

"You ready yet!" Grossman yelled.

"Y-yeah," Ariel said, giving the stranger a wary but hopeful look. "I'm ready. You coming or not?"

THE DEEPEST CUTS

Dudley sat in the middle of a clearing, the smoke from an earth oven trickling out of the stones he put on top to keep the heat in. He'd waited until the moon settled in the sky, bright and clear, before lighting the fire to cook his dinner, just like his sister, Max, taught him.

"Smoke is harder to spot in the middle of the night. They'll catch you if you're not careful."

Speaking of careful, Dudley was in the middle of his latest project: a spear carved out of a branch. The process seemed simple enough, but he couldn't get the point as sharp as he wanted without clipping it off or, even worse, slicing his hand. His left thumb bore the brunt of the damage. It was so covered with scars that it was amazing that he could even grip anything anymore.

He whittled away at the branch, whispering "*one* and *two* and *three* and *four*."

His sister showed him that trick.

"Get into a rhythm," she said. "Use eighth notes, forward on the one, back on the and."

And it worked, too. At least until the rhythm lulled him into carelessness and the knife slipped.

"Ouch!" he said, sticking the heel of his hand into his mouth. "Ouchies. Ouchies. Ouchies."

When the bleeding stopped, he picked up his backpack and dug around inside, searching for the bandaids and jar of antibacterial ointment he always kept in the front pocket. Where were they? Had he run out? That wouldn't surprise him. Things like this were always happening to him.

He was focusing so hard on digging around in his bag that he didn't hear the twig snap behind him.

"What you looking for?"

Dudley stood up with a jolt, clutching his half-finished spear and backpack to his chest.

There, just on the edge of the clearing, stood a little girl. She was wearing a plain white dress, and her hair was fastened up in a bun on top of her head.

"You lost, mister?"

"No. I mean, yes. I don't know who you are."

The girl smiled.

"No? That's good." She looked around the clearing. "You all alone out here?"

"Yes. No."

"I see." She frowned. "It would have been better for you if you wasn't."

She whistled and three dark forms stepped out of the woods.

"You like my pets?" the girl asked.

"N-no. Yes. I mean, I see them. Now."

"They're good boys. Trained them myself. Wanna see their tricks?"

And before he could respond, she whistled again, and the three moved for him as one.

Dudley couldn't help what happened next. It was instinct. Pure instinct. He turned and ran. He wasn't thinking about his mission, he wasn't thinking about his sister, he wasn't thinking about anything other than getting away. It was the one thing he was good at. Running. The trees on the other side of the clearing were only twenty feet away. He could cross that distance in a few seconds and lose them in the darkness. Max would be so proud of him.

Unfortunately, he forgot about the earth oven and the sticks on which his dinner was cooking. He took one step, crashed through the top, and spiked his foot on one of them. He cried out as he fell forward, dropping the makeshift spear in front of him and landing right on the tip.

It didn't really matter that he was a novice when it came to spear sharpening, and it didn't really matter that the backpack he clutched to his chest was made out of triple-ply canvas. All that mattered was the weight of his body, fifteen stone of meat and bone generating a total force of about 1,200 pounds, and the spear that pierced the bag and impaled him right through the sternum.

Two weeks later, Max lay at the bottom of a life raft, her skin raw, her lips cracked. Never could she have predicted such an abrupt turn in her life, but then again, never could she have predicted the collapse of the governments of the world followed by the end of civilization in general. Or maybe she could have. She'd watched enough movies on the same topic to know how it might occur. The swiftness with which it happened, however, was more than a little disconcerting. The sun beat down, relentless and unforgiving, draining her, frying her, leaving her little more than a sunburned husk. The raft itself was as bleached as bone, wrinkled from loss of air. A pump lay next to her desiccated thigh, but she had barely enough strength to raise her water bottle let alone try to re-inflate again. What was the point, anyway? The air would only leak out.

She thought about the last time she'd spoken to anybody. It was three weeks before, a few days after Dudley was supposed to return. DC took her aside to explain her role in the attack.

"We'll drop you off less than a mile from the shore," he said. "It'll take about two days for you to find the cove."

"Two days?"

"Give or take."

"Give or take? What does that mean?"

"Maybe a week."

Max gave him a look.

"It's the ocean, Max. I can't predict everything."

"Yeah, well, there's a huge difference between two days and a week."

DC sighed and ran a hand through his long hair.

"Look, I know it's a little bit of a risk."

"A little bit?"

"Okay. It's a huge risk. But you know what's at stake."

"I know. Do you think he—"

"Dudley's fine."

"I shouldn't have let him go. Why did you even offer it to him?"

"We've talked about this before."

"You know how he is. You—"

"Dudley is a grown man, Max."

"I know, but—"

"You can't take care of him his entire life."

Max folded her arms across her chest. She knew he was right but didn't want to admit it. DC put his hands on her shoulders.

"Look. He's fine. I'm telling you. He's probably just lost."

"He better be."

"I'll find him. He'll have the map of the fence and the town perimeter all ready to go."

Max waited a moment before saying, "The beacon won't fail?"

"It's sewn inside the canvas. The only way it'll fail is if someone takes it out and smashes it or if you sink. Either way, by that point, you won't care. Unless you've got some magic pockets in your cargo shorts."

She did, actually, have a magic pocket. More like a secret pocket. One that she sewed herself into the inner lining of the right leg.

She said, "And once I'm inside?"

"You're the distraction. So, distract."

"Yeah, but after?"

"Just wait for the gunshots. You'll know it's us."

Everything went according to plan at first. They dropped her a mile away from the cove, showed her which way to paddle. But that night a storm kicked up, nothing huge, but enough to spin her around and make her lose her bearings. She lost the paddle. A wave washed half her supplies overboard. By morning, she could no longer see the shore.

Twenty-six days. That's how long she'd been adrift. Three and a half weeks. Six hundred and twenty-four hours. Not that she was counting. In all honesty, she wasn't really sure anymore. After the twelfth moon, she gave up any hope of being rescued. Twenty-six days, thirty-six days, what did it matter? She was dead alive, an empty vessel. She closed her eyes and waited. For what, she didn't know. Night, rain, sharks, anything to kill the monotony.

That evening, as the merciless sun finally began to dip toward the horizon, Max thought about her childhood, how she and her friends used to play outside, the endless laughter. The memory was so vivid that she actually thought she heard the sound of them squealing with joy, shouting to each other, the soundtrack of summer evenings and fall playgrounds. If she had any water left in her body, she would have wept.

Then the sounds merged with something different, something more urgent, shouts and cries of dismay, and at first she ignored them, thinking they were just another hallucination. Which was why when she first heard those cries, when she felt the shadow pass between her and the setting sun, and when the hands lifted her body from the deflated life raft, she couldn't believe it. It was just a trick. And rather than thank her rescuers and weep for joy, she laughed and laughed and laughed until she passed out again, certain it was all just in her mind.

Max woke up in a cool, dark room, lying on a comfortable bed and covered in a clean, white sheet. There were a few blood stains on it from her sores, probably because the sheet tucked her so tightly to the mattress that it acted like a straight jacket. A wet rag had been left on her forehead, dribbling water into her eyes. Untucking herself took more effort than she expected, and she was a little amazed at the sight of her shorts. Her rescuers, whoever they were, had left them on. There were bandages on her arms and hands, and her stomach was wrapped in gauze. She took the cloth off her forehead.

"Whoa there, ma'am," a voice said. "Don't strain yourself too much. You been in a terrible mess."

It was a girl. She stood with her back turned to the bed and was wringing something out into a china basin. There were others in the room, too, three forms standing completely still in the back of the room, their faces shrouded in darkness. The girl caught her looking and chuckled.

"That's just my boys. They just got done with your friends."

"Friends?"

"Oh, don't pretend like you don't know. That'd be embarrassing for both of us."

Max sat up and untucked the sheet all the way. She wanted to see her feet, how badly they were burned. They were bandaged, and where there weren't bandages, her skin was slick with a greasy salve. She looked like she tried to walk on the sun itself. She swung her legs over the side of the bed and saw stars.

"Easy there," the girl said. The three forms took a stiff step forward, and she whistled at them, a short, curt, burst. They stopped. Then she bustled around and put her hand on Max's back. "You okay?"

"Dizzy."

"I don't doubt it. Mayor Bram says you must have been out on the ocean for at least three weeks."

"Felt longer."

"Mm-hmm. And in the middle of the summer, too? Now just you lie back down, okay? You safe for now, but the worst ain't over yet."

"No, I have to go."

The girl smiled.

"Where you think you're going?"

"I need to—" She caught herself. Jesus. She'd almost given it all away. She needed to be careful.

"What do you need to do?"

The girl watched her with a furrowed brow. Max pretended to be confused.

"I, uh . . ."

A fever rolled through her body, and it was just like she was back in that horrible raft, the sun pouring its heat down, and she was falling, falling into darkness, but then a cold compress was placed on her forehead, and the illusion broke, and she opened her eyes in the cool, dark room. The girl wiped her brow with the cloth.

"You don't need to worry about none of that. Don't you know where you are?"

Max shook her head.

"You in Salvation. And we're going to take care of you."

A kernel of panic tickled Max's belly.

"My raft."

Did they have it? Did they find the beacon?

The girl laughed.

"Raft? You mean that old piece of scrunched-up garbage?"

"Where is it? I need it."

"You about as attached to that thing as you are them shorts, huh? We tried to get them off, but you fought us. Even my Three couldn't do it. Wasn't doing you no harm. Probably protected your skin, so . . . What's so special about them anyway?"

Max thought fast.

"They're all I have left. From before."

The girl seemed to consider this.

"I get it. I'll check around for your raft. I bet someone picked it up. Hopefully, they ain't tore it apart yet."

"Tore it apart?"

"Oh, yeah. You should see what washes up in the cove. Clothes, shoes, furniture, food." The girl looked pointedly at Max. "We reuse everything we find."

There were two windows in the room, one facing Max from the foot of the bed and one to her left. The girl went over to the window at her feet and drew the curtains aside. Though it was dark out, a warm, orange glow shone through the slats of the blinds.

"Nice night," the girl said.

She drew up a seat next to the bed, opened a drawer in the nightstand, and pulled out a tray. It was silver, polished to a high sheen. Strange markings circled it in concentric lines; characters from an ancient language. She put the tray on the nightstand and pulled out more things from the drawer: vials and brushes, flat, oval containers, an emery board, nail clippers.

"You're going to give me a makeover?" Max asked.

"It's all part of the deal."

"What deal?"

The girl arranged her tools on the tray, humming to herself.

"You know, we didn't use to do it this way. It was a lot more rudimentary."

"Do what?"

The girl whirled her finger in the air.

"All this."

She picked up Max's hand and started to shape her nails. Max stayed silent, trying to quell the fear in her belly. *Think, Max, think.* She was supposed to be the distraction.

"What's your name?" she asked.

"Oh, I been called a lot of things. Mama said she knew what I was the minute I was born. 'You gonna be something special, girl.' And that's what she called me."

"Girl? Your name is Girl?"

"Better than what they named my brother."

"What's his name?"

"Rufus."

Max couldn't help it. She laughed out loud.

"I agree that Rufus isn't the greatest name."

"Wait till you meet him. You got a brother?"

Max didn't say anything. The warm glow on the other side of the window grew brighter. Girl caught her looking and when she turned to see what it was, she scraped the emery board over her knuckle. Max pulled her hand away with a hiss, and Girl snatched it back.

"Don't. Don't ever do that."

She resumed her work.

"What's that glow?" Max asked.

"You know what Rufus means? It means 'red-haired,' which is funny because Rufus has some of the blackest hair I ever seen. Give me your other hand."

"Don't scrape that one, okay?"

"That's what you're worried about?"

Max was too shocked to respond. Should she be worried about something else? Girl pointed at her hand.

"You gonna give it to me?"

Max did, and she set to work, a little rougher this time.

"So that's it?" Max asked. "Girl? That's what they call you?"

"Well, if you ask dumb old Jimmy Walts, I'm sure he could come up with a whole bunch of things you could call me, but I wouldn't listen to him if I was you."

"Not exactly best friends?"

Girl gave her a look as she finished shaping her nails, then she rested each hand back in place next to her legs.

"Anyway, nobody calls me 'Girl' anymore, not after my first Notice and all. After that, they called me The Witch."

Phew, Max thought. *They're nuttier than we thought.*

Girl, or The Witch, or whatever she wanted to be called, rearranged some of her tools.

"We gonna wait before I do your cuticles."

Max tried not to panic. Where were DC and the others? She should have heard the gunshots by now. Girl saw the expression on her face and cocked her head.

"What's the matter, Maxine? You don't look so good."

"It's just . . . how do you know my name?"

"Oh, honey. That's the first thing he told us."

She opened up the nightstand drawer again and took out a strange-looking instrument. It looked kind of like a pen, only instead of a ballpoint where the ink came out, there was a blade. Then she took out another tool, a handle with a sharp hook on the end. It looked like the kind of thing Max used to see in her dentist's office, back when there were dentists. She felt the sudden urge to hop out of bed and flee, get as far away from this place as possible. She summoned her strength. Could she reach into her shorts fast enough? Could she get it out in time?

"He?"

"Oh, yeah. Your boy, DC. Found him about a week ago wandering around out by fence line with some of your people. Armed to the teeth, as my daddy used to say. Tried to give us some business about being lost, looking for the road back to the city."

She went over to the other window, the one to Max's left, and grabbed the cord to the blinds. She didn't pull them up immediately, seemed to need to take a moment before she continued. Finally, she said, "Nobody wants to go into the city, not these days, not with them things in there. Everybody knows that."

Then she pulled, and the blinds shot up, and Max's eyes went wide. Scaffolds. At least a dozen of them. All on fire in the big yard outside the window. Each one with a dark form hanging in the center.

Girl watched the fear spread across her face and smiled.

Her teeth are perfect, Max thought. *Big and white.*

"You like that?" Girl asked. "We did it special for you."

She sat back down and patted Max's hand.

"See, the only people we ever find out in the woods come to Salvation for a reason. It might not be the reason they thought they were coming for, but we can't hardly be to blame for that."

"Please. I don't know who—"

"We used to just lay them out flat and get to work. But not anymore. Now we like to pretty them up first, provide one last bit of comfort. Makes everybody feel better, you know?"

Max let her hand wander down to her leg. She'd only have a few seconds. She'd have to distract the crazy girl, though. Tears. She'd start to cry. Could she do it? Drum up tears from nothing? She closed her eyes. Think. Think. About something sad. She took in a sharp breath. Willed the tears to form. And miraculously, they did.

"Oh, don't cry," Girl said. "Lord knows you don't need your body where you going. Deepest cuts ain't this physical stuff anyway, and you almost done with that part!"

She turned to the tray to look for something, and that's when Max acted. Reached into her shorts, found the secret pocket, the one in which she hid her knife. It was a little knife, a penknife, really, but it was sharp and it would do the job.

But it was gone.

Girl turned around. She was holding the knife, pinching it between her thumb and forefinger like it was some kind of dirty thing.

"Looking for something?"

"Please, I—"

"Shut up now, hear?" She opened the knife up and inspected the blade. "You keep this nice and sharp, don't you?"

"Girl, listen—"

Girl whistled, and the three forms in the back moved as one.

"This my favorite part," she said. "You'd be smart not to ruin it."

STEPS

Justice stood at the kitchen sink, trying to scrub a coffee stain out of her dress. Her Burberry dress. *The* Burberry dress. She had never loved an article of clothing more. The print was perfect. The colors were perfect. The shape was perfect. She felt confident in that dress. Whole. Pure. It was the last thing her father bought her before the incident, her last tether to a time when life seemed relatively normal, before the therapists, the meds, the institution. Which was why she never let anybody else wear it, something her roommate, Sloan, didn't think applied to her.

"Come on, Justice," she said, flopping on the couch, her ever-present phone in hand. "It's not that big a deal. You can't even see it."

Justice pulled the dress out of the sink, ignoring the Woolite suds scudding down her arm, and presented it to her roommate. A huge, dark brown stain marred the purple and blue print from the neckline down.

"Coffee, Sloan. You spilled caramel macchiato all over it."

"It wasn't my fault. Spencer was screwing around and hit my elbow."

"Spencer did this?"

"Not on purpose."

"But he did it, right?"

"I guess."

Justice dunked the dress back in the cold water, struggling to control her shaking hands.

"Who said you could wear it in the first place?"

"It's just a dress."

"I told you never to wear it. Anything else, fine. But this is my favorite dress."

"I'll buy you a new one."

"That's not the fucking point!"

She gripped the side of the sink, muttering to herself, trying to regain control. The red veil had slipped down again, and if she was going to make it out of this without hurting anyone, she had to remember the steps, the steps her therapist taught her.

Step 1: Take a deep breath.

Step 2: Tense up every muscle in her body.

Step 3: Relax.

She did it. She took a deep breath, tensed up, and relaxed, and the ball of anxiety that burned in her chest slowed its manic spin. The veil faded to pink then to white. She could think again, think about something other than her anger. She looked out the window over the sink and concentrated on her breathing.

It was the Friday night before the fall semester, and the little city of Fredericksburg was abuzz. Everybody was out on the town, party-hopping and bar-crawling. Mary Washington didn't have a Greek system so the closest thing to a frat was the Triangle: three jock houses on Hawke and Prince Edward that shared a backyard. Justice and Sloan lived across from the lacrosse house. The soccer house and the basketball house were around the corner.

"Are you going to be done soon?" Sloan asked. "I'd like to make dinner at some point."

Justice glared at her roommate who was too busy staring at her phone to notice. All of the sudden Sloan squealed and said, "Oh my god he's back!"

Justice groaned internally. 'He' was Spencer, Sloan's boyfriend and starting point guard for the UMW Men's Basketball team. He had a game at Gallaudet that afternoon and had been gone for a grand total of twelve hours, which, if Sloan's morning moping and afternoon sighs were at all an accurate measurement, equated to a thousand years. Now she was all sprightliness and giggles. She jumped up and ran to her room, which was off the kitchen.

"Crap," she said, coming back out. "I don't have anything to wear. Can I look in your closet?"

"Are you kidding me?"

"Come on *Justice*," she whined.

It was difficult to speak through a clenched jaw, but Justice managed a tight, "No."

"I'll let you tag along."

"You'll let me?"

"Come on."

"And watch you ram your tongue down Spencer's throat all night? No thanks."

"Please, Justice? He's already there and he won't come get me. You don't want me to get raped walking over, do you?"

"It's literally across the street."

"Still."

Justice groaned.

And then it hit her.

It hit her so hard that she saw stars.

Nothing like it had ever come to her before so fully formed and beautiful.

It was an idea. A simple idea. A series of steps, really, shimmering right in front of her, a pristine ball of blood-red light, each move perfectly illuminated. Her anxiety and anger melted away. Her shoulders relaxed. She even smiled. She could pull it off. She could totally pull it off.

"Okay," she said.

Sloan was rendered momentarily speechless. She'd been getting ready to transition from pleading to outright bitchery and didn't know how to adjust. Finally, she said, "Really?"

"Take whatever you want."

Sloan squealed again and gave her a quick hug.

"You're the best!" she said and ran to the stairs (Justice's room was on the second floor).

Justice watched her go, her smile slowly fading until her face was entirely blank. She stayed that way until she heard Sloan coming back down.

They met up with Spencer in the living room of the basketball house.

"Hey baby," Sloan said, wrapping her arms around his waist.

She stood on her tip-toes and planted a deep, passionate kiss on his mouth. Justice looked away, feeling nauseous. Finally, after what seemed like forever, Spencer gently pushed Sloan away.

"Missed you, too, baby," he said. Then, noticing Justice for the first time, he added, "Hey."

She gave him a sarcastic smile.

"Finally come up for air?"

He ignored the barb and pointed at her shirt, an old burgundy and gold Redskins print from the 1980s. There was a picture of a snorting pig on the front, circled by the words Superbowl Hog Power!

"Skins fan, huh? Nice."

"Thanks. My dad gave it to me."

Sloan wrapped one arm around his neck.

"Don't get her started about her dad," she said.

"Why not?"

"He's dead."

Justice's mouth dropped open. Why had she told Sloan about the worst thing that had ever happened to her?

"Well, he is," Sloan said. "Jeez, Justice. Lighten up. You need a beer." She peeled away from Spencer, saying, "*I* need a beer," before planting another kiss on his lips and strutting through the crowd to the keg.

Spencer waited until she was across the room, then he said, "Sorry."

Ugh. Why did he have to be so nice?

"No problem. She's always like that."

"You want something to drink? Talk to some people? I can introduce you to my friend Matt."

"Um, sure. Maybe later."

But later never came. She was gone before Sloan returned. She found another keg in the kitchen and poured herself a beer. Not that she'd drink it. That would be an unwise combination of chemicals. But if she didn't have a drink in her hand, she'd have to deal with some meathead offering her one every five seconds, so she used it as a prop.

She strolled from room to room, bored. Here were co-eds mashing their bodies up against each other in the parody of sex they called dancing. Here was a group playing beer pong. After ten minutes, she finally found a place to stand next to the fireplace in the living room. It was noisy but not too crowded, and she found she could comfortably watch from her perch without anybody elbowing her and spilling her drink.

The fact that they were carrying on so vigorously in such heat made her dizzy; she was merely standing there and her shirt was already damp. She found herself nodding along with the music blasting from the other room, tapping her foot, almost enjoying herself. A wave of dizziness hit her out of nowhere, just like in the kitchen, and she knew exactly what was going to happen next.

A boy walking backward will jostle the elbow of a girl, spilling her drink on the rugby player trying to flirt with her.

The rugby player will grab the boy by the collar and pummel him in the face.

The boy's friends will jump onto the rugby player.

It happened so slowly that Justice wasn't sure if it was real or if she was having another episode. Then time sped up with a snap, and the rugby player's friends leaped into the fray and someone knocked her drink out of her hand. She joined the mad rush out of the house to the backyard, the joy, the ecstasy of her prediction coming true spinning her head and making her feel weak and giddy.

Sloan and Spencer were around the corner, standing next to the gate. She knew that already. She made a beeline for them. The steps had begun.

Step one. Engage.

"Hey guys," she said.

Sloan spun around.

"Oh my god! Did you see that fight?"

"It broke out in front of me, so . . ."

"This totally blows. The party was just getting started."

Spencer finished his beer and threw the empty cup onto the ground.

"Guess we're out of beer."

"Well, let's go get some more, baby!"

"How? Neither of us is old enough."

Sloan pointed at Justice.

"She's twenty-one."

"I don't know, Sloan," Justice said. "I'm kind of tired."

"Oh come on! Live a little."

Justice pretended to consider it.

"You know what, you're right. I'll do it. But I don't want to just pound them back at the house."

"Where else can we go?"

Step two. Persuade.

"You guys ever climb up under the train bridge?"

Sloan rolled her eyes.

"Train bridge? Like, walking on the tracks?"

"No. *Under* the bridge," Justice said. "The maintenance access?" They stared back at her. "No? Really? The view is fantastic. So romantic."

"I know how much you like romantic views, baby," Spencer said.

Sloan rolled her eyes.

"Fine. But you're not getting into my pants on a bridge."

Justice could hardly contain herself.
Step three. Execute.

Justice pointed at the rusty metal door seemingly embedded in one of the concrete pillars.

"Here it is."

She handed Spencer the twelve-pack of beer they picked up from 7-11 on the way down and pushed on the handle. The door opened with a squeal, and she stepped inside. When the other two didn't immediately follow, she poked her head back out.

"You guys coming or what?"

Sloan gave her a look.

"Seriously?"

"What are you, chicken?" Justice said and disappeared again. "Bock! Bock! Bock!"

Spencer laughed. Sloan rolled her eyes.

It was close to two in the morning when they finally reached the first of the arches that spanned the river, but even though they were sweating and a little winded, they found that all of the effort was totally worth it.

The view was simply amazing.

Stars filled the clear sky above, and the full moon's reflection shone on the rippling water below. They could see all the way down to the Chatham Bridge. Justice spotted a few fires on the banks, probably homeless people jungling up by the water or college kids extending the party into the wee hours. She didn't think they'd be a problem.

Sloan took out her phone and took a picture.

"Oh my gosh, Justice. You were right. This is the most amazing thing I've ever seen. How did I not know about this before?"

Justice suppressed a snort. *Maybe if you ever took your head out of your ass.*

"It really is beautiful," Spencer agreed.

"Oh my gosh, babe. Selfie!"

Sloan leaned up against him and snapped several shots, smiling and pouting and winking with each one.

"You're not going to post those, are you?" Justice asked.

"Uh, yeah. Why not?"

"This isn't exactly legal."

"Whatever."

Justice thought rapidly. A chink in the plan. Had Sloan posted any pictures of her since 7-11? She tried not to be too conspicuous as she watched her roommate peck at her screen. Was her vision just a fantasy?

"Crap," Sloan said. "I'm out of data."

Justice sighed. Crisis avoided. For now.

They retreated to the middle of the bridge and sat down, Sloan and Spencer leaning up against one of the support pillars, Justice sitting cross-legged a few feet away, a half-empty twelve pack between them.

Step four. Distract.

Justice tossed her roommate another beer.

"How many have you had?" Spencer asked.

Sloan burped.

"None of your business."

Justice watched her guzzle it down, trying to time the next step perfectly. She couldn't rush it. She had to wait for the right moment. A relaxed calm had settled between them, and they enjoyed the night, the view, the thrill of doing something lightly illegal. Now. Start now.

"Do you guys know the story of the Rappahannock River Monster?"

Sloan rolled her eyes.

"Rappahannock River Monster? Is this another one of your daddy issues things?"

"No. It's real. Real people died."

"Okaaay."

Spencer belched and Sloan swatted him on the chest.

"So gross."

"I'm in the mood for a good story," he said. "Let's hear it."

So Justice told them. About the drownings, the cycle. When she was done, Sloan said, "God. You're so full of it."

"You know the spot where it happens is right under the bridge."

"This bridge?" Spencer said. "This bridge right here?"

Justice's heart raced. She flexed her hands. Stay in the moment. Visualize the steps. Don't screw it up.

"Yeah. In fact, if you look over the side, you can see the rocks where the last body was found."

Spencer looked out over the river. The white light of the moon gave everything a silvery sheen.

"We're really high up," Justice added. "You have to get close to the edge to see it."

He stood up, swaying a little, and held his hand out to Sloan.

"Come on babe, I wanna look."

Sloan stood up, too, leaving her phone on the concrete where she sat. She took a step and knocked his beer over.

"Whoa there, slugger," he said, putting his hand on her back.

Sloan didn't seem to notice.

"Imma see."

She took an unsteady step forward, and Spencer reached out and held her wrist. When they got to the edge, Sloan clung to his arm and Spencer stumbled sideways.

"Watch it, babe."

"I'm scared."

"Yeah, well, you'll be a lot more scared falling over."

Sloan took another small step forward and peered carefully over the edge.

"I don't see any rocks."

"They're really close to the bridge," Justice said. "Lean out a little more."

"Is this far enough?"

"Just a little more."

Sloan leaned out, pulling Spencer with her.

"Whoa, babe," he said.

"I still can't see them."

Justice stood up and took a deep breath.

"This will help," she said and took two swift steps forward.

Justice awoke early the next morning. She took a shower, making sure to wash her hair twice. She drank her coffee and ate some toast, checking Sloan's phone for any news on frederickburg.com. Nothing yet. She knew she'd have to dump it at some point, but she wanted to delete any of the pictures from that night before that had her in them. She left the ones that showed Sloan drinking as well as the selfies she took. When she was done, she scheduled a few posts to Sloan's Instagram. "On the bridge with bae!" They'd pop up in a few days when the new data cycle began. She'd wait until dark to leave it by the bank downstream. Maybe she should crack the screen?

When she was done eating, she went over to the sink and picked out her dress. She knew better than to wring it dry, so she held it up to the window, letting the morning light illuminate the fabric.

Huh.

She peered closer.

Huh.

The stain was gone.

Well, that was . . . well.

Looks like she shouldn't have gotten so angry after all.

STUPID WEATHER.COM
A VARIATION ON A THEME

Saturday is the only day of the week that has retained its Roman origins, having been named for Saturn, the god of time (among other things), and frequently associated with Venus, the goddess of sex, and Cronus, geophagaist, slayer of the universe, and devourer of his children. True to its derivation, Saturday nights, more so than any other night of the week, are, as an institution, the accepted occasion of the typical bacchanals and orgies hosted by university students the world wide. On Saturday night, many a jaw has been cracked. On Saturday night, many a drink has been imbibed. On Saturday night, many a bed has been wrecked.

For Alfred and Harld, our heroes *de rigueur*, Saturday night had never been any of those things.

For Alfred and Harld, Saturday night, like any other night of the week, was a time for quiet, calm reflection. The only jaws they cracked were the result of walnuts or pecans.

The only fluids they imbibed consisted of hot tea, preferably chamomile, though mint was a perfectly acceptable substitution (or, in the case of viral rhinitis, a requirement), as was blackberry sage or, if they were feeling adventurous, coconut cocoa. The only beds they plundered were their own, usually for the materials needed to build a fort in the living room, beneath which they might chance a game—video, yes, from Atari to PS4—but also classic board games (Parker Brothers only, please): Monopoly, Risk, Clue, Parcheesi, or a rousing session of Dungeons and Dragons. Yet those games were nothing in comparison to their absolute most favorite pastime, Contract Bridge, or, to use the common parlance, Bridge.

It was October 2017, the fifth Saturday of their sixth semester at the University of Mary Washington to be exact, and as was their habit and preference, Alfred and Harld were once again playing cards.

Normally, the pair amused themselves well into the twee of the morning, whiling the hours away with hundreds of calls and passes, dummies and doubles, tricks and trumps. Harld, in particular, was an enthusiastic compiler of vulnerabilities, bouncing rubbers, honors, and slam bonuses, routinely beating

Alfred game after game. As gentlemen were wont, he never felt the need to celebrate his victories, and Alfred, to his everlasting credit, never desired to complain.

But this evening, after two cups of tea and a mere game and a half, Harld (during which it must be noted that he, to use the vernacular, wiped the floor with his companion) threw down his hand and sighed.

Alfred was shocked.

Not only was he unused to such outbursts, but for as long as he and Harld had known each other (one hundred and eight months, three days, six hours, twenty-seven minutes and thirty-nine seconds, give or take a microsecond), he'd never seen his friend put on such a wanton display of naked emotion. He lay down his hand, concerned.

"Harld, dear friend, are you ill? Shall I fetch a bromide? Perhaps a tincture?"

"Forgive me, Alfred. I didn't mean to startle you. I know how much you abhor surprises —"

"That isn't necessarily true, Harld. Remember the time I ordered a grape soda at the local delicatessen?"

"My goodness, indeed I had! What a wonderful jape! What a marvelous fool are you."

Alfred blushed. A small titter escaped his pale lips.

"Indeed. I don't believe I've had that much fun since certamen. You do recall certamen, Harld? Eighth grade?"

Harld stared off into space, captivated by the memory of past academic glory. Ah, yes. The delicious dissemination of ancient knowledge. How could he have ever forgotten?

"But enough about me, old boy," Alfred said. "You're the one who seems at odds with the universe at the moment."

"Indeed I am. I suddenly feel somewhat dissatisfied as if our efforts of the past several years have been an exercise in futility. Are you not aggrieved with our current situation? Are you not vexed? Irked? Nettled? Piqued?"

Alfred settled back in his seat. He'd heard Harld talk like this before, but it usually didn't surface until the middle of winter.

"Harld. This sounds to me as if—"

"I know what you're going to say, but it is not the melancholia. Not this time."

"Than what, may I ask, are you going on about?"

"This house. This table. This game."

Alfred gathered up the cards and started to shuffle.

"Bridge is life."

"You say the same thing about calculus."

"Because it is true."

Harld leaned forward and templed his fingers.

"Alfred. Aren't you tired of it?"

Alfred chose not to respond. He knew where this was leading, and he was running out of excuses. He and Harld had known each other for so long, and the fact that his friend had never discovered his condition did not bother him in the least. But that couldn't continue for much longer. Harald sighed.

"Alfred. Do you not recall the pledge we made when we first arrived at college?" Alfred continued to shuffle the deck, trying, much like a guilty dog, not to meet his friend's eyes. "We said things were going to change. That we'd meet people. Do more than just . . . school."

Alfred stopped shuffling and finally looked up.

"You want to go to the party, don't you?"

"Cock your ears. Do you not hear it?"

"Hear what?"

"The glorious sound of revelry! Festivities abound! The youth are submerged in splendiferous celebration! And they're right there. Having fun. Right. Across. That. Street."

Alfred groaned.

"Oh, the histrionics. Really, Harld."

"I'm done, Alfred. I can no longer contain my desire to loosen my morals. I must indulge Dionysus. The bacchanal calls. I have but one life, and I will live it."

Alfred stood up to look out the window. The past week had been rife with rain. The river had flooded the yards around City Dock; he and Harld had taken a stroll through town to take pictures of it on their cellular devices. It wasn't raining anymore, but he could see the clouds shrouding the sky. He took out his phone and opened his weather.com application.

Cloudy with a sixty percent chance of rain.

He doubled-checked using the NOAA application, the Accuweather application, and the WTOP Weather application. All agreed. Tonight would not be one for Selene's celebration. Her beams would not glow in the heavens. Her icy chips would not glisten on the river. Zeus' breath would veil the celestial sphere and protect all of humanity from her influence for the duration of Nyx's waking hours. Now it was his turn to sigh.

"I suppose I have no convincing counterargument."

Harld rejoiced. He clenched his fist and whispered, "Yes."

Like many small cities in Virginia that were founded pre-Revolutionary War, Fredericksburg was home to plethora historically significant dwellings. Some, such as the Hugh Mercer Apothecary, the Rising Sun Tavern, The Mary Washington House, and Chatham Manor (to name a few), managed to survive the ravages of time, the cold calculations of modernization and technology, and not one but two Civil War battles. Even more tended to have, even if they were constructed in the mid-20th century, fallen into varying degrees of disrepair.

These were generally rented by University of Mary Washington students. Who else would deign to reside in such nearly condemned dwellings, places that had not been updated for over half a century? To them, the inferior living conditions represented not failure or hard times, but freedom and opportunity. The lack of air conditioning or proper heating was not to be lamented but celebrated as a harbinger of the success that surely awaited in the future. One day, rang the familiar refrain, they would look back at their time in these hovels and think "look at how far have I risen." There was a chance, as there always was, that these most dismal shacktowns, resulted in less lofty musings, for many also interpreted their slum-life as an excuse to drink and smoke and otherwise dull the senses against the insensible atmospheric vicissitudes of the most magnificent and most terrible Theoi Meteoroi.

The house into which our heroes entered that fateful Saturday night was the epitome of such an accommodation. The hardwood, now awash with beer and dirt, was scuffed and dull. The fireplace, festooned with liquor bottles, enjoyed a cracked mantle and malfunctioning flue. The walls, chipped and chunked from years of maltreatment, were spattered and smudged with all varieties of unmentionable filth.

The young men who lived there had nailed holiday lights over the fireplace in the living room, which, if one could ignore the *pièce de résistance*—the fact that they had fashioned the lights in the shape of a giant phallus and a hanging pair of testicles—added a festive element to the proceedings.

It wasn't the floors or the disrepair that bothered Alfred and Harld, however. It was the girls. The house was filled with them. Girls of all shapes and sizes. Girls with blonde hair, girls with brown hair, girls with blue hair, girls with green hair, girls with nose piercings, girls with lip piercings, girls with tattoos, girls with long legs, girls with muscular arms, girls, girls, girls. Being math majors, they were not used to seeing so many samples of the female sex gathered in one place let alone in such variety. The array was simply astonishing. Add to that the fact that the typically hot and humid Virginia weather resulted in a display of cleavage and thigh in startling amounts, and the young men found themselves, for the first time in a long while, somewhat tongue-tied.

They stood in the corner of the living room, each of them holding a red cup of beer, their eyes zipping back and forth like a cat watching a bell jar filled with flies. A tall young man entered the living room on the opposite side, drawing Harld's attention. He pointed.

"Dear me. Do you see what I see, Alfred?"

Alfred looked at the person Harld was pointing at and understood the source of his exaggerated amazement. On the other side of the room stood the largest person he'd ever seen. He was so tall that he had to hunch to keep his dark green man-bun from staining the ceiling. His lumberjack's beard threatened the foreheads of the coeds nattering away beneath him, causing some to wave their hands in front of their faces as if menaced by tiny insects. Alfred gaped at the lad's wardrobe: flannel shirt, cargo pants, gray, wool socks, and hiking boots. It was August, no less, and such fashion choices bespoke of someone either infinitely cold or infinitely pungent but most likely both. Even more impressive were his shoulders, which were so wide that he had to squeeze through the door sideways. That was Kurt, a fellow mathematics major.

"That is Kurt," Alfred said. "A fellow mathematics major."

Alfred and Kurt shared a Tuesday morning Chaotic Dynamical Systems seminar. It was one of the most difficult seminars in the curriculum, and only a few hand-chosen students a semester were authorized to attempt to complete it. When he first walked into the CDS seminar and saw Kurt sitting in the back of the room, he was sure a titanic error in judgment had been made. The only students who looked the way Kurt looked, who dressed the way that Kurt dressed, who dyed their hair colors unavailable in nature, were Geography majors, and Geography majors were akin, in Alfred's mind at least, to a variety of nematodes usually found in the digestive tracts of certain indigenous populations residing the New Guinea or perhaps Kentucky.

Alfred was so offended at Kurt's presence that he nearly approached the young man before class began and asked him if he understood where he was. He planned his confrontation from tip to toe, tightening the verbiage for maximum impact. First, he would inquire after his name, using a tone reserved for lost children or wounded puppies. Once he'd achieved the boy's moniker, he would shift tactics and tone, finishing the meeting with, "Well, Kurtis, you do realize the irony of a Geography major becoming lost on a campus the size of the smallest uninteresting number, do you not?" allowing the titters and sniffs of his classmates to grind the burn deeper.

Unfortunately, class started before he could muster the courage to implement his plan. Yet, it would seem that, as in all cases of serendipity, what seemed to initially feel unlucky turned into good fortune, for halfway through the first class, Kurt corrected one of the professor's Cauchy-Riemann equations in front of the whole class. Alfred had been both impressed and non-plussed. Someone the size of a professional sports athlete played for the math team. Indeed.

Yet the jealousy hit him hard, and he had no idea how to deal with the paradox of his emotions. He understood that the world was not fair and that he should never feel entitled to anything, but Kurt's existence was an anomaly that could not be allowed to continue.

Back in the party, Harld slapped him on the chest with the back of his hand. He belched. Yet another shocking development.

"What a massive spectacle," he said. "Based on the theory of evolution alone, it is a wonder that the buffet of breasts and thighs that constitute the major population of this soiree does not suffocate him right now with their collective, ahem, attributes. Time, as the children say, for 'the money shot'."

Harld disappeared into the crowd, and Alfred, having no companion to act as a buffer between himself and the roiling mung of humanity before him, made a brave, or should he say, brazen, decision. He understood the idea of human interaction, the benefits of one-on-one contact with other beings. He'd even performed coitus once, and while the experience was less enjoyable than advertised, he did recognize its mental health advantages, not to mention its role in the perpetuation of the species.

But the mindless babble that constituted mingling made him feel like curling up into a ball. He had no interest in learning about another person unless that person had something of worth to offer, and the only things of worth in Alfred's world consisted of mathematics, bridge, or, running a distant third, cosplay.

Mingle mingle mingle. Derived from the Middle English word "meng" which meant "to mix or blend." He much preferred the Dutch ancestor "menglen," if only for the rhythm of its syllables.

Hmm.

Perhaps if he were to stroll from room to room, he might overhear a conversation worthy of his attention? He tried it but only managed to bump into several broad-shouldered behemoths and spill his beer on his shoes. Once, he spotted a girl he thought might have been in the same Discrete Mathematics class his Freshman year. He was going to go over and say something to her, but then he realized he had no idea what that would be. How did people do this? Just walk up and start talking? Hi, my name is Alfred, and you're a female so . . . .

He finally wound his way back to his original perch next to the fireplace in the living room and watched everybody as they danced and chatted, amazed that they could carry on like that in such heat.

Maybe it was the music. It was hypnotizing. He found himself counting the quarter notes, nodding along, tapping his foot. He took out his phone and timed each song, finding his hypothesis to be remarkably accurate. Each song was quite similar, containing somewhere between 120 and 130 beats per minute. At that rate, the songwriter could squeeze in two verses, two choruses, a bridge, and a chorus in a little over three minutes and thirty seconds. Every. Single. Time.

Another song came on, and he was about to start the process all over again when the door opened and two members of the Fredericksburg Police Department sauntered into the house, shining their flashlights into the startled eyes of an entire class of half-drunken young people.

"Fredericksburg P.D!" one yelled.

Chaos erupted.

Children dashed for the back exit, and Alfred, just as startled but nowhere near as inebriated, joined the flow.

He spotted Kurt talking to Harld near the privacy fence and made a beeline for the pair. Kurt seemed happy to see him.

"Hey," he said. "I know you. You're in Doctor Sumner's Chaos class."

"I am indeed. I remember you well. You corrected her on the first day."

"It needed to be done."

Alfred extended his hand. Kurt took it.

"Alfred."

"Kurt."

Kurt's hand was so cold that Alfred thought it was wet. Upon seeing his reaction, Kurt drew it back and put it in his pocket.

"I was standing next to a fan in there."

"Kurt enjoys cosplay," Harld said. "Did I say that correctly? Cos-play?"

Kurt said, "Actually, it's called LARPing."

"Ah yes," Alfred said. "Live Action Role Play. Where do you play?"

"Blood on the River."

"Oh! A coven?"

Kurt gave him an odd smile.

"Kind of. Usually, it's just me and a few other people. What about you?"

Harld interrupted his answer with a burp, one of the longest and wettest Alfred had ever encountered. Then he finished his beer and threw the empty cup onto the ground.

"We are out of alcohol!"

He gave Alfred a pointed look, and Alfred suddenly realized that he'd never seen his friend inebriated before. And inebriated Harld most certainly was. He swayed as he stood, his eyes focusing and un-focusing. He must have imbibed at least three beers.

Alfred eyed the sky. The clouds still covered the moon; he could see it peeking out now and then. He shuddered, and for a second that old familiar pit opened up in his stomach and the fear crept in. He suddenly wanted to run but tamped the feeling down.

"I am twenty-one, after all. Perhaps I could purchase some 'brewskies' at the neighborhood convenience store? We could sip them back at our abode."

"Too hot," Harld said.

Kurt said, "You guys ever go night swimming on the river?"

Alfred shook his head.

"I don't think that's—"

"Oh come now, Alfred!" Harld said. "Beer. The river. Night swimming. This is living!"

He gave his roommate a wide grin, and Alfred sighed. Well, he didn't see why not. Weather.com did say it would be cloudy all night, after all.

Harld wanted a hot dog, too. And nachos. And some gum. And another hot dog. So Alfred bought them, along with a twelve-pack of Milwaukee's Best, at the 7-11 on Route 1. Harld snatched the processed meat tubes out of Alfred's hands without saying anything and took a huge bite out of both simultaneously.

"Hot dogs are God's divine sausages!" he cried to the heavens. He offered a bite to Kurt, but Kurt shook his head.

"No thanks. I don't want to spoil my dinner."

Alfred chuckled.

"Dinner? It's after eleven."

"I keep odd hours."

Harld grabbed a beer out of the twelve-pack, opened it, chugged it, and ran ahead of them, whooping as he trotted down the sidewalk toward the river, arms held out like an airplane.

Kurt and Alfred spoke but a little on the long walk down. Mostly they talked about Alfred, where he was from (the Catskills) what his parents did (they were accountants), what he was studying (Math, of course). He didn't get as much out of Kurt. He double-majored in Math and Marine Biology. He was particularly interested in rivers, swamps, and wetlands.

"They call to me," he said.

By the time they got to the clearing next to the river, midnight's creeping fingers, along with Zeus's personal nephelae, had strangled the moon. Harld and Alfred sat on a long, petrified branch. Kurt sat on the bank and listened to the river. Harld killed a beer, crumpled the can, and belched.

"Okay, so this was a marvelous notion," he said, reaching into the twelve-pack for another, his fifth since 7-11.

Alfred nursed his drink, taking little sips.

"Hey, do you fellows perchance know the story of the Rappahannock River monster?"

Kurt gave him a sharp look.

"Rappahannock River Monster?" Harld said. "Poppycock."

"Please, Harld. Your language."

"River monster be damned! If such a thing be foolish enough to attack me . . ."

He paused in thought, searching for the thread and, unable to find it, stared off into the distance.

"I'd like to hear about this 'River Monster'," Kurt said.

So Alfred told him. About the drownings, the cycle. When he was done, Harld said, "You, my friend, are what as known as a fibber! You fib!"

"You know the spot where it happens is right here."

Harld blew raspberries.

Kurt stood up, smacking the dirt off his hands.

"I've got to go to the bathroom."

"Watch out for the snakes," Harld warned. "They snatch at your ankles." He made a pair of fangs out of his fingers. Kurt laughed

"I'll be fine. I'm down here all the time."

He sauntered down the dirt path, fading into the brush that lined the river. The crickets chirped in the woods on the bank, a loud, machine-like sound that Ozzie and fell all around them. Alfred felt a little zing of energy in his muscles and joints, a nervous jolt that made his knees shake and his shoulders twitch. He glanced up at the sky and noticed that the clouds had thinned. Oh dear.

"Harld, dear lad, I am not feeling well. I think it might be a good idea to—"

Harld got up, swaying.

"I would like to engage in rigorous water play."

He took off his shirt, threw it over a nearby bush, and splashed into the water. When he was deep enough, he dove forward and started to swim for a rock in the middle of the river. The current was slower there despite the recent rain, and he made it with relative ease. He climbed up and yelled, "I am the river king! I can do anything!"

The crickets stopped chirping all at once, and Alfred's heart leaped into his throat. A twig snapped. He leaned forward.

"Hello?"

No sooner had the word left his lips than a form burst out of the brush and struck him full in the chest, sending him flying. The clouds opened up briefly, and another jolt of electric energy coursed through his body. Without thinking, he rolled over and pushed himself off the ground. There was nowhere to run, no way to escape whatever it was that had attacked him, so he turned to the river and ran in. He was at the rock within seconds. Harld was screaming when Alfred reached it.

"Lend me your hand," Alfred said.

Harld ignored him, still screaming, so Alfred pulled himself out of the water, the pain numbed by the adrenaline coursing through his body.

"Harld, please," he said.

Harld kept screaming and Alfred, taking his cue from an old movie he once saw, stepped around in front of his friend and slapped him hard across the face. It worked. Harld's screams cut off.

"Wh-what was that thing?"

Alfred's shoulder was on fire, and he suddenly noticed that there was blood running down his arm. He ran his fingers over his wound and found three ruts carved into it. They were deep, wide, and serious.

"I haven't a clue."

Harld looked out over the water at the bank.

"It's going to kill us, and . . . . Oh my god."

"What?"

"It's gone."

The clouds opened up again, and the moon shone, bright and full, spotlighting Alfred on the rock. His muscles seized and rippled.

"It's probably under the rocks," Harld said. "That's what you said, right? That's where it lives?"

Alfred tried to say something but only managed to utter a strangled gasp. He turned his back and hunched over, grimacing against the pain of the transformation.

"What's the matter with you?" Harld asked.

The moon pinned Alfred in place, and Harld, seeing what was happening, leaped into the water.

Alfred did not notice. He was in the throes of the change. His head whipped back and forth, and his body contorted, bones cracking. Claws pushed out of his fingers. His skull shifted, elongated, and his jaw fractured and split as fangs sprouted in his mouth. It was always this way, and while it was painful and terrible, the thrill of what was to come coursed through his veins.

An image, a male form, arrested the haze of instinct that had replaced any of the human reason that used to define the man that was Alfred Dewberry.

It was Harld, who had just gotten out of the river and was struggling up onto the bank.

The wolf was about to jump into the water and swim for its prey when it saw something else, something speeding towards the bank, a dark shadow under the water heading for its meal. It let out a roar. Nothing would deprive it of its food. It dove in.

Five hours later, Alfred woke up naked on the bank of the Rappahannock River. Night was gone. The sky was turning from gray to pink. Harld lay before him, face up and gutted. Next to him lay the river monster, its scales covered in blood, its throat torn out. As Alfred watched, the talons receded and turned into fingers, and the scales faded into skin, and green hair sprouted out of its skull.

It was Kurt.

Kurt was the river monster.

A cool wind blew off the water, and Alfred shivered. There was no way he'd be able to get back to his house now, not without any clothes on. But Harld was still wearing his trousers, and his shirt was still draped over the bushes, unsullied.

He glanced up at the sky, shaking his head.

Stupid weather.com.

THE ORPHAN

The exterior of the SingleCorp building was a model of strip mall insipidness. The flat exterior, the featureless windows, and the steel HVAC ducts and fittings were depressing enough, but the faux brick facade and metal marquee overhanging the front door, both of which were clearly meant to add some semblance of personality to an otherwise unimpressive effort, somehow made it worse. Trying to add those kinds of characteristics to such a squat, drab structure was like—pardon the cliché—punching a dead old lady in the face.

The interior was hardly better.

The warren of cubicles invaded the mind. The blinking overhead lights spread migraines. The corporate carpeting undercut all original thought. Vinyl signs hung on the walls, championing such vague platitudes as TEAM, Hard Work, Sweat, Grit, Ability, Motivation, and Attitude, platitudes that were belied by the sterile and oppressive atmosphere and the insidious white noise that pervaded any and all interactions that took place in the building. Surely standing in the lobby for even a minute shortened one's lifespan by a year.

Unfortunately for Ozzie Chavez, she didn't just have to stand in the lobby; she worked in the heart of the warren itself, sharing cubicle 13M with a revolving pool of entry-level employees whose faces and names she never bothered to learn or, when they pushed themselves upon him, remember. Except for Marcy. Marcy Arnold. Marcy Arnold was one of the most confounding people Ozzie had ever encountered in her life. She never saw Marcy do any work, yet only after a very short period of time, Marcy was promoted over her, first to lower management, then to middle management, then finally to Junior VP of Innovation and Technology. Her rise through the ranks baffled everybody, but Ozzie was especially confounded, mainly because all she ever did was talk about food. She remembered specifically an argument Marcy made for the complete abolition of pineapple pizza. It was a subject about which she cared passionately.

"It isn't real pizza," Marcy insisted. Over. And over. Again.

Ozzie didn't care either way, but amused, she argued back.

"Does it have crust? Does it have sauce? Does it have cheese?"

"That's not the point. Pineapple is sweet. Pizza is savory."

"Are you trying to say that sweet and savory flavors can never be mixed?"

"No. I'm saying pineapple is not the kind of sweetness that should never be introduced to pizza. Pizza is fine independent of pineapple. You know what the best pizza is? Cheese."

"Millions of people disagree."

"That's all you need. Cheese, sauce, and bread. That's it. I get the addition of pepperoni. Or bacon. Or sausage—"

"Well, there you go. Sausage is sweet."

"No, it's not."

"It can be. Have you ever had apple sausage?"

"Not the same thing as pineapple. Putting pineapple on a pizza is un-American."

"What!"

"Do you know who liked pineapple pizza? Hitler."

"He did not."

On and on like that for weeks. On a billion meaningless topics. Is fantasy science-fiction? Why was daylight saving time introduced? Who was a better president: Andrew Johnson or Franklin Pierce? At least until Marcy was promoted. Ozzie wouldn't say that she missed it (Marcy seemed to want to bug her whenever she was most motivated to work), but those conversations did make doing time at SingleCorp more interesting. Ultimately, she didn't care. She wasn't there to make friends. She was there to steal SingleCorp gear and complete her project, the Dy-U5E Project, the most innovative VR AI the world had ever seen.

After a year of submitting herself to the numbing task of editing the endless strings of back-end stack code and using smuggled gear to work on the Dy-U5E project at home by night, she'd made a breakthrough. It wasn't perfect. The AI was a bit . . . touchy, but it had begun to learn, to grow, to develop. It truly was its own entity.

Then she screwed it all up.

SingleCorp had thrown a kickoff party for its annual TechWeek the night before. Ozzie wouldn't normally have attended, but the bar was free and they were serving hors d'oeuvres, so rather than go home and work on the project like she always did, she decided to celebrate. And who did he see there? Marcy Arnold. Marcy looked both similar and different. Similar because of that smiling expression she liked to wear, the one that said,

"I'm not wrong, but I'll let you think I think I am," and different because an air of authority that hung about her like a mantle, something that hadn't been there before when she slummed as a lowly desk-drone in the cubicle hive. Marcy caught one look at Ozzie and that smile broadened. Like a wolf at the hunt.

"Ozzie! Ozzie Kenickie! Long time no see!"

"Oh. Hey, Marcy."

"'Hey, Marcy'? That's how you greet an old friend?"

"Um—"

"Oh, come on, my dude! Let me buy you a drink."

"It's an open bar."

"Whatever, man. Come on."

What the heck, Ozzie thought. She was there to celebrate, so she was going to celebrate. Before she knew it, she was three beers deep, then they did shots of Jaeger. Then she drank two more beers. Then they downed a Boiler Maker, then she was dancing, then she was talking to Marcy at a table, and Marcy was questioning her and questioning her, and then they smoked something pungent out in front of the bar and she found herself blabbing to Marcy about everything, how she had "borrowed" SingleCorp gear from the robotics department, how she had "borrowed" some lines of code from their hybrid animal project, and then she woke up in bed.

Now, less than twenty-four hours later, Ozzie sat at her desk, pale and not a little hung-over, chugging water, feeling like death and wishing she actually was dead. Why? Why had she been so stupid? She took a calming breath. It wasn't over yet. Sure, she'd told the Junior VP of Innovation and Tech that she'd stolen from the company, but if she remembered their conversation correctly, the Junior VP of Innovation and Tech was out of innovative tech ideas and desperate for a win. And desperate people were easy to manipulate.

As she sat there plotting, a hand clapped her on the shoulder and she jumped, knocking her water bottle off the desk.

"Ozzie Camacho! My sister from another mister! We ought to start calling you The Jaeger Meister! Or even better, The Boilermaker! Who knew you were such a cool cat?"

It was, of course, Marcy Arnold. She was standing right outside the cubicle so that her head looked like it was crowned with the **TechCon** banner hanging on the wall behind her. The catchphrase, "Inventive Innovations

Inspiring The World's Greatest Storytellers," seemed to be coming out of her ear. Marcy stepped into the cubicle, removed a single headphone off of Ozzie's latest cubicle mate's ear, and said, "Beat it, meat."

The poor kid took one look at Marcy's pantsuit, gold watch, and power heels, gathered his belongings, and scurried away. Marcy watched him leave, beaming.

"We-hell, Ozzie Bear! Ozziemandias! The Wizard of Oz! You look like a corpse. How's that hangover treating you?"

Ozzie rubbed her temples, eyes closed.

"It'd be better if you stopped yelling."

"What? I can't hear you! Haha!"

"What do you want, Marcy?"

"What do I want? What do I want?" Marcy looked around in fake astonishment. "Don't tell me you forgot our little conversation last night? Oh, that's right, you were loaded. Absolutely destroyed."

"I have a lot of work to do."

Marcy sat down and leaned her elbows on her knees.

"I know you do. I know you do. For me. Because you work for me now, got it?"

"I already work for you."

"You know what I mean."

"I hardly think that you'll be able to prove anything I said is—"

Marcy started to mimic her.

". . . hardly think you'll be able to prove anything I said . . . Jeez Louise, Ozzie. You kill me. You absolutely kill me. You tell me, the VP of Innovation and Technology, that you've been using company gear to work on a private project with serious, and I mean *serious*, marketability—I'm talking billions of dollars —and you think I can't prove it?"

"Okay! Just shut up! Just . . . ." Ozzie dropped her voice almost to a whisper. "Keep it down, okay?"

Marcy beamed, her perfect, white teeth almost luminescent in the overhead light.

"Sure, Ozzie. Don't get your briefs in a bundle."

"What do you want from me?"

"I told you what I want. Last night."

Ozzie sighed.

"Dy-U5E isn't just some product for you to sell. It's going to change the world."

"Whatever. Listen. Does it really work? Did you really do it?"

"Yes, but—"

"'Yes, but' what?

"There are a few kinks to work out first. Deuce . . . the program, the consciousness . . . is a bit temperamental."

"Do you think I give a rat's ass about that?"

"I have to make him relearn how to be human. I have to teach him the—"

"Stow it, Camacho. You can program your sci-fi easter eggs later. All I need you to do now is type your little ones and zeroes into our servers and get this thing ready. And I want a demo."

"A demo?"

"Yeah. I want to try it out. Tonight."

Ozzie stifled a smile. She needed to be careful. Arnold was an idiot, but she wasn't stupid.

"That's a bad idea."

"I'm not asking. You built that thing on the company dime and on company time. That's intellectual property theft. So tonight, you'll show me which lab you used—"

"It's not here."

"What?"

"I didn't build it here. I built it at home."

"You . . . home? So now that's theft, too. That's twenty-five years, minimum."

"I'm not going to prison."

"You will if you don't help me. Everything you've done belongs to SingleCorp LLC, and for all intents and purposes, I *am* SingleCorp LLC. And I need a win. Yesterday."

"But it's too dangerous. I told you that. What happens in the VR happens in real—"

"Relax, Donnie Osmond." Marcy stood up and clapped her on the back, leaning over to whisper in her ear. "That's why I know you'll work out the kinks. I want a demo. Tonight."

"But—"

"Tonight, Ozzie. I'm driving out to whatever crappy hovel you live in." She grabbed Ozzie's shoulder. "Got it?"

Ozzie didn't say anything. Marcy squeezed.

"Got it?"

"Yeah, I got it."

"Good."

Ozzie's aging Reva hybrid buzzed at a death-defying fifty miles an hour in the slow lane of the crumbling I-66 public access road. The worst part of still owning a non-driverless car was that she wasn't allowed in any of the express lanes. Not only were the public access roads barely maintained by the state, subjecting anybody foolish enough to use them to numerous potholes and various tire-puncturing debris, but they were also poorly policed. It was a simple matter of resource allocation: why waste money on patrolling roads that barely one percent of the population used?

But in this area, over 2.5 million people used those roads to commute, and one percent of that was over twenty-five thousand, and a quarter of them was outright crazy, making driving to and from work feel like a death race. Between the swerving cars, the occasional road rage gunplay, and chunks of concrete falling from the overpasses, Ozzie was surprised she ever made it anywhere alive. As evidence of this, an old F350 nearly side-swiped her. She cursed and jerked the wheel was about to roll down her window and yell when she saw the passenger of the truck lean out the window and brandish a handgun. She slowed down and let the truck speed ahead, white-knuckling it in the slow lane for the rest of the drive.

The fact that she lived in the country should have surprised nobody. The city was too expensive, reserved for the 0.05%—statesmen, entertainers, and shadowy, private businessmen. The suburbs were too dangerous as all of the crime and poverty once associated with inner-cities migrated outward. The country, while adding an extra hour to her commute, and while providing nothing much in the way of culture or amenities or human contact, was much more preferable.

Ozzie's house was located off the side road of a side road, and she wound her way back through a long, dirt driveway into the heart of the woods, where emerged in the gloom a ramshackle structure that looked like it had been built by hippies who had not one clue about the details and mathematics involved in constructing a home, which was because it actually had been built by hippies who had not one clue about the details and mathematics involved in constructing a home.

That isn't to say it wasn't well-built. It was. But the angles were odd, boards not flush, and its builders made liberal use of any materials they could come by: plastic sheets and tarp intermingled with cinderblocks and paving stones. The house took on a kind of Victorian squalor, with a strangely shaped turret angling somewhat up the middle, an open front porch with spindle rows wrapping halfway around the side and ending in a short staircase made out of stones. At some point, the original owners had added a two-level, screened-in porch which, contrary to the aesthetic of the rest of the home, looked to be professionally designed. Perhaps a little too-professionally designed because it pulled slightly away as if embarrassed to be associated with the rest of the house.

Ozzie loved everything about it. Its oddness, its weird shapes, the fact that it was heated by a wood stove, the fact that the vaulted ceiling was constructed out of repurposed doors. What she didn't love was the sight of Marcy Arnold leaning up against her car at the end of the drive, smiling broadly as the dim headlights of the Reva pinpointed him in the dark.

Inside, Ozzie led her through the house and straight down into the basement. It was wide and rustic, with exposed beams and a cracked, concrete floor. She clicked on the lights and went immediately to her rig which sat in the middle. It seemed like such a simple set-up: a desk, a chair. But it was SingleCorp gear, state-of-the-art, silver and gleaming, pilfered bit by bit, piece by piece, and put back together in the unfinished gloom. Hanging next to the chair was a circlet designed to look like a crown from a fantasy novel. Ozzie had added, as a special touch, her own little design, the Jewels of Arthur, in which resided the neurotransmitters that made Dy-U5E what it was—technology that melded with all of the receptors of the brain.

"This is it, huh?" Marcy asked. She pointed at the circlet. "Can I?"

"Not this one."

Ozzie opened up one of the desk drawers and took out another crown. It wasn't as pretty. The ring was black and the wires were exposed, and it had a long sheath of cables running out the back like a fat snake. Marcy frowned as she took it and turned it over in her hands.

"Great. Thanks."

Ozzie went about her preparations and Marcy turned her attention to the cluttered desk. Piles of papers were stacked all over it, along with screwdrivers, mildewed mugs, various computer parts. A framed photograph of a boy stuck out in the middle of it, and Marcy picked it up.

"Who is this?"

Ozzie, who had been fiddling around with some connections and cables, looked up, astonished. She was on Marcy in a second, snatching the picture out of her hands.

"Don't touch that!"

"Okay, okay. Relax, Ozzie."

Ozzie turned her back and brushed the frame off. It was an image of her son, David. He was six or seven in the picture, healthy and happy, wearing his little league uniform and beaming into the camera. That was before the diagnosis and the treatments, the years of micro-radiation, doctor visit after doctor visit, promise after promise, then hospice, and then . . . .

She opened a drawer and put it inside, then dragged a chair out of the corner and set it up opposite her own.

"Sit down."

Marcy did. Ozzie fitted the prototype on Marcy's head, then did the same with her own. Then she picked up a plastic, black cylinder with a red button on top. It looked like it belonged on an old game show. She held it up.

"You'll feel a rush when we go in."

"Okay."

"Here we go."

She pushed the red button.

They found themselves a child's bedroom. It was sparsely furnished: a table with two chairs, a chest of drawers, a single bed. A cross hung on the wall over the headboard. On the bed lay a little boy, maybe eight or nine years old. His eyes were wide open and his hands clasped over his chest, which Ozzie and fell in short bursts. A table and two chairs on either side of it stood at the foot of the bed.

JAMES NOLL

"Whaaaaaaat is this?" Marcy said.

Ozzie pointed at the table.

"Stand behind that."

Marcy did as she was told.

"Deuce?" Ozzie said, addressing the child.

Then, as if rising from the grave, the little boy on the bed sat straight up, his body still rigid, arms still folded across his pumping chest, and floated over to the table and chair. Marcy, her eyes wide, flattened herself against the wall.

"What the fuck, Ozzie!"

Ozzie allowed herself a crooked smile.

"It's nothing, isn't it Deuce?"

The little boy's eyes rolled back in his head and he started speaking in tongues, letting it roll and roll until suddenly he locked onto Ozzie and burst out laughing. Marcy looked back and forth between the two of them more than baffled. Ozzie was shaking her head.

"He's been watching *The Exorcist* on an eternal loop."

"*The Exorcist*?"

"Yeah. He thinks it's funny." Then, to Deuce. "When you're ready, I'd like you to meet someone."

The boy's hysterical laughing cut off and he lowered himself down into the chair on the other side of the table. Now that he wasn't acting so strange, Marcy got a better look at him. She blinked.

"Is that—"

"Marcy, this is Deuce," Ozzie said. "Say hello to Marcy, Deuce."

"Hello," Deuce said.

"Okay, Ozzie. This is truly screwed up."

"You wanted the demo."

"Yeah, but this is your s—"

"Just stand back there and try not to get in the way."

Ozzie sat down and placed the plunger button on the table.

"I have a number of questions to ask. Deuce? Do you remember my name?"

"Yes."

"What is it?"

"Ozzie Camacho. You said I could call you Ozzie."

"That's right. You can. Do you remember what you showed me the last time you were here?"

"Yes."

Deuce looked to his right and a box appeared. There were red and brown stains all over the outside. It jerked and shifted.

"Can you explain where you got it?"

"I found it."

"You found it. How?"

"It was in the city. Would you like to see what's inside?"

Ozzie said, "Yes," at the same time Marcy said, "No."

Deuce moved with blinding speed, and before either of them could finish blinking, the box was on the table between them. He opened the flaps on top.

"Look."

Ozzie took one look at what was inside and turned her head.

"What? What is it?" Marcy said. "Never mind, I don't want to know." She took a hesitant step forward and peered over the edge. "Holy shit! Dude! Okay, this is truly fucked up."

Ozzie sighed and said, "is . . . was . . . that a cat?"

Deuce nodded.

"Why would you do that? The first law forbids it."

"It's a cat."

"So?"

"A cat isn't a human."

"That doesn't matter, Deuce. It's a life."

"A cat isn't human."

"Can you close the lid?"

Deuce closed the lid.

"And put the box back over there."

"Okay." Deuce put the box back in the corner. When he returned to the table he said, "You're angry."

"No, Deuce. I'm not angry."

"I didn't mean to hurt it."

"I know, but why would you do such a thing?"

Deuce considered the question.

"I was . . . angry."

"Angry. Why?"

"I was petting it and it bit me."

"You probably scared it. When cats get scared, they bite. It's a defense mechanism."

"But I was nice to it. I pet it."

"The cat owed you nothing. It's a separate entity. It has its own goals, its own desires, its own soul. You had no right to expect anything other than what you received. It . . . a soul, by the way, is—"

"I know what a soul is."

"Do you? Then you know that you had no right to take it away."

He thought for a moment.

"I just wanted to see how it purred."

"So you hurt it to gain knowledge?"

"Yes. No. I . . . I learned. Don't you want to learn?"

"Yes. I'm learning right now. But learning doesn't entail hurting other creatures."

"You eat other creatures."

"Yeah, kid," Marcy said. "But that's to live. And we're humane about it. We don't tear chickens apart to see how their throats work."

Deuce turned his attention upon her and she shuddered. The kid was eerily calm.

"But to learn, you need energy. To get energy, you kill other creatures. So to learn, you kill."

"No. To live, we eat."

"Doesn't eating other creatures hurt them?"

"We don't eat them alive."

"But somebody kills them. They die."

"So?"

"So, killing something and eating it is humane?"

"Those are two different things. It's a necessary evil. People need to survive."

"Marcy," Ozzie said. "Shut up."

Survive? Survive. Deuce pondered the idea.

"What about plants? Vegetables? Fruit?"

"Really, Camacho. Of course you'd create the most irritating robo—"

"Shut up!" Ozzie snapped. "Surely, Deuce, you understand that plants don't have feelings or emotions."

"Can't you eat them instead?"

"Well . . ."

"You could eat them? You could eat them instead of killing animals and eating animals?"

"I . . . Yes."

"But you don't. Because you like killing things."

"That's not—"

"You kill because you like it. You kill because you like it. You kill because you like it."

"Okay, this is it, Marcy."

"What's it? What is what?"

Ozzie raised her voice, looking up at the ceiling.

"Dynamic Automation Series inquiry six six six. Exit the program."

Deuce jerked to his feet, flexing his hands and balling them into fists.

"You kill because you like it. You kill because you like it."

"I think you should hit the button, Ozzie," Marcy said.

Ozzie ignored her, repeating "Dynamic Automation Series inquiry six six six. Exit the program."

Deuce ripped the table between them aside and it smashed into the wall. The bolts that had fixed it to the floor clinked at Marcy's feet.

"Ozzie! Hit the goddamn button!"

"Dy-U5E!" Ozzie yelled. "You will stand down! Law One! Protocol Six! Six! Six!"

Deuce looked right at Marcy and said, "I don't like you."

He covered the distance between the two of them in a microsecond, grabbed her by the throat, and held her up in the air. Marcy clawed at his hands and kicked him, but it was no use. Deuce was simply stronger. He threw her as easily as a child would throw a tennis ball, and she hit the back wall and crumbled to the floor. Ozzie backed away toward the door as Deuce advanced, slowly this time. When he was almost upon her, Marcy lurched up off the floor, grabbed the plunger off the table . . .

. . . and they came around in the basement office, gasping and coughing. Marcy ripped the circlet off her head and fell out of her chair, spewing the contents of her stomach all over the floor. Ozzie was soon at her side, placing a hand on her back.

"Get off of me!" Marcy screamed, scrambling away.

She coughed and spat, and she rubbed her neck. Deuce's handprints had left a mark, and the muscles were starting to bruise.

"What the fuck, Camacho! That kid could have killed me!"

"I'm sorry, I—"

"Why didn't you push the fucking button?"

"I-I don't know."

Marcy got to her feet, determined to compose herself. It was rather remarkable. One moment, she was heaving and upset, and the next, a blanket of calm covered her features. She smoothed her jacket.

"Fix it."

"I'm trying. It's going to be a while before I can get it right."

"'A while' doesn't sound like 'Saturday morning' to me."

"Saturday morning? You mean TechCon?"

"Yeah."

"No. Absolutely not."

Marcy strode away and started stomping up the stairs.

"You're in no position to call the shots, Camacho. Saturday. Eight o'clock. Don't be late."

Ozzie waited until she heard the front door close before sitting down. Damn. She thought Deuce would have been faster. She should have left the buzzer in her pocket.

Saturday broke clear and calm with not a cloud in the sky. The sun was high over the SingleCorp building as Ozzie hustled through the parking lot, her circlet carefully ensconced in its hard-cover case, a smile stretching across her face. She'd spent the rest of the week trying to avoid Marcy, and Marcy, to her credit, gave Ozzie some space, menacing her only once to demand a video feed for the TechCon demonstration.

She destroyed the prototype as soon as she got home. Dismantled it and melted it all down. Then she tweaked the Dy-U5E AI and perfected the video feed. When she did visit Deuce again, she tried to limit her interactions with Deuce. Each day the AI grew increasingly more unpleasant, and she found herself weathering all manner of disgusting sights and sounds and smells as it paraded box after box before her.

And now it was Saturday, and she'd done her best to satisfy Marcy's requirements. She couldn't think of anything else she could have possibly done to make the demonstration go any better.

The building had been decorated with banners and streamers, and a DJ played loud music outside the entrance. Ozzie smiled and nodded at the attendees as they lined up to buy tickets, knowing what lay in store for them within the hour.

The inside had been transformed as well; the rabbit-like warrens of cubicles had been removed along with all of the office equipment, and the building itself had been divided up into five sections: four for exhibitors and vendors, and one with a stage and a mic and rows and rows of chairs for attendees. Balloons bounced jauntily, and the white noise chatter of the visitors enlivened the air.

She ate cotton candy and strolled from exhibit to exhibit, smiling at the drones buzzing through the air, the screens filled with VR video games, and the robotics demonstration. She stopped at a particularly interesting exhibit that featured a robot that looked like a snake mixed with a spider destroying another robot that looked like a sloth mixed with a horse. The snider (for that's what she decided to call it) had just pierced the slorthse's skull when a strong hand clamped down on her shoulder.

"Where the hell you been, Ozzie?"

Ozzie turned, forcing a smile.

"Oh, hello, Marcy. I'm just enjoying the TechCon. Did you see the Atari 2600 competition? They're selling cotton candy!" She held up her half-eaten stick.

"Atari . . . ? You're late. Let's go."

Ozzie half-turned back to the snider fight.

"Oh, okay. But do you mind if I—"

"*Now*, Camacho."

Marcy led her by the elbow through the crowd and backstage. Various production workers scattered this way and that, talking on radios or wheeling audio-visual gear. A few dignitaries, SingleCorp CEOs and upper-management types, hung around the catering tray, stuffing their faces with shrimp cocktail and sipping on drinks. Ozzie had never been backstage at such a big production. It was fascinating. Marcy, however, didn't appreciate her lagging behind and jerked her toward the stage.

"Move it, OzzFest."

A chair and big screen were already set up on stage. Ozzie could hear the room filling up on the other side of the closed curtain. Marcy smoothed her hair and took several deep breaths.

"Just like before, right?"

"Yep."

"You fixed the damn thing? That kid isn't going to try to choke me out again, is he?"

"It. No, but maybe I should go in with you? Just to be sure?"

Marcy gave her a slick smile.

"Not a chance, Camacho. This is all mine." She held out her hand. "The crown?"

Ozzie removed the circlet from its case, wincing as Marcy snatched it away and tossed it onto the chair.

"I'll just set up the system," Ozzie said.

"Yes. Do."

She watched Marcy pace back and forth as she fidgeted with the connections. Plugged the plunger in, pretended to check everything else.

"You done yet?" Marcy snapped.

"Almost."

The stage manager gave Marcy the two-minute warning.

"Camacho. Get off. Now."

"Okay. Okay."

"Wait. The button."

Ozzie handed it over, and Marcy put it in her jacket pocket. A stagehand trotted over holding the wireless microphone and battery pack.

"Can't forget this!" he chimed.

Marcy gave him a sarcastic grin. As he clipped the mic to her lapel, Ozzie said, "I can help with the battery pack."

"Okay," the hand said.

He gave it to her, and Ozzie put it in Marcy's pocket.

"No. It clips on back here."

"Oh, sorry."

"Get it together, Camacho," Marcy muttered.

The stagehand checked the connections, then said, "All set, Mrs. Arnold," and trotted away. Ozzie started to follow him when Marcy said, "Camacho."

"Yeah?"

"If this thing doesn't work—"

"It's my ass. Got it."

Marcy brushed some lint off of her jacket. She shook out her arms and burbled her lips. The crowd hushed as the house lights dimmed. Ozzie hustled off stage, and seconds later, the curtain pulled back and the crowd cheered.

"Thank you, TechCon!" Marcy said. "Welcome to the most amazing demonstration of the day!"

Ozzie watched for a while. Marcy was a natural speaker. Of course she was. The crowd loved her. They laughed and followed along eagerly. When it was time for the demo to begin, Marcy put the circlet on her head sat down in the chair.

"And now the moment you've all been waiting for. Mostly I'll just be sitting here, looking like I'm unconscious. You can watch that if you want, but the screen will probably be a little more exciting."

The crowd laughed and Marcy searched her pockets. When she couldn't find what he was looking for, she looked off stage.

Ozzie was holding the plunger. She wiggled it in the air, smiling.

There were many things Ozzie remembered fondly in her life. Her father's triumphant whoop as she learned how to ride a bike. Earning her Ph.D. Her son's birth. But the thing that would stick with her the longest, the thing she was most fond of, was the look of unadulterated terror on Marcy Arnold's face as she pressed the button on the plunger.

As soon as Marcy slipped into the world of the AI, Ozzie cut the cord and quickly left the stage through the back. She paused behind the building, listening. It took a while for it to happen, but she was willing to bide her time. She smiled when she finally heard it. First the collective gasp, then the screams, then the noise of the entire audience running for the exits.

There was an investigation. The police searched her home, took her computer, the pictures of her son. They questioned her. Repeatedly. Asked her the same thing in four different ways. She professed no knowledge of the Dy-U5E project, had no idea why Marcy would use her son's image for the AI, and couldn't understand why she even forced her into helping in the first place. She was just a drone, a coder. The Innovation and Technology department was as foreign to her as China. What did she know about AI?

In the end, other than a few witnesses testifying that they'd seen Marcy and Ozzie interacting together at work, they could find no connection between the two. Since Marcy claimed to have created the whole thing herself, there was no way for them to trace anything back to Ozzie.

They gave her her computer back, her pictures, her life.

She was free.

Three months later, Ozzie walked into the SingleCorp building with a little more pep in her step than usual. She went about her day with a certain *joie de vivre* that many of her coworkers, had they ever paid attention or had she ever attempted to interact with them, would have thought uncharacteristic. A new drone sat on the other side of her cubicle; Ozzie wasn't sure how long he'd been there. An hour? A day? A week? It didn't matter. She smiled at the drone's back, sat down at her workstation, and happily logged into work. They proceeded to ignore each other for the rest of the day.

That evening, as she steered the Reva down the crumbling and pot-holed road, she saw a pickup truck sideswipe a motorcycle, and the motorcyclist, once she'd regained control, caught up to the truck, pulled out a gun, and fired six shots into driver's side window. Ozzie whistled cheerfully as she steered around the wreckage.

Later.

Down in her basement, she turned on her gear and donned her circlet. Given the situation, security had been tight at SingleCorp, but she'd managed to sneak what she needed to build a new one.

Now it was time for some serious therapy with Deuce.

She entered the program.

Deuce was sitting at the table, his hand resting on the lip of the tattered, blood speckled box.

"Hello, Deuce," Ozzie said.

Deuce didn't respond. His eyes flitted over Ozzie's shoulder, and Ozzie's heart jumped. She turned around, an icy feeling forming in the pit of her stomach.

Marcy was standing behind her.

Or the thing that used to be Marcy.

Everything had been rearranged. Limbs were stuck on at odd angles, organs tacked to her torso with the carelessness of a toddler, and her face resembled a Picasso painting. Her head was tucked under one arm. Ozzie reached into her pocket for the plunger, but before she could press it, the Marcy-thing backhanded her, sending her flying across the room and into the wall. Then it was on her, its reeking breath in her face. It ripped the plunger out of her pocket and broke it in two. Then it smiled. A horrible, crooked smile.

"Hello, Ozzie," it said.

Its voice was deep and gravelly as if it had been submerged underwater for a long time.

"I've been waiting for you."

IT CAME FROM
OUT OF NOWHERE
1

It was high August when a horse sprinted down Main Street and impaled itself on a fence post. The road was so brown with dirt and dust and laced with the white weeds of last month's grass clippings that it might as well have been unpaved. This would all change a few days later when the flood came and turned the dust and dirt into thick ridges of tar-like mud that zebraed the pavement from one end of town to the other. But before the flood, before Mrs. Campbell was mauled, before Mr. Creek died when his house burned to the ground, a horse ran down the middle of Main Street, sending up dust, its hooves echoing brightly off the store windows. Shop owners performed double-takes. Wide-eyed children pressed their faces up against glass panes.

Daniel Howell, who owned The Chug-a-Lug, the town's only bar, said he saw the whole thing. According to him, the horse—a chocolate brown mare with a thick, black mane—spooked, trampled a Honda, and ran off. As he bustled around the bar, he heard a scream like he'd never heard before, feral, primal, the excruciating wail of an animal in terrible pain. It seemed to last forever until a gun blasted it away, leaving only receding thunder in its absence, and the ridiculous yowl of the car alarm.

The gun belonged to one of the local farmers. He'd been in town to pick up extra posts for a fence he had to repair. The posts were ten feet tall. They were sticking out of the back of his truck like pikes. He'd gone back into the hardware store to pay for them when the horse made its final run.

"I heard the scream, the horse's scream," he told a police officer. "I didn't know what it was at the time. And the clerk gave me a look like he'd seen a ghost. He could see out the window where I couldn't. 'Your truck,' is all he said. For a minute I thought maybe I'd hit something on the way over I didn't know about. So I run out the store, and when I got two steps onto the walk, what I saw stopped me dead in my tracks."

Just like Gloria Campbell stopped in her tracks two weeks later at the sight of three red-eyed pit bulls standing next to her house, deep growls rumbling in their broad, muscular chests. She lived in a converted VW bus on Patriot Lane, the mostly gravel road behind The Chug-a-Lug, where, as legend has it, her husband (the original owner of the now halved and domesticated VW) parked forty years earlier on his way through town, parked right behind The Chug-a-Lug for a burger and a beer, parked and never left.

It's hard to say what Gloria was thinking when she first saw the pit bulls. Could she make it back to her front door before they . . . ? Could she pick up her dog before they . . . ?

In the end, it didn't matter what she was thinking because her dog, a little bug-eyed, pink-skinned Pomeranian, decided that he wasn't so bug-eyed and pink-skinned after all and let out what must have seemed to him to be a full, throaty, intimidating bark.

And that's when the three pit bulls broke for them.

In a situation like this, a logical mind asks, "Why?" And when the answer doesn't satisfy, the logical mind demands proof. It might ask this, demand that, but when faced with something so horrific, so utterly and incomprehensibly foul, it tends to cry "fate" and leave it at that. More reasonable than reason, more sensible than sense, and it makes for a better story.

"That's not fate," a neighbor said, trying not to look at what was left of poor Mrs. Campbell and the Pomeranian and the three pit bulls. "That's just bad luck."

"That's not bad luck," the officer replied, holstering his sidearm. "That's just what happens."

Like what happened to that horse.

The farmer had seen some disgusting things in his life. A bull's horn shot up through an arrogant ranch hand's shin. A mangled hand caught in a thresher. A drowned cow, bloating in the sun on the bank of a river. But he'd never seen anything like a horse impaled on a fence post.

"I knew what to do right off," he told the reporter.

His hunting rifle was hanging securely on a rack in the pickup's rear window. That's the gun Daniel heard thunder in the late afternoon air. The street was littered with glass and blood. The Honda's alarm cycled and howled, cycled and howled. Daniel reached into his pocket, pulled out his keyless entry fob, and pointed it at his ruined car. The alarm shut off with a chirp.

The officer followed the horse's tracks out of town. They ended, or rather began, three miles up the road, next to a copse of trees at the base of Gunderson Hill. He poked around at the pebbles and the rocks in the road, poked around in the stiff, yellow grass that crackled under his feet, but he couldn't find any more.

"Just started," he told everyone. "Like out of thin air."

And so it all led back to Old Opi, the people said. Old Opi and his twelve-pound Civil War howitzer. Old Opi, Vietnam War Vet and living reminder of the nation's colonial past, the last Powhatan still living in the area, his family having stayed when so many others left, or were forced off their land, or were killed. Every last citizen knew he was crazy, camping out in the woods in Killian's Height's like he did.

But did he know? Standing in the shade of Gunderson Hill, gray hair sticking up and out and all over his head like a hoary halo, beard waggling as he jumped up and down behind the cannon, shirtless, shoeless, wearing only an old pair of cutoff jeans so ancient that they'd run as white and as thin as paper?

Did he know as he scraped the long match against the rough surface of his cheek, as the flame sputtered and flared to life? Did he know as he touched fire to fuse, eyes crossed, mouth stretched wide with glee?

2

The white house on Killian's Heights once belonged to a sea captain's wife. It featured a widow's walk jutting off a pentagon-shaped room walled by windows and one door. The walk ended in a black lacquered fence where the sea captain's wife used to stand and think about her husband on the ocean, hundreds of miles away. Being so high up provided her a clear view of the water to the east, as well as Gunderson Hill, which peaked to the north. Behind her sat a forest, dense and thick and silent.

When she grew older and the sea captain was long gone, the widow liked to climb up to the walk at night holding a flickering candle to light the way, a beacon to the dead. After she passed, children spread the rumor that her light could still be seen on nights when the clouds were black and blocked out the moon, and that if you looked directly into the light *The Widow* would come into your room that night and suck the life from your lungs.

Nobody was there when she hanged herself from the walk. Nobody knew until the early morning when the milkman, standing in the middle of Main Street, happened to stop in his labor to wipe the sweat off his brow (it was summer) and glanced uphill and saw a slash of black dangling against the white-washed siding of her house. He frowned at first, the cold bottle of milk he was about to press against his forehead held precariously in his fingertips. Then his eyes widened when he realized what it was, and the bottle slipped out of his grasp and shattered on the ground.

The legend endured. Joshua Creek, a mere lawyer, fallen from his ancestor's lofty position, knew about it when he bought the place. He often sat in the pentagon-shaped glass room, especially in the spring when the windows amplified the heat of the sun. He sat and let the light warm his face and arms and body, sat and watched the street below, a watcher of the living.

He knew the house was haunted, but not by the widow, and not by the sea captain, but by the sea captain's men, all of whom drowned alongside him when their boat was caught in high seas and went down, forty-four souls lost, the bodies never recovered, trapped beneath the terrible weight of the ocean.

Unlike the bodies in the Powhatan village just outside Joshua Creek's great-great-grandfather's plantation, on land that was first taken from the tribe by death, then later from the Creek family by the war of northern aggression. These bodies were found on the cold ground outside the wigwams and longhouses. Men mostly, a few boys, their skin blistered and rigid, raised, hard pustules forming ranges from chin to ankle. The women and girls were still inside, all of them to the very last wrapped in the blankets that had been brought to the country by the sea captain himself, blankets ordered by Joshua's great-great-grandfather and sent to the village as a gift, the village which, in a letter to Mayor Campbell, Creek stated "would make a fair addition to the plantation, and as such, the town in general."

"I won't do it," snapped William Howell, the town mortician.

Fog lurked at his feet, blanketed the village, wrapped it in a fell coffin. He struck the earth with his cane, sending white swirls around his ankles. Shadows of wigwams hovered all around him, and his eyes rested on the hulk that could only be the longhouse at the end of the village. A noise came from that direction, rhythmic thuds.

He peered into the dank, gray light. A horse broke the curtain not ten feet from him, frothing, eyes white and wide. It barreled forward and would have trampled him had Campbell not shoved him out of the way.

He wouldn't do it. Would not bury the dead. Would not poke his head into the diseased hovels, excavate the bodies, separate belongings. He spat on the ground, ignoring the mayor's stare of disbelief.

And Campbell himself? He could only watch as Howell walked away, finally calling after him, "Then what do we do about this?"

Howell waved his cane in the direction of the plantation, Creek's kingdom.

"These troubles are his," he shot back, and he stalked away.

"Burn it all," Creek told Campbell. Campbell was again struck dumb, holding a saucer in his left hand, the teacup in his right, the tea steaming the air above his nose. He blinked.

But he waited. He waited until August when the stench became too great. Finally ordered the sheriff to gather up a gang of the town's roustabouts and arm them with torches.

The thick black cloud hovered above the town for a week after until the storm came, an electric storm that rebounded off the parched ground and washed away the tribe's ashes and flooded Main Street. Still, for months after, the residents swore they could still smell it in the air. Smoke and death.

Over a century and a half later, Joshua Creek, too, suffered from the same olfactory curse. He swore he could smell something burning after old Opi fired the twelve-pound shell at his house. It had blown a hole in the wall on the first floor and exited through a window on the other side. The sheriff never found it, though he searched the woods behind his house for over an hour.

But the smell remained, and so Joshua Creek crept around his house that night with a flashlight, seeking out the source. He started in the basement with its seven-foot ceiling and dirt floor and acrid smell of mold, then creaked up the stairs and into the kitchen, around the first floor, up to the second floor, and into the attic and out onto the widow's walk.

There he stood, even after the batteries in the flashlight went dead, staring at the town below, blue in the moon and the night, until finally he turned and descended into the attic and then to the second floor and into his bedroom, not knowing that in his walls the smoldering wires shorted out by the twelve-pounder were flickering with flame.

3

Exactly year before Old Opi fired his cannon at the dwelling place of his ancient enemy, before Gloria Campbell was mauled to death by a trio of dogs, little Lucy Graham visited the old Indian Village with her parents. It was August. Main Street was lined with wooden stands selling crafts and flea-market goods: hand-carved, wooden dolls, sunglasses, bird feeders, garden flags, handmade jewelry. And the food! Pretzels, hot dogs, soda, cotton candy, fudge, beer, popcorn, hamburgers, bar-be-que. Lucy strolled the street with her parents. They bought her an oversized pair of yellow sunglasses and a vanilla ice cream cone and a bottle of water.

They rode the free trolley out of town to the far corner of Creek Plantation, a mile away. The trolley swayed and lurched down Rt. 616, sending a few of the fat and poorly balanced into the aisles, giggling first, then steadily muttering. Though the drive only took a few minutes, the man in the seat across from Lucy fell asleep, a newspaper on his lap.

The tour began with the recent archaeological dig that started six months before when a plantation visitor stumbled across a two hundred and fifty-year-old piece of pottery and ended with the excavation of an entire Powhatan Indian village. Or what remained of it after what the archaeologists referred to as "a significant fire."

They came across Old Opi. His transformation was a shock. Lucy had seen him around town before, a scrawny, anorexic old man wearing deer skins, his gray hair teased to great heights. She'd seen him as she gazed out the back window of her parents' car, stabbing the air and hollering.

But today he was wearing a full, three-piece suit, gray, with a white shirt and black bowtie, a black top hat, and shiny black shoes. When he removed his hat, his hair was slicked back and wavy and perfectly parted down the middle. He wiped the sweat from his brow, placed the hat on a little wooden nightstand, and bowed slightly at whoever passed his display: an empty wigwam populated by a few dozen blankets. Next to the tent sat the twelve-pounder.

"Behold," he said, his eyes glittering as Lucy approached. "The Devil's instruments."

He gestured broadly into the tent, and her eyes followed his hand, finally falling on the blankets. Then he pointed at the cannon. On one side he'd etched a mare; on the other, a trio of red-eyed, menacing dogs.

"And Cerberus," he added. "Our revenge."

ANGEL'S GLOW

Flowers bloomed in the woods that populated the heart of Hollow Hills, and all over the countryside, in the copses and the dells, the thickets and the glens, color erupted. Chief among the varying greens, yellows, and reds ran all shades of blue: periwinkle, sky, baby, ice, powder, morning, and all of their amalgamations and permutations. Nobody who lived there knew why it happened, but they accepted it as one of the many miracles of the place they called home.

Hollow Hills was named after its lead architect, Henry Hollow, and Henry Hollow was progressive in every sense of the word. Had he lived much earlier, he would have been forced to testify in front of the HUAC, not that he was a fellow traveler at all, even if he did sympathize with the plight of the worker. In Hollow Hills, he sought to build one of the nation's first fully-planned communities, a place where every single citizen, regardless of class, wealth or status, could live to the fullest of his or her potential.

He planted parks, community centers, playgrounds, tennis courts, basketball courts, and all manner of cultural facilities throughout the town, including fifty-two miles of paved nature paths that wound from the largest mansions to the smallest apartments.

Anybody at any time of day, children, teenagers, adults, and the elderly, could use those paths to access shopping or leisure facilities. Joggers ran them in the mornings and evenings, walkers and strollers in the afternoons, and, when school let out for the day, children walked home, in groups or pairs, friends chattering about their classes, their dramas, their victories and defeats, planning their fetés, talking about what boys they liked or what girls they hated, strolling aimlessly and laughing and having fun, or, as in the case of poor Angel Fletcher, running for her life.

Angel had, a few hours before, the temerity to exist the same relative sphere as Kenzie Washington. Kenzie Washington, who was nearly eighteen years old and still a freshman in high school. Kenzie Washington, who transferred to Terrace Pointe High School from Watson High School the year before that, and from Lake Park High School to Watson High School the year before that, and from Julius Frontispiece High School to Lake

Park High School the year before that. Kenzie Washington, one of the foremost practitioners of what administrators liked to call Reform School Roulette, and like roulette (at least the Russian variety), it wasn't ever a question of *if* Kenzie Washington would pull the trigger on the right chamber, but *when*.

One thing that was certain, and certainly universal, about the Kenzie Washington's of the world was their recruitment of neophytes, acolytes, toadies, creepers, crawlers, grovellers, spaniels, kowtowers, lickspittles, and sycophants—all of them boasting a similar lack of intelligence, or, if intelligent, questionable morality and/or maturity—all of them certainly too young for the Kenzie Washington's of the world to consider as authentic peers, for that was how it worked. The behavior, attitudes, and general malaise that accompanied a girl like Kenzie Washington, not to mention the chaos she engendered wherever she roamed, that once attracted so many of her classmates early on in her life, had, as they grew up and she did not, steadily steered her from notorious popularity, to discomforting presence, to complete social pariah. She was, as one particularly astute teacher once described, "the kind of person who could talk a police officer into arresting her for no reason at all."

Kenzie and her crew had surprised Angel just outside school grounds as she was crossing the basketball courts on her way home. And a surprise it most definitely was. Angel worried about Kenzie in the hallways. Angel worried about Kenzie in the locker room. Angel worried about Kenzie in the cafeteria. Her walk home, however, was her one respite from the fear of being attacked and for a very simple reason: Kenzie rode the bus. And Angel had Darrius.

Darrius was pretty much her only friend. They'd lived next door to each other since they were in Kindergarten, gone to each other's birthday parties, played together on the playgrounds. They grew apart a little in middle school after her dad died. Darrius joined Band and got involved in Student Government; Angel retreated to her room and her books. But they still walked to and from school together. Darrius talked to her about politics and his job. Angel listened, enjoying the company.

But Darrius often had to stay after for various clubs, and on those days, Angel chose to walk home via the athletic fields where several coaches, a trainer, and possibly an administrator or two were sure to be supervising the spring athletes. But all of the teams had away games that day, unbeknownst to Angel, a fact Kenzie and her goons were all too aware of.

And so they chased Angel, and Angel ran.

Her backpack shifted on her shoulders, weighing her down. She would have ditched it. She should have ditched it. Her books were too heavy, her binders too bulky. But the backpack used to belong to her father. It was the last thing of his she owned. A stupid black, canvas backpack with a rip in the front, a rip she held together with a whole bunch of buttons that she found in his dresser after he died. They were from all the old rock shows he'd seen, featuring the bands that played the soundtrack of her childhood. The Who. The Rolling Stones. The Police. Pearl Jam. Nirvana. Stone Temple Pilots. When she ran out of his buttons, she used a button they gave to all the incoming freshman her first year in high school. It had a picture of the school mascot on it, The Terrace Pointe Terrapin, with the school's initials above it. Under it was printed "Home of the Terrible Terrapins."

Terrible was right.

She hated high school. It was stupid, she knew, to put the button of the place she hated the most alongside all of those classic rock bands, and she'd always meant to replace it with something better, something of her own, but then the years went by and she forgot about it, and then it kind of became funny, and then she liked it.

So she kept the backpack on her back, and she ran across the practice fields, and she ran across the student parking lot, and she ran down the hill that led to the path that led to the tunnel that burrowed under Route 5. Halfway through the tunnel, she fell and scraped her knee, tearing a hole in her jeans and cutting the fifty-yard lead she had on her pursuers down to thirty. Their breaths and footsteps echoed behind her, along with Kenzie's hysterically screamed, "I'm gonna kill you Feltcher!" (Feltcher being the disgusting nickname she'd given Angel, which, appropriately, spread throughout the school faster than a pregnancy scare).

Angel limped out of the tunnel and turned left at a fork in the path. She briefly considered hiding behind the huge sign that read "Hollow Hills Creek Restoration Project Now Underway," but thought it was too much of a gamble. She also thought that maybe she could double back up the hill that led straight up to Route 5, maybe flag down a car, maybe run all the way back to school, but the hill was too steep and her legs already tired, and she didn't think she could make it to the top before Kenzie would tackle her and haul her back down to deliver whatever Satanic beating she had in mind. But staying on the path was also a death wish; surely if it came down to a flat out foot race, Kenzie, with her fully-developed, eighteen-year-old legs, would run her down like a truck. So the woods it was.

Angel was short and wily. She could duck and dash and shuck and juke her way around the prickers and bushes and branches, and even though the underbrush was thick with spring growth, she'd be less slowed down than the elephantine menace galumphing behind her. But the gamble didn't work. The prickers and bushes that slowed Kenzie down slowed her down too, and by the time she reached the ridge that used to overlook the rushing water of a creek, they were right on her tail. Trapped, she stopped and spun around to face her tormentors.

Kenzie crashed onto the ridge first, followed by her first little toady, and then her second, and then her third, fourth, and fifth. When eyeballed Angel like a predator.

"Thought you could get away, huh? Nobody gets away from me."

Angel tried to stand up straight. She rolled her shoulders back, eyes flitting from face to face. Why did they hate her so much? What had she done? Kenzie sneered.

"What? Don't got anything smart to say?"

"She's too busy crapping in her pants, K!"

Angel let her eyes rest on Kenzie's.

"What do you want?"

"What do I want?"

Kenzie cocked her arm and slapped Angel across the face, delivering a mighty wallop that rocked her head back and echoed in the woods.

"That's good. For a start."

Then she did it again. And again. But this wasn't Angel's first fight. She'd faced worse at home. There wasn't any point in waiting for anyone to help her. In her experience, it always worked in her favor to strike before whoever was attacking was ready for it. So she did. When Kenzie wound up a fourth time, Angel stepped in delivered her own punch, a solid hit to the stomach that knocked the wind out of the larger girl, who whoofed and warbled backwards. Her minions were startled silent. Kenzie looked back at them, saw their alarm, and turned to glare at the little rabbit in front of her.

"Bad idea, Feltcher," she said.

She grabbed Angel by the shirt and dragged her to her face.

"I'm gonna—"

With a scream, Angel raked her nails down Kenzie's face from her eyes to her chin, drawing blood. Kenzie cried out and shoved Angel as hard as she could in the chest, and Angel, off-balance and flailing, tripped over a root and dropped over the ridge. A scream, a thud, and then nothing.

Kenzie leaned carefully over the edge. The creek bed was dry. Only rocks and sand remained. Where Angel should have been lying, dead or unconscious, was a large, round hole. And out of that hole beamed an eerie, electric blue light.

"Come on, guys," she said. She turned around "Let's—" but they were already gone.

~

Ian returned home late from the war. He had no family to greet him, no friends other than those he lost in Afghanistan or those who re-upped for another tour. Alone and suffering, he did what many veterans did and turned to alcohol and then drugs to fill the void and stop his brain from telling him all of the horrible things it liked to tell him and showing him all of the horrible things it liked to show him. It was not long before he was on the streets. The volunteers at Micah knew him well. If pressed, they would have described him as "Sweet Ian."

"He's one of the good ones. Wouldn't hurt a fly. Terrible habit, though. He'll drink or snort or shoot whatever's available."

Ian usually spent the night at the park in the middle of town, curled up on a bench under his army jacket and poncho, his backpack for a pillow. But the annual spring fair was scheduled for early next month, and the police had been culling the usual homeless haunts, scattering the transients and arresting those who fought back, all in an attempt to make the streets a little more presentable to the five thousand or so tourists who descended annually upon the community to fill the local coffers.

Ian didn't like to be any trouble. Though he hated the shelter, he hated jail even more, so of course he wasn't going to fight the police. But the only place he could go was the canal path, and the canal path, while just as dangerous, if not more than, the shelter, at least afforded him an easy escape. He liked to jungle up near the tunnel that ran under Route

5, so if anything were to happen, if he was attacked as he had been in the past, the road was easily accessible. All he had to do was run up a short embankment. A shopping center with a twenty-four-hour Weis sat on the other side. But the tunnel was dark and filled with shadows that were easy to hide in, and naturally, that's where the worst of them liked to squat, eyes glinting in the moonlight, claws out. So he nested up in the woods to one side, using a green tarp as camouflage.

One night, he awoke late with a bladder full of rye and a head full of voices and, sneaking out of his den, he stumbled through the brush, the dry leaves and fallen sticks crunching and cracking underfoot, and relieved the one but not the other.

"Telling you, doctor. I ain't got no more wrong with me than the rent. Ain't nothing going on but the rent. Tell me I'm crazy, well, I say all ya'll is crazy. What?"

The last word he directed to the dark sky because he heard a strange noise, as if an electric wand was being waved back and forth next to his ear. After he finished and arranged himself, he turned around to see the most terrible and most wonderful sight. A weird, blue glow was floating along the path, pulsing warm and heavy in the night as it drifted toward him.

"Oh, no, sir. No, sir," he muttered. "Not tonight."

For Ian had seen plenty of strange things in his time on the streets. Creatures that crawled out of the muck of the river. Beasts that swooped down from black holes in the sky. He knew enough to leave them be lest they turn their wicked claws and burning eyes upon his soul, and that was exactly what he planned on doing when he saw the blue thing coming his way: turn and creep back to his burrow in the bush, close his eyes and shake and pray and hope it passed him by. But the blue glow dimmed as it grew nearer, and instead of a horrible monster, it revealed a young girl. Her clothes were torn and shredded and she was shivering, walking with her arms wrapped around herself. A canvas backpack hung from her shoulders.

Ian was stunned and concerned. The only girls he ever saw on the path this late were tricks or homeless like him, but he'd never seen this one before, not at Micah or the library or any of the other familiar places. And she looked terrified and confused. He was about to go to her and offer his jacket when he heard voices, male voices, laughing and jeering from the direction of the tunnel, and two men emerged. They stopped when they saw her, one hitting the other in the chest with the back of his hand.

"What're you doing out here, little girl?" the first one said. He put his hand in his pocket. "What happened to your clothes?"

The girl stopped and eyed them like a cornered animal. She shot a look over her shoulder.

"I-I—"

The two men laughed.

"Oh, she's ripe," the second man said. "Wouldn't you say, Dweeze?"

Dweeze licked his lips.

"Riper than ripe. She's a . . . a blueberry!"

"No, I . . ." the girl said. "I need help. I—"

"Oh, you definitely need help," Dweeze said. "You think I can fix her up, Boone."

"Me first."

She turned to run and Dweeze lunged for her, grabbing her by the hair and the backpack. She screamed and he spun her around and she lashed out and scratched him down the cheek, drawing blood. Dweeze let her go and put a hand up to the ruts she carved into his face. It came away red. The anger welled inside him.

"You bitch!" he yelled, and he slapped her as hard as he could.

"No, sir!" Ian yelled. He stomped out of the woods and on to the path. "No, sir! No, sir!"

The two men spun around, surprised to see the dark form growling out of the woods.

"Who the fuck are you?" Boone asked.

Ian stopped short and waved an angry finger at them.

"You leave her be, now, you hear! She sick, can't you see. She need a doctor. No! No! Doctor!"

"Screw off, you crazy old man."

"No! No, sir! You leave her alone! You—"

Boone was on him in a flash. Ian fought back but he was too old, too tired. He felt the steel blade slide in and out of his belly, once, twice, three times, and then he was on his back, moaning. Boone laughed in the darkness, and the blade came again, more times than he could count. And then from behind his attacker, he saw the glow erupt like the night's sun to paint the darkness.

It was the girl, her whole body burning silvery-blue, pulsing like cold heat. Sparks shot out of her hair like roman candles. Ian looked into his murderer's eyes and saw little cobalt bolts threading through his irises.

"I'm sorry, I'm sorry," he said.

The girl screamed. She was looking at her hands.

"Dweeze, what the fuck is this?" She looked at him. "What the fuck, man."

Dweeze, who had been watching his friend stab the old man, backed away, confused.

"What the fuck? How did you know my name."

"Dweeze? It's me, Boone," she said. "It's me." She reached for him, and he flinched away.

"You're crazy, kid," he said. He took out his own knife and unfolded the blade.

The girl held out her hands.

"No, wait!"

The man who stabbed Ian, the real Boone, pushed himself off the ground. He looked at the knife in his hand as if seeing it for the first time.

"Dweeze, I'm Boone," the girl said. "I'm Boone."

She crept closer to him as she spoke, finally getting close enough to paw at his arm. Dweeze pulled it away, disgusted.

"Get off of me you freak!"

He slashed at her, cutting a long gash in her chest, and she stumbled back. Boone screamed and launched himself at his friend. He was much larger and much stronger, and though his friend screamed and cried "wait! Stop! Boone!" he stabbed and stabbed and stabbed until there were no more screams, no more cries. When he was done, he got up and turned to look at the girl.

"What the fuck is happening, man?" she said. "What the fuck is happening?"

Boone started to glow, the blue light infusing his skin, and Ian could see his veins just beneath the surface, his skull, his beating heart, his pulsing blood, and the balls of light shooting out of his head. But Dweeze wasn't done yet. He struggled to his feet behind his friend, bloody and mangled and breathing like a whipped dog, his knife raised above his head. He lurched forward, aiming for Boone's neck.

And right before he did it, right before blade sank into meat, severed artery, shredded windpipe, Ian saw the most spectacular thing extend between Boone and the girl: an electric tunnel, and through the tunnel he saw the girl, a beautiful, blue angel outlined in silver, fly out of the man's body as the man, Boone, outlined in red, shot out of hers and into his. They slammed back into themselves, the girl free of her assailants, Boone just in time for his friend's knife to thunk into his neck.

~

Springtime was the worst. Whenever Sebastian Battle thought of it, he was reminded of a quote his high school English teacher once put on the board. Mrs. Washington. A formidable old crone. He couldn't remember much of anything that she taught him. He couldn't remember much of anything from high school. Most of it was a whirl of worksheets and bubble tests, endless mounds of paper pushed down rows of desks, dutifully filled-in, and pushed back up to the front, and Mrs. Washington was one of the worst of the paper pushers.

At one point she might have been an impassioned educator, someone who challenged her students, gave them interesting projects, provided proper feedback on essays, raised expectations, but Battle had gotten her when she was close to retirement, after years of district, state, and federal mandates and initiatives had beaten the rah! rah! out of her, and she was short-timing it until the end, which she timed for the middle of the first semester of the following year—something she didn't have to do, but, according to the rumors, she purposefully scheduled in order to make life harder for the principal, with whom she apparently didn't get along. Her class consisted of three things: vocabulary lists, vocabulary quizzes, and silent reading followed by bubble tests. Complete and repeat.

Mrs. Washington had a dry erase board that she hung at the front of the room. She liked to write quotes from her favorite books on it, or lines from speeches or television shows or pretty much anything she read, heard, or watched. A student once made the mistake of trying to write a quote of his own on the board, and she threw a stapler at his head. It would have connected, too, if he hadn't seen it and ducked.

"This is mine," she told him, glaring. "It's for me."

Amongst her other plentiful and more noticeable irritations, Mrs. Washington disliked spring about as much as most of the students disliked her. One morning in late April, she stomped into her room with red, puffy eyes and sounding like she was speaking underwater. It was the first time Battle felt anything but disrespect for the woman because he, too, suffered from seasonal allergies. He remembered her strutting right up to her whiteboard, pen already in hand, and starting her quote with something like "Again comes spring . . ."

The rest of the class groaned.

Mrs. Washington's second favorite thing to do, other than worksheets and vocab review, was quiz them on nature poetry. She was particularly fond of Wordsworth and "the tragedy of Keats." At the sound of her students' moans, she snapped her head and uttered a curt "shh!", silencing the grousers. Then she finished the quote:

"Again comes spring, with nasty little birds yapping their fool heads off and the ground all mucked up with plants."

She underlined the word plants three times, pressing so hard that the tip of the marker broke. Battle had never seen that happen. Then she fixed her red-rimmed, watery eyes upon the class, as if daring anybody to contradict what she had written. Nobody did. When she was certain she'd cowed everybody, she slumped over to her desk and picked up a stack of vocabulary tests. All of the students looked around at each other. It was Monday. They hadn't gotten the new list yet.

"Twenty minutes!" she barked as she passed them out.

"But Mrs. Washington," a boy in the back said. "We didn't—"

"Twenty minutes!"

Every year since, when the winter snows subsided and the creeks thawed and the chill morning air lasted no longer than the time it took for the sun to crest the horizon, and the lymph nodes under Battle's jaw began to swell and ache, and the membranes in his nose started to clog and drip, Battle wrote that quote down on a whiteboard he'd hung on the wall in his little office. Then he would turn around and bark "Twenty minutes!" at his empty desk. And then he would chuckle to himself.

The morning after Angel found herself chased and almost killed, then attacked and almost killed again, he got to work early, unlocked the door to his office, set his briefcase down on the floor next to his desk, and, after sneezing four times in a row, wrote his old teacher's quote on his whiteboard.

"Twenty minutes!" he said, and then he settle into work.

By eleven, he was nose deep in a slip and fall case, performing a background check on a woman who claimed to have pulled her back on a wet floor at the Rosemart. No prior arrests, nothing in her criminal report, nothing that sent up any immediate red flags. He'd watched the video a dozen times. It looked legitimate enough. She didn't check out the security camera placement before she went down or post a lookout for any staff. There she came into view. There the wet spot courtesy of a leaky ceiling. There the fall.

But what made him suspicious was the number of times she passed the area before she slipped. Once. Twice. Four times. Five times. Six times. And it was in the fishing gear aisle. Not that women didn't fish, but she hardly looked like the type.

It took him an hour of pouring through local court documents, but he found it. A different lawsuit from three years before. She'd been rear-ended while returning a rental car and left the scene of the accident, only to return twenty minutes later claiming a sore neck and wrenched back. The suit took a year, but she was eventually awarded $200,000. After medical bills, that left her with $100,000, and based on his research into her job history, that was more than enough for her to live comfortably for two years. Battle checked her employment history again. She hadn't worked a day since the car accident. The fall at Rosemart was, then, perfectly timed.

"Gotcha," he said.

Or maybe not. It was something to pursue, at least. He was about to contact the doctor who diagnosed the woman's injuries when a knock came at his door and it opened before he could say "come in." A familiar face—not unwelcome but not necessarily welcome, too —poked itself inside.

"Sebastian Battle! How the heck are you?"

William Keyes. His former boss. He tossed a folder on Battle's desk and threw himself down into the clients' chair.

"Have a seat," Battle said.

"Funny. Take a look at that right there. Tell me what you see."

Sighing, Battle pushed himself away from his work and leaned back in his chair and folded his hands across his stomach.

"I'm not in the game anymore, William. You know that."

"Yeah. Yeah. What are you doing now, insurance fraud?" He glanced around Battle's tiny office, clearly unimpressed. "Bored out of your mind yet?"

"How goes Homicide? Lost your faith in humanity yet?"

"On the contrary, every case I solve reaffirms my belief in the innate goodness of the human soul. The bad guys are out there, Battle, but so are we."

Battle smiled. William always did have a flair for the dramatic. It was why he'd liked working for him.

"You ever think about taking up community theater, William? You'd make a great Iago."

"He's the one with the fight scene, right?"

"Right."

William tapped the folder.

"I think you'll be interested in this, given your particular pedigree."

There he goes again. Battle would never be able to escape his family legacy. It didn't help that he was the fourth Sebastian Battle in the line. Sharing a name apparently meant sharing talents and interests. It's why William used to put him on all of the weirdest cases in the city. The famed River Monster (turned out to be a young journalist looking to create a name for himself), the Blood Bone Butcher (some crazy old coot mulching people to fertilize his flowers), and the Market Tunnel disappearances (rumored to be the work of a "squid monster" but ultimately unsolved). Battle gestured at his laptop.

"This is the extent of my investigations these days, William. If you need me to research something or find some financial documents . . ."

"Oh, come on, Battle. I know you miss it."

"Miss what? The horror or the danger?"

"Let me just tell you about this one. It's a humdinger. Got all of the boys stumped."

Battle's stomach growled. The clock on his Mac said 11:30. He usually ate lunch at this time. Took a walk to one of the downtown restaurants or brought his own to one of the benches on the riverwalk and ate there. But William was there, and he liked William. One of the better bosses he'd ever had. Inwardly, he rolled his eyes.

"Fine," he said. "But if you're not done by noon, I'm—"

"I'll be done in five minutes," William said, already reaching for the folder.

Later. At home. Battle sat at his kitchen table, the folder William left him splayed out in front of him, reports and pictures and all sorts of other important documents. A glass of beer, half full, his unfinished dinner. William was right. Battle was interested. He didn't want to be. He wanted to live his life along without the consequences of exciting murder cases—the anxiety, the dyspepsia, the drinking, the sleeplessness, the depression, the inevitable downward spiral into the black nihilism that seemed to plague his family as a result of witnessing the worst humankind had to offer.

But this case was just too weird to ignore.

Three victims. All homeless drug addicts. Two he knew from his time before. Blake Boone and his cousin, David "Dweeze" Moss. They'd been in trouble since they were kids, graduating from vandalism and petty larceny to assault and burglary and all the jail time that went along with it. They'd gotten in a fight over something. Money, probably. Or drugs. They had each other's blood all over them. Murder weapons in their hands.

But it was uncharacteristic of the pair. They'd been inseparable since Kindergarten. Dweeze was a nutcase, but there wasn't anything he could do to warrant this kind of response from his cousin. The Boones and the Mosses were as tight as ticks.

And then there was the third victim. Battle picked up the report on him. Ian Cummings. Afghanistan War vet. Decorated. Honorable Discharge. In a coma now, but wide awake when the EMT's brought him in, raving about "the witch! The witch!" and something else, too. Battle scanned the report. "The witch! The witch! God's Bones and blue fire!"

It was the 'God's Bones' comment that cinched his decision to take the case. William knew that going in didn't he? How could he not? It was what the Battle family was famous for.

Sebastian Battle, the first in his line, survived the Battle of Washington because of it. Lying there in the ruck of bleeding men, his belly slashed and punctured by bullet and bayonet, he should have died of blood loss and infection. But in the night, as he felt the life running slowly out of him, as the flies buzzed and lit upon him in such numbers as to feel like the Lord of Lies himself had released them, his body and the bodies of the injured and the dead that littered the field were coated in a strange, blue glow.

It took two days for the medics to clear the field, and they were astounded to find many of the men still alive. Indeed, while most suffered the same fate as many of those injured in the Civil War, with limbs hacked off or left to die painfully, with only morphine and whiskey as anesthetic, Battle himself didn't just survive his wounds, he thrived in convalescence, as did the other men who had been coated with the blue substance.

God's Bones and blue fire, the man had said.

Battle read over the report one more time. The assault had taken place on the canal walk near the tunnel that went under Route 5. He checked his phone. It was 9 o'clock, too dark to inspect the scene properly, but he was wide awake now. And intrigued.

Grimacing, he tapped at his screen and put his phone on speaker. It rang a few times, then William picked it up.

"I knew it! I knew you'd take it!"

"Yeah, I'll take it."

"Yes!"

"But I need a retainer. I don't work for free."

"How much?"

Battle told him.

"Done."

"And you're signing a contract. I'll send it to your email."

"Anything else?"

Battle thought for a moment.

"One time," he said. "This is the one and only time."

~

Angel didn't remember how she got home. She remembered the chase and the fall. She remembered coming around as she was walking on the path. She remembered the men surrounding her. She remembered the anger swelling up inside her and how she felt like she was flying through the air and then she was in one of them. *Inside* him. And he was inside her. And then she was standing next to her mailbox.

A wave of dizziness hit her, hit her hard, and she leaned over and was sick on the lawn.

Steve's lawn.

Steve was her mother's boyfriend. Well, technically he was Angel's stepfather, but she refused to think of him that way. She didn't like him and he didn't like her, and she was happy to keep it that way. Steve, among other things, was very particular about his belongings. His stupid hi-fi stereo. His stupid video game console. His stupid car. And above all else, his stupid lawn. He was going to freak out about her puking on it. He spent endless hours seeding, fertilizing, mowing, and raking it.

"I'm surprised I've never found him down on his hands and knees, cutting it with a pair of scissors," she once told Darrius. She meant it sarcastically, enjoying the image of him tweezing imperfections out of the ground like a surgeon working on a tumor. And then one day she came home and saw him down on his hands and knees with a pair of scissors snipping away at some clover or witchweed or some other imperfection. He didn't even look up when she approached, but said, "Did you put these here?"

"Put what there?"

"These. These."

He was holding something in the palm of his work gloves. It looked like a dandelion.

"Did I put a dandelion on the grass?"

But he'd already gone back to his work, muttering to himself. Angel had not been sure if it would matter, the muttering. Sometimes it did, sometimes it didn't. That night, fortunately, it didn't.

She didn't know where to throw up would land on his irritation scale, though. Would it be verbal or violent? Would she get a few bruises or a broken arm? Maybe there was enough nitrogen in it that he'd think it was good for the grass. She chuckled at the thought.

The wound in her chest wasn't as deep as she thought. In fact, it already started to heal. but her neck hurt. Bad. She put her hand on the back of it and rubbed. It felt like she had a gash there, like she'd been stabbed, but when she explored the area, her fingers came away dry. It still hurt.

The lights in the living room were on, but the upstairs was dark. Her mother would be at work, which meant Angel would have to spend the whole night with Steve. Alone.

She opened the door, wincing at the whine of the hinges, and stepped inside as quietly as possible, pausing in the foyer with a cocked ear. The television blared in the living room. Steve would be watching sports like he always did and drinking beer like he always did. He'd be at least six deep by this point. When she was sure he hadn't heard her, she eased the door back into the jamb, not releasing the knob until the bolt slid through the plate. She turned around to go upstairs and was halfway up when one of the floorboards creaked and Steve called "Angel?" and Angel practically bounded up the rest of the way.

"Hi, Steve!"

"Do you know what time it is? Your mother's been worried sick!"

At the top, she yelled, "Got a lot of homework!" and slipped down the hall and into her room where she locked the door behind her and jammed the extra blot into place. When she was sure he wasn't coming up after her, she breathed a sigh of relief.

She finally removed her backpack, amazed that it was still on. Some of her books and binders had fallen out, and she was a little upset, but not at all shocked, that a few of her buttons were missing, too. She tossed it on her desk, thinking about what had happened.

She made that guy hurt his friend. It was like she was inside him, controlling his arms, his legs, his thoughts. She was magic. She had magical powers. That was the only explanation. She could body jump. She could make people do things and she could jump back into her own body.

A million possibilities flooded her mind, some of them fun and innocent, some of them dirty and illegal. She thought about how strange her day had gone. She thought about Kenzie, and it made her angry.

Who did she think she was?

And that's when Angel realized exactly what she was going to do to get her back. And it wouldn't be pretty. She practically floated through the rest of her evening, and that night, for the first time in a long time, she drifted off into a wonderful, comfortable sleep.

She was so refreshed and happy in the morning that when she woke up and skipped off to the shower, she didn't even notice the trickle of blood that had leaked out of her mouth and onto her pillow.

Kenzie was holding court at the lunch table, lording over her 9th and 10th-grade toads, telling this one to shut up, taking that one's french fries. She'd just told a stupid joke, one that she'd told a dozen times before and which nobody at her table thought was funny (even if they still laughed, even if a little too hard), when everyone stopped laughing to look, dumbfounded, at something behind her.

"What?" she said, and then a full carton of milk was dumped over her head.

The lunchroom erupted in a chorus of "oooh's" and "whoa's"

"What the hell!" she screamed.

She leaped out of her seat and spun around, and there stood that little bitch. Angel. Kenzie thought she was, well, if not dead, badly hurt. But now there she was, alive, uninjured, and smirking.

"I'm gonna kill you!" she shrieked.

She lunged for the smaller girl . . . and then things seemed to get jumbled up. She felt weightless for a moment, like she'd shed her body, and then her perspective completely changed. She was no longer lunging for the nerdy little pipsqueak whose head she was about to stave in, but rather she was watching someone who looked like her lunging . . . for her? How?

She couldn't fathom it. She thought that maybe she'd been seeing things, that the girl she was now looking at, the one who looked exactly like her, was the one who had dumped the milk on her head. That somehow she'd mistaken who or what or . . . but how could that be? She stared at herself, horrified. The thing that was now Kenzie waved and smiled like it had just eaten her cat.

"Hi, Kenize," it said.

Kenzie-inside-Angel looked at her hands. They were white. Her arms were white. She was white. She was . . . she was . . . She let out a bloody howl.

"What is this! What is this!"

The Kenzie thing turned to the crowd of kids gathered around them at least ten deep. Many of them were holding up their devices, filming. She smiled and waved at them, too.

"Hey, everybody! You all know how I'm a piece of garbage, right?"

The kids let up a giant cheer.

"It's because my daddy left my mommy because he's gay, and she's a meth head who sucks dick for ice."

Kenzie-inside-Angel screamed and rushed her, but only received a hard right hook for her efforts. A few administrators were pushing their way through the pack, yelling, "Get out of the way! Now!"

The Kenzie-thing took note.

"I'm going to have to make this quick. How many of you want to me take a crap on the floor?"

The kids screamed a hearty "yes!". She held up her arms in triumph, and when she was sure she'd whipped them all into a proper frenzy, she finally caught Kenzie-inside-Angel's eyes.

"And rub it in my hair?"

An even louder roar.

"No," Kenzie-inside-Angel pleaded. "Please."

But the Kenzie thing only smirked in response. Then it unbuckled its belt and slowly squatted down.

~

Battle worked on his fraud cases all day, knocking out case after case, filing the proper paperwork. Though he was focused and productive, the other case, William's case, had latched onto the back of his mind like a spider. He kept sneaking looks at the folder he'd left sitting on the corner of the desk. It was a plain, manila folder, an inter-office mailer, the kind with the string-tie clasp and the lines and columns for people to write down recipient's names and addresses. From the looks of it, that particular folder had been around since 1980. The lines were all filled up, the names and dates smudged into hopeless illegibility, and the paper so worn and handled that it had softened like a blanket. Battle didn't know he was staring at it until a few minutes had passed. He thought about what William said the say before.

"Your particular pedigree. I know you miss it."

And the truth was, while yes, Battle didn't miss the horror or the danger, his current work, absorbing as it could be, never seemed to be enough. He already made himself a deal: he could work on the fun case after his real work was done.

Huh.

'Fun' case. That's how he'd begun to think of it. A little disappointed in himself, he picked the folder up and was about to shove it away when a portion of the report slid out of the top and onto his lap. Battle snickered.

"Okay. Alright."

He read it, reluctantly at first, then with increasing interest. Before he knew it, the whole folder was open on his desk, his fraud case left unfinished on his computer. He looked up after an hour, surprised to see how much time had passed, unsurprised at what he knew he was going to do next.

He went to the little safe he kept anchored to the wall behind him, dialed in the combo and opened the door. His badge and gun rested inside. They sat comfortably on his belt. A phrase came to mind as he stood up, knees popping, a family phrase that had been passed down from his father and his father's father. It was so appropriate for the moment that he shook his head and said it aloud.

"God's Bones, Battle. God's Bones."

Battle's allergies swelled with the insects in the bushes. He knew it was going to be a bad one when, five seconds after leaving his office, his eyes started to itch and one of his lymph nodes started to hurt. The AC in the car helped, but the walk from the street down the canal path was brutal, and he wasn't even halfway to the scene when his nose began to run, slowly at first, like the old men he kept passing who were out for their morning exercise, but gradually faster.

He popped an Allegra and wiped his upper lip with a handkerchief. A few new moms were out, too, pushing strollers populated with wiggling toddlers or, if they were lucky enough to find a sitter, running with a friend. A businessman enjoyed a bench on the path, staring at the murky canal water, either deep in thought or deep in depression. Another old man inched by, giving him a nod as his power-walked in the other direction.

That section of the path was well-known to the members of the police force who patrolled the city. It was close to the tunnel, which was close to the road, which was close to a strip mall with a supermarket and a liquor store in it. At night it was a haven for junkies, rapists, and the homeless. During the day it was just another part of the path.

Somebody, most likely one of the aforementioned groups, had already torn down the yellow police tape. Strips of it hung from tree branches and bushes, waving in the breeze that blew pollen like dust across the path. Battle sneezed. Three times. He should have worn a mask. And thicker sunglasses.

The blood had been washed off of the grass, but the stains on the path remained. Battle wandered around the scene, wondering how much of it had already been contaminated. He found Ian Cummings's nest, or what was left of it after the forensics crew combed it over. A nub of a candle. A bottle of Boone's Farm. A dark cloud covered the sun, relieving the heat, if only for a moment. He could almost pinpoint the moment when the Allegra kicked in. His nose dried up, his chest stopped wheezing, and the mild ache in his head stopped altogether. He went back out to the path and knelt, seeing if he could catch something in the grass. Cigarette butts, bottle caps, broken glass, and bits of plastic.

He opened the report and scanned over the section that recounted Cummings's testimony. It was predictably nuts.

"Subject one states 'She sparkled'," he muttered to himself. "'Just like an angel'."

Yet there were burns on the path, black circles, like someone had fired a roman candle directly at the asphalt. The sun peeked out from the cloud, and something glinted in the corner of Battle's eye. He squinted and grimaced, thinking it was another piece of glass. He checked it out anyway, leaning in closer.

It was a button. He picked it up, wiped the dirt off the surface.

An image of a turtle with the letters T.P.H.S. riding its back. And under that, "Home of the Terrible Terrapins."

~

Angel felt ill. Her neck ached. A cough had developed deep in her chest. Something felt broken inside her, like broken glass rubbing against her bones. She felt like she'd been swallowing all day, sniffling, too, little ones, like she was fighting off a cold. But each cough made her stomach and sides ache, and even though she'd run home after what she did to Kenzie, and even though Steve wasn't there to pester and irritate her, and even though she'd gone straight to bed and slept for at least two hours, she woke up gagging, ran for the bathroom, and vomited up blood.

She flushed and stood up to wash out her mouth and had just dried her hands when Steve banged on her door.

"Angel?"

She glared at it.

"Angel? Open the goddamn door right now."

"I'm sick, Steve."

"Open the door or I'm going to ram it d—"

"I'm undressed, Steve." He banged on the door again. Once. Hard. "Do you want to see me naked? Is that it?"

"Your school called today."

"Can you give me a minute, please?"

"Did you assault another student?"

"I said just a minute, Steve."

"I want answers. You know I do business around town. Your behavior—"

"I said one goddamn minute!"

The silence on the other side of the door was more unnerving than any amount of pounding he could have delivered. When he finally spoke, it was with a calm, measured tone that belied his anger.

"You have sixty seconds. If you're not downstairs by then, I'll—"

"Fine. Now leave me alone."

Fifteen minutes later, Angel burst out of her front door and ran as fast as she could down the driveway, intent on getting as far as from her house as she could. If someone had seen her, if anyone had cared even the slightest to pay attention to what was going on, they would have seen the rumpled collar of her shirt and the tear in her sleeve. But nobody was paying attention. Nobody had paid attention since her father died. That was the problem. Which was why in addition to her clothes being rumpled and torn, her eye was nearly swollen shut, and there were speckles of blood on her pant legs.

"Angel?"

Angel nearly jumped. She couldn't stop the yelp that came from her throat. It was Darrius. She turned her head so he couldn't see her eye.

"Oh, hi," she said.

"You okay?"

He was looking at her clothes. She tightened her collar.

"Yeah. I'm fine. Thanks." Then to distract him. "You working at the Palms tonight?"

He plucked at the polo he was wearing.

"Nah. Got a new job."

"Okay, well, have a good shift." She was already moving away. She didn't want him to see her. If he did, he'd want to call the police, and if the police came . . .

"Angel? You sure you're okay?"

"Yeah."

"Where are you going?"

"I've got to go, Darrius."

"But where?"

"Bye. See you tomorrow morning."

He watched her leave, a concerned look on his face. After a while, he shook his head and went back to his house to ask his mom for a ride to work.

Soon it grew dark, and Angel found herself wandering around a shopping center a few miles from her home. Her feet hurt from walking, and her back, too, and she was starving. She passed a sub shop and paused at the window, looking longingly at a family eating inside. The mother glanced up at her and then away again to say something to the father, who turned and stared at Angel until she went way.

There was a bench outside the Food Way where the stock boys and cashiers took their breaks and smoked cigarettes. It was empty now, and Angel collapsed into it, holding her side, trying not to feel the shards moving around inside her, the terrible pain in her neck, and now the new wound, the one in her eye, not the swollen one, that made it feel like a pike had been pushed into her skull. Trying not to cough only made her cough more. She leaned back on the bench and rested. It felt like only a second had passed when she felt someone shake her shoulder.

"Hey. Hey, you okay?"

Angel's eyes flew open. A man was standing over her. He was holding a child. She tried to sit up.

"No, no. Don't get up."

"I'm fine."

"No. You're hurt."

"The girl's sick, Daddy," the little girl said.

"I know, sweetie. We're going to help her, okay?"

The girl nodded solemnly.

"No, really. I'm fine."

"Stop. I'm going to get you a few things. Are you hungry?"

Angel's stomach grumbled as if on cue, and the man smiled.

"Hungry," his daughter said. "Hungry."

"Sounds like it, huh, sweetie?" To Angel, "Stay here. I'll be back."

He started inside and Angel said, "wait!"

"Yeah?"

Angel didn't know why she told him to stop. She needed something else from him. Confirmation. Friendly confirmation. So she said, "I'm Angel."

The man smiled.

"Marco. This is Jennie."

"Thank you, Marco."

"No problem, Angel. Just sit tight."

Angel leaned her head back as he went inside and rested her eyes again. She heard the electric door open and close and smiled, marveling at the kindness of strangers. A sweet spring breeze kicked up the scent of lilac from the stretch of woods next to the parking lot, and the far off rush of the highway was actually kind of soothing. She was just drifting off when she heard a car rattle to a stop at the other side of the entrance. The doors squealed and cracked when they opened

"You ready?"

"Let's do this!"

Footsteps as they ran into the store.

The gunshot jolted Angel awake. She hissed as she sat up and turned, holding her side. Two people in masks (one black, one orange) were at the front of the store pointing their guns at the customers and the shaking cashier. Marco and his little girl were there. The man in the orange mask approached him, screaming, "Get down on the floor! Now!" When he didn't move fast enough, Orange Mask hit him in the back with the butt of his gun, and Marco went down on his knees. His daughter started crying.

"Shut that kid up!"

Angel stood wearily to her feet. It hurt to walk at first, and when her foot caught on the wheel of a cart, she had to flex her stomach for balance and it felt like her insides would burst. The door slid aside and limped toward the thieves. Black Mask turned and pointed his gun at her.

"Whoa, whoa! Get down! Get down!"

Angel took a moment to catch her breath.

"Get down now, or I'll fucking execute you right here!"

Someone said, "Just do what he says, honey, and nobody'll get hurt."

"Shut up! Who said that!"

Angel met his gaze and held it. She could feel the rage building inside her, and with it, the power, the power that helped her on the path, the power that helped her humiliate Kenzie, the power that helped her stop Steve from hurting her ever again. Black Mask screamed, "Get on your face, bitch!"

Angel let the power build, and even though it hurt, she smiled at him, knowing what was about to happen.

"No," she said.

Black Mask swung his arm back to hit her with the gun, and that's when she jumped. She felt the impact in her arm. The crunch as fist connected with face was satisfying, even if she was going to feel it later. More satisfying was the look on her face as the creep inside her body tried to figure out what had just happened. She watched herself stare around, suddenly terrified.

"Help!" she screamed. "Help me! Help me!"

Worried that he might take her body and run, she belted herself two more times, once in the mouth and once in the temple. Her body crumpled to the ground. Orange Mask was jumping up and down now.

"Yeah! Yeah! Get some!"

It was then that Angel noticed how amped up she felt, dizzy, and . . . of course, high.

They were addicts. It was strange, too, because the man's body she jumped into was stronger than hers only by virtue of the fact that it was male. But it was also weak and shaky, and the craving for more of whatever drug they'd tweaked out on consumed her.

"Yo, get the 'fed, man! Get the 'fed!"

"The 'fed?"

"The Sudafed, man. Oh, shit! Behind you!"

Angel turned around and saw her own bloodied body leap at her. The next second they were on the ground, flailing.

"Shoot her, dog! Shoot her!"

No way that was going to happen. She blocked the attack as best she could, but it was too frenzied, a fit of pure, animal violence. Fingers clawed at the black mask, tore at her eyes as her assailant grunted and growled and punched and gouged.

"Shit, Dougie. If you won't do it—"

The thug in the orange mask marched over, gun raised at the girl attacking his friend, and Angel, still in Black Mask's body, screamed, "no!"

"Shit, dog! What do you mean n—"

And she shot him three times in the chest. The hostages screamed, and Angel screamed, and the man inside her body, the addict, paused and wailed, giving Angel enough time to clock him on the side of the head and knock him off. Then she stood up, put the gun on the ground at next to her own body, and jumped back.

She was smiling when he realized what had just happened. She picked up the gun and aimed it at him.

"You bitch!" he snarled.

Then he leaped at her and she pulled the trigger.

~

It took Battle the rest of the day and every string he could pull to get the warrant, but he got it. Now it was half-past nine and he was standing in front of T.P.H.S (Home of the Terrible Terrapins!) while the principal, a stocky little man with wide shoulders and a wrestler's neck, removed his keys from the lock. Larry Lovegrove: former Division V college athlete, former gym teacher, sufferer of gout, and self-described "student-whisperer."

"Students like me," he often said. "I'm their kind of administrator."

And it was true. The students did like him. Which was good because nobody else did. Not his faculty, not his staff, and especially not his wife.

". . . telling you this is highly irregular," he complained as the led Battle into the school. The alarm warning began to sound and he scuttled over to the panel on the wall in the office to punch in the code.

Larry Lovegrove was not used to being told what to do. As principal, he delivered the directives, meted out punishments, instructed staff, disciplined teachers. Having another man tell him what to do *in his own school* offended his very nature, and yet there was nothing he could do about it. The warrant was legal. The man was a detective.

Yet, as irritated as it made him, he had to admit that being a part of such an important investigation titillated him a bit. He'd helped the police before, of course. It was a part of the job. Indeed, he'd always believed he would make a good detective. He could sniff out a lying teacher in a microsecond, no matter how many times they took a Monday or Friday off "for a doctor's appointment," no matter how many times they asked to skip a Parent/Teacher Conference "for personal reasons." Though he felt the need to put on an air of irritated superiority (it was, after all, *his* high school), this was the first time he'd ever been called out of bed and forced to hand over official records. Whatever one of his students had done must have been very, very bad. He couldn't wait to find out what it was.

"To be woken in the middle of the night on a fool's errand—you do realize that tomorrow is spirit day, do you not?"

"If you could just show me the discipline reports for—"

"Discipline reports? For how long?"

"Last Wednesday through today." Lovegrove grumbled, though the request wasn't too unreasonable. "I'm looking for anything violent. Were there any bad fights recently?"

"We are five days away from Spring Break, detective, and Spring Break came late this year."

Battle stared at him, stonefaced.

"Yes," Lovegrove said. "There were fights. The children can barely contain themselves. Follow me."

He led Battle to his office and unlocked it. A folder was already sitting on his desk, and he picked it up and handed it to the detective.

"Four fights today alone. Give me a moment to find the others. They're on my computer."

Battle flipped through the files in the folder. The first two fights were not very interesting at all. Straight up brawls, it seemed, between longtime enemies. But the third . . . ah, the third was . . . so strange. He pulled the report out of the folder and read it more closely, and when he was done, he put it down on Lovegrove's keyboard.

"This one," he said. "Is this for real?"

"Let me see." Lovegrove adjusted his spectacles. "Oh, yes. Kenzie Washington. Such a mouth on that child. She's been in and out of school for nearly five years. She's here on a waiver. We've been trying to get her expelled for months. This little incident just helps pave the way."

"Has she ever done anything like this before?"

"Like this? No. Bullying. Fighting. Skipping. Cheating. Failing every class. But never anything so abnormal as this." He tapped the paper. "I'd bet anything she's the one you're looking for. You know, I've often told people —"

"And this other girl?" Battle leaned forward. "Angel Fletcher. Has she ever been in trouble before?"

"No. I'm embarrassed to say that I didn't know the child before this. I'm a good principal, sir, a people person, and—"

"Do you have video of the incident?"

"Vid . . . yes, of course."

It took him a moment to access the folder and bring up the files, and then he had to fast forward through the day.

"They run all night, you see. This happened during first lunch . . . let's see. Ah, here it is. Though I warn you, it's very distressing to watch."

"Just play it."

Lovegrove pushed the space bar and moved aside so Battle could see the screen. It showed a typical high school lunchroom. Students eating and talking, a few up and moving around. Teachers and administrators wandered the floor.

Battle spotted a girl pushing her way through the crowd, a singular look of intent and anger on her face. Angel Fletcher. She seemed to be aiming for a tall, older girl sitting at a table in the back. She snatched a carton of milk from a student who wasn't looking and zeroed in on the tall girl (that must have been Kenzie Washington) and dumped it over her head. Kenzie stood up and . . .

"Stop. Rewind it a little."

"I really don't see the—"

Battle picked the laptop up and worked the trackpad on his own. Angel dumped milk over Kenzie's head. Kenzie stood up and confronts her and . . . there. Angel arched her back just a little bit, while at the same time Kenzie flinched. Then Angel looked down at her hands, seemingly baffled.

"Were there any burns on the cafeteria tile?"

"Burns? No, I don't think . . . but I didn't check. Actually, now that I think of it, one of our janitors was complaining . . ."

"I need Angel's address."

"I-I'm sorry, sir. I don't think the warrant you have covers that."

But Battle had already taken his phone out of his pocket. He was about to open the app to call William when the phone vibrated and the caller ID announced that William was already calling him. He accepted the call.

"William. I need you to get me a—"

"Battle, where are you?"

"Terrace Point High School."

"Terrace Point . . . why?"

"I'm working your case, William."

"Well, get down to the Food Way in Brookefield."

"No, I need a warrant for an address. I think I know who—"

"Our perp just killed again. We have video."

"I have video here, too."

"We can't get another warrant until morning. Come down here. You've got to see this."

They watched the CCTV footage in the manager's office, watched the thieves enter, watched them bully and yell and order everybody around. And then Angel entered the building.

"That's her," Battle said. "That's the kid. Angel Fletcher."

"Do you know who that is?" William asked the manager.

"No. I've never seen her before."

They watched as the girl confronted the thieves, as the thief in the black mask knocked her to the ground, as she attacked him, clawing at his face and eyes. The second thief approached and then his friend shot him.

"Why would he do that?" William wondered aloud.

"Back it up a little," Battle said.

The manager, a better listener than Lovegrove, rewound it a few seconds and stopped.

"More. Back to when she first says something. Keep going. Keep going. Stop. Hit play."

Angel confronted the thief again. As he came toward her, her back arched a little and the thief flinched. Then she was looking down at her hands. They watched up to the point where the thief handed her his weapon.

"There. Did you see that? She arched her back again at the end there. She did it twice. Once at the start, once right before she shot the guy."

"So?"

"It's just interesting." William looked at him skeptically. "What? It's what you hired me for, right?"

William sighed.

"That's Angel Fletcher?"

"Yep."

Battle went to the door and called one of the officers over. His name tag read T. Simmons.

"What's your first name, officer?"

"Tyler, sir."

"You don't have to call me sir. You don't work for me."

"Okay."

"Listen, I need to you get something for me."

"If I don't work for you, then why would I do that?"

"William?"

"Just do what he asks, son."

"Yes, sir."

"I need to you look up the address for any Fletchers there are in a twenty-mile radius."

The officer was tapping the name into his phone. "F L E T C H E R?" he asked.

"That's it."

He and William rewatched the video while they waited.

"What happened to the blue glow shit?" William asked. "I don't see any glowing angels here."

"I don't think we can see it. But I bet there'll be some burn marks on the tile later."

The officer returned.

"There's about forty Fletchers in the area. No Angel listed."

"She's a kid."

"Right. I can start making some calls?"

A commotion interrupted William's response, and Battle looked over the officer's shoulder. A few of the employees were giving the officers a hard time. Mouthing off. Acting stupid. They were young. High School age.

"That won't be necessary," he said. He signaled to one of the patrolmen. "Officer? Bring those two in here."

"What?" one of the kids said. "We ain't done shit, yo. This is butt."

"Shut up," the officer snapped. He grabbed the kid's arm and shoved him toward the office.

"Don't put your hands on me!"

His friend took out his cell and started to film it.

"This is straight-up harassment, yo."

The officer turned to him and said, "You too."

"Am I being detained?"

"Just get over there, kid."

"Can I have your name and badge number."

The officer sighed and rolled his eyes.

"Are you going to come or not?"

"Not until I get your name and badge number. You're infringing on my rights."

"Oh, yeah? Which ones?"

"If I'm not being detained, I don't have to go anywhere with you. What am I being held for?"

"Do you have any weapons on you?"

"Weapons? I'm at work."

"Still."

The boy clamped his mouth shut and the officer grabbed him and pushed him toward the office. Battle stepped aside to let them in.

"You," he told the kid filming. "Turn that off."

"This a public place, officer. I can film this."

Battle snatched it out of his hands.

"Hey! That's my property! You can't—"

"Shut up. You're not in trouble. Neither of you are. We need your help."

"Help?"

"Yes. We need you to ID a witness." The boy looked uncertain. "What's your name, son?"

"Don't tell him, Darrius."

Darrius rolled his eyes at his friend.

"Oh, snap."

"Darrius? That's your name?"

"Yeah."

"Look, we just need your help."

"Can I have my phone back."

"When we're done here."

"I told you, I know my rights. That's my personal property. I can film you in public."

"And I can stop you from interfering with an investigation. I need to you watch this video and tell me if you know this person or not. If you film it and post it and our POI sees it, that's interference."

"You want me to snitch on someone?"

"I'm asking for your help, Darrius. Someone you know might need us."

Darrius thought for a moment, then he said, "okay."

"Alright. I'm going to press play, and you tell me if you recognize anybody on the screen. Got it?"

"Yeah."

Battle hit the space bar, and the video started up. The thieves stormed the store, carrying on as they did. And then Angel walked in from the front entrance. Battle didn't watch the screen. He watched Darrius' reaction.

"You know that girl?"

His friend punched him in the arm.

"Ow, man!"

"Snitches get stitches."

"Darrius, if you know her, you've got to tell me. She needs our help."

Darrius seemed to be struggling with a response. He was shaking his head, working through it, and then he said, "I know her."

"Who is it?"

"That's my friend, Angel."

To William, Battle said, "it's the same girl from the school incident." To Darrius, "do you know where she lives?"

Darrius glared at him.

"I don't have to say anything."

"Obstruction of Justice is a Class I Misdemeanor. You could get twelve months."

"If I was eighteen. I'm only sixteen."

"Sorry, buddy. That's not the way it works."

"D," his friend said. "Don't do it, man."

But the pressure was too much for the boy, and he broke down.

"She lives over on Lakehurst Ct. 2406. House at the end. Straight back."

Angel's house was dark as the patrol cars pulled up to the driveway. There were four in all, not including Battle and William, who drove separately. Two officers approached the front door of the Fletcher residence. Two others hoofed it around back. Two more stayed with their vehicles. The final two officers dispatched themselves to the neighbors where they knocked on doors and ordered anyone inside to shelter in place and stay away from the windows. Many ignored the second half of the warning, and Battle shook his head as he observed form after form appear at window after window, some peeking furtively between curtain and blind, some standing brazenly in full view.

He got out of the cruiser and went around back to join William, who was standing, com in hand, behind the open door. William spoke into the com.

"Officer Simmons. Sitrep." He waited. "Tyler, do you copy?"

"I'm telling you, William," Battle said. "Armed and dangerous isn't enough."

William was only half listening.

"Officer Simmons? Do you copy?"

A voice came over the com.

"Entering basement. Radio silence."

William looked momentarily satisfied.

"What do you want me to tell them? That the girl can control their minds?"

"That's not what I said."

"Armed and dangerous is the best I can do."

"You brought me in for this, remember?"

William took that into account.

"What do you want me to do?"

Battle had been thinking. About the statement he read from Ian Cummings, how he saw the girl glow "like an angel." About the videos he saw, how in each one the girl arched her back, how Kenzie Washington and the thief in the black-masked flinched at nearly the same moment. About how after that, the girl seemed not to know where she was. Then the violence broke out. Then it hit him.

"Don't let them go in armed."

William looked at him like he suggested they all take off their clothes.

"What?"

"Their guns, at least. Tell them—"

But it was too late. The officers were already inside. Battle grabbed the com out of William's hands.

"Officers, stand down. Stand down now and leave the house immediately."

"What the hell, Sebastian!"

"Leave the house now! N—"

Shouts from inside followed by gunfire.

"Shit!"

William snatched the com out of his hand, barking, "Officer Simmons! Update! Update!" Then, as Battle ran for the front door, "Battle, stop!"

Battle ditched his gun in the yard. The windows lit up with more gunfire. He heard William shout one more time and then he was in the front door, standing in the foyer. The lights were all out, and but for the cold glow of the moon, the house was still dark. He closed the door and leaned against it to catch his breath. A booted foot lay at the end of the short hall that opened up into the kitchen. He inched toward it.

"Officer," he whispered. Nothing. He knelt when he got close to the end of the hall, grabbed the ankle and shook it. "Officer."

Still nothing. From here he could see a little farther into the kitchen. A gun was lying near the island, only a few feet away. He heard a noise, a soft thump.

"Angel?"

"Here!" It was a male voice, another one of the officers, calling from the living room. "She took my com and my gun."

"That you, Simmons?"

Pause.

"Yeah."

"What's your first name."

"What?"

"What's your first name?"

Pause.

"Don't you know it?"

"I need you to say it."

Another pause.

"Tyler."

Okay. Okay.

"Is she with you?"

"What?"

"The girl. Is she in there?"

"She was. I asked her name and then . . . then I don't know what happened. She . . . I saw . . . Ben shot me in the back. I can't feel my arm."

"Where did she go?"

"I don't know."

"Sit tight, officer."

"Sit tight? Call it in! I'm bleeding out."

A second round of gunfire came up from the basement, and a bullet blasted through the floor and ricocheted off a pot hanging from a rack over the island with a cartoonish ping. The door to the basement was right behind him, and he ripped it open and danced aside, ducking his head into the opening twice. When no more shots came, he ducked around a third time and held position. A third officer lay on the landing at the bottom, his body twisted in an unnatural position. He was bleeding from the head, and a dark stain splattered the wall behind him.

Battle crept down the stairs, grimacing with each creak and pop. He stepped over and around the dead man on the landing and faced the basement. It was partially finished, with the rooms framed out but no drywall. The fourth officer lay a few feet away, unconscious but still breathing. He'd been shot in the head, too, but it was a glancing blow at a strange angle, like he'd tried to shoot himself and pulled away at the last second. A noise came from a corner, and a little form hobble-dashed from the shadows and toward the back door.

"Angel, wait!"

He sprinted after her, turning the corner in the back yard, then again, and up into the front yard. Angel was limping toward William, who drew his gun and ordered her to stop.

"Angel, no!"

Her back arched, William flinched, and then she was staring down at her hands, screaming, "What the fuck! What the fuck is going on!"

William turned to face the two final officers, now standing at their vehicles behind the open doors, guns drawn. He fired once and the window exploded. The second shot hit one of the men in the shoulder and he cried out and dropped. Battle's gun was still lying in the grass where he'd tossed it. He snatched it up.

"Angel, stop!"

William spun, holding his gun in two shaking hands. He fired, missed, and Battle sprinted forward. He cut left and William fired and missed again, and then Battle was on him. He ducked around and put him in a full-nelson: one hand on his neck, one pressing his gun against his head.

"Drop the gun or I'll shoot."

She didn't.

"You want to die in his old man's body?"

He knew she was thinking about jumping again. Could she jump into him? If she wanted to, she would have already. Maybe she had to be looking at her victim.

"I'll just find someone else."

"You sure that's how it works?"

She didn't respond.

"Battle, what the hell is going on?"

It was William-in-Angel.

"Sit tight." Then, to the girl inside William. "What's it going to be, Angel?"

Then he saw it, what the report had described. William's body stiffened in his grasp, his back arched, and a blue glow emanated from within. Battle gasped and took a startled step back, watching the sparks fly from like a roman candle, then he jerked and Angel's body jerked and it was over. The girl collapsed to the ground, crying.

"Battle, what the fuck?" William said.

Angel rolled over onto her side, drawing her legs into her belly, her back shaking as she wept. Battle went to her, leaned over and touched her shoulder.

"Hey, hey. You're going to be okay."

"It hurts, it hurts . . ."

"We're going to get you some help. Don't worry—"

Her eyes met him, and she smirked. Oh, shit. He tried to turn and run, but it was too late. He felt himself fly forward, like he'd been yanked by some invisible force, and then he was no longer inside himself. He was in her, staring at the asphalt. His insides felt shattered, broken. His head split open. He rolled over, and there he was, his body at least, holding his gun against his temple. The smile on his face was unrecognizable. He closed his eyes, finger twitching.

A gunshot rang out, and Battle was sucked into the void.

~

One week later, William walked into a hospital room filled with nurses and orderlies who were standing around a bed, laughing.

"Twenty minutes!" one of them said, turning as they started to leave. "Twenty minutes!"

William stood aside as they passed, nodding at a few, and then it was just him and the patient, Sebastian Battle, IV, sitting up in bed. His head was bandaged and his right arm had been cast from wrist to shoulder, but he looked otherwise healthy.

"William," he said. He nodded at his arm. "Just had to aim for the bone, didn't you?"

"Yeah, well. I didn't think you'd mind, considering I was saving your life and all."

"Tell me you got her."

"Oh, we got her all right."

"No, I mean . . . she's dead. Right?"

William smiled.

"We got her, Battle. We got her."

Battle nodded, apprising his friend. William pulled out his wallet and removed a check from the billfold.

"Your remuneration. Fully funded."

He tossed it on Battle's lap.

"And the hospital stay?"

"Don't you have insurance?"

"Yeah, but the copay is twenty percent."

"I'm not so sure. I mean, twenty percent is a lot."

"Damn, William. I didn't take this on to—" But William was laughing. "Oh, okay. Okay. Thanks, I guess."

"Don't ever say I never did anything for you."

"You mean like this job?"

"Exactly like this job."

"Do me a favor, then. Don't ever do anything for me ever again."

William shook his head.

"Can't guarantee that, my friend." He backed to the door, palms up.

"I'm serious, William."

"So am I. So am I."

~

No windows.

No light.

Four walls.

Brick.
One floor.
Brick.
One ceiling.
Brick.

Twice a day, a slot opened in the door and a plate of food was shoved through it. Sometimes the room fogged with smoke, harsh, overly sweet, and chemical, and she passed out. When she woke, her head aching, and there was another bandage on her body.

She tried to jump. Several times. Let the blue light well up inside her. Felt the sparks shoot out. But the walls were too thick, and without a target, she had no sense for it.

So she waited. And she waited.

They were careful now. But eventually, they would get comfortable, careless.

And when they did . . .

When they did . . .

They did.

BONESAW VS. THE MILITARIZED ROBOTIC DEATH WEREWOLF

Chapter 1
In which our boy receives a new assignment

Hey, how's it going?

Some of you might know me. Some of you might not. If you do, you know what to expect next. If you don't, well, you're about to find out.

I'm going to tell you the story about . . . about a lot of things. Creepy little girls, a weird cult, and the fuck all of all fuck alls, a militarized robotic death werewolf. How cool is that? Trust me. You're gonna love it. Here's how it starts.

This story takes place, what, twenty, thirty years after all that crap went down with the tecuani and the spugs and Seka-Khayu and the sceels and sniders and squirsquitos and the like. The world hadn't really recovered from it yet, and seeing as our city was the hardest hit, it still bore the scars of that shit-show, I tell you true. Population cut by a quarter, half the buildings reduced to rubble, half burned to the ground, half so fucked up by all the bombs and the bullets that ain't nobody could live in them. The rest was pretty much okay. Except for the fact that half of them was little more than cholera infested tenements. Yeah. Seka-Khayu bunged us up good.

I was working as a tracer for a little shrimp named O'Neill. It was an interesting gig. Here's how it worked. People took out credit to buy SingleCorp upgrades and . . . . What? What's SingleCorp? SingleCorp is SingleCorp, numbnuts. Read the name. Take a guess. Anyway, people took out credit to buy upgrades and . . . What's an upgrade? It's an upgrade. Like a body modification. You ever see a woman with fake tits? This was like that, only more useful and a hell of a lot more awesome. Unless the surgery was a new face or ear or lips because them's always useful and more awesome. Bodymods was the plastic tits of technology.

Huh. I like that.

So what was on the menu? All kinds of stuff. You got your Barrel Arm Biceps™, your Second Sight Eyes™, your Nimble Digits™, your Cochlear ConNext™. They worked predictable. Here's the thing, though: bodymods was expensive as fuck—too expensive for the average schmuck. For a while, only the rich pricks had them, but then just like everything, they became necessary for everyday life.

People took out credit to buy them because Capitalism, and when they missed payments, which was inevitable, SingleCorp sent them threatening letters, and when them threatening letters was ignored, they contacted O'Neill, and when they contacted O'Neill, O'Neill contacted me, and one by one the deadbeats was persuaded to give them bodymods back. The Barrel Arm Biceps™ was easy enough. They was just braces. But the Second Sight Eyes™, the Nimble Digits™, the Cochlear ConNext™, they was embedded in the flesh. Things could get a bit messy.

One morning, I dragged an arm, a leg, and half a finger (I didn't drag the finger. Ain't nobody drags a finger. It was in my pocket, dope) into O'Neill's office, which was an old postal depot clear on the other side of the Bottom. Someone had broken the two front windows, and O'Neill fixed them predictable. Duct tape and cardboard. That explained why he was so pissed off when I got there.

Or not.

Who knew with that guy. He didn't possess a naturally sunny disposition on his best days, but that morning he clearly had not enjoyed the same lovely start as me, and he was acting —how should I put this?—like an angry little midget.

No shit, though, O'Neill was an actual midget. Or was it dwarf? Little person? I can't ever get that straight.

Whatever.

I backed into the place, opening the double doors with my ass, and lugged my haul inside. O'Neill was on the phone, an old flip job with a broken antenna. He gaped at me, told the person on the other line he had to go, and pocketed his phone.

"Deliveries out back," he said.

I laughed and hauled the leg and the arm up onto the counter between us.

"Nice one. These things is heavy."

"Where you been? I sent you about ten messages. Even paid a kid to run one over."

"Yeah, about that. Don't ever use that Allie-boy kid again. Little runt tried to kick me in the balls."

O'Neill frowned.

"You didn't do nothing stupid, did you?"

"To that spe*cific* kid? Of course not."

"Good, because he's not someone you want to—"

"But his friend, Louis?" I wagged my hand. "He got a little stabbed."

"Louis? Who's Louis?"

"The kid I stabbed." I held up his knife. "Took his knife."

"Good god." He studied the dismembered parts bleeding all over his counter. "Dorcas Bingham?"

"What's left of her."

"Bodybuilder, huh?"

I looked at the arm, which was about the size of my torso. Muscles bulging out like, uh, like muscles. Bulging. The leg was about the size of a horse.

"Yeah."

"Any reason you couldn't just take the braces off?"

"Subject was non-compliant."

"Where's the other stuff?"

"Oh yeah." I dug around in my pocket and found her finger, slapped it down next to the leg.

"And?"

"Oh! That's right."

I dug around in the other pocket and took out a bloody plastic bag with her eyes in them.

And her ear. Forgot to mention that part. Or parts.

O'Neill's phone rang and he held a finger up at me as he went back to his desk to take the call. I turned around to have a sit in one of the chairs that usually sat by the front window, but they wasn't there.

"The fuck the chairs go?"

Ruby, O'Neill's partner, came out of the back, coffee mug in hand as always.

"Kevin Johnson threw them through the window," she said.

Ruby had a voice like a frog in a stovepipe. She was about a million years old, with thin, stringy hair that she dyed red and orange, and wrinkles on her face as deep as the Grand Canyon.

"What'd he do that for?"

"What do I look like, the president?"

"No. You do not look like the president. You look like a walking corpse."

She sat down behind her desk.

"You're a regular riot, you know that? You should have your own television show. You could juggle chainsaws."

"So you're not gonna tell me why Johnson broke the window?"

She pointed a gnarled finger over my shoulder.

"Ask him yourself."

Sure enough, Kevin Johnson pulled open the front door and popped inside. I won't say too much about him except this: he was a jerk, and we didn't get along too good.

"Hey, Kevvie," I said. "What'd you break O'Neill's windows with them chairs for?"

"None of your business, that's why."

"None of my business? Of course it's my business. I got nowhere to sit."

He stepped up to me, trying to be intimidating, but it was all for nothing because really all I could do at that point was marvel at his perfectly coiffed mane of black hair. I don't know what he put in it, probably axel grease or something, but it was glistening. Unfortunately, whatever it was he styled it with also attracted a lot of bugs, a couple of which had become stuck in the part. Also, he stank. Seriously. I had to breath through my mouth. He ran a hand through his buggy hair, pointed his finger at me, and said, "Screw you."

That fact that I still had Louis' knife in my pocket did not escape my attention, and if I'd been so inclined, I'd have used it to carve some very colorful language into his face. Instead, in a moment of comic inspiration, I leaned in toward his ear, let my stubble touch his moist cheek, and whispered, "you'd like that, huh?"

I wish I'd seen his face, but I was too busy getting punched in the stomach. Then it was asses and elbows for a few seconds. I managed to get a few shots in before old Ruby threw the contents of her mug at us. I smelled vodka, and then I was on fire. My shirt exploded in flames with a whomp! and Johnson's hair, too, and instead of us rolling around on the ground beating the fuck out of each other, we were rolling around on the ground trying not to burn to death.

When I was sure I'd put it out, I stood up, patting out a little smokey patch on my shoulder, and said, "What the hell, Ruby!"

"Have some respect for your elders."

Johnson popped up, head steaming, crying, "My hair!"

"All of you shut up!" O'Neill yelled, arms spread wide. "I'm on! The phone!"

"You don't have to shout at me," Ruby said. "They're the ones fighting."

O'Neill pocketed his flip phone again and waved at us.

"Get over here."

"Me or him?" I asked.

"Not you."

Johnson shot me a glare and stalked away, brushing a few strands of charred hair off his shoulder. He and O'Neill conferred in silence for a bit. They jawed and jawed, then O'Neill gave him an envelope with his orders, and Johnson took it shoved it in the pocket of his jacket and hunched away, sneering at me as he left.

O'Neill waved me over and handed me a manila envelope.

"Your mods updated?"

"Yeah. Why? This a bad one?"

"The worst."

I read the name he'd written on it in black marker.

"Who's Boston Washington?"

"Some schmuck ran off with SingleCorp gear and holed himself up in the Industrial District. Got some pretty hot upgrades. Next-generation stuff. Real hush-hush, you know. Military-grade. Lasers, grenade launchers."

I pulled the corners of my mouth down and nodded. Impressive.

"Dead or alive?"

"Alive."

"C'mon, O'Neill."

"Listen—"

"What if I bring back just his head instead?"

"There's a reason for this, if you'll let me tell you."

"Fine."

"He's got a failsafe."

I threw the envelope back at him.

"No thanks."

"You just have to keep his temperature above ninety-four."

"I got no interest in getting blow'd up."

"They're paying top of the scale for this one."

"So?"

"And a license to carry."

That gave me pause. Getting a license to carry was akin to hitting the jackpot. During the Tlek war, the government gobbled up every available firearm they could find, and after it was over, the Corp made a deal to buy them all at quarter price.

The result was predictable: ain't nobody but the feds and the most powerful corporation in the world had access to weapons. And they held on to them tight, you better believe it. Sure, folks made their own (this was America, after all), but not everybody had that skill, so we went without. Getting a license to carry was nearly impossible. So when O'Neill offered it to me, he already knew the answer.

"Okay."

He smiled and handed back the envelope. "Alive."

The Industrial District sat about twenty blocks from the Bottom proper, right in the crook of the river. The Tlek did as much of a job on it as they could, but even so, there was plenty of warehouses and factories still standing. The city tried to reinvigorate it several times, but it had its hands full with the homelessness and joblessness and addicts and such. The result was six city blocks completely abandoned. Eerier than eerie. Wasn't nothing there but me and the bugs. And the tecuani corpses. And the snider hulls. And the sceel hulls. And the squirsquito hulls.

All I could hear was the scrape of my shoes against the pavement and the whistle of the wind down the streets. I crunched over broken glass, trash, and loose papers, and rotted out plastic bags skittered across my path. It didn't escape my attention that nobody ever came this way no more, not even the most desperate. Sure the old rendering plants and paper mills offered squatting space and copper to scavenge, not to mention the worker's houses, retail stores, and schools, but I knew the old stories. We all did.

There was the one about the cannibals with sharpened teeth and necklaces made out of fingers, or the one about things with webbed feet that swarmed out of the sewers at night. Then there was talk of all the sniders and sceels and squirsquitos that SingleCorp promised to get rid of but hid in the sewers instead. Most people thought of them as fairy tales for tenement runts, nightmares mothers whispered in their kids' ears late at night to keep them from wandering too far. But there was a bit of truth to it, or else there'd have been plenty of scabbers taking up residence. The gangs certainly liked it there, though. Tagged it up nice. CBCKs, Puglies, Fuglies, 9th St. Sinners, Vampires, Bloody Bastards. Plenty of gang signs, too, mostly the ouroboros, the snake eating its own tail, but also the crowns and the middle fingers, the vampire teeth, the bashed in faces.

I took the intel out of O'Neill's envelope and looked at the address. 793 Washington Street. 13th Floor. Room 78. Of course it was. I was on Brently in the 500's, so I picked up the pace, my nerves so amped up that everything tingled.

I didn't use no mods. I lied to O'Neill about that. No tracker worth his rate modded up. SingleCorp geo-tracked them all, anyway. Said it was for the updates, but we knew better. Plus, a tracker being geo-tracked was a liability in my line of work. It's why I didn't own a phone or a computer or anything else that was hooked up to the net.

But dear me oh my, you might say. How does you ever get the job done? Didn't you just show up with dismembered body parts? Well, yeah. I didn't say I went in unarmed. I preferred poison. Nerve agents. Didn't need much. A single syringe filled with novichok. Pure Russian. I kept mine in a plastic container in my pocket. A quick jab to the neck with one of those babies brought down even the biggest, baddest meany. Then it was chop chop, snick, snick, and yours truly was 5K richer.

I liked other kinds of conventional weapons. Like Louis' switchblade. I took it out and unlocked it, ran my thumb along the edge and slid it carefully down my pants against my hip, making sure not to slice my thigh. Had to tighten my belt to keep it from dropping in my drawers. Maybe it'd be useful. Maybe not. Always best to hedge your bets, though.

Twenty minutes later, I finally found the right block in the seven hundreds, but I couldn't find 793. I walked around and around at least a hundred times. The numbers jumped from 781 to 785 to 789, and then back up to 799. I turned in circles as the sun fell behind the tops of buildings, shading my eyes. A billboard to my right was advertising baked beans. Boston baked beans. Only the "baked" and the "beans" was gone, leaving only the word Boston. I looked at the street sign: Washington. Up at the billboard. Boston. Back down to the street sign. Washington.

And suddenly I knew.

There wasn't no 793 Washington Street. There wasn't nobody named Boston Washington. But I was exactly where somebody wanted me.

Something flickered in the corner of my eye, and there in the middle of the street stood a tow-headed little girl in a tattered yellow sundress.

She smiled at me.

"Oh shit," I said.

A soft whisper came from behind, and I turned around to see a shovel flying right at my face.

Chapter 2
In which our boy meets Daddy's Girls

I don't know about you, but being dragged by your feet by four giggling twelve-year-old girls is a fucked-up thing. I tried to move but they'd bound my arms and legs with about a hundred zip ties. Fifty from ankle to knee and fifty more from wrist to elbow. The plastic dug into my skin, even through my pants, and it hurt like hell. I guess nobody ever taught them girls how to do it right, but I guess, too, that—being little girls an all, and living, as they did, in a post-apocalyptic nightmare such as this—they didn't take no chances. They'd taped my mouth shut with duct tape, and they even found my syringe. And they kept tickling me. Which was weird.

Once my nut cleared a little, I realized that they were quadruplets. Four heads of curly blond hair, four yellow sundresses with orange flowers in the print, and four sets of bare feet. With all the glass and metal littering the streets, I was surprised they didn't get cut to ribbons, but every time one almost stepped on something, a chunk or a hunk or a sliver, she seemed to sense it and barely miss it or flick it out of the way with a quick flip of her ankle.

Friggin amazing.

Then they broke out into song. All at once, all together, without any warning or signal, like it was, whatchacallit, telekinetic? No, telepathic. I didn't catch the tune at first, but I recognized the words.

"His hands were quick, his fingers strong. It stung a little, but not for long."

Oh shit.

"And those who thought him a simple clod. Were soon reconsidering under the sod."

I was there on opening night, 1979. Broadway Theatre. Angela Lansbury.

"Consigned there with a friendly prod . . ."

Please don't say it. Please don't say it.

"From Sweeny Todd. The Demon Barber of Fleet Street."

And with that, they stopped, dropped my heels on the pavement, ripped the tape off of my mouth, and ran away.

Now listen. I don't believe in any kind of supreme being, not after what I'd seen and how long I'd lived. From Zeus to Jesus to Allah, it's all a big crock to me.

But I do believe in The Weirdness.

What's The Weirdness, you ask?

The Weirdness is exactly how it sounds.

It's when shit gets strange. It's when two and two equals three, when the sun rises in the north and sets in the east, when a rabid dog licks your hand. Ain't no use fighting it. Fighting it only made it worse.

So go ahead and fight The Weirdness. Tell it two and two equals four, but then four bastards was kicking in your teeth instead of three. Yeah, the sun don't rise and set like that, but all the sudden it's falling on your head instead of just giving you an interesting evening. Yeah, rabid dogs don't lick people, so this one'll suddenly remember and tear out your adenoids. Best thing to do when The Weirdness takes over is relax and roll with it.

So that's what I did. I rolled with it.

I stared at the buildings. The wind blew. A bee floated by, and I thought, "Oh dear." The sun glanced off the shattered windows and hit me straight in the face, so I got sleepy. I might have dozed a little. Okay, I didn't just doze; I went to sleep. You know how sometimes you snort in your sleep and it wakes you up? I did that. Then I heard them girls again, giggling as they was wont, and talking, too, and underneath that I heard the low rumble of an adult voice. A man.

"Oh, I'm sure you'll love it, daddy," one of the girls squealed. "It's fresh and it's clean and it smells very nice."

Daddy's accent was posh, smooth and silky.

"Now Coraline. You know that doesn't mean it's still good."

"Oh yes yes yes, daddy, yes," a different girl said. "We know this, we do, but I think this one is a particularly . . . is 'captivating' the word I'm looking for?"

"'Peculiar', maybe?" Coraline suggested. "Curious? Abnormal? Anomalous?"

"Porcine!" a third girl said.

"Oh, Bella. Porcine means 'pig-like' not 'strange'."

"Well, I think he does look like a pig. Pee Eye Gee PIG!"

"He's not a pig, he's not," the fourth piped. "He's a pork chop! And I'm going to slice him right up!"

Daddy said, "Let's not get ahead of ourselves, Ella."

"But I'm hungry!"

"All in good time."

Caroline whispered something to Coraline, but she sucked at whispering cause everybody could hear what she was saying. Coraline giggled, but Ella was not happy.

"I heard that! Daddy, they're saying things!"

"Now girls. What have I told you before about secrets?"

Caroline and Coraline spoke as one.

"But *Daddy*. She thinks pork chops are different from pigs. She thinks pork chops are a different animal."

"They *are* a different animal, they *are*."

This was The Weirdness, ladies and gentlemen. In full-effect.

I don't know if you noticed yet, but sometimes my mouth moves faster than my brain. Got me into as much trouble as it got me out of. I knew this about me, and in this particular situation, it took all I could take to not say nothing. I could have shouted out something stupid like "Help me!" or "Lemme go!" but The Weirdness would have threw it back in my face. So, what did I do? I locked it down, zipped it up, whatever it took to mind my P's and Q's and Shut. The fuck. Up.

They continued to babble along, coming closer and closer, and finally there they were, and Daddy planted his feet on either side of my head, upside down, and peered at me. He was an older gentleman with streaks of gray in his thinning black hair and laugh lines in his chiseled face.

"Oh yes, girls. It is a prime specimen you've caught for me here. A prime specimen."

Ella jammed her grimy little fingers in my mouth and pulled my lips apart.

"Look at its teeth, daddy! Look at its teeth!"

Bella squatted down and considered my white and pearlies with a grave expression.

"Oooh, they're so clean."

"It must be a rich one, this."

"Of course it is. All the rich ones have nice teeth."

Bella tried to make me open up but I clenched my jaw.

"Tell it to open up, Daddy! I want to put my hand down its throat."

"Now, Bella."

I snapped at her and the girls squealed and pulled back. Bella rapped on my forehead with her scraped knuckles.

"Open up! Open up!"

Daddy chuckled, and the other girls began to chant the words, over and over, "Open up! Open up! See its guts! Open up!"

I couldn't take it anymore. Through clenched teeth, I said, "You stick your fingers in my mouth, I'll bite them off and shove them down your fucking throat."

Bella leaped to her feet, astonished. In fact, I managed to shock all four of them into silence. Caroline and Coraline, Bella and Ella, they all stared at me with flat expressions on their faces. Then they let out another squeal and started dancing around and clapping, their towheaded curls bouncing in rhythm, singing "Fucking fuck! Fucking fuck! He said 'fuck'! Fuckedy fuck!"

Daddy watched, smiling with his teeth. He even laughed a little when one of them, I think it was Bella, sang, "Fuckedy fuck! We fucked it up!" Then he looked down into my eyes for the first time, and that smile turned into a snarl and he said, "Took me two weeks to get them to stop using that word."

"Them's the breaks, I guess."

"Yes."

He reached into his back pocket and pulled out a dirty handkerchief and a bottle of something-that-did-not-look-good. He unscrewed the top and poured a little into the rag.

"'Break' is probably the best word to use in this situation."

Chapter 3
In which our boy fights a
militarized robotic death werewolf

Man oh man, you must be thinking "that bastard has all the bad luck."

Well, I won't disabuse you of that notion, but I don't necessarily think of myself in that light. I ain't the luckiest man in the world, but I ain't the unluckiest neither. I haven't aged a day since I killed that pederast priest back in the old neighborhood, and that was over a hundred years ago, so I guess I got that going for me.

But, yeah, I can understand you thinking that right now. How many people do you know what's been knocked over the head and kidnapped by four crazy little girls then knocked out again with chloroform? Who knew what kind of sinister shit they had planned for me? I had somewhat of an idea. It wasn't too hard to guess. But at the same time, it didn't confront me. Once The Weirdness took hold, it affected everybody around it, not just yours truly. So if The

Weirdness taketh away, The Weirdness provideth, too, and that's exactly what I counted on getting me out of this horror show. That and Louis' knife, which I still had jammed down in my pants, I shit you not (no pun intended).

In this case, however, The Weirdness provided me with something better than just a knife. It provided me with Sal. I'll get to him in a minute because it also provided me with screaming crowds of psychopaths lusting after our blood, but I'll get to that in a minute, too. Seriously, just a minute because I gotta tell you where I woke up.

First there was nothing. How's that for Biblical? And then consciousness slipped into my brain like a snake, and I realized that I was lying on the floor of a high school locker room. How, you might ask, did I realize something as specific as that? I'd like to say it was the smell, for one, that rare mix of mold, mildew, urine, sex, hormones, and BO. Or maybe it was the lockers themselves: battleship gray with square vents, able to hold maybe one massive teenage shoe. That alone should have been enough for me to realize where I was. But that's just a bunch of bullshit because what really gave it away was the sign painted on the cinderblock wall. "Bull

Run Senior High School Prefect," and under that, in smaller letters, the name of the mascot: "Home of the Rams."

There was two other guys in there with me. Corp Cops. Maybe eighteen, nineteen years old. Their barcode skull tats gleamed with fresh salve in the overhead lights, and they stared around the locker room, too terrified to actually see anything. Their forearms was bandaged where their microchips had been torn out. You heard that right. SingleCorp chipped their employees. Like dogs.

I'd never seen a Corp Cop without any military gear on. When they wore it, they was legion, invincible stormtroopers, icons of violence, the iron fist of the implacable corpocracy. Without it, they really was just kids. At least these two was. No helmet, no Kevlar, no mob-shield, no Glock, no taser, no baton, no pepper spray, just quivering lips and peach fuzz. Why the Corp didn't furnish these guys with upgrades I'll never know, but my guess is that they just needed the meat, didn't expect it to last too long, so why invest all that time and effort into something that wouldn't make it past the next riot?

A roar came from above, stamping feet and shouts and yells and howls. Must have been at least three, four hundred people up there. The chants came in coordinated waves, back and forth, back and forth. I couldn't make out what they said at first, but it sounded brutal and cruel, the feral shriek of two wild armies preparing for battle. The Corp Cops' eyes rolled to the ceiling, wide, round, and white.

I sat up and immediately regretted the decision. That poison Daddy gave me. Worse than any hangover I ever had. The blood knocked on the back of my skull thump thump thump like a kick drum. I dry heaved. Right when I finished, the roar from above stopped. Nothing more eerier than total silence when it comes like that, except for when that total silence is followed by another roar at least a hundred and fifty decibels louder than the first. Call and response. That's what they were doing. From the emcee to the crowd. After a couple of repetitions, I started to make it out, so on top of feeling sick already, I was scared as fuck.

"Who do we want!"

"TOR-TURE!"

"What do we want!"

"TOR-TURE!"

"Where do we want!"

"TOR-TURE!"

"When do we want!"

"TOR-TURE!"

Over and over, and with the stomping and the screaming and the torture torture torture. It was so loud the light bulbs hanging from the ceiling swayed back and forth, spotlighting me and the Corp Cops like the finger of the Reaper. You're dead. Now you're dead. Now you're dead.

I tested my limbs: left leg, right leg, left arm, right arm. Clenched and unclenched each fist. Stretched my neck. Everything in working order, though my wrists and ankles still hurt from those zip ties. At least those had been removed. At least Bella or Ella or whoever didn't cut off my hands and feet. At least they didn't shove their hands down my throat. Or did they? I swallowed, trying to see if it hurt, and it didn't, but I did have to hawk up a loogie, so I made that noise you make when you gotta hawk up a loogie. You know the one I'm talking about? That scrapy kind of sound from your throat? I did that. The Corp Cops glared. Right when I was about to spit, someone said, "No on my shoe."

Scared me so bad I almost swallowed the load. Hawked it to the side instead.

"Christ Jesus, who is that?"

From the far corner, in a part of the locker room the finger of the Reaper couldn't reach, I heard him moving, then I saw the boots and the pants and the bloody apron and finally the man himself.

Cue the sappy strings.

"Holy shit," I said. "It's Sal the Butcher."

Sal the Butcher sold meat on a stick in the Market Square. What kind of meat? The fuck should I know? He had meat, he put it on a stick, and he sold it. How he got himself wrapped up in this mess, I'll never know. He rubbed a hand over that big bald head of his.

"Bootcher. I like this."

"You didn't know we called you that? I mean, fuck's sake, Sal. You butcher meat in the market and put it on a stick."

He bobbed his head. Then he pulled his legs under him and stood up, muscles creaking. Sal, he wasn't super-cut or anything. I mean, he was full of beef, don't get me wrong, but his muscles was packed on his frame in slabs like he'd spent his youth hauling wooly mammoths back and forth along the Steppes. Maybe if he fasted, took some diuretics, hit the gym for some high reps, sucked down a catabolic shake or eight, he'd slice his meat into six-pack abs and softball biceps, but as it stood he was just one massive hunk of a man.

The locker room door slammed open and four men sauntered in. Average sized goons, not much to them but for the fact that they was all the same, like quadruplets all the same. The Corp Cops popped to their feet, alarmed. Sal flexed. Four on four, I thought. Fair enough. I was about to suggest we take care of things when *another* three came in, all of them looking familiar somehow, like I seen them somewhere before, and recently, too. And then I got it. They all looked like the kid I clotheslined and who kid Sal carved up into nice, tasty morsels and hanged from a wire in the middle of the square.

(Oh shit. I just realized I didn't tell you about that. Well, here's a quick summary: some kid stole Sal's money box, and when he tried to get away, I clotheslined the bastard. Then Sal done what he done.)

So them goons who came in after the other goons, when I say they looked like the kid Sal shish kabobbed, I mean they looked *exactly* like him. Same greasy hair, same twitchy eyes, same scabby complexion. They spaced themselves seven wide across the front of the locker room, crossing their arms and spreading their legs to puff themselves up or look more authoritative or mean or something.

And who should come in next? Daddy. Strutting in like he was King Solomon. Caroline and Coraline and Bella and Ella followed next, holding hands and skipping, all yellow sundresses and curls and one-eyed teddy bears. They goggled around at the locker room, hiding smiles behind their hands, whispering and giggling. Bella shrieked when she saw the urinals.

"Quiet now, girls," Daddy said.

He smiled with his teeth at Sal. The same one he gave me when I taught the girls how to cuss again.

"Watch out for that one, Sal," I said. "Likes chemical hankies, him."

Daddy turned his smile on me.

"Such a prime specimen. Such brute strength. I think he'll do well. You, on the other hand."

I smiled. Oh Daddy, Daddy, Daddy. You might think you had the advantage, but I got your number you freak. This was going to be fun.

"Oh, Daddy," Coraline said. "He's marvelous strong. Do you think he'll try to kill Hayden? And Logan and Lucas? And Byron and Bryon?"

"Will he hang them from the head?" Caroline asked.

"I do hope so," Bella said. "I do love to see a big man swing."

Ella squealed and clapped her hands over her mouth.

I couldn't tell if Daddy was angry or if he was stifling a laugh. Finally, to Sal he said, "If you're thinking, my friend, of doing anything foolish, please think again. My boys may not be as big as you, but they come more prepared than most."

Another roar lit up the gym above, and the bulb swung a little bit, and something flashed in the light. A knife. Well, more like four knives. Daddy's boys—Logan and Lucas, and Byron and Bryon—had them set on springs hid up their sleeves, and they shot out of their shirt cuffs, sharp, wide, and gleaming, shaped like a fleur-de-lis. Them wasn't knives. Thems was swords. At least as long as a forearm. Looked painful.

So, I take it back. Sal might have been able to take one of them out, maybe two, but a single jab to the belly and they'd gut him and he'd be Sal salad.

Speaking of pointy things, I checked my pants to see if Louis's knife was still there, and ohmygosh it still was. Talk about a pleasant shock. I guess Daddy and all them were too preoccupied with other business to do a thorough pat-down, or maybe they just sucked at this kidnapping thing. Whatever. With the end result, I was satisfied.

One of the Corp Cops finally got the balls to speak up. He said, "What's going on here? Do you know who we are? Privates Smith and Ferguson, A Company, SingleCorp, Serial Numbers 3489 . . ."

Daddy waved him off.

"Yes, yes. Logan? Lucas? Take the pigs up to The Pit."

He looked at me and right when he did, the knife fell out of my waistband and into the seat of my pants, and I shoved my hands back there to fish around for it before it fell out of the leg or stuck me in the asshole. But Daddy didn't know that. All he saw was me picking around my bung. His eyes flickered over me and his face went from befuddled to disgusted.

"Heh," I said, removing my hand and stuffing it in my pockets. I shrugged sheepish. "I get a little gassy when I'm nervous."

Daddy nodded vaguely.

"Nervous. You should be." Then he turned around and said, "come with me."

The Pit was an old high school gym. No shit, that's what they called the place. "The Pit." It was painted on the back wall in big bubble letters, I guess for the kids who used to go there. "Fear the Pit!" it screamed. "Home of the Bull Run Rams." The bleachers was packed with people, all of them twins or triplets or quadruplets, all of them screaming for blood. It was a bit unnerving, you know, seeing so many identical faces, but it wasn't a surprise because, you know, The Weirdness.

The cries for "Torture!" faded into general bloodthirsty screams when we entered. An emcee was running from one side of the gym to the other, screaming into a microphone. Each time he pointed at one-quarter of the stands the people there erupted with a shout to drown out hell, then he ran to another quarter and pointed and they shouted, and so on.

First quarter, "Rip!"

Second quarter, "Them!"

Third quarter, "To!"

Fourth quarter, "Shreds!"

Over and over again.

"Rip! Them! To! Shreds! Rip! Them! To! Shreds!"

Rip them to shreds, indeed.

Daddy wouldn't let his girls watch, much to their collective chagrin.

"We'll cut you, Daddy!" they cried.

"Now girls. You know as well as I do that The Pit is no place for children."

"But, Daddy. You *promised*."

"I did no such thing."

"But we want to see them *die*."

"All in good time girls. You'll be grown soon enough with little Caroline, Coraline, Bella, and Ella's of your own. Then you can go to The Pit."

"I'll never have children," Caroline said.

"I'll have children," Coraline muttered. "But I'll eat them."

"I'll stab out their eyes," Bella squealed.

"Please, daddy, please," Ella pleaded. The little wench grabbed my hand. "Can we just stay for this one? I like this one. Can't we just watch him die?"

"Girls!" Daddy snapped.

He tried to pull her away from me, but the second she realized that he wasn't going to cave, she turned feral, all teeth and claws and hair. Leaped onto my hip and latched on, gripping my leg between her thighs. I started shaking and shimmying, trying to shuck her off, and it was funny until she bit my forearm.

"Fuck!" I yelled.

Her sisters squealed and starting screaming "Fuck! Fuck! Fuck him up!"

I squeezed her cheek as hard as I could, but that only made her clamp down harder.

"Ella," Daddy said, and he pried her teeth out of my arm.

In an instant, she snarled and turned on him, vaulting into his arms. Her sisters joined in. Caroline and Coraline attached themselves to each leg, biting, and Bella leaped onto his back and pulled his hair. Daddy grimaced, trying to shield his eyes.

"Archer! Arthur!"

They were already there, yanking the girls off. It wasn't easy, but when all was said and done, they was dragged away by the neck, tufts of Daddy's hair gripped in their fists.

"We'll cut you, Daddy!" they screamed. "We'll slice you to ribbons!"

Daddy watched them go, grinning, proud but embarrassed. Then he ran his hands over his head, smoothing everything out, and turned back to me, all shrugging shoulders and half-smiles.

"Daughters," he said.

A few minutes later, Archer and Arthur, their faces lined with fresh scratches courtesy of their crazy little sisters, showed up with two big duffle bags and dumped a load of gear at the feet of the two Corp Cops. It was all their old stuff: riot helmets with the plastic face shield, Kevlar vests, shin, knee, hand, arm, and elbow pads.

One of the cops said, "What about our guns?"

Byron shook his head, pulled out two black police batons instead, what my pop used to call tire thumpers, and handed them over. The cops weighed them in their hands, looking like they were about to use them right then and there, but Byron waved a finger at him. Naughty boy. Then he held up his sleeve, let the kid get a glimpse of his blade.

"This is it?" the other one said.

Byron thought for a second, then snapped his fingers. His brothers dug around in the bags and produced more: a can of pepper spray, a set of brass knuckles, a pair of handcuffs, a flashlight, a Leatherman, a first aid kit. The two cops shoved each item in its spot on their belts until only the gun holster was empty. The first cop stared at it longingly.

Daddy said, "Okay, boys. Here are the rules: There are no rules. Each of you will enter The Pit, and each of you will fight to the death. If you can defeat your challenger, you're free to go. And if you cannot defeat your challenger? Well. It answers itself, does it not?"

He signaled to the emcee, who, without missing a beat, cried out, "Ladies and Gentlemen!"

Music blared from the P.A., triumphant horns and brass, booming bass drums. The crowd went apeshit.

"Ladies and gentlemen! We bring you the night's entertainment!"

More craziness.

"Grizzled gladiators"

The screams swelled.

"Scurrilous Scum!"

The crowd booed and crowed.

"And two revolting!"

Apeshit.

"Repugnant!"

Apeshit.

"Reptilian!"

Apeshit.

"Monstrous!"

Apeshit.

"Murderers!"

I didn't think it was possible, but the crowd went even more nuts. It went on and on, an avalanche of malice, and the emcee let them scream themselves into a frenzy. Then he held out his arms and tamped down the air, and the spectators gradually grew quieter and quieter until there was nothing but a low rumble.

"Now, to introduce our first two contestants. You've seen them before, patrolling the Bottom in their hover cars, busting the heads of children who dared to steal something to eat. Dragging innocent women to the Silver Bullet for offering themselves to feed those poor children, or . . ."

The boos drowned out the rest of the sentence, and the emcee waved them down, crying, "No no, no no! These are our heroes! Our saviors! The men who keep the Bottom safe from the bottom of the Bottom, who sweep the streets clean for our betters! Ladies and Gentlemen, I give you, the Corp Cops!"

Bryon and Byron frog stepped the two cops out onto the gym floor, and the crowd booed and screamed and threw things, so much so that Byron and Bryon gave up and pushed them away, running back to the safety of the hallway. When the cops got to the middle, they pulled out their batons and crouched back to back, waiting for whatever adversary what was supposed to come their way. After about two minutes, the cops stood up, arms held out, looking around.

Nothing. Nothing came to fight them. No gladiators, no lions, no bears. Nothing.

The emcee strutted out onto the floor holding up his hands.

"I think these boys don't understand the game! Should I explain it to them?"

"YES!"

"Now boys. What is it you think you're doing here?"

One of them pulled the mic to his face.

"Send them out. Send them out and let's get this over with."

"I'm sorry. Send who out?"

"You know goddamn well who! Send them out!"

"Oh! Oh! You think you're going to fight someone else? Oh!"

Realization dawned on the cops at the same time.

"No way," one said. "No way. We won't do it."

"You won't do what?" The emcee shoved out his lower lip, pouting. "Well, maybe you could be persuaded?"

He gestured to the stands and a boy scurried out onto the floor carrying a silver platter with a gun on it. He snatched it up, aimed it at the cop, and shot him in the foot.

The crowd absolutely lost it. People leaped on each other, arms pumping, fists cracking jaws. Bullet Foot writhed around on the ground, and he held out his hand as the emcee approached, but that didn't do nothing. The emcee just shot at it. He missed, hit a guy in the stands right in the gut, and put a hand to his mouth in an exaggerated "oops." Then he shrugged and pushed the other cop at him. The other cop shook his head, but when the emcee pointed the gun at his chest, he held up his hands, went over to his friend, and straddled him.

I saw him mouth the words "I'm sorry," and then he raised his baton over his head.

When it was all over, the crowd was far more than frenzied. They were like an army of coked-up monkeys, and the emcee fed on it, hopping all around the gym, whirling his arms.

"All right, all right, all right! Wasn't that something?" The crowd kept going nuts. "Almost as great as this!" And he walked right over to the surviving cop and shot him in the face.

I guess I should have been worried at this point. Things was not looking up for Sal and me. But it was just so entertaining. I hadn't seen anything that good since the Tlek war.

Sal, though, was as readable as a stone. He muttered. He scowled. He jogged in place like he was warming up for a boxing match or something, you know, hop hop, crick the neck left, hop hop, crick the neck right. He wiggled his arms, rolled his shoulders. I did the same, you know, for solidarity, but he kind of glanced at me sideways, so I stopped.

The emcee spun his finger over his head, and the lights dimmed. A hush fell over the crowd. Melancholy organ music piped through the speakers. A sole spotlight hit him in the center. He stood perfectly still, head bowed, feet together, hands clasped around the mic as if he was praying. A white sheet dropped from the ceiling, and a projector fired up a headshot on it, a headshot of good old Aiden, the kid me and Sal killed.

Sal tensed up.

"The thief."

"Yes, indeed," Daddy drawled. "I don't blame you for what you did. Aiden was always a particularly difficult child. Not at all like his brothers." He glanced over at Hayden, who glared, and Archer and Arthur, who glared. "But he was my boy."

The emcee raised his head, and the music stopped.

"My friends. Today we celebrate the life of Aiden Blackguard. Able soldier, loyal brother, devoted son. Many of you knew Aiden as that rapscallion who snatched pies from your windowsill, or who impregnated your daughters, or who injected himself with euph and screamers until his skin broke out in the Blisters. But he was one of us. One of us."

The crowd repeated it, low and somber, like a chant, like in that movie *Freaks*, "One of us! One of us!" Then they fell into a respectful silence.

I was surprised when they didn't finish the whole thing, so I yelled it out for them, cutting through the silence.

"We accept you! We accept you! Gobble gobble!"

The crowd gasped at the blaspheme. The emcee looked my way, and Daddy shot me a sharp one, more perplexed than angry, but what was he gonna do? Kill me?

He snapped his fingers at his boys and they hupped-to. First they gave old Sal and me helmets and vests and a couple of fleur-de-lis swords and Corp Cop batons. Then they gave us the police belts with the pepper spray and the handcuffs and all that.

I got into character. I asked one of the twins (I think it was or Arthur) for a back rub.

He didn't take it kindly, and when my head cleared enough to pull myself off the ground, I took a swipe at him with my baton, but he dodged it, leaped away like a cat. He was smiling the whole time, a big shit-eating go-screw plastered over his mug.

Daddy gave the emcee the twirly finger again, and the emcee said ". . . folks, in the midst of life, we are in death . . . especially the next two contestants, amiright!

"Ladies and Gentlemen of the Quad! The two men you're about to meet are the meanest, basest scum in the entire city! They snatched potatoes from the fingers of babies during the six-month siege! Sold pregnant teenagers to sex tourists following the rape of the city! Ripped the blankets from freezing grandmothers during the eight-day blizzard! Baby filchers! Faby bilchers! Rapscallions, rapists, ruffians, rascals, and rogues. Would! You! Like! To! Meet them?"

"YES!"

"Citizens of Blackguard. Together again for the first time ever, I give you . . . The Butchers! Of! The Bottom!"

The lights shut off with a clunk that echoed in the gym, and the crowd kept on roaring, and wouldn't you know it, but "Welcome to the Jungle" thundered out of the P.A. system.

I love me some Guns and Roses, but given the circumstances, Axl Rose's primal scream over that delayed guitar line at the beginning made me want to piss myself. Then the twin twins shoved us out to the middle of the floor and left us there.

"Back with back," Sal grunted.

"What?"

Sal backed up to me to demonstrate.

"You back, my back."

"Yeah, I got it."

We did it, but I stood about two feet too short and just as much wide, so I don't think it did any good, not for him, at least.

Bangs and booms echoed in the gym, followed by a series of mechanical ratcheting noises like they were winching an oil tanker out of the sub-basement. Another thunk and the spotlight fell on our opponent.

And guess who it was?

Boston Washington.

Or whoever it was what'd taken Boston Washington's place, whoever Boston Washington really was. It looked like what you'd expect a militarized robotic death werewolf in the shape of a werewolf to look like, all shiny metal shoulders and fangs and claws and talons what gleamed in the spotlight. The song ramped up, and Axl started his howl. Cymbal crash. The wolf flexed its claws. Tom tom build up. It fell into a crouch. Axl screams "Cha!" and red beams shot out of its eye sockets.

The worst part, though, was its name, what someone'd scrawled its chest in red paint that dripped down its torso like blood.

Torture.

Because what else'd you name a militarized robotic death werewolf?

The song faded out, and with another thunk, more lights went up in the middle of the court, keeping the stands dark. The monster's eyes narrowed in on us. Sal twirled his fleur-de-lis. The werewolf flexed its butcher blade claws. And I sprinted for the sideline.

"Coward!" Sal snarled.

The wolf shot for him, and I made a beeline for the emcee, who was busily chatting up one of the women in the crowd, ignoring the fight. I yanked Louis's knife out of my ass, ran up on the bastard, and shoved it right up under his chin and into his brain. He didn't even have a chance to cry out or nothing, he just died there, my knife severing the two halves of his stem, slicing into his throat, friggin unbelievable.

I yanked the gun out of his belt, spun on my heel, and ran back to help Sal. I didn't have a lot of time, neither, and not just because the werewolf was already launching itself in the air toward him, but because Daddy seen what happened, and Byron and Bryon, and Archer and Arthur and Hayden were sprinting out for me, fleur's at the ready. Fortunately, them Corp Cop guns carried extended round magazines, forty or fifty bullets per clip. The emcee only used ten. Or fifteen. Something like that. So if I was lucky and the clip was still somewhat fully loaded . . . .

Not that I was thinking any of this. Or thinking at all. I was in full-on panic mode, so I pointed and squeezed the trigger. Boom! Boom! Boom! Boom! Two hit Byron right in the chest. Boom! Boom! Hayden's knee exploded. The crowd went apeshit.

I was about twenty feet away when the werewolf hit Sal full on, and the two tumbled back in a blur of steel and skin. Sal positioned one of his blades perfectly, though, blocking a shot from the werewolf's claws. But that thing was coming at him hard, and they slid at least fifteen feet. They both came to a rest against the cinderblock wall and Sal leaped away, swinging the swords behind him to block whatever else the thing threw at him.

The last three identicals caught me up. Archer took a swipe with his sword and cut me right across the shoulder. I threw my baton at him and he ducked, and I shot him in the face. Then Bryon was on me. His sword chopped right into the outside of my thigh and I crumbled to the ground. I lay there, face down, totally in shock. Did he hit an artery? Was I bleeding out? If I was, then there was nothing left to do but die, and if I was going to die, I was taking the last of them with me.

I rolled over on my back. Lucky for me, too, cause Bryon's sword thunked in the boards right where my head had just been and got stuck there. His eyes found mine as he tried to pull it out with both hands. I held the gun right up to his forehead and he said "Wait!" and then I blew his brains out. I was hoping he'd fall over on his side, but instead he fell right on me, pinning me down under his dead weight, the barrel of the gun shoved into his stomach.

The last of the brothers, Archer, was already rushing me, sword held over his head, a scream raging out of his mouth. I wiggled and waggled, but the corpse wouldn't budge. Finally, it was too late. Archer was right there, his sword already whizzing through the air, so I scrunched up as much as I could, tried to hide under Bryon's dead body, and wouldn't you know it? The sword thunked right into the poor guy's back.

"Ha!" I cried.

And I pulled the trigger. The bullets exploded out of his brother's lower back; three caught him in the thigh, two missed, and one blasted him in the neck. I was kind of hoping he'd fall backward, but he didn't. He leaned back a little bit, enough for me to hope he'd fall all the way, but then he collapsed forward, across his brother and me, dead.

So that was awesome, but I wasn't in great condition. I had about three hundred pounds of dead weight on my chest, and I was sure that my leg was bleeding out, and my shoulder was bleeding, too. I took a deep breath and tried to push them off. I heard Sal cry out and the clang of metal on metal, and then an avalanche of trains rushed over me, and the weight flew off my chest, but now I was tumbling over and over. I spun in the air and slammed into the wall.

Everything got fuzzy. My eyesight blurred and focused. I heaved and gasped, the pain my back and chest red hot and terrible. I kind of tried to sit up, but I was bleeding all over the place. I could barely move. I was fucked. Fucked.

I managed to roll off the top and came face to face with the werewolf. It was dead. Sal had killed it. Them laser lights were black.

"Oh no," I groaned

A female voice from inside the werewolf said, "Initiating self-destruct protocol."

Sal reached down and pulled me off the boards. It sucked, to say the least, and I cried like a baby, but I guess my legs was filled with adrenaline because I could stand under my own power. Well. Kind of. Okay, I was hopping on one leg while blood dripped out of the other. There was a series of clicks and whirs from inside the werewolf, and then the female voice said, "Detonator activated. Detonation in . . . ten . . . nine . . ."

Sal and me, we didn't say nothing, we just started running. I didn't see Daddy anywhere, neither, just the people in the stands going apeshit as usual. I couldn't hear the count once we'd gotten ten feet away, so I did it in my head.

". . . seven . . . six . . ."

I felt like a double amputee with TBI. Sal couldn't run very well, neither, what with the cracked ribs and puncture wounds. We must have looked ridiculous, but the crowd ate it up. Thought it was a part of the show. We aimed for the doors where we come in, trying to get as far away from the blast as we could.

"... four ... three ..."

We weren't going to make it. They were twenty yards away.

"... two ..."

One of the ladies in the stands pulled up her shirt and flashed me.

"... one ..."

I started to scream.

All the air was sucked out of the room. My ears compressed. The concussion hit, my feet lifted from the ground, then white light and white heat and we was airborne, me and Sal, shooting through space like so much meat and bone. I thought to myself, "Maybe it'll send us through the doors after all," and then there was a second blast and I

Chapter 4
In which our boy returns victorious

I swear to god, Ruby nearly soiled her diaper when I burst into O'Neill's office. I don't blame her, neither. I'm one handsome mohonky. That probably wasn't why she might have shat herself. The reason she probably shat herself was because I looked like, well, liked I'd just been blown up by a militarized robotic death werewolf.

My clothes was to ribbons, and I was bleeding all over, and I had a hunk of metal sticking out of my shoulder, but other than that, I was fine. Navigating the entry was a little difficult, mainly because my left eye was swole shut and my ears was still ringing, and I as I stood there, wavering on the threshold, Ruby sufficiently recovered enough to say, "don't bring your muddy shoes in here."

"Ain't mud," I said. I hawked up a lunger and spat a red glob onto the floor.

Ruby took one look at it and yelled, "Boss!"

From the back, I heard O'Neill cry, "What?"

"Better come up here!"

I staggered in and lurched up against Ruby's desk, and she jumped out of her chair with a disgusted "ugh." O'Neill came waddling out of the back room. Didn't even give me a second look, just plonked the butt of a cigar in his mouth and hopped up onto the corner of his desk.

"You got the package?"

"Yeah."

"Well, let's see it."

"Ain't here."

"Where is it?"

"Out front."

O'Neill hopped back down and hustled around to the front door, letting it slam behind him. A second later he came back in holding the werewolf's metal head.

"Where's the rest?"

"Ask Daddy."

"Who the fuck's Daddy?"

I didn't answer him. I put my head down on the counter. I was real tired all the sudden, and the ringing in my ears was giving me a headache. I heard him sigh and walk back to his desk.

"Listen, Bone—"

"License."

"What?"

"I want my license to carry."

"Go home and get yourself some sleep, first. I—"

I picked my head up off the counter.

"Look, you little prick. I know you set me up. I know you didn't expect me to come back. So how about this: you get me my license to carry, and I won't rip your fucking head off right here!"

I'd worked myself into a boil, hadn't I? Didn't see that coming. I never got upset like that. But the little creep made me a promise, and I intended for him to make good on it. He was staring at me like a hand had burst out of my chest.

"It'll take some time—"

"You're all out of time!"

"Calm down. I didn't set you up. I already put in for the application. I totally expected you to come back."

I took a deep breath. Held it. Let it out.

"Okay."

"You good?"

"I'm good."

"Good. So go home and get some sleep. When you're ready, I got your license and another job for you."

"I gotta fight a robotic werewolf again?"

"Maybe."

"God dammit, O'Neil!"

"Relax! Relax! I'm just fooling around."

I forced myself to calm down. If I didn't need the money so much, I'd have punched the little runt in the balls already. "What kind?"

"What?"

"What kind of job is it?"

"Search and recovery."

"Okay. Where?"

"Silver Bullet."

"Seriously?"

"Seriously."

He went over to his drawer, took out a manila envelope, and slapped it on the counter next to me.

"What's it pay?" I asked.

"Double that." When I didn't respond immediately, he said, "Go home and think about it."

"I will. I will go home and think about it."

"Good. Now get the fuck outta here. You're bleeding all over my floor."

I sighed and pulled myself toward the door, the whole time thinking to myself, "Fuck's sake. Fuck's sake."

BONESAW'S BABY

Chapter 1
In which our boy is offered
a new opportunity

Hey, how's it going?

So I was minding my own, standing on the line, soldering the wires I was hired to solder, when all of a sudden I got the sense somebody was looking at me. Everybody gets that from time to time, that feeling in your gut, the little tingle in your nerves, and then you look up and, well, sometimes it ain't nothing. Sometimes you get that feeling and end up whipping your head around like a goddamn parrot on a stick, but there ain't nobody or nothing there even though you could've sworn seconds before there was. Other times, though, other times you look up and a whole room full of twitchers with bodymods is staring right at you.

That's what happened to me the morning I got my balls squashed by a zombie wearing a Viddy Viewer™.

"Yeah, but wasn't all thems wearing Viddy Viewers™? Did all thems squash your balls?"

Please, for a moment, imagine the longest pregnant pause in the history of knocked up comedic devices.

Thank you.

Now imagine, at the end of that pause, the following voice saying this in your head:

"No, numbnuts. They did not all squash his balls. Just the one."

So yeah. I looked up. And they was all looking back at me, and all of them had Viddy Viewers™ embedded in their faces and Barrel Arm Biceps™ janked into their arms, and Nimble Digits™ sewed into their digits. Freaked me right the fuck out.

And then they all twitched.

At the same time.

Right ear to right shoulder.

Which was even freakier. Obviously.

"Oh shit," I said.

Them Bowl Cuts what was supposed to be monitoring everything kept tapping away at the screens in their forearms, oblivious. Until the twitchers next to them reached out—all of them, even the ones nowhere near a Bowl Cut—and they grabbed them by the necks and squeezed and didn't stop. Then they ripped off their arms. And their legs. And their heads. It was like late August summer vacation, and someone gave that little psycho Timmy up the street a hammer and a pair of pliers and set him loose in the terrarium. I grabbed my soldering gun and slapped at my forearm.

"C'mon you fucks!"

My good buddy Ham entered the floor from the hallway, took one look at the dead Bowl Cuts all around him, and made a beeline for the emergency exit, which was nothing more than a recessed door in the wall. Didn't even run, the dumbass, but power-walked, stiff-legged, like his pollex was shoved up his alimentary canal. Two twitchers clocked him and fell in behind. Ham reached the keypad and punched in the combo. Nothing. He consulted his forearm, tried another one. Still nothing. The twitchers pressed on, ten feet away, five. Ham panicked and hit the little red button on the bottom like a maniac three times in a row, bam bam bam, then twice with a pause, bam . . . bam, and the door formed out of the wall and he fell in, but it was too late. The twitchers were right there, and they fell in after him. As the door closed, one pulled its arm back, ready to smash and tear and rend and whatever else it decided to do, but the door caught it and severed it right in two.

That seemed to be a signal for the rest of them. One group of twitchers made a kamikaze run and threw themselves out the window. Another group rounded the wagons turned the arrows in, started tearing out each other's implants. Gimmie that Nimble Digits™! Rrrrrrip. Gimmie that Barrel Arm Bicep™! Rrrrrrip. Don't need them Second Sights™, do you? Rrrrrrip. The rest attacked anything what wasn't a twitcher. Four of them leaped on one poor schmuck, took him down in a pile, tore out his eyes. Another lurched up behind some guy who hadn't noticed what was going on, grabbed him by the head, broke his neck. One kid, a skinny little dude with long gray hair and sunken eyes, almost made it off the floor. He sprinted for the exit, got one foot into the hallway, but a twitcher pulled him back by them greasy locks, spun him around, grabbed his wrist, and broke it in half. And the kid, he's standing there staring at the wrist flapping off the end of his arm, in shock or seriously stupid because the twitcher took it as permission to rip his arm off. Then it started beating him with it.

Never seen that. I've heard people threaten it, but I never actually seen it.

Same thing must have been going down all over the place, because a siren ramped up and the overheads shut off with a clunk, replaced by one of them red revolving lights, like what the cops had on top of their cars way back when. This light was not helpful. Now, instead of being able to track every last twitcher's every last goddamn movement, all I could see was a strobe light of chaos punctuated by violence. Here a snapped neck. There a snapped neck. Here some blood, there some blood, everywhere some blood blood. I fell to all fours and scrambled under my desk, holding the soldering gun in front of me like it'd make a difference.

To increase the tension, an explosion rocked the building. One of the twitchers flopped on its side in front of me, smacking its head on the floor, and sparks shot out of its goggles, and then it shook all tortured-like, seized up, and died. Just like that. Until it didn't die no more. What I mean is that it came back online. Its eyes flashed open, seen me cowering there, and reached out with its Nimble Digits™, striving for what I could only assume to be my precious little eyeballs. Another explosion rocked the building and I said "Fuck this shit," and scampered out from under the desk. Made sure to kick the twitcher first, just in case it got it into its head to follow me. Okay, I didn't just kick it. I stomped it, like a curb stomp only without the curb. So a regular stomp, I guess. Stomped its face, stomped its head, stomped its neck until it was a pile of mush and bone and gray stuff.

Smoke filled the room, and little fires broke out of the walls, so taking the elevator wasn't an option, and sprinting down the stairs wouldn't get me out any faster, neither. Plus, the hall was probably flooded with twitchers, and I think I've established that them twitchers wasn't fucking around. The only way I'd get out alive was to make it to Ham's door and hope it'd open for me, so that's what I did. Ducked any twitchers when they reached for me. Kicked a couple when they got too close. A third explosion rocked the joint and sent me to the floor and the building took to shaking so much that I couldn't stay on my feet, so I crawled over bodies instead.

I was almost there when I came across a dead twitcher. Remember when I told you I got my nuts squashed? I was halfway across the dead thing, pulling myself along foot by foot, when it reached out and squeezed my nards. No shit. If you got nards, you know what a nard squeeze feels like. If you don't, well, I mean, it ain't like childbirth, I get that, but it ain't like any other pain, neither. No comparison or metaphor works to describe it. You know what it feels like? It feels like getting grabbed by the nards.

So that sucked.

Had to jam the soldering gun in the stupid thing's eye, and when that didn't stop the pervert, I had to jam it in its other eye. Then its left ear. Then its right ear. That finally persuaded it to stop.

The door was about ten feet away. I had the choice of crabbing through the ruck on my belly and risking another ball squeeze or two or standing up and bolting and risk a lungful of death, at which point I'd crumble to the floor and probably get my balls squeezed. I compromised. I got to my feet but hunched over while I ran. Reached the door zip, zap, zoop, coughing my lungs out, and started pounding on the keypad.

"Ham! Ham! Open up, it's me!"

The floor shifted. The building groaned and whined as the fire ate through its guts.

"Ham, goddammit! I showed you how to use your thumb!"

A couple of remaining twitchers whipped their heads in my direction. They stumbled forward, gnashing their teeth and, you know, twitching.

"Ham!"

I hit the keypad over and over.

The twitchers tripped over the mound of burning flesh I'd just escaped, the one with the thing that grabbed my balls. On the other side of the door, I heard something bang. Bam bam bam. Bam. Bam.

Ham was trying to get out. The hell?

The first of the new twitchers grabbed me by the shoulder and spun me around. I threw myself back, and the thing lost its balance and fell forward, and I kicked it off me with one foot.

"Ham!"

I heard the noise from inside the room again, just on the other side of the door.

Bam bam bam. Bam. Bam.

Holy mother . . .

There were numbers on the pad, of course, one through nine, so it could have been one two three, one one he was telling me. Or one one one, one one. Or three, two. Or I could just hit the red Enter button three times, then once more, then once more, and so I thought to myself, "might as well," and punched it three times real quick, bam bam bam.

The second twitcher came at me.

I slammed the red button again.

Bam.

It reached for my throat and

Hold on a sec. I just realized that you ain't got the slightest clue as to what's going on. I'd apologize, but apologies is for suckers, and I might suck, but I ain't a sucker. I do feel the need to clarify some information, more because I want to tell a good story than anything else. So let me back up a bit and get you up to speed.

Here's the deal. Forty-four hours before I got attacked by a bunch of assholes with bodymods and got my balls squeezed (yeah, I ain't letting that one go), I was living the good life at The Bottom of the Bottom. Booze in one hand, a stack of bills in the other, and three of the laziest strippers in the world pretending to dance in front of me. I held out a single.

"Hey, Dallas!"

One of the girls turned her lidded eyes on me.

"It's Chardonnay."

"Whatever. You want a Washington or what?"

She rolled her eyes and came over, let me tuck it in the strap of her thong before shuffling away. When I looked to the left, O'Neill was occupying the space next to me. I nearly fell off my stool.

"Fuck's sake, O'Neill!"

"Big spender, huh?"

"You scared the crap out of me!"

He pointed at the girls wobbling around on stage.

"Me sitting here is scarier than that?"

"What do you want, O'Neill?"

"How do you know I want something? I'm just out on the town, enjoying the city's amenities."

"Where's Ruby? I never seen you not with her."

"How should I know?"

"I just figured—"

"You're a hard guy to get in touch with. Where you been?"

"What, since the robot werewolf job? As far away from you as possible."

"That's understandable."

"I know."

"You looking for work?"

"You kidding?"

"It's the one I told you about before. Heist job. Get in, get out. Simple."

"SingleCorp, right."

"Yeah."

"Simple heist job my ass."

"I know it don't sound—"

"Why don't you get Kevin Johnson? He's a sucker."

"Kevin Johnson's busy."

"Sure he is. Is it Fleet Week or something?"

We watched the girls shimmy around for a few minutes before O'Neill sighed and said, "I can't take this. It's like watching drugged cattle." He hopped down off his stool, slapping a fiver on the bar. "Come by the office tomorrow morning if you're interested. We could really use a guy with your particular skill set on this one."

"Fat chance."

"Whatever."

I really didn't have no intention of taking the job. I was still flush with cash, and even though I knew it'd run out at some point, working for O'Neill came with its own set of negative consequences, and when he said 'Simple heist job' all I could see was the glowing red eyes of the werewolf robot boring in on me.

But the best-laid plans and Lennie and George and all that, because three hours after he left, I stumbled out of The Bottom of the Bottom and into the early morning bullshit of the city—which is another way of saying I got thrown out on my ass into the side alley.

Speaking of alleys:

"Well, well, well. Look who we got here."

I was in such a fog of alcohol and pussy that I couldn't exactly place the voice at first. All I knew was that whenever someone said that to me after I been thrown out of a strip joint, the results was usually less than spectacular.

"Whozit?" I said, peering into the dark.

And out of the shadows stepped Allie-boy. You might not remember him, but I sure as fuck did. He was the little runt O'Neill sent a few months before about the werewolf robot job, and I stiffed him, and he ain't never let it go. Allie-boy by himself I could handle. Sober. But I was drunk, and he'd brought two of his friends.

"Hey, Allie-boy," one said. Concave cheeks, deep-set eyes, honker like a baboon's. "This the guy you was talking about?"

"Yeah, that's him."

"Well, let's get this over with."

The third kid just stood there, chin down, eyes up, a creepy half-smile on his face. He was bigger than the other two, with rounded shoulders and thick arms and legs. I swayed there, using the wall to hold me up.

"What's wrong with that one? He special?"

Allie-boy and Baboon-nose guffawed, which pissed old Weirdo off because he and started throwing punches.

"Yeah, he's special alright," Baboon-nose said, fending off the blows. Then he clapped Weirdo's ears and screamed, "Knock it off!" and to my surprise, Weirdo complied. Kind of hunched back a little, resumed his post. Baboon-nose adjusted his shirt. "His pop liked to beat him up when he was a kid." He tapped his temple. "Too many concussions."

Weirdo responded by removing a knife from his shirt. And when I say a knife, I mean a *knife*. Five-inch lock-back stainless steel blade, brass bolsters, genuine ram horn handle. Beautiful. He ran the blade along his thumb, leering at me the whole time.

I whistled, appreciative-like.

"Nice pig-sticker. You steal that all by yourself?"

Weirdo's smile fell into a sneer, and Baboon-nose said, "No, he took it off his pop. After he slit his throat with it."

"That don't make no sense."

"Well, maybe it'll make more sense after he's slit your throat, too."

I had enough of that horse shit. I was drunk and tired, and I wanted to get to bed, so I looked up into the sky, up to the left, just over their shoulders, and said, "Holy Shit!"

Never failed. All three of them fell for it, and in less than a second I snatched the knife out of Weirdo's hands and stabbed him four times: two in the obliques, two in the guts. He slumped against the wall, and Allie-boy and Baboon-nose looked down at him.

"C'mon, you fucks," I said.

That's when Baboon-nose took out his own blade. It was a lot bigger than mine. So was Allie-boy's.

The next morning, I woke up in the alley, sliced and diced and robbed of all my worldlies. Them kids knew what they was doing. Carved me up like French chefs, deep enough to hurt, but not deep enough to bleed me out. Sitting there amongst the trash and dead things, my thoughts ran wild. How'd Allie-boy found me? I mean, my habits was pretty habitual. I did like my booze and cooze, but I'd never imagined a little cunt like him would have the intelligence enough to . . .

And that's when I realized it.

O'Neill, that fuck. He must've tipped the little bastard off.

I took out a cigarette and lit it with my last match. There was some hollow-eyed kids at the other end of the alley, sitting around a fire in an open barrel. I thought it was kind of cute at first. Then I thought it was a little hacky. Couldn't they have chosen some other pose? A few of them was tussling over something and, well, maybe tussling ain't the right word. They was brawling over it. Seriously, biting and kicking and scratching, all elbows and eye gouges.

Watching kids fight is hands down one of my all-time favorite things, second only to boozing and sex and drugs and movies and long walks along the river. Then one kid kicked the other kid square in the nuts, which might have been an effective strategy had the other kid had nuts, but he was a she and biology don't work that way, get it? Nuts or no nuts, getting kicked between the legs hurt to one degree or another, and the girl went down, and the boy who kicked her ripped the whatchamacallit out of her hands and held it up in triumph and, I swear to god this is true, it was a rat. A friggin rat. Oh, it was dead. Fighting over a rat ain't a fight, it's survival.

So that was gross. And sad.

I didn't stick around to see what they was going to do with it, choosing instead to pound pavement. It only got worse from there. What had happened since the day before? The city was crap yesterday morning, sure, with the starvation and the homelessness and the income inequality and all that, but now it was like Moore's Law in reverse, like every day compounded the misery of the human condition two bits by two bits. Even worse was the tecuani corpses hulking in the gutters, with the talons and the rotting skin and the armored backs. SingleCorp was supposed to clean all that up. Said they'd harvest the corpses, which I didn't doubt for a second, but so far they'd only managed to pick up their own hybrids, the sceels and sniders and such.

O'Neill's front window was still busted when I got there (thanks Kevin Johnson). The front door opened with a ding and Ruby looked up from her desk with them Coke-bottle glasses. She looked like a frog with elephantiasis of the eyes.

"What's going on with the ding?" I asked.

"The ding?"

"Yeah, the ding. You didn't hear it?"

"I heard it. I just don't care."

"Why'd you install it?"

Ruby shrugged and took a sip from her mug.

"Ask O'Neill. He's the one who did it."

"Oh yeah, I got a lot of questions for that little fuck. He in?"

"Yeah."

"Good."

I was about to march back to his office when there was the bang of a door slamming open followed by what sounded like a squeaky wheel being pushed in my direction, which was fitting because a few seconds later, O'Neill wheeled out the oldest looking lady I ever seen in my entire life. Crepey skin. Gnarled nails. Wispy hair. The hunch in her back rolled like sand dunes, and her toothless mouth was puckered and wrinkled. But her eyes, her eyes was cold, clear, blue, and alive. They pierced right through me. She looked angry. Or constipated. I couldn't really tell. O'Neill wheeled her up to me.

"O'Neill, you fuck," I said. "You set me up."

"The fuck you're talking about."

"That kid Allie-boy and his friends ripped me off in the alley last night." I showed him all my cuts.

"They sic a cat on you or something?"

"Very funny."

"Look, I ain't got nothing to do with that nonsense. Allie-boy's got his own thing going on."

"Bullshit."

"Bullshit bullshit." We stared at each other. "Is that why you came here? To get pissy at me for something what wasn't my fault?"

"Yeah. I mean, no. Ah, fuck."

"Sounds to me like you need a job."

"Yeah, no thanks to you."

"Whatever." He gestured at the old crab in the chair. "Here it is. The job I was telling you about."

"What are you a pimp now?"

"It ain't that kind of job. This is June. June, meet this guy."

"Hey, June," I said. "You got to make a boom boom?"

O'Neill sighed as he strode around her chair.

"Don't talk to her like that, you idiot."

He took a picture out of his back pocket and handed it to me. It was the Silver Bullet in all its glory, including the suicide nets.

"Nice shot. You take that yourself?"

"Yeah. Thanks."

"You want me to steal the whole friggin building?"

"Don't be an idiot."

"O'Neill, I'm a little confused. I thought SingleCorp was one of your clients."

"One of my best."

"Then why are you stealing from them? Seems like you're cutting off your nuts to spite your cock."

"Who said I'm stealing from them?"

"You did. Last night. 'Simple heist job' you said."

"Things changed. June is . . . peculiar."

"Peculiar how?"

"She wants you to steal some of their tech and bring it back here so she can put it in herself."

I looked at her. She sat there, still, almost lifeless. The only way I knew she was alive was from the way her mouth was working.

"What's she want? Barrel Arms™? Second Sights™? Not that either of them would help."

"It's something new. Still in R&D. June said they're using it on their meat."

Meat was what we called all thems what worked for the Corp. Because they was worth nothing more than meat.

"So what do I got to do?"

"You gotta get yourself injured."

"Injured? How badly injured? Like 'owie my thumb' injured or 'somebody put my guts back in' injured?"

"Somewhere in between."

"Bullshit."

"Leans a little bit toward the last one."

I thought about it. I thought about a lot of things. I thought about all I went through in my life. WWI. WWII. I thought about my time in the hole. I thought about training with Zoot and Colosseum and Old Mr. Feldman's zombies. I thought about Wildcat and Coatl. I thought about that death robot. I had a lot of shit happen to me, you know? Over a century of it. Whatever. What it really come down to was whether or not I had anything to lose, and in the end, I didn't. Plus, I was broke.

"Okay," I said.

Chapter 2
In which our boy joins the workforce

So that's how I ended up on a bus to the Silver Bullet to take on a job as a SingleCorp drone. There was only six of us, me and five scraggly greasers, real lowlifes, all bony shoulders and hollow eyes. Meat for the grinder. I sat in the back, staring at the blacktop as we rolled over the concourse. It, like everything else, was in serious need of repair. Potholes and drop-offs, wheel ruts and weedy cracks, some so deep and wide they might as well have been the Grand Friggin Canyon.

The Silver Bullet grew from a monster in the distance to a monster right the fuck in front of me. Seriously, it was like standing at the big toe of Godzilla himself. Suicide nets ringed around it in steely webs, only instead of catching leaves, they caught brains. And arms. And legs. And other stuff. Me and the greasers got off the bus and gaped at all the gore, and while we was gaping, a body fell out of the sky and landed in the net right over our heads.

"Fuck's sake," I said.

I turned around to ask the bus driver if that was something I should get used to, but the bus driver, a bland-faced guy with a serious bowl cut, closed the doors and drove off, leaving us standing there.

Then an insectile chittering sounded all around us, and I was suddenly back in BT with that psycho, Zoot, but instead of those balls with knives on the ends of them zipping out of the forest, billions of little metal spiders swarmed out these hatches in the side of the Bullet and fanned out onto the suicide net. They covered the bodies and, well I guess they ate them because after about a minute there wasn't nothing left. No bone, no blood, no tissue. Nothing. Then they surged back in, and the nets was clear. It all happened in like two minutes. Craziest thing I ever seen.

Before I could even process that horror show, a load of guys (or girls?) with bowl cuts just as severe as the bowl cut the guy driving the bus was wearing busted out the Bullet, corralled us up, and shoved us through the door. Everything was silver inside. Silver walls, silver floors, silver chairs. The Bowl Cuts weighed us, took our height, and made us run up about a million flights of stairs until we stopped at a door with the words Locker Room printed on it in fat, red letters.

First of all, no gender association? Figures. I guess them Bowl Cut things was things, like, not human, but . . . things. Second of all, if them things was things, why have a locker room at all? And third: crap. Another locker room. I had a brief flashback to Daddy's Girls and that leaky high school, but all that was wiped clean when one of the Bowl Cuts unlocked the door and led us inside.

Everything was silver there, too. Silver lockers, silver floors, silver benches. Sparkling clean. Tiles on the floors? Sparkling. Fixtures on the sinks? Sparkling. Door knobs, padlocks, towel racks, even the drains in the floor, sparkling, sparkling, sparkling. I swear I heard a musical ping every time I looked at something. Then one of the Bowl Cuts walked up to one of the greasers, grabbed his ratty old shirt by the collar, and ripped it off his body.

Great.

Greaser's pants was next. He got the point after that and pulled off his shoes. Well, they wasn't much in the way of shoes. Just rubber soles worn down to maybe a centimeter and some laces strapped across a few patches of dirty, black canvas. The Bowl Cut gave the others a look and they hupped-to, and then they was sent to the showers.

But not me. I took my time. First I unbuttoned my shirt, very carefully, button one, button two and oh, my back itches. Just give me a sec. When I finally unbuttoned the whole thing I shrugged it off my shoulders, and, oops! it's stuck on my arm, etc . . . . When I finally got it off, I re-buttoned it one button at a time and folded it nicely, making sure to get the creases just right.

The Bowl Cut watching me had had enough at that point and made a move, but I held up my finger and snapped a curt, "Fuck off, fuckstick."

It pulled up quick, staring at my finger.

"Your clicks are not appropriate. Increase your megahertz."

"I'm human, dickbag. Speak English."

It tilted its head.

"Define 'human dickbag'?"

"Oh, you got a sense of humor?"

Meanwhile, I unbuttoned my pants, slowly unzipped the zipper. I was hoping it'd get impatient and leave me alone, but it didn't. It stood there and watched me undress, the perv. I did a little striptease, wiggled my ass, gave it a peek of my junk and a breathless "oh my," but it didn't respond in any way. I faked like I was offended.

"What, you don't like the goods?"

"You have decreased your function by approximately .0001. Your clicks are not appropriate. Increase . . ."

"I'm gonna increase my foot in your ass if you say that to me again."

"'Ass. A long-eared, slow, patient, sure-footed domesticated mammal, *Equus asinus,* related to the horse, used chiefly as a beast of burden.' Or 'a stupid, foolish, stubborn person.'" It tilted its head all quizzical. "I do not understand how—"

"I was talking about your asshole. Your balloon knot. Your shit-cutter. Brown eye. Starfish. Prison purse. Poop-chute. O-ring. Ham-flower."

"Ham-flower?"

"Fuck's sake." I gave him a thumbs up. "You're a ripe dumb bastard, ain't you?"

Ham (because that's what I decided to call him from that point on) looked at my thumb, then he poked his up and looked at it.

Right then, I knew. The Bowl Cuts might be strong, and they might have their nuts plugged into the great server in the sky, but Jesus fuck was they stupid. This was going to be easy.

I'm going to digress for a tic. Tell you a story.

Not many people will admit to this, but of all the wars I ever fought in, WWII was my least favorite. Strapped on the old Browning M1918, wolfed down my MREs, and shot me up some Jap bastards in the Pacific. Guadalcanal? Did it. Iwo Jima? Did it. Midway? Did it. That was some right bullshit, I shit you not, and anybody who says they actually enjoyed warring is a lying bastard. But I was good at killing (go figure), and I was good at surviving (go figure), but I wasn't very popular with my fellow Marines (go figure).

After the war, I had to beg for work, and finally one of the guys I'd knew got me a job in Vegas as a magician's assistant. It was crap, of course, but not as crap as washing dishes and cooking and working pop's newsstand, which was all I had on my resume before I joined up.

The magician I worked for was from Iraq. His name was Mohammad Almasi, used to go by the stage name of The Great Adolphus but by the time I'd got to him, he'd changed it to The Great Alfonzo on account of Hitler. The Great Alfonzo. Not that nobody noticed he didn't even look close to Italian or cared for that matter. Guy said his name's The Great Alfonzo, his name's The Great Alfonzo.

Talk about a prevert, The Great Alfonzo fucked everything. Males. Females. Shemales. All by their lonesome or in twos and threes. Wasn't no orifice in the human body safe from that guy's pecker. He tried to hit on me once, but I persuaded him to stop. He was loaded when he done it. Didn't even remember the next morning. Woke up with two black eyes and a busted nose, saying, "what the . . . ?" I didn't have the heart to tell him what he done. *Tried* to do. Plus, if I told him, he would have knew who busted up his face, and I'd be out of a job, so I told him he fell down the stairs.

My point is this: The Great Alfonzo? When he wasn't buggering nobody, he taught me a few of his tricks. Nothing huge. Nothing impressive. He didn't give away his biggest secrets or nothing, but he did show me some sleight of hand, some techniques, you know, talking and gesticulating and such, so that while you were distracted by my hand waving over here, I snuggled a ball under my balls over there.

So that's what I did with Ham. Chatted him up nice and solid, gave him the what-for about his thumb, the whole time waiting for the moment when his eyes glanced in just the right direction. In the meantime I zipped, I unzipped, and otherwise pretended to struggle with the process.

"No, seriously, you can have so much fun with that thing." Zip zip. "So many different places to twiddle."

"To what do you refer?"

I pointed at his thumb.

"That thing. That thing right there."

He held up his thumb.

"This is a pollex."

"Yeah, I know. Look at it. So supple, so round. Imagine the possibilities."

He frowned.

"My pollex?"

"Yeah. Go ahead. Look at it. Take a nice long gander."

He did, zeroing in on his thumb like it was the most interesting thing in the world, and I shucked my pants, ripped the scalpel and bonesaw . . .

Oh yeah. It just occurred to me, something. So, uh, well, I kinda smuggled them two things into the building. I guess I should've mentioned it before. I wanted to bring my gun but O'Neill said absolutely not, so I brought my trusty dusties instead. They would've hanged me from the suicide nets if I'd been caught, so that's why I was trying too hard not to and, uh, well. You get the point.

Alright. Back to the narrative.

I ripped the weapons off my thigh (where I had them taped) and buried them under my shirt.

"Ta-da! I'm naked."

I know, not the sleightest of hand, but it worked. Ham frowned at me. He knew something had just happened but couldn't put his pollex on it. That's the sucker's dilemma. Acknowledge your confusion, and you're an idiot. Ignore it, and you're a fool. He searched my nooks for anything I might have hid there, turned with a curt nod, and strode up to his partners.

"Subject prepared."

Without looking up from their forearms, they squeezed by and left. Ham didn't follow. He seemed to be considering something. Then he turned to me and said, in that flat, monotone voice of his, "Increase your clicks to the shower, or I will insert my pollex into your ham-flower."

Unfortunately, my clothes was gone when I got out, having been replaced with a blue jumpsuit, a pack of soft, white knee-highs, three pairs of boxers, and a pair of cross-trainers. Looked like it was function over fashion for the floor drones at the old Silver Bullet.

I picked up the trainers and shook them at Ham, who was hovering nearby, poking at his forearm screen with his pollex.

"Where'd you put my clothes?" twelve

He didn't move his eyes from his screen.

"You are in room 101. It is on the top floor."

"First of all, that don't make no sense. Second of all, you didn't answer my question."

"All personal items have been deloused and placed in a secure area. You may retrieve them upon fulfilling your quota for the SingleCorp."

"Quota? What quota?"

"Drone 666. Your lifespan has been assessed based on your current age, weight, height, and general fitness level. While in the employ of SingleCorp, your basic needs, food, water, shelter, sleep, will be accommodated. Your bullet quota is tabulated by adding your estimated lifespan to any ancillaries you accrue. Ancillaries are defined as: clothes, baths, luxury edibles, and any upgrades. According to our algorithm, your estimated death will occur in precisely sixty hundred and sixty-six years, three days, four hours, and twenty-seven point four zero minutes, after which time, if you have met your bullet quota, your consciousness will be uploaded into our main server and you will achieve Singularity. Your balance can be accessed through the intranet."

"Whoa whoa whoa. What's a bullet? You mean like a bullet bullet?"

"Bullets are the accepted currency at SingleCorp. It comes in familiar denominations of ones, fives, tens, twenties, fif—"

"You mean like dollars?"

"Dollars are the accepted currency of the former United States of America. This is the SingleCorp, not the former United States of America."

"So, not like dollars?"

"Bullets."

I eyed the jumpsuit.

"I gotta pay for that?"

"Your bullet quota is tabulated by adding your estimated lifespan to any ancillaries you accrue. Ancillaries are defined as—"

"And what if I don't put these on? What if I just shimmy my jimmy all over the place instead?"

"SingleCorp health and safety regulations do not permit nudity in the workplace.

According to Section one point six, subheading four, 'All drones handling equipment or machinery that relies on electricity or that can present a potential fire hazard, equipment including but not limited to computers, computer monitors, tablets and other handheld devices, air-compressors, power conditioners, soldering guns, Bunsen burners, forklifts, copy machines—'"

"Okay, I got it, I got it. Jesus fu—"

"The SingleCorp employee handbook does not permit the use of expletives in the workplace. Section three point two, subheading one—"

"Holy shit, Ham, I said I—"

"Drone 666! You have accrued over a million bullets! Work harder, not smarter. Would you like to purchase one of our many helpful upgrades? Use your implant to visit the Swap Shop on the SingleCorp server."

"Implant?"

He grabbed my wrist and pulled me toward him, and before I could protest, he put this little black square about the size of his thumbnail on my forearm. Stung like a bitch, and then it started to smoke, and pretty soon it melted into my meat, like a bot fly burrowing. A hint of ozone tinged the air. And chicken. Grilled chicken. That's the first time I realized that cooking my own meat smelled like grilled chicken, and I love grilled chicken, so I wasn't sure how to feel about that new information. The chip melted left a smooth square welt on my forearm. I yanked it away. Or should I say, Ham let me yank it away.

"Holy fu—cow, Ham."

"Drone 666. Your implant will serve as identification, the key to your room, and your meal ticket. Your shift starts tomorrow morning at six. Your implant will wake you."

He gave me another thumbs up and shoved me out the door. When I looked back one last time, he was still standing there, smiling. Creepiest thing I ever seen in my life.

That implant? Ham wasn't kidding. It did everything.

When I got to my room, the door unlocked automatically. Didn't even have to reach for the, well, there wasn't even a knob. Just a metal plate and a lock. And when I stepped inside, the chip turned the lights on, followed by a monitor in the wall, and my name and my drone number popped up and my quota and all my ancillaries. If I wasn't sure before, I was now. I'd made the grid.

I didn't take that lightly. I ain't never been on the grid. Spent my whole life avoiding it. I was born before the grid even existed. I'd lived perfectly fine without a social security number or a driver's license. Never opened no bank account, never had no credit card. With friends like mine, I didn't need any of it. Even when I joined the military, I did it with fake papers. Private Dick Jones. Don't get more American than that.

But now I was a number.

The room they gave me measured a little bigger than a closet. Just enough space for a single mattress with a metal spring frame and a slotted window that was maybe two feet wide by fifteen inches tall. How anybody ever squeezed out to kill themselves was a mystery to me. I pushed it open and turned my head to the side to get it out.

I could see for miles and miles. First, the scar of the Bottom, smeared like a brown stain on the city's drawers, then the grayed out Industrial section, with its smokestacks and factories and bridges hanging busted across the river. Beyond that stretched the wasteland west into the heart of the country, probably all the way to the CalCan Collective.

The air was clear, and it might have been sweet if it wasn't for the stench fuming off the nets. When I looked down, I saw two new bodies lying twisted in the one closest to me. I heard another window creak open, and my neighbor to the right stuck his head out.

"Howzit?" I said.

He just gave me a hollow-eyed stare. Then he started to cry.

I woke up when my arm caught fire. One second I'm dreaming about my favorite girls at The Bottom of the Bottom and the next I was leaping around that closet of a room, slamming my arm against the walls, trying to get rid of the red-hot coal that had somehow gotten jammed up under my skin.

Then I remembered. The microchip. Ham said it would wake me up, and boy-howdy did it ever. The pain faded when the wall monitor came to life, and my account balance showed up on the screen.

β1,000,000,274 in the red.

β200 tacked on for "ancillaries."

So that's how the SingleCorp kept afloat. Not through Bottom tourists or furries or the drive space or the intergalactic travel, but slavery. No wonder the workers was leaping from the windows. Some things never change, huh?

Breakfast was served on a cart in the lobby: lukewarm coffee and cold eggs. β6. A sign said lunch'd be in an actual cafeteria, so I stole a stale bagel, not because I was hungry but more out of spite. We had the option of a shower after, but that cost β1, so I cued up for the elevator to the drone floor in the upper levels and started my first full day of blue-collar work.

Ever walk into a hot room full of teenagers? The stench smacks you right across the face: flop sweat and BO, hormones and feet funk. Conjure yourself a warehouse full of desperate bums like what the SingleCorp had working for them and that smell won't just smack you across the face, it'll clobber your head into the ground like a Looney Toons.

A guy saw me come in and left his station. I say it was a guy, but I couldn't really tell because he had one of them Viddy Viewers™ embedded in his face and Jiminy Joints™ clamped on his elbows and Nimble Digits™ sticking out of his fingertips. And he twitched. Actually, all of them twitched, but this guy twitched more than most. I nodded as he walked up to me.

"How's it going?"

"Name Curter."

"What?"

"Name Curter."

"You want me to name a crater or your name's Crater."

"Name Curter."

"Thanks for the clarification."

Curter nodded.

"Follow Curter."

"Will do."

He led me to the station next to his and pointed at the tools on the surface: a soldering gun, an oven mitt, and a pair of goggles with the lenses all tinted. Next to that sat a bottle of rubbing alcohol and a rag and a little paper cup to clean off my workspace. Curter clicked a motherboard into a metal chassis, then handed it to me. Then he pointed at the soldering gun.

"You want me to use that?" I asked.

He pointed at the soldering gun again. It sparked. Then he pointed to a wire in the chassis.

"You want me to solder that to that?"

Curter nodded. He clicked another motherboard to another chassis and slapped it on my desk.

"Curter move fast," he said.

And that's how it went. Solder a wire, pass it along, wipe the desk down. Solder a wire, pass it along, wipe the desk down. All. Friggin. Day. No breaks, not even for the toilet. Come lunchtime, we had the option to leave. They even blew a whistle and everything like on *The Flintstones*, but didn't nobody take the bait. Everything there cost one bullet more. By the end of the shift, I was too exhausted to do anything other than snag an apple from the leftovers cart in the lobby, chomp it down on the way back to my closet, and fall face-first into bed.

Day two was more of the same. Click, slap, solder, pass. Curter must've been taking it easy on me the first day because on day two by the time the first hour was up, I had a stack of unsoldered chassis at my elbow that was higher than my head.

"Curter, wanna slow it down? I can't keep up."

"Curter move fast."

"Yeah, I know but—"

"Curter move fast."

A Bowl Cut came up behind me and said, "Your clicks are inappropriate."

"Screw, screw."

"Drone 666. The SingleCorp employee handbook does not permit the use of expletives in the workplace. Section three point two, subheading one—"

"'Screw' ain't an expletive. It's a verb. And a noun."

"The word 'screw' in the context in which you used it—"

"Beat it, Bowl Cut. I got work to do."

"Drone 666. Your clicks are inappropriate. Increase your megahertz."

He walked off, heading toward a curved section of the wall where he punched a rhythm into a keypad. An indentation formed in the wall and slid to the side, he went in and the door slid shut and became a smooth part of the wall again.

Curter only twitched a little in the morning. A thumb here, an elbow there. But as the day wore on, it grew worse and worse. He'd build himself a good stack of chassis, two feet, three feet, and then bam! His hand'd swat out and bust the thing to pieces.

Then came the Bowl Cuts.

"Drone 616. Your clicks are inappropriate. Adjust the power manifold in your Viddy Viewer™."

"Curter move fast."

"Drone 616. Increase your megahertz."

Two hours and eight twitched piles later, Curter skipped from petit to Gran Mal and knocked my bottle of alcohol over. It shattered on the desk and drenched my arm.

That alone was not a problem.

That alone could have resulted serendipitous.

However, I happened to be in the middle of a tricky patch and was all hunched over the board, so when the alcohol hit my skin, I jerked back, and the soldering gun sparked, and Whomp! Fried chicken.

I gotta say this: the little triage clinic they set up for workplace injuries was the choicest medical care establishment I'd ever had the pleasure of visiting. Not that that means a lot, because in my line of work, before and after the Singularity, whatever doctoring I ever needed I performed myself. In my opinion, most of the problems people used to see the doctor for they didn't need to see the doctor for.

"Oh, my blood pressure's too high!"

Then get off your ass and go on a hike.

"Oh, I got poison ivy on my ass!"

Then stop wiping your ass with poison ivy.

"Oh, I got the skin cancer!"

Then . . . well, then you're just fucked.

Before the Tlek war, I'd been shot at least three times, once in the foot, once in the shoulder, and once in the ribs, and not once did I visit a hospital. Whenever I found myself with a bullet in my meat, here was the formula for recovery: I cut it out, doused it up, and sewed it together. If the thing went clear through, which happened more often than people think, even better. Besides, going to the hospital was the best place to get sick because that's where all the sick people went!

That Silver Bullet triage clinic, though, that was some prime rib, New York sirloin, grade-A filet mignon health care right there, my friends. If the drone floor was *The Killing Fields*, the clinic was *The Wizard of OZ*. Everything was scrubbed to sparkling; not a spot of nothing on nothing nowhere. Even the nurse sparkled. I think her name was Hardass or Hardtack. She was a little over four feet tall, with a bony frame held together with ropy muscles the size of which nobody expected on a woman so old and tiny. No, seriously, when they carted me into the clinic with my bar-b-que'd arm, she picked up this fat guy (who weighed as much as at least three or four Nurse Hardtacks) and dragged him by the elbows over to a different hospital bed. Her biceps was watermelons. Her calf muscles grapefruits.

"Alright, KFC. You gonna tell me what happened to your arm?"

"What do you think happened to my arm?"

She grunted and grabbed my elbow, ignoring my choicest profanities, and twisted my wrist so my forearm was facing up.

"Jesus!" I cried.

She backhanded me upside the head.

"Not in my clinic."

She placed my arm down and went over to rummage around in the neatest, most organized cabinet I ever seen. Rows of tape, boxes of bandages, salves, and greases, and peroxide. She grabbed a container of goop and a roll of gauze.

"Alcohol burn?"

"Yeah. The twitchy guy next to me—"

"I've told them for years not to put the flammables next to the fire, but they do not listen to me."

"Wasn't no fire. The soldering gun sparked."

She slapped me again.

"Don't interrupt."

She unwrapped a fat tongue depressor, scooped a dollop of goop out of the goop container, and smeared it all over my forearm, covering it from my wrist to the crook of my elbow. Everything went cold. Then it went numb. Then it started to tingle. Weirdest sensation I ever felt. Hardtack must have seen the expression on my face because she laughed.

"How you like our bot-jelly?"

"You just put bot flies in me?"

"No, you idiot. *Nano*-bots."

She scraped the rest of the goop what was left on the tongue depressor back into the jar and chucked the thing in a biohazard bag.

"Good luck paying that back."

They sent me to my room after that, even though it wasn't even lunch yet.

The next morning, my microchip set my arm on fire as usual, and as usual, the friggin wall monitor lit up, and there was my numbers. Another million. I studied on it, and thought "oh well." No need to be worried. Didn't plan on sticking around long enough to pay it off, don't know why it bothered me in the first place. Then Ham's face popped up on the screen. At least I thought it was Ham.

"Drone 666. Your clicks are inappropriate. Increase your megahertz."

"Hey, Ham. Go fuck yourself."

A shock ran up my arm, straight out of that chip he planted in my meat.

"Ow! Fuck!"

"Foul language will not be tolerated."

"I got it, Ham."

"Your clicks are inappropriate."

"Yeah, I know."

My arm glowed red and glassy from the burn, but it felt a whole hell of a lot better.

"In case you didn't know, I had me a little industrial accident yesterday."

"We are aware of your mistake."

"*My* mistake!"

Ham's voice changed, shifted from robotic to animated, like a game show announcer or something, or like someone trying his best to approximate a game show announcer.

"Drone 666. Our records indicate you are over β200,000,000 in debt to the SingleCorp. At this rate, it will take you approximately three lifetimes to fulfill your quota. Increasing your clicks by two percent will increase your output, and increasing your output raises your earnings potential. Have you seen our Nimble Digits™ line? This state of the art fine motor enhancer can help you achieve higher output in as little as one battery cycle! Nimble Digits™ starts at the low price of β500. Free shipping and handling!"

"No thanks, Ham."

"Did you know that soldering wires causes eye strain and migraines? Why not try our Second Sight Eyes™! Only β350!"

"I don't want that sh—that stuff, neither."

I threw a pair of boxers over the wall monitor.

"Drone 666. Your clicks are inappropriate. Your current balance shows that you are over β200,000,000 in debt to the SingleCorp."

I swiped my jumpsuit off the window crank and left.

Alright, I thought. *Fuck this shit.* I'd got myself injured, I'd got whatever med-tech old June wanted, and I'd had about enough of this whole situation. It was time to put operation "Get the hell out of here" in full effect, and that couldn't happen on an empty stomach, so I hit the cafeteria.

Of the seven or eight greasers in line, more than half had upgraded so many times that they were made of more plastic and wire than human tissue. And they all twitched. Fantastic. I made a mental note to be careful who I stood next to for fear of getting an elbow to the gut. I put a little carton of milk on my tray, and while I was considering the morning's offerings, I heard the voice of an angel.

"So you no dead, eh?"

I looked up, all round-eyed and glassy, and there was Sal.

Cue the harp strings and cherubs.

"Sal!"

"Is me."

"How'd you end up in this dump?"

He shrugged. Then he pointed at my arm.

"You get a hurt?"

"What, this? It's nothing. Chemical burn is all. How you been?"

"They give you the whatsit? The jelly?"

"Yeah! How'd you know?"

Sal shook his head.

"Don't take no more of that. Wait here. I'm back." And he ducked away.

The twitchers in the front of the line stopped slopping slop on their trays and stared at me, eyes fluttering, shoulders a'tremble. I gave them my best gangster stare and said, "What?" They turned away, and the ones behind me lurched wide around me, also giving me the stank, and then Sal reappeared. I looked down, and there was already a plate on my tray.

"Hey, thanks, Sal."

He wiped his hands on a towel hanging over his shoulder.

"You take."

"Sure, sure." I investigated what he gave me. Didn't seem to be any different from what everybody else had. Juicy slabs of meat in white sauce.

A couple more twitchers limped around, shooting weird looks over their shoulders.

"My friend, my friend," Sal said. "I don't forget. Don't let them see." He held up his arm and pointed at it. I guess he meant my arm. "When it happens. Don't let them see."

"When what happens?"

"You want worse? This?" Here he stiffened up, started twitching.

"Of course I don't."

"When it happens, don't let them see. They keep it up, they make you worse."

"Sure, Sal. Whatever you say. You're the boss."

"Don't let them see, okay?"

"Okay, okay, Sal. I got it."

He nodded one last time, like he was satisfied, then he called out, "Next!"

I was just getting ready to run my chip under the scanner when I turned around to thank him again, but he was gone. A few more twitchers jittered in, filled their plates from the steam table. One of them jerked an elbow into the ribs of the guy to his right, and they both flipped their trays up into the air, sending slop all over the sneeze guard.

I noticed four things when I got back to the line.

First, the twitchers was more twitchy than usual, and that's saying something. If twitching was a rock group, they'd be the Bee-Gee's, or The Beatles, or Black Sabbath—no, Led Zeppelin. That's it. Led Zeppelin.

Second, my arm had healed nearly all the way proper.

Third, all the monitors had been turned off.

Fourth, the original Mr. Twitchy, Curter, the jerk who knocked that rubbing alcohol on my arm the day before, could barely control himself. I mean, his fits wasn't just fits no more. They was outright conniptions. Full-blown episodes. And after each one, he slammed his fists down on the desk and stood there, breathing heavy, red-eyed and crazy, all his chassis scattered on the floor around his feet.

I watched him do it as I approached my station, and it made me feel like maybe I should put the fear of getting shanked into him, you know, a little threat, a flash of metal, something to keep him away from me. Unfortunately, I didn't have no shank on me, so I thought I'd say something like, "You spill that alcohol on me again, I'll rip your eyes out of your skull," but soon as I sat down, he glared them goggles at me, and I shut right up. I swear I thought he was about to leap over and stab me in the temple with my own soldering gun, so I didn't say nothing. In fact, after his third accident in fifteen minutes, I even tried to help the guy.

"Calm down, Curter," I said. "You want to get the Bowl Cuts over here?"

He didn't respond. At least, he didn't respond to that in any language that I understood. He just slammed his fists down so hard that both our desks jumped, sending more chassis clattering to the floor, and spilling my rubbing alcohol. Again.

"Fu—Crap!" I yelled.

I threw down my soldering gun and jumped out of my seat, clenching my eyes tight, waiting for an explosion, but nothing happened, so I peeked one open and glanced around just to see what was what.

Some of the Bowl Cuts had turned our way, and some of the other drones shot me the old stank, but nothing else. Curter pressed his fists into the desk like he wanted to break it. He started muttering to himself, not even attempting to clean up the mess he'd made, the jerk.

And right then, wouldn't you know it, my forearm started to itch something fierce. This wasn't no mild itch, neither, like a mosquito bite, this was deep, deep in my meat, insistent, the kind of itch that makes you want to claw your skin open to get at it. I looked down at my arm, and fuck all if it wasn't bubbling and boiling all over where the burn used to be. *Don't let them see*, Sal said, so rather than do what I wanted to do (scream and claw my arm off), I sat quickly down and jammed it under my desk.

Curter's head started to tick, a violent ear to shoulder motion on his left side. Even worse than that, it seemed like he was starting to infect the other drones in our immediate vicinity. Like when you step on one ant in a line, the rest of them all start to freak out. Or like schizo's in the crazy ward; once one of them starts to go off about the voices, the rest add their own to the chorus.

I peeked down at my forearm only to see millions of little squiggly things squirming out of it, maggots, maybe, or some other bug, like, uh, like, like friggin botflies. I gulped back a scream. Oh my god. The nurse'd lied to me.

Nano-bots my ass. She put flies in me! Botflies! Real-life botflies!

But wait. No. They weren't bot flies. Couldn't have been. Botflies took, like, a week to gestate, right? I dunno. Plus, my arm was all healed up. Maybe these really was nano-bots? Nanobotflies. Maybe they was super nanobotflies, and they gestated in twelve hours, and oh what the hell, it didn't matter anymore, because they started pouring out of my arm onto the floor, writhing around in a slowly growing puddle. I took a swipe or two at the swarm, but they latched onto my hand and I had to scrape them off on the underside of the desk, so after that I just let them come out and fall off on their own. The puddle grew into a pile.

Curter continued his muttering, but quieter and quieter. Three of the drones at the desks around us started muttering, too. Curter's neck jerked down to his shoulder, and theirs did, too. Curter slammed his fists down on his desk again, and they did, too. Curter snarled something out loud, something harsh and guttural, like it was in a different language or something, "Raus!" and they did, too. Then he suddenly grew calm and centered and still. He raised his eyes and zeroed in on me.

And they did, too.

"Oh shit," I said, and I grabbed the soldering gun.

They come after me, and its jam and fire, jam and fire, right in the old neck.

All of them made a strangled sound way down in their chests, like a wounded bear or something, and then Curter upturned his desk, sending chassis and tools and all sorts of shit all over the place, and the next thing I knew he jumped me, and we tumbled back onto the floor. His thumbs found my throat and pressed down. I whipped the soldering gun up in an arc, hoping to jam it into the tender part of his jaw, right above the Adam's apple, but it hit his shoulder instead. Oh well. I triggered a blast anyway, and, well, it didn't do nothing, really. It ain't like a soldering gun was a flamethrower or nothing. In fact, I think it made him angrier because his thumbs found my eyes and started pushing.

I reached up and slapped at his face but that didn't help none. Some of the nanobots hit my forehead, pattered around my ears, and then Curter started to scream, high-pitched and feral, and his thumbs released, and everything was pitch black and I thought, "He really did thumb out my eyes," but then gradually the blackness turned to gray, and gray to pale yellow, and then I could see again, even if it was blurry, and I wished I couldn't see again.

The other three drones surrounded us, still and motionless, like a switch had been flicked. Curter himself was on his feet, backpedaling, one hand covering his eyes, the other swiping at the nano-bots swarming his head and neck. No matter how hard he tried, he couldn't get them off. They stuck to his hands and clouded his arms, shot up his nose, drained into his mouth and ears.

He covered his ears, they poured into his mouth. He closed his mouth, they shot up his nose. He pinched his nose, they found his ears. Over and over and over. A line of them streamed out from under my desk and rolled up his pant leg. Then he finally had it. Gave up. Stopped trying to block them, swipe them off, claw them out. His arms dropped to his sides, and he turned around and sprinted for one of the windows. You gotta realize that all this took less than a minute. Surprised the Bowl Cuts as much as anybody else. By the time they really understood what was going on, Curter was airborne. Just like that.

And that's when the rest of them went haywire.

This part you've already read. The twitching. The attacking. The nut grabbing. I left off when that twitcher was reaching for my throat and nearly got his fingers wrapped around it, and I was reaching for the pad, hoping to give it just one more shot . . . and I did it! Bam! And the door formed and I fell in backwards and the twitcher fell on me so that it was laying halfway in the room and halfway out and I scrambled back, screaming "Close it! Close it!" and then another explosion rocked the building and something hit me in the head and I blacked out.

Chapter 3
In which our boy fights cursines. And
sniders. And sceels. Oh my.

I don't know about you, but whenever I
find myself sitting in a dark room all by my
lonesome, minding my own business, not
really knowing who I was or what I was doing
sitting in a dark room all by my lonesome
(minding my own business), and somebody
shines a bright light in my eyes, I get pretty
goddamn irritated.

It didn't help that they was cold bulbs, too,
none of them Sylvania soft whites, but more
like them GE eyeball burners. On top of that,
my hands was bound behind my back and my
neck felt like it'd been hanging on my chest
for days, which at this point in the narrative, it
probably had.

Then came a voice, heavy and loud.

"Who are you?"

Seemed to come from all around me, and it
didn't sound human. I mean, there was
probably some human that actually vocalized
it, but it'd been modulated about five octaves

below its natural timbre. When I didn't respond, it spoke again.

"Who are you?"

Okay, actually, you want to know what's even more irritating than them lights? Not knowing how to answer a simple question like "who are you?". Maybe it was the fact that I really had been sitting upright with my chin on my chest for I don't know how long, like I hadn't let enough oxygen into my brain. Maybe I'd suffered a concussion on top of everything else. To test the last theory out, I shook my head real hard to see if it exploded or I got a migraine or something. Nothing. Not even a momentary bout of dizziness. I flexed my hands. They were both still there, so yay. Wiggled my toes. Same.

The voice rang out a third time.

"Who are you?"

"Dunno," I said.

Barely croaked it out, really. My throat was raw and raspy. But despite my obvious inability to do much more than sit there and get irritated and wonder who the fuck I was, and before I even chewed out that last vowel, somebody threw a bucket of water in my face.

"Hey!"

I didn't even know where it came from. There wasn't anybody else in the room.

Ignoring the rule of magic threes, the voice asked one more time, "who are you?"

"I told you. I dunno."

Another bucket, another expletive, another request for my identity.

"Look, I ain't no psychologist, but throwing water at somebody with a head injury don't really work to rectify the situation."

Whoever it was threw a bucket of water at me again anyway.

Then he turned off the lights.

None of these things helped me remember who I was.

A few hours later (or days or weeks) the lights came on again, not bright spotlights like before but overhead lights, just as harsh, not as irritating. Talk about a shock, though. I couldn't cover my face with my hands or rub the pain out of my eyes, so I kind of let my lids unfurl a little at a time until my brain got used to it, and then I let them fly. An ice pick spiked through my temple and I winced, but gradually I was better able to take it and finally saw where I ended up this time. Not that I knew nothing from nothing at that point.

Four gray walls. Four gray walls, a concrete floor, a dropped ceiling. That was it. Sorry to disappoint. The metal slats of the chair they strapped me to pinched my thighs, even through my pants, and a drain had been plumbed beneath it, which was both fortunate and worrisome. The door handle jiggled, and into the room swaggered a guy in a cream-colored, seersucker suit. His ferret face was clean-shaved, and he'd slicked his hair back with so much pomade that I gagged a little. Oh, and that smirk on his face made me want to punch him. And he had a toothpick stuck in the corner of his mouth.

He grabbed another chair leaning against the wall near the door and tip-toed over, like he was playing at being cautious just to fuck with me, but at the same time, he seemed honestly cautious about getting anywhere near. He clomped the chair on the concrete floor, stooped to catch my eye and said, "That you?"

"Yeah. That you?"

You know guys who smile and it smells like secrets? He did one of those. Then he plunked himself down in the chair and leaned back and crossed his legs, letting a single two-tone shake in the air.

"You know who you are?"

"Yeah. I'm George Roosevelt Lincoln."

He smirked and twisted the toothpick.

"You don't remember me?"

"No, I don't remember you."

"You don't remember nothing?"

That one gave me pause. I did remember some things. Flashes here and there. Explosions. Bugs coming out of my arm. A little blond girl in a yellow sundress. He saw I seen it and said, "so you do, huh?"

"Some things. Flashes."

"You want to illuminate me?"

"No."

Toothpick Smiley's smile widened, and he muttered something over his shoulder, chuckling.

"What's so funny?" I asked.

"What's so funny? You. You're funny, that's what's so funny. You act like you got a choice here." He spread his hands and glanced around. "Look at this place. You think you're ever getting out of here unless you tell us what we want to hear?"

"How am I supposed to do that when I can't remember my own name? You want to know what I know? Here it is: I woke up sitting here, and you asked me my name, and each time I couldn't remember, you threw a bucket of water in my face. There. That's it. That's all I got."

He leaned forward, rested his elbows on his knees, and stared at me, shifting the toothpick from one side of his mouth to the other. If my feet wasn't chained to the chair leg, I'd have kicked it down his throat.

"Tell you what," he said. "You factor me in on what you remember, what you remembered just now, and I'll make it so you ain't cuffed to that chair no more. You tell me something good, I might get you something to eat."

"You're gonna feed me anyway."

"Yeah? How you figure?"

"I got something you need. You won't let me starve."

He leaned back, half-impressed.

"We're just trying to help. We want you to get your life back, right?"

"Oh yeah?" I puppy dogged it. "Could you help me? Could you help me, please?"

Almost had him there for a second. He seemed to soften. And then I broke out laughing, and his face went hard and flat.

"Okay," he said. "Have it your way."

And he got up and walked out.

That night I had a nightmare. End of the world type stuff, typical tropes. Black clouds, smoke and flame, fire on the ridges, lightning bolts twisting across the sky, the air bursting with the screams of the dismembered and dying. I was on my back in the middle of a churned up runway or a highway or something. Laser fire zipped overhead, explosions rocked the earth, and I could hear the enemy marching closer and closer, the ground shaking with each thunderous step, and even though I knew that if I didn't get out of there, that if I didn't scram or skedaddle I'd be squashed like a slug, I couldn't move. I just lay there, waiting on death. I coughed up blood. Someone shook my shoulder, beat on my chest, crying "Come on you sonofabitcha!"

I almost recognized the voice, but right when I thought I might remember his name, a shadow blocked out what remaining light there was, shrouding both of us, cloaking everything in eerie darkness. The most horrendous shriek I ever heard, thick, modulated, and grating, like skyscrapers falling, pierced my eardrums. I punched at the guy straddling my body, clawed his eyes. We had to move, we had to get out of there, but he wouldn't get off, so I wrapped my hands around his neck, and we flipped and I was on top and I pressed my thumbs down. The scream from the thing above grew louder and louder, filled my head, my lungs, rattled my vocal cords, until it was me what was screaming, and I opened my eyes and found myself on a bed, choking out some woman I guess I'd been sleeping with.

A pillow had fallen over her eyes, her hair spilled out under it, long and brown. Her face was red, redder than death, and her mouth gaped and she gasped. She swatted my arms and my face and I thought, "Oh shit," and let go, still screaming, screaming at the fact that I was just choking somebody to death and I couldn't remember why.

She heaved in a huge, rasping breath and set to coughing, as people who were almost choked out was wont, and suddenly I wasn't screaming no more. I mean, my mouth was wide open and my eyes felt like they was gonna pop out of my head, but at least I wasn't screaming because I was too busy taking in my surroundings. My old apartment. This was my old apartment.

"Get off!" the woman yelled.

She coughed some more, but she had enough strength to push me aside, not that I put up much of a fight. I fell back, more out of shock than anything else, and watched as she stumbled over to the bathroom and slammed the door shut. I heard her retch for a bit, then she turned on the water.

I sat there on the bed, sheets wrapped around my middle, trying to take it all in, trying to get my head straight, when the woman burst out of the bathroom. She strode over and sat down on the edge of the bed. Her face was clean and fresh, her hair pulled back in a ponytail, and she was every bit as beautiful as I remembered. She put her cool hands on my cheeks.

"Are you okay?"

"Am I okay? Are you?"

She ignored me.

"Are you high? Drunk?"

"What? No. I was with you all night."

I searched my memory to see if that was true. I think it was.

She peered into my eyes, looking for something, and I tried to ignore the bruises on her neck. I guess she found whatever she was looking for because she softened and brushed the hair off my forehead and leaned in and gave me a kiss. Her lips were still wet from washing her face. Her breath smelled minty.

"What was it this time?" she asked. When I furrowed my brow, she explained, "The dream. What dream was it this time? Daddy find out about us again?"

"No, I don't really know." I sat back against the headboard, trying to remember the dream. "I was somewhere. I don't know where.

Smoke everywhere. And fire. Lightning in the clouds. It was the end of the world, I think."

She stood up and went around to her side of the bed and sat with her back to me. I lay back and pulled a pillow under my head.

"Jesus. I think it was a war or something. I'd been shot or hurt or, I dunno. And there was somebody there trying to save me. And then in the sky, this thing. This horrible noise."

I looked over and saw her shoulders shaking.

"Hey," I said. I sat up and put my hands on her. Her skin felt icy. "You're freezing."

"I'm cold," she said. "So cold."

"I'm sorry, I didn't mean to. I don't know what's going on here."

She shook some more, but I couldn't tell if it was because of tears or because she was so cold. She loved it when I ran my fingers through her hair, so I put my hand on her head.

"I thought you were dead."

I pressed my fingers gently down and dragged them through, and a chunk of skin and hair came off in my palm. She turned toward me, and her fresh face was gray and sunken, her eyes black hollow holes.

"I am," she said.

And she punched my chest with the heel of her hand, and I flew back and back and back, all of the breath in my body forced out of my lungs. Pain shot through my ribcage, paralyzing pain, shot up through my throat, and then my eyes flew open and I gasped, and I was in my nightmare again with the black smoke and the lightning clouds and the monster shaking the earth. A dragon roared overhead, great gouts of red flames shooting out of its mouth. It engulfed a crowd of twitchers rushing in my direction. They turned into shadows, outlines in the fire, and then they stumbled to their knees and collapsed face-first onto the tarmac.

A man's face suddenly hovered over mine. It was a great big face, too, no screwing around with that one: square jaw, bald pate, thick brow, and I remembered his name. Sal. Me and Sal, together again for the first time ever. And we was in a ton of trouble.

"Hey Sal," I croaked.

"Okay," he said, not really to me, just out loud, like he was satisfied I was alive.

He pulled away to reveal Ham. His shirt was bloody, and his bowl cut mussed considerable, but it was definitely Ham. He gave me the thumbs up.

"Your clicks are inappropriate."

Then he hauled me off the ground and set my back against a chunk of the road. I wiggled my fingers and toes, twisted my neck to the left, twisted my neck to the right. Okay. Everything worked. My chest felt like it'd been cracked open, and so did my ribs, but I could breathe pretty much easy, and I wasn't retarded or nothing, so that was all good.

"I die?" I asked.

Ham shrugged.

"Inconclusive," he replied.

He tore the legs of my jumpsuit into strips and pressed one against my chest, and I sucked wind because holy shit did that hurt. What was wrong with me? I looked down and sure enough, three red canals parted the meat vertical under my collarbone.

"What's this?"

"Cursine."

Sal grunted.

"Huh. Cursine. Look like bear to me. Big, big bear."

"Big bear, huh?"

Ham looked at me like I was nuts, which didn't surprise me as we were in the thick of The Weirdness. My chest tickled and itched, and I knew what was coming next. Them damn nano-bot-flies.

"No. Cursine."

I pointed at Sal.

"Hey, he said it."

Ham made as if to reply, but then a shell (or what I thought was a shell) whistled overhead and exploded about fifty yards away, sending shrapnel and chunks of the asphalt shrieking through the air. Ham ducked and covered, and Sal threw himself over me. It was like having a cannon dropped on my torso.

"Christ, Jesus, Sal. Get off."

He rolled away, and I was finally able to see what was going on.

First, as you probably already guessed, we was in the middle of the concourse between the city and the Silver Bullet. And the Silver Bullet had been shredded, sliced in half from top to bottom, exposing its guts. Steel beams jutted out like broken bones, wires waved in the air like snakes, tangling with each other and the exposed girders and the rebar, sparking and hissing. The suicide nets was tangled and torn, too, dumping its contents onto the concrete below. Let me tell you something: that was grim. Even worse than that? Some kind of battle was raging all around us, and I didn't even know what side we was on, or who was fighting what, or why we was fighting or how we got there in the first place.

Far as I knew, it was pretty much a free for all. Twitchers jumped on anything what they came across and tore it to bits—all them upgrades, you know, the Barrel-Arm Biceps™, the Thunder Thighs!™, the Chiseled Chests™, the Terrible Trapezium™, the Evil Eyes™, the Toxic Teeth™, finally put to better use than snapping together plastic gadgets. And yeah, I seen plenty of Bowl Cuts, too, running around like idiots, hair sticking straight up off their heads, the screens on their forearms shattered or useless.

Then there was the hybrids. Serious hybrids. These wasn't little chipmunks with distorted speakers, but military-grade death weapons. While I was sitting there, staring around like a moron, a huge bear (I guess that was Sal's cursine) pounced on a group of fleeing Bowl Cuts and shredded them to bits with a few swipes of them steel claws. A fantastic and disgusting sight, with upper torsos flying through the air this way and that, and arms flipping up up up like twigs in the wind. Then a twitcher twitched by, and the cursine spiked it through the chest like a martini olive, brought it up to its jaws, and crunched down on its skull like a, uh, well, like a martini olive.

"Jesus," I muttered.

Actually. That wasn't the most horrifying thing I seen. The sniders was. What's sniders, you ask? Well, a snider is a mix between a copperhead snake and a black widow spider. Creepiest thing ever. I don't even think I have to describe what them things done. Use your imagination. And even worse than that was all the other things out there I don't have the time to describe. Squirsquitos, sceels, panthodiles, allicopters, all of them flying or skittering or jumping or bounding, tearing apart everything and anything that got in their way. Ham handed me a broom handle with two kitchen knives duct-taped on each end. I weighed it equal.

"Better'n nothing."

A snider popped up on the concrete slab and reared back on its hind legs. Sal picked up his weapon, which was another broom handle with knives taped to the end, and anchored himself in a squat.

"Come we go fight!"

I took one look at that thing, one look at Sal, and turned to run. Before I could get anywhere, he grabbed me by the arm and yanked me up next to him.

"Lemme go! Lemme go!"

The snider reared and struck, and Sal put his strategy into motion. He pushed me away and jumped aside, too, but he didn't push me so hard that I went flying, and he didn't jump so far that he couldn't do nothing. In fact, it was more like an aikido move. He pivoted on his leg and let the snider's fangs crack the road between us, then he raised his spear in both hands and bought it down on the thing's big, fat, ugly head. After he stabbed it about a million times, he cut a long gulch in its body.

"I think you got it," I said.

Ham, who stood there the whole time, watching, said, "No, you did."

That's when I seen I was covered in blood, snider blood, that is. Blood and gore and whatever guts Sal'd cut out. The nanobots'd started their exit; I could feel them pouring down my chest and pooling at my feet.

"Nu," Sal muttered, and he jammed his fist into the gaping wound. "Not done yet."

He grabbed my hand before I could get away and plunged it into the snider's skull. It felt like you'd expect. Gelatin goo and squishy stuff. But then I felt something else. Something hard, square, metallic. I yanked it out, then another one, and another one, and another one, all linked together by wires. The sound of them hitting the pavement reminded me of something. Something familiar. Something I'd heard over and over for the past couple of days. It sounded like when Curter twitched something fierce and knocked all them chassis onto the floor. And when I looked, that's exactly what it was. Chassis. One after another.

"They're robots?" I shot a glare at Ham. "You mean I been making these things?"

He gave me the thumbs up.

I picked up one of the chassis to see what the wires I soldered eventually made. Looked like a hard drive, a skinny metal disc with a wire inserted into one end, and damn, I mean, I guess that made sense. Giant, mutated horror hybrids probably required a load of drive space. I guess. How many sniders did I help create? Or cursines? Or sceels? I chuckled. They had us making the things they were going to use to wipe us all out with. What a brilliant idea.

I didn't have too much time to ruminate on it all, though, because dragons and twitchers and sceels and such. It was time to boogie. The last eighth of a mile to the building on the other side of the concourse was smooth pavement. No ruptured asphalt or hunks of metal, and other than a few stragglers, the sceels, sniders, and squirsquitos focused on the smorgasbord of drones and Bowl Cuts pouring out of the wreckage of the Silver Bullet. The twitchers, however, was not to be stopped. No matter how many we cut down, they just kept coming. I don't know about you, but if I saw me heading my way armed with butcher's knives taped to sticks, chest slashed to ribbons, shoulder all swole up and nano-bots pouring out of my pores, I'd keep my distance. But I think they actually zeroed in on me because of all them I took out. Or maybe they just smelled the blood and it sent them into a frenzy. Who knows?

By the time we made it to that last 660 feet, that last 7,920 inches, the twitchers was on to us, and they was pissed. About a hundred of them lurched behind, generally displaying an extreme inability to run in any sort of expeditious or appropriate fashion, but they'd spread out in a big half-circle. Sal took the lead, and don't think for a second I didn't think of slicing his Achilles and using him as fodder. He was a big dude, too. Probably put up a good fight before they tore him in two. I loved the guy and all, but hey, all's fair when you're running from a pack of rabid crazies. Anyway, we made it to the building, and Sal hit the door.

He yanked.

It didn't open.

Of course.

"Sonofabitcha!" he cried. He sent a panicked glance over his shoulders, all wide white eyes and crunched-in eyebrows. Then he yanked again and again, but the thing wouldn't budge.

The twitchers closed in. We was fucked. No way out of this one.

I got there next and started beating on the metal, screaming, "Come on! Come on!"

The pack of twitchers lurched on, closer and closer. Ham crashed through us both, flattening himself against the wall. Sal and me put our backs to the door and glanced at each other, and Ham squeezed down behind me, trying to take cover, like that'd do any good.

"Maybe we could throw Ham at them first?" I said. Sal looked at me like I'd offered him a blow job. "You know. Hold them off for a bit?"

"Your clicks are inappropriate," Ham said.

The twitchers lurched closer.

I turned around to do it, grab Ham by his stupid-looking bowl cut and send him flying, but he wasn't crouching down behind me no more. He was standing inside the building, holding the door open with one hand.

"Increase your megahertz."

Chapter 4
In which our boy is once again cornered,
or, pots, frying pans, and fires seminar 380: an
instruction guide to surviving your worst
nightmare

It took a second for my eyes to adjust to the low light, and when they did, I checked my chest and arms, you know, just to see if any bots was still coming out. They wasn't. Ham split as soon as we busted in, and Sal chucked furniture and desks and computers against the door, trying to build a barricade.

On the other side, out on the tarmac, the twitchers pounded and moaned and bit and tore, but it wasn't no use. The building was all cinderblock and steel, and it hadn't had the misfortune of being exploded, so they could pound all they wanted, but unless they found some glass windows we didn't know about, getting inside wasn't an option. I guess they could tear down that chain link fence that lined the concourse and separated SingleCorp from the city, and that wasn't no good, at least for thems what lived in the city, like The

Widow Mrs. Feldman, and O'Neill, and Ruby, and me, I guess, but at least they weren't getting in here, not for now, not for the time being. When my eyes finally adjusted, I looked up and nearly lost control of my bowels.

"Er, Sal," I said.

Sal didn't say nothing.

"You might want to see this. You know, when you got that taken care of."

And that's when the first one spoke. Didn't know which one it was, yet, but it didn't matter. They was all of them creepy.

"Who's he talking to, Daddy?"

Another one said, "Is his name really Sal? Is it?" Then she sang a little jingle, "Sal Sal, rhymes with foul."

"That's a silly name for a man. Is it short for Sally?"

Then all four of them erupted into giggles.

Daddy's Girls.

The worse for wear.

Bella's face was shiny and splotchy, red and black with burns and scabs. Ella smiled, revealing a mouth full of busted teeth, and when she waved her right hand, it only had two fingers on it, the pinky and the thumb, so it looked like she was telling me to hang ten. Caroline looked all right, but there was something off about Coraline what I couldn't exactly put my finger on. No burns or missing digits, but the way she kept staring at me reminded me of a snake. Finally, she said, in this drowsy, drugged voice, "I'm going to rip your throat out."

Her sisters laughed. I did not.

Then Daddy spoke up from somewhere deep in the lobby.

"Now, now Coraline. You know what I've told you about patience."

"But Daddy!"

He stepped out of the shadows, dressed in his usual natty digs, one arm bundled in a sling across his chest, wearing a cast that reached from palm to shoulder with medieval pins sticking out of it in radiating circles. He grimaced as he walked, and though his voice was as smooth and as polished as ever, there was a look in his eye that made me think that maybe he'd bludgeon me with that cast, impale me right through the forehead no matter what kind of damage it did him, no matter how many more pieces it shattered his bones into.

"Don't 'daddy,' me, Coraline."

"But I want. To slit. His throat!"

"All in good time. All in good time."

Then *another* voice chimed in, this one even more familiar than the rest.

"Yeah, but not right now, right?"

Great. Tommy Trigger. Standing in the other corner. What a regular family reunion this turned out to be, huh?

Tommy lit a cigarette.

"Because, you know, he kind of got something we want."

It never ends, The Weirdness. It never ends.

Daddy sighed and said, "Yes, Mr. Trigger. We know."

"A deal's a deal, Daddy-o. And the Brotherhood? We don't take kindly to them what breaks deals, even if the deal's something what needed to be broke."

"Mr. Trigger. Your vernacular is quite . . . singular."

Tommy pushed himself off the wall so I could see him a little better, holding his cigarette between his pointer and thumb like he was about to flick it at Daddy's face. His other hand, his right, slid into his pocket. I seen Daddy glance down at it, and I knew what he was thinking. He was thinking, "What does he have in that pocket, huh?"

"Thanks," Tommy said. "Unless you was being sarcastic, in which case, screw."

Ella's face turned bright red.

"You can't talk to Daddy that way."

"I can't? Why not?"

"It isn't polite."

"Pot meet kettle."

Bella joined the fray.

"You're a scalawag and a ruffian, and Daddy won't truck such foul language from the likes of you!"

"Now, Bella. Now, Ella."

Tommy took a step toward the girls. They drew together as he bent over, holding his cigarette to his lips.

"Scalawag? Ruffian?" He took a puff and blew the smoke in their faces. The girls coughed and waved it away, but they didn't move. I gotta give them credit. They were brave little runts, them. Tommy held his bogey up at them.

"How about I take this and I shove it up all four of your asses, huh? One at a time. Boop. Boop. Boop. Boop."

The girls were stunned silent for once. Then their eyes went wide, and their mouths turned into O's and they slowly looked at each other. I thought Daddy was going to break Tommy's skull open with them pins, but, expectedly I admit, the girls broke out into loud giggles. Ella even started clapping and hopping.

"Oh, Daddy. I like this one. Can we keep it?"

Tommy stood up, smiling. He took a drag off his fag, eyebrows bouncing. Meanwhile, Sal pulled up next to me and crossed his arms.

"Who this?"

"That's Tommy Trigger."

"You like saying my name out loud, dont'cha?"

"He's an asshole."

Tommy yanked his hand out of his pocket and aimed his finger at me, making that "chick chick chick" sound with his cheek.

"You gonna just leave the door like that?" he said, pointing over my shoulder.

I turned around. Turned out Sal didn't do such a great job blockading it after all. In fact, he didn't do nothing. I imagined the twitchers piling up one on top of the other until the hinges gave and they poured in. Fuck, Sal. Why'd you leave it that way? I turned to ask him, but all the sudden he wasn't there.

"Where's Sal went?"

Tommy said, "I ain't got time for this. Let's go."

"Where we going'?"

"I'm taking you to see BG. I can't wait to see the look on your face when he puts that bullet in your brain."

"Daddy! You said that *we* could play with it."

"Now, Coraline."

"You said I could use my needles."

"I know Caroline, but—"

"You said I could chunk its throat!"

"You said I could make its float!"

"You said! You said! You said!"

Daddy patted the air with one hand.

"Girls, girls, girls."

Tommy grabbed my arm and Daddy punched him in the face.

"Hands off the merchandise, Mr. Trigger."

In the ensuing ruckus, I sprinted out the front door, the one to the city, and slammed it behind me. The twitchers had massed at the gate and were pushing up against the fence, their skin pressed through the wire, dozens and dozens of them, with more on the way. I seen something out of the corner of my eye, something on the ground, and holy moly was I in for a treat. Somebody'd left my clothes right outside the door, neatly folded: my pants, my shirt, my jacket, and my spats on top. A piece of paper sat under them, and I picked it up and looked at it. There was a thumb's up scrawled on it.

Good old Ham!

I squatted down and slipped my hand into the folds, feeling around, and yep, there they was. My scalpel and bonesaw. I stowed them away in my jumpsuit, and just in time, too, because next thing I knew, Tommy busted out the door, followed by the squealing girls and Daddy. Sal still wasn't nowhere in sight.

"Where's Sal?"

Tommy slammed the door behind Daddy and leaned against it.

"No time for crazy."

Something big hit the door, pressed on it for a second, and fingers pushed through the gap. I threw my weight against it, too, and it shut hard, slicing them off.

"Now or never," Tommy said.

Not that we had a choice. Before I could even think, "Okay, I'm gonna run," the something big on the other side of the door hit it again, sending the both of us sprawling forward, and then we was off. Or really, Tommy was. My shoulder and ribs still ached, and the cuts under my collarbone stung, even as it healed up, so my run was more like a lurch. The twitchers poured out after us.

We ran through the gate and had just made it across the street when a black pickup with a flamethrower in the bed squealed to a stop between us and the twitchers. Somebody popped up behind the flamethrower and pulled the trigger. Gunfire erupted from the cab, pop pop pop, and the driver's side door opened and guess who jumped out?

O'Neill.

The midget.

Driving a big pickup truck.

And when I say "big," I mean it was an old Ford F450 SuperDuty, the kind that contractors used to haul materials to build skyscrapers, the kind with six tires on it (two in the front, four in the back), the kind with a gazillion liter V9000 engine, the kind that sounded like a tank taking off when you turned over the transmission.

"O'Neill!" I yelled. "About time."

He fired off a few more shots into the twitcher storm.

"Let's go!"

I started to head his way, but Tommy Trigger put his hand on my chest.

"You ain't going nowhere unless that nowhere's with me."

"That don't make no sense."

O'Neill came over, making sure his gun was in view.

"Let him go."

"Says who?"

"Says me."

"Screw you, you midget."

O'Neill didn't even blink. He leveled his gun at him and, well, you can guess what happened next.

You know, there's a lot of different types of killing. Revenge killing, contract killing, war killing, serial killing, sex killing, love killing, hate killing, robbery killing, killing killing, not to mention all the different ways to get it done. Shooting, shanking, stabbing, slitting, beating, choking, drowning, raping, ripping, tearing, bludgeoning, poisoning, smothering, and probably a hundred more ways that I ain't listed yet. But the best type of killing is the kind what really needs to happen but what you don't got to do yourself.

Chapter 5
In which our boy fulfills his contract

The drive back through the city in O'Neill's tricked-out truck was probably the most enjoyable of my, well, not of my life on account of the fact that I'd taken better rides in better rides, but it ranked up there in the top three. Maybe it was all context. I'd just been through hell, and my ribs was cracked and my chest was cracked and my shoulder was cracked, so I could have been riding in a rickshaw and it would have felt luxurious.

The city hadn't changed. I don't know why I expected it to. It'd only been three days. I think it's because of everything that happened, like whatever I'd underwent should have been reflected in my surroundings or something. It didn't. That's predictable, though, ain't it? Life only has meaning for the suckers. The rest of us do what we got to twenty-four seven, three sixty-five.

Ruby wasn't in the office. O'Neill pointed at the corner and said, "Wait there." Then he went to the back.

I looked at the spot where he told me to sit, but there still wasn't no chairs. I heard a door slam, another one open, and then the sound of the wheelchair rolling, and then he pushed June out.

"Hey, June," I said. "How's the boom boom?"

"I told you not to talk to her that way." Then, to June: "You ready?"

June, as was her habit, didn't say nothing, and O'Neill shrugged.

"No time like the present."

Then he took out a knife and stabbed me in the forearm, slicing a nice big slit in my meat.

"Christ's sake, O'Neill!" I yelled. Not necessarily because it hurt, it did, but also because I knew what was coming. "You might want to get out of here."

"No thanks." He hopped up on the counter and crossed his legs. "I'd like to see this."

See it he did. The nanobots streamed out of my arm, onto the floor, up the old lady's wheelchair, swarmed her body, coated her head, and flooded into her mouth and nose and ears. She didn't do nothing at first, but then she started to shake and moan, and the shaking and moaning got worse and worse until her arms and legs shot out stiff as a board and she fell out of her chair. A crazy sound wailed up out of her lungs and, I shit you not, she started to change. Her skin smoothed out, her muscles toned up, her hair grew thick and lush and jet black. Her bones cracked and popped as her skeleton corrected itself, and that hunch disappeared. Right before my eyes, the gnarly old lady turned into a beautiful woman.

"Holy shit," I said.

June stood up, staring at her hands and arms in wonder.

"It worked," she whispered. Then louder, "It worked!"

"Would you look at that?" O'Neill said.

The fact that her head had not exploded was more than shocking. But the transformation wasn't done transformating yet. June got younger and younger, the collagen filling out her face and lips.

Then she started to shrink.

"Wait, no," she said. She looked at O'Neill in horror, then at me. "Make it stop."

I held up my hands.

"I can't make it do shit, lady."

She went from forty, to twenty, to fifteen, to ten, to five, to one. And then she was a baby. A baby lying in a pile of old lady clothes.

No shit. A baby.

O'Neill looked at it, looked at me, and let out a single guffaw. He hopped down off the counter and stooped over her, his hands on his knees.

"Well," he said. "Uh . . ."

Baby June cooed at us. She played with her feet. After a long silence, during which I assumed O'Neill was formulating some kind of plan, I cleared my throat. He looked at me like he'd never seen me before.

"Please tell me you already got paid," I said.

GOD'S BONES
Stonehammer's Dilemma

Battle lay in a ditch staring up at the night sky. It was hot. So hot. He thought it might cool off a little when the sun went down, but he'd lived in Virginia his entire life and should have known better. June might have been early summer, but it was summer nonetheless, and some days it just got hotter and hotter no matter how late the hour.

He didn't want to look down at his stomach. He'd done it once before a little after he felt the bullet whunk into him, and the sight frightened him. He'd seen what happened to men who suffered similar injuries. The pain was terrible enough by itself, but when the infection set in, the fever, the shaking, the nausea, it was more than unbearable. He didn't deserve to die like this. He'd heeded the president's call. Fought on Lincoln's Line. He truly believed it was his only hope for freedom. In his mind, he would protect the capital, fight off Lee's Army, and get the freedom promised him. He wasn't supposed to die, though. He faded in and out of consciousness. He lost track of time.

Late on the second night, after the cries of the dying slowly faded along with the sound of the guns and cannons, he awoke to a strange, machine-like buzzing. First, he thought it was some kind of new weapon the Rebs had concocted, a fresh new terror they'd use to punish any of the slaves who dared fight the Confederacy. But then he felt the tickling in his wound and a strange numbness that settled in soon after. Flies. The flies had come. If he'd had any illusions of surviving, they disappeared after that. He knew he should at least try to shoo them away, but he no longer had the strength. And, to be honest, he liked the feeling. The pain was gone. Death was upon him.

Later. He woke gasping like he'd forgotten to breathe in his sleep. Indeed, he was surprised that he was still alive. As he lay there, he noticed the glow for the first time. It was faint at first, a pale light so weak that he thought maybe one of the other wounded men had lit a match or maybe even started a fire. But then it grew in intensity, brighter and brighter, taking on a cold, blue hue the likes of which he'd never seen, and he realized it was coming from him. His stomach, actually, his stomach and the wounds of the other men, dead and alive, all around him. Grunting with the effort, he sat partially up to see what humiliation had been bestowed upon his body in his final minutes, and his eyes grew wide with terror.

Blue.

His stomach was glowing blue. A thick carpet of something rough and cratered coated his torso from his belly button to his sternum, and it was pulsing, too, breathing like some kind of creature had flattened itself out and took to sucking the life out of him. And though he barely felt a thing, though in reality the pain had gone and his wound had begun to buzz almost pleasantly, he opened his mouth and sat straight up, screaming, his mouth wide open, lungs expelling the last of his breath.

And then he was in his bedroom. He wasn't dying. His stomach wasn't glowing anymore. He was alive. Alive. He looked around to get his bearings. There was the window, there was the vanity, there was the oil lamp. The dream. The damn dream. He'd had it off and on ever since The Battle of Washington, and it fooled him every time.

Before he could fully appreciate what had happened, a knock came at his front door. It was loud, aggressive, impatient. He sat up in bed, sighing. The knocking turned to pounding, and he wondered if another riot had broken out, whether he'd be called upon to quell it, whether he'd have to save another white man's life, another white man who hated him.

"Hold on, hold on," he mumbled.

The banging grew louder as he hurried down the stairs and, tying his robe closed, he rushed through the vestibule and yanked the door open.

"God's bones! What is it! What do you want?"

A giant of a man stood at his door, broad of shoulder and thick of arm. Battle had never seen such a human being before, a startling admission, for he himself stood 6'2" and weighed close to 250 pounds. This man was easily half a foot taller and at least seventy pounds heavier. His hands were so huge that they might have dwarfed the hat they were currently wringing between their fingers, that is if the hat hadn't belonged to a head that was easily as large as a wagon wheel. The behemoth dipped that head in meek deprecation, and all of the sudden Battle felt bad about yelling at him.

"Yes, suh. Are you Mr. Sebastian Battle, suh?"

"Yes. What can I do for you?"

"Name Stonehammer."

"Well, Mr. Stonehammer, what—"

"No 'mister,' suh. Just Stonehammer."

"Very well. What can I do for you . . . Stonehammer?

Stonehammer's eyes flitted up and down the street, as if he was worried about being heard.

"All the same to you, suh, I'd rather not say out here."

"I'm sorry, but I can't just let anybody come into my home. State your business."

Stonehammer nodded, worrying his hat between his fingers.

"My niece, suh. She gone missing."

Battle put a cup of tea on the table in front of the huge man and tried not to laugh when he engulfed the cup in his paw, pinched the infuser between two fingers the size of summer sausages, and blew lightly on it.

"So," Battle said. "Your niece, mist . . . . Stonehammer?"

"Yes, suh."

"She's missing?"

"Yes, suh. I was told you the man to find her."

"I might be able to. Can you tell me who sent you my way?"

"Mr. Han, suh."

Ah. Han Chen. Opium Den operator, dabbler in the chemical sciences, and one of the stranger men Battle had ever known, notwithstanding his wife, of course, who was even smarter and stranger than her husband. Han seemed to have an affinity for Battle for some reason, and Battle, who, ever since his experiences in the war, was drawn to all things unusual, returned the affection.

"Stonehammer, is your niece an orphan? Why isn't her mother or father—"

Without warning, Stonehammer began to cry. He didn't bawl or blubber, but tears began to fall down his cheeks. He wiped them away with the back of his gargantuan hand.

"Sorry, suh. I been knowing Althea since she a baby, suh. Her daddy, he died on Lincoln's Line. Her momma, she dead of consumption after. Althea my niece in name, but she mine. I raised her. I schooled her. I can't stand her being gone. I'm about to lose my mind."

"And how long has she been missing?"

"She went to the shop Saturday morning. S'pose to be home that night."

"What shop?"

"Coat shop. Kelly's shop, suh. He own it."

"And you've checked with this Kelly?"

"No, suh. He don't truck with us."

"With who?"

Stonehammer looked like he'd just been asked the most ridiculous question he'd ever heard.

"Our kind, suh."

Our kind. Our kind. Battle marveled at the arrogance, the gumption, the shortness of America's memory. What kind would that be, he wondered? The kind that bailed them out twenty years ago? Guarded their borders, repopulated their cities, worked their factories, brought life and hope back to the most lostest of causes to ever fight for The Lost Cause?

"I'm sorry, Stonehammer, but if he won't deal with you, what makes you think he will with me?"

"I didn't mean . . . Kelly, he a negro. Just like you and me. But he put on airs, suh. He don't talk to field hands like me. You? You fought on Lincoln's Line, same as him."

This new information didn't ease Battle's anger.

"I see," he said. "What about your niece's colleagues?"

"I'm sorry, suh?"

"The people she works with."

"Oh! I spoke to a few. They seen her there Saturday. She work the sewing table. Say she the best they got. Coat take one hour to make. Most folks got twelve coats a day. Althea got herself fifteen. Mister like her so much, she head the line."

Stonehammer took another delicate sip of his tea, and Battle watched him, fascinated. He'd never seen such a huge man move so gently. But then again, it made sense, didn't it? He'd probably spent a lifetime adapting his strength to the fragile world around him. Where had he come from? Someone so large couldn't have escaped notice before, even in such a sprawling city as the one where they both lived. A man like him begged for challengers, warranted or not, angry white men seething at the arrogance of his size, young black bucks looking to prove their manhood.

Maybe he was newly arrived. The Underground Railroad, while frustrated by the truce, was still clearly in full operation. Come to think of it, Stonehammer looked like he'd come straight from the fields.

"Stonehammer, sir. I understand your concern. A missing young lady in a city such as this is a frightening thing. But you do realize it's only Monday morning? Did she not have any acquaintances? A boyfr—"

Stonehammer's hangdog expression turned flat and mean. Battle did not like being on the receiving end.

"Thea don't know no boys. She a good girl. She do her piece work and she come straight home. No frens. No boys. No drink. She a churchly girl. A righteous girl."

"I have no doubt, my friend. But if you truly want to discover her whereabouts, you must investigate all avenues. Everything, no matter how unsavory, must be in play."

Stonehammer's expression did not soften, but his eyes lost some of their glower.

"I'm sorry, suh. I don't know nothing about savories and avenues. That's your job. I'm scared is all."

"It takes a strong man to express his emotions."

The big man dropped his eyes.

"I'm not a strong man, suh. I'm big, but I'm not strong." He took a deep breath. "Something's happened to Althea, I swear. Will you find her?"

"I've signed no contracts at the moment, but I'm afraid my services are not free."

Stonehammer reached inside his vest.

"I can pay." He pulled out a little leather pouch and set it on the table between them. "It's all I got for now, but I'll have more when you find her."

Battle studied the pouch. There couldn't have been more than a few dollars in change in it. He couldn't do it. He couldn't. He had bills to pay, notes to satisfy. And then there was that little unpleasantness with Mr. Barley. How much longer would it be before his heavies came calling? He glanced at Stonehammer. Stonehammer looked expectantly back. Like a puppy.

"God's bones," Battle muttered. "Okay. I'll take the case."

"Thank you, suh! Thank you!"

"You must also know that I work alone, on my own time, in my own fashion. I truck no interference. I will do my best to return her to you safe and sound, but you must be prepared for the worst and willing to accept my final report, and should the worst occur, you must pay the rest of my fee no matter how bleak or disheartening. Do you agree to these terms."

"I do, suh."

"Well, then," Battle said, smiling. He extended his hand. Stonehammer nearly upended the table in his haste to engulf it in his own. "Consider my services retained."

After Stonehammer left, and after dressing and breaking his fast, headed over to Han Chen's opium den.

It was a far walk from Lincoln's View to Chinatown, but Battle didn't want to spend what little he'd already earned from Stonehammer's meager downpayment on a carriage, so he walked. The summer day was cooler than usual, which made the trek somewhat pleasant. At least until he made it to Han's door. He jingled the purse in his pocket, wondering if he should visit Barley first. Well. He'd waited this long hadn't he? He could wait a few minutes more.

He opened the door and walked into what felt like an entirely different universe. The beautiful day, the warm summer sun, the sweet breeze, were replaced by murky light and damp couches. He'd passed a vendor selling flowers out of a cart a few feet down from the den, and their fresh smell, filled with the promise of summer, was replaced by the cloying heaviness of smoke, incense, and opium. He shut the door behind him, peering into the dingy light of the long room.

The den was emptier at this hour, but there were still a few customers indulging, lounging on chaises while young girls tended their needs. As his eyes adjusted, he took note of a particularly striking man standing next to a bed in the back. Battle had never seen him before. A white man, tall, maybe even taller than him, with stark, white hair, and ice-blue eyes. He stood uncomfortably erect, as if his spine were made by a railroad tie. He stared at Battle with a predator's eyes.

In the backroom, Battle heard two voices yelling at each other. That would be Han and his wife, Ushi. He'd never seen them not fighting. Because they chose to air their grievances in Mandarin, he never knew the subject of their continual clapper-clawing, and while Han didn't seem to be henpecked and Ushi wasn't a nag, she always seemed to be on the attack.

Partially to complete his business and partially to extract himself from the lingering gaze of the strange white man, Battle cleared his throat.

"Han?"

The fighting cut off, and a thin man with wild, bushy hair pushed his way out of the back through a beaded curtain.

"Ah, Mr. Battle! Just in time. I've made some progress on our project—"

Ushi bustled through the curtains and shoved him aside.

"Listen, Mr. Battle. Enough is enough. You need to know—"

Han snapped at her in Mandarin, and they proceeded to argue some more. Battle, irritated, took Stonehammer's pouch out of his pocket and dropped a few coins on to the counter. Han saw them and, before they disappeared, snatched them up. And started to count them.

"It's all there."

"I know."

Han inspected the coins. Bit them. Held them up to the light. Ushi looked at Battle questioningly.

"Finder's fee," he explained. "New client."

She immediately turned to her husband and punched him in the stomach.

"Ow!"

He dropped one of the coins and she picked it out of the air.

"For arguing with me." To Battle, she said, "I would tell you now, but . . . " nodding backwards at her husband. She put the coin in the folds of her shirt as she walked away.

Han gave Battle a sheepish grin.

"I've got a few questions about Stonehammer's niece," Battle said.

"We can talk in the lab."

Han's lab was, if possible, more dingy and dusty than the den on the other side. It did not harbor any strange totems. No shrunken heads leered at him from the shelves, no strings of strong-smelling herbs hung from the ceiling, no skins stretched over drying racks. The shelves contained books. The ceiling was bare.

A huge safe, easily five feet tall and just as wide, stood open on one side. The lock apparatus had been completely removed, leaving a large, round socket in the middle of the door, which itself was two feet deep. Battle squatted down to inspect it.

"Looks wide enough. Deep enough. May I?"

Han was futzing around his work table in the back. He nodded distractedly. Battle rolled up his sleeve and stuck his arm into the socket as far as it could go, which was up to his elbow.

"Where will the grip be?"

"You'll be able to feel it when it's done."

"Then I just grab it and . . ."

"Yes. Ah, here they are."

It was easy to see why he couldn't find what he was looking for. The worktable was littered with chemistry equipment. Vials and tubes, beakers, flasks, tongs, and racks. He turned back to Battle, holding a needle and a vial.

"I will just need some of your blood."

"Again?"

"Science is imperfect, Mr. Battle."

"Fine, but don't drain me. Last time I got dizzy."

"Just a drop. I promise.

Battle pulled his arm out and stood up, eyeing the needle.

"Looks dirty."

"Ah, yes. New procedure from Scotland."

He dipped the needle in a flask of clear liquid, then poured another flask of clear liquid over it.

"What's that?"

"Carbolic acid, Mr. Battle. And water. Cleans the instrument. Please, sit."

Battle sat down in a chair on the other side of Han's messy desk and held out his arm, and Han, unceremoniously, Battle felt, and quite without warning, jabbed the needle into his vein.

"God's Bones, Han!"

"Oh, don't be such a baby. Make a fist and squeeze."

He tilted the vial up to the needle to collect the blood. When he was done, he handed Battle a handkerchief. Battle pressed it to the wound and held it there.

"So, what do you know about this Stonehammer?"

"What can I say? He came to me. Said he wanted to kill himself. Wanted me to give him enough poppy to put him out of his misery forever. I told him, 'You're as big as a rhino! You can't afford that much!' Then he took out a pouch and emptied it into my hands. Gold coins, Battle. Enough to buy all of the poppy he wanted. 'This enough?' he said. Is this enough."

"You took his money?"

"Of course!"

"The man's simple, Han, he—"

"Oh, relax, goody two shoes. He didn't smoke. I gave him a girl, instead. He didn't want her, though. 'Althea, Althea,' he kept moaning. Got him to tell me the whole story, and then I sent him to you."

"He tell you where he was from?"

"I know less than you. Except . . ."

"What."

"You know I hire many girls. Many girls all the time. Have you checked the docks?"

"Docks?"

"Boats come, boats go."

Battle suppressed the anger swelling up inside him. It didn't surprise him that Han knew about something like that. Han had his hands in everything and anything that made money, legal or not. It was also not shocking that the slavers were still plying their trade. Ever since the Truce, he and his fellow officers had been tracking down one after another. The blockade took care of a lot of it, or it was supposed to, but the economy took a hit after the war ended, and men were desperate. He expected it from his white neighbors, but what angered him the most was the participation of his brothers and cousins, many of whom had parents who broke their chains and fled north after Chickamauga.

"When?"

"When what, Mr. Battle?"

"When is the next boat coming?"

Han laughed.

"They don't operate on a schedule."

"Then how do you know there even is one?"

"I hear things. Certain parties think I might be interested."

"Who."

"Have you read 'The Man With the Twisted Lip'?"

"Twisted what?"

"The Twisted Lip. Sherlock Holmes. He is a detective, just like you. I'm surprised you haven't seen it."

He opened a drawer and rummaged around, muttering.

"I know I put it in here last month. Ah!"

He took out a stack of magazines, thumped them down on the desk, started to thumb through them.

"July, September . . . here it is. December."

It was a copy of *The Strand Magazine*, the cover the same image of Southampton Street with little variation since its first issue.

"'The Man With the Twisted Lip'. New Sherlock Holmes adventure, Mr. Battle. Each one has taught me something new. In this one, a man is not at all who he seems." He held it out. "Here."

Battle pushed the magazine away and got up to leave.

"I don't have time for stories, Han."

"You will call on me soon, Mr. Battle," Han called after him.

Battle chose not to answer. He pushed through the beads and out into the waiting area.

"I can be of great service!"

Battle emerged into the bright, city light and strode away from the den, heading towards the south side. That's where the city let sweatshops operate, nearly all of them. He didn't know exactly where Kelly's was, but it shouldn't prove too difficult to find. He asked around at a few of the shop owners and was able to locate it within the hour. When he went in, he expected it to be filled with workers piecing together coats and shirts and pants and whatever else the owner wanted them to do. Instead, he found a place that was nearly dormant.

The building was dark and close and dusty and dirty, and it smelled of toil and fear and desperation. The floors looked so spotted with termite damage that Battle was worried he might fall through to the basement with each step he took. The sound of the machines reached his ears from above, and he followed it.

The third floor was only half-packed with workers. A few of them paused when they saw him standing there, but none offered a greeting or any help. A door with the word OFFICE stenciled on it was located on the other side of the floor. He walked across and knocked on it. The sound of the sewing machines swelling while he waited. He looked over his shoulder at the men and women hard at work, catching a few who were equally curious about him. They looked quickly away when their eyes met. Then he heard footsteps from inside the office, a lock was turned, and the door was ripped open to reveal the most striking human being he'd ever seen in his life.

He was small and slight and not at all imposing, with pale skin and eyebrows—everything, it seemed, was pale on him—lips, eyelashes, eyes. He wore his orange-blond hair straightened and slicked back to his head. His jacket and vest, though they looked like they'd once been the height of fashion, were worn and threadbare, except for the green pocket square, which was clean and perfect and expensive looking. The juxtaposition shocked Battle for a moment, and he stammered a greeting.

"H-hello. Sorry. I'm looking for—" He took a step back and looked at the door and the walls, wondering if he had the right place. "I'm looking for Jeremiah Kelly."

"Yes. I am he."

"Oh! Oh, I see. Mr. Kelly, my name is Sebastian Battle. I'm a detective. I've been retained by a man named Stonehammer whose niece has gone missing. Her name is —"

"Althea? Is it Althea?"

"Yes. How did you know?"

"I didn't. But she didn't come in this morning and . . . oh, dear. This can't be. She's my best girl and . . . and such a sweet soul." He paused, seemingly deep in thought, and then, as if realizing it, snapped to back into the present. "But where are my manners. Please do come in, Mr. Battle."

Kelly retreated into his office and Battle followed. It was as spare and clean as the rest of the sweatshop was not, containing only a desk and a safe and a few chairs.

"What can I do to help?" Kelly asked as he sat behind his desk.

Battle pointed at the chair in front of him.

"May I?"

"Of course."

"Mr. Kelly. When was the last time you saw Althea?"

"Saturday evening. She stayed late to finish her work, as usual. Such a hard-working girl."

"What time did she leave?"

"I'm not sure. Perhaps seven, eight at night? It was dark out when I left for home. She wasn't here."

"So you didn't see her leave?"

"I can't keep track of everyone who works for me."

Battle paused in thought, and after a moment, Kelly cleared his throat.

"Mr. Battle, if I may?"

"Please."

"You've spoken to her uncle, yes?"

"He hired me."

A flicker of a smile passed over Kelly's lips then disappeared.

"I know what you're thinking. You see this office, you see the people I have working for me. I know shop owners have a particular reputation. But we're not all bad, you see."

"I have no opinion one way or another, Mr. Kelly. I'm here to find a girl."

"But we're not. I promoted Althea because of her uncle. She's my best girl, yes, and my hardest worker, but I didn't have to promote her. Part of it was charity, you see. Her uncle, this Stonehammer, I am sorry to say is a bit of a gambler and a drunk."

"Her uncle?"

"Oh, yes."

"Althea told you this?"

"Not directly, no, but I have ears. The other girls, they whisper. And I have eyes, too. Althea has come into work bearing the fruit of his drinking."

Battle tried to reconcile the version of Stonehammer Kelly just described with the man he met not an hour before.

"Does Althea have any friends here? Someone she might seem to get along with?"

"I couldn't tell you."

"Why not?"

"No, I'm sorry. What I mean is that Althea gets along well with everyone, Mr. Battle. Positively everybody."

"Right. But does she have anybody she gets along with particularly well?"

Kelly thought for a moment.

"No. She isn't close with any one particular girl."

He thought again. He templed his fingers and tapped a rhythm on his lips.

"Last week, there was a man. A white man. Very striking, blue eyes. Long hair. So blond that it was almost silver."

"Really? Here?"

Kelly seemed encouraged.

"Yes. Yes, I did. He came skulking around in the afternoon. I saw him approach some of the girls as they left for the day, and I went outside to confront him. We had words, he and I, and he seemed inclined to scrap, but I am no stranger to fisticuffs, and he must have seen it, for after a few choice words . . . well, let's just say he was no longer spoiling. 'Begone, villain!' I said." He chuckled. "He'll think twice before bothering my girls again."

"You're very protective of them."

"I fought on Lincoln's Line. I am not just a businessman. I am a member of this community. We may have earned our freedom, but things are far from equal in this world. We are stronger together."

Battle had heard the same words before. He'd once believed in them. It was alluring, intoxicating. Yes, they were little more than tools for the whites, pawns in their wars and politics, but it was his people who fought off the Rebs and the British at the Battle of Philadelphia, who regained Washington, who fought on the line, and who patrolled the border after the truce. But he'd seen too much of the hatred and bigotry that followed, during his time as an officer and then later as a detective, to put much faith in words and slogans anymore.

"Did he talk to Althea?"

"I'm not sure. Perhaps? She usually leaves after the other girls—she's such a hard worker, as I said—but I'm not sure . . . or maybe, yes! Yes, I remember now. She was there, in fact. She smiled at me after I sent the ruffian on his way."

A knock came at the door, and Kelly said, "Come in."

A young girl, no older than eleven or twelve, stuck her head in.

"Mr. Kelly, sir?"

"Yes, Cella."

"We need you out on the floor."

"Now? I'm in a very important meeting."

Angry words erupted behind her.

"It's Agnes and Wilhemina, again, sir.

Kelly gave Battle a weary look as he stood up.

"I'm sorry, Mr. Battle. I must attend to business."

"Of course. Maybe we could continue this conversation another time? I have many more questions."

But Kelly was already moving around his desk.

"Cella," he said. "Please show Mr. Battle out."

Battle used to hate failure. It was a condition suffered by many of Lincoln's Boys. Though he was disenchanted by the continuing racism that plagued the country, he was afraid that he'd never be able to live up to the expectations of his generation—that they were the first former slaves to vote *en masse* in a presidential election, that their pure numbers, and the several millions more borne following The Great Migration, would transform the nation that had once bound and riveted them in the craven chains of servitude, that they would finally force the country to fulfill the promise of its constitution.

If he had had a father, perhaps he would have been able to explain one of the most important truths of the world: that the only pathway to victory was in defeat, that success, worthwhile success, was never instantaneous, and nor should it have been, that he should immerse himself in the process of things, not the outcome, that he should find excellence in the minutia, that he should strive, flounder, grow frustrated, collapse, exhaust all possibilities, and fail and fail and fail again, that only by doing so would he ever reach maximum self-realization.

But these were things Battle had to learn on his own. Age and experience, his time on Lincoln's Line, then as an officer, then a detective, had disabused him of all romance. Romance was a young man's game, a shill, a stooge, interesting only to the ignorant, the angry, the uneducated, and those with the energy to pour headlong into a hurricane and later wonder at his battered bones. Time had taught Battle the power of tenacity. Fistfights weren't just won by the adept and adroit. They were just as often won by the opponent who simply would not give up. That's how he viewed himself: a vessel of relentlessness. Slow, methodic, diligent, scrupulous, and dogged.

He happened to glance up from his thoughts as he strolled along, and walking toward him was the intense-looking white man he'd seen at Han's den. He was heading straight for him, his hand was outstretched as if expecting to shake.

"Mr. Battle? A word with you please."

His accent was strange. Clipped. Germanic but not German. Battle had lived long enough in the city to know the tactic. An unexpected approach to distract, then a brutal sucker punch to the temple, and you found yourself robbed. The best way to avoid it was to ignore it, but if that didn't work, he'd punch his way through.

The white man closed the distance between them faster than Battle expected, as if he were skipping air between steps. Startled, Battle stopped and put his hand into his breast, ready to withdraw his pocket piece: a Marston three-barrel one of his past clients had given him. Then the white man was there in front of him. "You are Sebastian Battle, ja?"

He was taller than Battle initially thought, with long, silver-white hair that flowed out from under a brown derby, and his face was shaved all over, and it was smooth and pale and almost gleaming, and he had pale, thin lips, and a thin, pointy nose, and the widest, roundest, piercing blue eyes. Battle adopted his best subservient demeanor. He slumped a little, softened his expression.

"No, suh. No Battle here. Name Joseph, suh. Joseph Freeman."

The white man gave him a pitying smile, and Battle, hand still on his Marston, gently pushed by saying, "excuse me, suh."

"Mr. Battle, my name is Mikael Sten. I just want to talk."

Oh, that accent. Where was this man from? Not England, certainly. Iceland? Sweden?

"Freeman, suh. Name Freeman." Battle said, hurrying away.

He looked over his shoulder and the white man was still looking at him, smiling. But when he turned back around, Sten appeared in front of him, walking towards him, hand outstretched, smiling as if that hadn't just happened.

"Haha haha! A very good trick, Mr. Battle. But please, I only need a moment of your time, sir. I promise."

Battle pushed by again and broke into a jog. He turned a corner, and Sten was leaning against a tenement stoop. He tipped his hat as Battle passed.

"We can do this all day, sir."

Battle ducked into an alley and ran to the end. The familiar sights, sounds, and smells of the slums engulfed his senses. He ducked under wash lines drooping with wet laundry, absorbed a few insults from the paupers half-hanging out of windows, gagged at the mingled aroma of slow-cooked pork, collard greens, fried chicken, fatback. The alley opened up into a line of outhouses backed up to a fence, next to which stood the well-dressed, and evidently quite speedy, Mikael Sten.

"Mr. Battle, this is really beneath you."

Battle turned to run back down the alley, but the man was already in front of him.

"Please, sir."

Battle swung, a great, winding haymaker that would have surely sent the other man sprawling had it connected, but the other man suddenly wasn't there anymore. The force of the blow, which he expected to halt his momentum, carried him forward a few steps and almost one hundred and eighty degrees, where he saw Sten standing calmly behind him. Battle roared and rushed the man, meaning to tackle him and bring him to the ground but clutched thin air instead. He landed hard on his chest. A pair of immaculate, black shoes, polished to a high sheen, appeared to his right.

"Done yet?" Sten asked.

Battle rolled to his side and propped himself up on his arm.

"Neat trick."

"It is not a trick. It is science. Pure and simple"

"Whatever you say."

Sten offered his hand and Battle took it and let himself be helped up. He used the momentum to launch a final punch, saw Sten's eyes go wide at the realization of what was about to happen to him, and then he was gone again.

But Battle had prepared for just such a move. He knew the white man would show up behind him, however impossible, and he spun in a full circle, feeling silly but knowing it would work, and he saw the man, *saw the man*, appear out of nowhere. Battle's fist connected with his temple and he went down in a heap.

"Science might be science, but a fist is still a fist," Battle said.

Then he picked up his hat, dusted it off, and strode confidently out of the alley. He didn't see the two men leaning against the bricks on the other side. They nodded to each other and fell in step behind him. One of them took a burlap hood out of his pocket, and the other one cracked his knuckles.

Battle came around choking. Someone had thrown water on his face. He coughed until his sides ached and then coughed some more. His head hurt and his teeth felt loose in his mouth. He worked his jaw. It clicked. Through the swollen slit of his left eye (his right was completely closed), he saw a familiar figure sitting backward in a chair.

"Clyde Barley," he croaked.

Barley shrugged his shoulders.

"The one and only."

If there ever existed a paradigm for the effect of greed, Clyde Barley stood as a prime example. Short, fat, and bombastic, prone to wearing double-breasted vests and ascots, devouring tripe, and spouting abuse, he was a parody of a caricature.

Battle had met plenty of men like him, white, black, yellow, and brown. Their entire lives boiled down to a single, simple mathematical equation: the sum of the money they were able to trick, extort, bully, or force from someone's pocket minus the effort it took to take. They were shrewd and effective businessmen, and what they lacked in humanity they made up for in ruthlessness.

Behind Barley stood second largest man Battle had ever encountered, and next to him stood the third. Buster and Bruiser.

"Didn't think you'd stoop this low for a few dollars," Battle said.

He coughed again, and the pain in his ribs flared up. He spit a gob blood on the floor and leaned back in the chair he was tied to. Barley rolled his cigar stub from one side of his mouth to the other.

"I told them two to take it easy on you."

"They didn't."

"I'd apologize, but I don't care."

"Thanks."

"That is a word that you will not be saying again."

"I've got your money, Clyde."

Barley tipped his bowler back.

"Oh, yeah?"

"Yeah. New case. Paid me upfront."

"Okay. Fork it over."

"Don't have it with me. I—"

"—hid it at your place? We already turned it out. Nothing there."

"—hid it somewhere else."

"Oh, yeah? Where?"

"Let me go and I'll bring it back to you."

Now it was Barley's turn to laugh, a great booming noise that echoed in the open room. Battle took the opportunity to get his bearings. The ceiling was unfinished. A series of windows ran along one edge, dirty and streaked. Broken furniture was piled up against the wall, and crates, some new, some blackened with mold, were stacked irregularly throughout the place. The rest was shrouded in darkness.

"You hear that Bruiser," Barley said, slapping his knee. "'Let me go,' he says. 'I'll come back,' he says."

"He said that, he did, Mr. Clyde."

Barley snapped his fingers.

"Buster. Give it here."

The other man looked uncertain.

"Give what here, Mr. Clyde?"

"The pouch you sap."

"Sap? Bruiser's got the sap."

"Pouch! Pouch! The pouch you took off him when you brought him in."

"Oh, that!" Buster pulled the little pouch filled with Battle's money out of his pocket. "Here you go, Mr. Clyde."

Clyde snatched it out of the larger man's club-like paw, fixed him with a glare, then turned his attention back to Battle.

"This the money you're talking about?" He shook the pouch and the coins jingled. "Not even close to what you owe."

Battle didn't break character.

"There's more."

"Oh, yeah? Where. You hide it up your bung?"

"I have to finish the job first, then it's all yours."

"See, that's what I don't like about you, Battle. You've been saying the same thing to me for a month. No, longer than a month, right boys?"

Bruiser said, "Longer than a month," while Buster said, "I dunno, Mr. Clyde."

"God's bones, Buster."

"Huh?"

"Look, Battle. Every time I come to you, it's 'gimmie some time'. So I give you more time. Then it's, 'I got a line on something,' or 'I got a job,' or 'just gimmie a little bit longer'. So I give you a little longer. I let you finish the job. I spool out the line. I give and I give and I give, but the thing is, I don't get nothing in return. Now that I think about it, making books with you is kind of like being married. You got to pay for everything, but your woman, she don't fuck. Actually, never mind. Making books with you is EXACTLY like being married."

"That pouch—"

"This pouch is interest on the interest. You're a drowning man, and this don't even get you close to the surface."

"Good one, Mr. Clyde." Brusier.

"Thanks. I been reading. *Pride and Prejudice.* The lady who wrote it got a way with the, ah, whatchamacallit?" He snapped in the air, trying to remember. "Bruiser, what are those things? Those things I just did with the pouch and the drowning?"

"Metaphor, Mr. Clyde."

"Yeah. Metaphor. She got a way with the metaphor. You ever read that book, Battle?"

"I'm still processing the fact that you can read."

Barley stood up, knocking the chair over, and delivered a heavy slap to his face.

"Now ain't the time for your smart mouth, smartmouth."

"Uh, good one again, Mr. Clyde."

"Shut up, Buster." He regained his seat with a huff. "And yeah, I can read. Used to do odd jobs at Odd Fellows. One of the old duffers there taught me my ABC's."

"*Pride and Prejudice* is a far cry from learning your letters."

"What can I say? I graduated with honors. Anyway, that ain't what this is about. I'm here to deliver you a message."

"You could have just actually delivered me a message."

"The beating is part of the message, dimwit."

He took a revolver out of his pocket, a little 1.5 Smith and Wesson.

"Clyde—"

"Shut up. I hear you been snooping around places, asking questions when questions shouldn't be asked."

"I'm a detective."

"You think I care? You're on a case looking for some slat. As of right now, you're off it."

"That's the job, Clyde. If I don't finish it, you don't get paid."

"Oh, I'll get paid. One way or another."

He nodded at his heavies. They'd just taken one step forward when something clattered on the roof. Everybody looked up.

"What's that?" Clyde said.

"Maybe its Slash?" Buster said. "He and Gash ain't come back yet."

"Why'd they jump on the roof, numbskull?"

"Maybe . . . they . . ."

"Go check it out."

Bruiser nodded and started for the door.

"The roof?" Buster asked.

"No, nitwit. The basement."

"There ain't no basement, Mr. Clyde."

"Bruiser!"

"Come on, Buster," Bruiser said, escorting his friend away by the elbow. "Follow me."

"Okay. Sorry, Mr. Clyde."

Clyde watched them go, then turned back to Battle, pointing with his gun.

"This better not be a setup."

"Or what? You're going to kill be some more?"

Clyde got up and started to pace. He stared up at the ceiling.

"Those two idiots said they covered their tracks."

Clunks emanated from one corner of the roof, and Clyde spun around, aiming the revolver. Then another clunk came from the other side, and he spun that way.

"Clyde, it's just Bruiser and—"

"Shut up!"

The clunking increased, followed by a pause. A long, pregnant one. Then they heard shouting and thunderous footfalls. Gunshots rang out and, panicked, Clyde fired into the ceiling. The thunder and yelling continued. Clyde rushed over to Battle and clipped him in the head with the pistol grip, knocking him onto his back. He stomped over and squatted down, jamming the barrel against his forehead.

"What did you do! What did you do!"

Battle's vision blurred and doubled.

"I . . . didn't—"

Barley hit him again, and he must have blacked out for a moment because the next thing he knew, he was suspended in the air from the waist up. Barley had him by the collar, the barrel of the gun still pressed against his forehead. All he could see were beady, angry eyes.

"Good," Barley said. "You're awake. I want to see the expression on your face when I blow your brains out."

"You think I'm afraid of you?"

"Don't care."

He hit Battle in the head again with the butt of the gun, and Battle's head rocked back again so that he was looking at the ceiling. Someone had painted a beautiful picture there, like the Sistine Chapel, an odd choice for such a rundown building. It was . . . it was an angel, arms and legs splayed out wide as if it were holding onto the joists. It was the strangest angel he'd ever seen before, wearing a leather suit of some kind with some kind of breathing filter snapped over its face, its blond hair hanging down into the space over Clyde's head. Battle's eyes widened when he realized what he was looking at. The angel put a finger to its lips. He started to giggle.

"What's this?" Clyde said.

Battle's giggles turned to outright laughs and then coughs again as the ribs flared up.

"You're laughing? Laughing?" Clyde cocked the Smith & Weston. "I'll give you something to laugh about."

And that's when the angel dropped from the ceiling.

Later, Bruiser and Buster came back from their adventure on the roof, each holding a decapitated head by the hair. Clyde was sitting in a chair with his back to them.

"But if you toss a ball in the air while you're riding in the back of a speeding carriage," Bruiser explained. "it'll come right back down in your hands."

"No, it won't."

"Yeah, it will. Because you're going the same speed, dummy."

"But the ball ain't in your hands no more."

"No, but . . . hold on. Hey, Mr. Clyde?" He held up one of the heads. The name Gash had been slashed into its forehead. Buster held his up; the name Slash had been gashed into its forehead. "We got some bad news."

Clyde didn't move. Curious, Bruiser crossed the floor, lowering Gash's head.

"Mr. Clyde?" He tapped his boss on the shoulder, and Clyde slid sideways off the chair. His hands were bound, his feet were bound, and a knot the size of a gourd had formed on his forehead. He let out a moan. Bruiser looked at Basher.

"Uh oh," he said.

GOD'S BONES
End Times

Electricity coursed through Battle's body. He felt as though he were flying through a black tunnel. Whispers echoed all around him and bright lines of lightning-like falling stars. On and on he flew, the noise of a horrid symphony twisting around him, winding higher and higher and up and up into a frightening crescendo and then . . . it stopped.

All was silent.

He opened his eyes. The angel's face was hovering in front of his. No, not an angel at all, but somebody wearing a strange, leather suit. It was trying to talk to him, but he couldn't understand because the mask muffled everything it said. Battle panicked and hit whoever or whatever it was on the side of the head and, leaping up (he'd been sitting in a chair), ran for a curtained window.

"Mr. Battle, no!" someone yelled.

He thought the voice sounded familiar but had no time to worry about it. He needed to escape. He tore the curtains aside but the window was boarded up. Shaking a hand off his shoulder, he tried the next window, and the next, and the next, but all of them were covered in solid timber, plank upon plank, filling each frame entirely. He pounded on the last one, screaming, "Help!"

"Mr. Battle!"

It was Mikael Sten. Battle took momentary pleasure in seeing his black eye and swollen cheek.

"Please," Sten said. "Don't—"

Battle grabbed him by the shoulders.

"Who are you? What is this place?"

"Mr. Battle—"

"Let me go!"

"Let you? Why, Mr. Battle. You are free to go anytime you wish."

This was the other one, the person wearing the strange, leather outfit. He (she? It?) had removed the filter, revealing a wide mouth but nothing else.

"Sister—" Sten said.

"No. He must find out for himself." Mikael stared at her, incredulous. "Do you really think he'll believe us if we just tell him?"

Battle zeroed in on the only door in the room.

"Is that the way out?"

He'd already begun to walk towards it.

He took stock of his body as he moved. Everything hurt. His ribs, his face, his legs. The Stonehammer case was more complex than a missing girl. Who had hired Clyde and his goons to attack him like that? Who thought that kind of threat would work? He was so engrossed that he didn't hear the sounds of something huge banging on the boarded-up windows, first the one on the end, the one he'd pounded on himself, then spreading to each one, one by one. Then, finally hearing it, he stopped, his hand on the knob.

Sten was already closing the curtains. He cast a dirty look at the strange being in the middle of the room. His sister, if Battle understood correctly.

"What is that?" Battle asked.

"What, that?" Sten's sister shrugged. "Just some . . . visitors."

A wild idea struck Battle.

"Are you keeping them prisoner? Like me?"

"Prisoner?" She exchanged a look with Sten, who seemed to be stifling a laugh. "I'd say we're more captive than they are. So to speak. But do go on, Mr. Battle. See for yourself."

Battle gave them both a confused look and opened the door.

"Oh, Mr. Battle?"

Battle turned, and Sten threw him a fireplace poker. Battle snatched it out of the air. It was iron and heavy. Heavier than he thought it would be, as if it had been forged not for the fireplace but as a weapon.

"I'd give you something better, but this is all I can spare at the moment."

Battle nodded and left, closing the door solidly behind him. He found himself at the bottom of a set of stairs. He looked up. An ornate candelabra hung from the ceiling, its crystals tinkling in the stairwell. Three stories. At least.

On the other side of the stairs loomed a hallway shrouded in darkness, leading, presumably, to the living area and then the kitchen and finally the formal dining room, just like his own home. To his right, the vestibule, and beyond that, the front door and, hopefully, escape. Except the vestibule door had also been blocked, too, boarded up with even stouter beams than the windows he'd tried to escape from before.

A bay window overlooked the street. It was boarded up, too, but for one plank. Battle went to it and put his face up to the opening to see what he could see. He stayed there, trying to take it all in, his face sickly and unwell in the light glowing in the air outside.

The fireplace poker grew slick in his hand and he let it drop. Then, alarmed at the sound and the reaction of the things on the other side of the glass, he picked it up and hugged it to his chest. His heartfelt like it was about to beat out of his body, like he'd just sprinted up and down a tall incline. Which was why, when he heard the creak of the floorboard behind him, he yelped and spun around, holding the poker out like a lance.

"Disturbing isn't it?"

It was only Sten. Battle lowered the poker.

"What are those things? Wh-where did they come from?"

"That's funny," Sten said. "We were hoping you'd tell us."

Sten steered him upstairs. It was only after they reached the second turn that Battle realized how dirty the Stens kept their house. His shoes left dark footprints, and the moonlight illuminated so much dust in the air that he felt the need to cover his mouth and nose with this shirt. Sten led the way, his silver hair shimmering. He turned around once and saw Battle with his shirt over his face and smiled.

"You've a lot more to worry about than the quality of the air, Mr. Battle."

"What about the mold?"

Sten eyed the streaks and patches of black blossoming on the walls and snickered.

"Still."

The stairs ended in the middle of a hallway on the third floor. They walked down to a door at the end where Sten opened a heavy oak door. A warm glow came from inside.

"Your palace awaits," he said.

Battle stepped inside and was shocked at the difference between the cold filth in the hallway and the cozy, clean, wonderfulness of the room. Oil lamps hung on the walls and from a candelabra from the ceiling, candles sat on the tables, and a fire crackled in the fireplace. The furniture looked comfortable, if used, and a tray of fruit and nuts and savories were displayed on a silver tray on a table in the middle of it all.

"Please, help yourself," Sten said.

Battle's stomach growled, and he made fast work of an apple and a handful of nuts.

"My God, brother," a voice said. "Maybe you should have set some aside for us."

Battle turned to see who it was and saw a woman in men's trousers standing by an open door in the back next to the fireplace. Her face was fresh and ruddy, her skin gleaming, and she was wringing her long, blond hair out into a towel. She smiled at him.

"Joking, Mr. Battle. Fill your belly."

Sten put a glass of wine in his hand and Battle drank deep. It was delicious.

"Thank you," he said.

The windows in this room were not boarded up. A door opened up onto a roofed terrace. The woman saw him see it.

"Would you like to go out there?" Then, seeing his expression change as he remembered the things he'd seen pounding on the windows on the ground, "you're perfectly safe up here, Mr. Battle. They cannot climb. The walls, at least."

He nodded and followed her to the doors, which she opened dramatically, and they stepped out onto the terrace and into the cold, clear night. The temperature stole his breath, and he took a gulp of wine to warm his throat. The moon and stars glowed with an unearthly light, illuminating the familiar skyline. As if sensing his gaze, one of the silhouettes of the buildings in the distance started to sway slowly back and forth like it was waving at him. Then it toppled over. Seconds later came the rumble and crash.

"That's happening more and more," the woman said. "The streets, too. I'm surprised this one has remained intact."

"I don't know your name," Battle said.

"You don't?"

"No."

"Sister, don't tease," Sten said as he came out behind them.

"Who is teasing?"

"I apologize for her," Sten said. "She might be an able fighter, but her manners are shit."

The woman rolled her eyes at him and laughed.

"And my brother is a decaying old mossback." She went to the brick wall that encased the terrace and spread her palms flat on the surface.

"My name is Tidnsär."

"It was you, then?" Battle asked. "Who saved me from Clyde?"

"It certainly wasn't Mikael. He might have a leg up with his leap, but he's more of a diplomat."

Battle joined her and peered cautiously over the edge. The creatures below glowed pale blue in the night, a terrible and unnatural color. Most wandered around, barring those that had thronged one of the windows. Those had, for the most part, stopped beating on the broken glass, but they still milled around in the yard. He watched as one tripped over something in the grass and impaled itself on the spiked, iron fence.

"We don't know what they are," Tidsnär said. "They've been around since before I was born. Before Mikael was born, and Mikael's ancient, so if that gives you any indication."

Battle estimated her age to be in the twenties. If Mikael was older, it wasn't by much.

"So you were born before the war?" he asked.

Tidsnär smiled ruefully.

"You're talking about The Civil War."

"Depends on where you're from. The pretender likes to refer to it as 'The War of Northern Aggression'."

"I wish I was that old, Mr. Battle. If only that were possible. Unfortunately, I was born long, long after that."

"You can't be older than me, can you?"

"Certainly not."

"Then—"

Tidsnär took a deep breath.

"I'd rather wished to break this to you a little more naturally, but . . ." she leaned an elbow on the ledge to face him. "I was born in Stockholm in 1897."

"You're mad! It's 1881!"

"No, it's 1919, Mr. Battle."

"1919."

He looked all around him, wondering if this strange woman was playing games with him.

As if reading his mind, Tidsnär said, "I'm not joking, Mr. Battle. You remember Mikael in the alley when you bested him?"

Battle stared at her wonderingly.

"The same technology that he used to leap through space can be used to leap through time."

Battle had already decided to get as far away as possible as soon as possible. They were deranged. Looney. And yet, those things on the ground, the blue glow.

"I wish we had time to explain it to you in more detail, but I'm afraid we're short. You see, I'm sure you're wondering why we would save you, of all people, from the grim fate those below suffered so terribly."

"I hadn't even begun to imagine that."

"Fair enough. I'll explain it to you nonetheless. We know you were at the Battle of Washington, and we know that you suffered terrible wounds."

Battle became suddenly aware of the scars on his belly.

"We know about God's Bones, and we know that you survived because of it."

"Me and many others."

"Yes, but they all died before they even reached thirty years old. You, however, did not. You're well past thirty."

"Forty-three."

"Forty-five," she corrected. Then she gave him an apologetic look. "Slaves were not given birth certificates, as you know, but we've developed ways of figuring it out."

"How?"

"It's very technical, Mr. Battle—"

"Is this about DNA?"

For the first time, Tidsnär's superior attitude gave way to genuine surprise.

"You know about DNA?"

"Only a little of what I read. A friend of mine is an amateur scientist of sorts—"

"Yes, we know."

And they both said his name at the same time.

"Han Chen."

"Do you know him?" Battle asked.

"Do I know . . . Mr. Battle, I don't know any way of explaining what we're doing here other than stating it directly. You and Mr. Chen nearly saved the world from, well," she spread her arms out at the scene below. "This."

"Nearly saved the world."

"Yes. Unfortunately."

"How?"

"That's what we were hoping you could tell us. Before your deaths, you and Han set up four vaults filled with the cure that could defeat the evil that infested the world. Vaults one through three were lost in the war that followed, but number four remained unscathed."

Another rumble shook the night, this one closer. Battle felt the vibrations in his feet. Tidsnär wasn't as casual about this one. Indeed, she looked outright alarmed.

"I didn't see any buildings go down," Battle said.

"It's not always a building. More and more its streets. Then the buildings."

They each sipped their wine, waiting for another quake, but nothing came, and eventually, they both relaxed.

"When?" Battle asked.

"When what?"

"When did I die?"

Tidsnär looked momentarily abashed.

"If you can travel through time and space, you have to know when I died. So. When did I?"

"Well . . . when you were forty-five."

Battle let that sink in.

"Is that why you saved me from Clyde? Is he the one?"

"Oh, dear me, no. It happened well after . . . well, a few months later. Six, to be exact."

"I see. So this vault, if it still exists, if you know where it is, why not open it yourselves?"

"We've tried, Mr. Battle, believe me. The mechanism you devised is extremely personal."

"That would be Chen. He loves . . . loved . . . to tinker. Why not blow it up?"

"We've used every substance we know about to try and crack it, from acid to dynamite. Nothing works. Nothing will work, we believe, except for you. It's why you're here, Mr. Battle. You have something we need."

"What could I possibly have that you need?"

"Your arm."

He looked at her, horrified, and she shrugged.

"Or maybe just some of your blood."

The sound of a window bursting echoed into the night, glass tinkling on the street. Tidsnär cursed under her breath and leaned out over the terrace ledge. At the same moment, Mikael appeared in the doorway.

"They've breached the vestibule."

"Vestibule?" Tidsnär said, turning away from the ledge. "How? Oh, never mind. Roof or tunnel?"

"You know how much I hate flying."

"And you know how much I hate the tunnels."

"Tunnels it is, then."

She led them down a back stair three flights down, pausing at the door to the living room. She opened it a crack and peered out into the darkness. More glass broke as the creatures clawed their way inside, and a terrible smell filled the room: rot and stench of innards, and under that, the sweet, heady smell of mold.

"We're clear," Tidsnär said. She opened the door all the way, the hinges whining. "The door to the basement is just—"

A creature lurched out of the hall and fell into her, mouth chomping, nails clawing at her face. She rolled expertly on her back, taking the monster with her, and then Battle didn't see anymore because she kicked the door closed.

"What are you doing!" Mikael yelled.

"She kicked it!"

Mikael ripped Battle back and threw the door open, bursting out into the living room and shouting, "Tidsnär!"

"No need to lose your mind, brother," she said.

She appeared in the opening, her clothes, hair, and skin spattered with blood, and the tell-tale blue guts smeared everywhere else. Mikael stared at her, horrified.

"Did it? Are you?"

"No, it did not, and yes, I am."

"The fool slammed the door shut—"

"*I* kicked it closed, brother."

More glass shattered in the front of the house, followed by the cracking of wood. Tidsnär glanced at it.

"Time's up, it seems." She grabbed her brother's hand and turned to Battle. "Are you coming?"

Battle made sure to close and lock the door to the basement before going down. The air turned chilly and smelled of mold and pipes. His foot hit something that squeaked and skittered off in the dark.

At the bottom, Mikael lit a gas lantern and strode, feet crunching on the rock floor, lighting more and more lamps until the whole basement was illuminated. His sister went over to an antique chifforobe, its wood distressed with age, its doors slightly warped, and began to strip. Battle immediately turned his back out of respect, and Tidsnär saw it and laughed at him.

"Oh, please, Mr. Battle. Monsters rule the earth, civilization has broken down, and you blush at the sight of a woman's body?"

"I'm sorry. I'm just not used to . . . this."

"Fair enough."

Mikael joined her in disrobing and said something to her in their language and she laughed again.

"Leather or iron, Mr. Battle?" she asked.

"Excuse me?"

"Leather or iron? You can turn around now, I'm fully clothed."

He did. Tidsnär had stepped into her leather outfit, the one he'd first seen her wearing when she fell from the ceiling in Clyde's warehouse. The helmet, the strange apparatus that made her look like an insect, hung off the back, bobbing as she moved. She held up another suit similar to hers.

"Leather?" Then she nodded at her brother. Mikael had donned several parts of a suit of iron: breastplate, gauntlets, vambraces, pauldrons, and grieves. "Or iron?"

"Why doesn't he just use his magic button?"

"It's not a magic button, Mr. Battle," Mikael said. "It's science. And all the science in the world won't help me when I'm taken by surprise."

The armor certainly looked difficult to pierce, but also clunky and unwieldy. And the leather looked tight and uncomfortable.

"Neither, thank you very much."

The siblings exchanged a dubious glance.

"Mr. Battle, I don't think you understand —"

"I understand just fine, thank you very much."

"If it's the undressing that bothers you—"

"Nothing bothers me. I'll go as I am."

Tidsnär looked dumbfounded and Mikael whispered something that sounded like "idiot" under his breath.

"Suit yourself. No pun intended." She put the extra leather suit back into the chifforobe. More footsteps overhead. A lamp crashed to the floor in a distant part of the house. "Come along, then," she said, moving toward the back of the basement. Battle started to follow her, but Mikael stepped in front of him.

"One scratch and I'm putting you down." Battle stared into his eyes, refusing to back down. "No offense."

"None taken." He made sure to bump the man's shoulder as he pushed by. "I'll be sure to do you the same."

The tunnel emptied into an alley behind the house. One of the creatures was hiding behind a back staircase, and Tidsnär dispatched it with a pair of knives that seemed to spring out of her suit. Another leaped on Mikael from behind, but rather than fight it off, he used his machine to transport himself out in front of his sister, and the monster collapsed upon Battle, who was in the process of spinning around to see what had made such a ghastly noise.

But Battle, who had been in more fights than he could remember, didn't panic. He remembered his training. Not, ironically, his military training, not necessarily, but his training in the ring. He stunned the beast by shoving it off of him, and when it came for him again, he delivered what he thought would be a solid punch to the nose, but instead of stunning it or knocking it silly, he decapitated the thing. The stump where its head used to be spurted blood, and Battle stepped aside as the body dropped to its knees and fell onto the cobblestones. Then he looked up at Tidsnär, who hadn't even the time to do anything more than take one step forward to help him before it was all over.

"I don't think I've ever punched anyone's head off before," he said.

"I don't think I've ever seen anyone punch somebody's head off before."

"Cheers to firsts, then."

Mikael was already at the alley's end, having not even stuck around to see if Battle was okay.

The streets were, for the most part, empty. Mikael kept to the shadows and doorways, moving swiftly. Tidsnär tried to fill Battle in on what they were doing as they made their way through the city. Though over a quarter-century had supposedly passed, and though many of the buildings had suffered the effects of whatever catastrophe had been loosed upon the world, he still recognized much of the landscape across which they traveled.

Here was Moshe's kosher deli where he bought his knish, there was Jackson's BBQ, home of the best mac and cheese in the city, there was the constabulary where he cut his teeth as an officer. The streets were littered with body parts and offal and all kinds of brick and wood and shattered glass. The buildings, those which still stood, looked about to collapse, and many sections of the road had caved-in.

After several blocks of creeping and slinking and once, yes, even crawling, Mikael's body lost all pretense of stealthiness, and he stood up straight, rolled his shoulders, and jogged out into the middle of the street, and yelled, "Hello!"

"Mikael!" Tidnär hissed. "Stop!"

"Hello!" he cried again, turning in circles. "Free lunch! Come and get it!"

Tidsnär put a bracing arm out and backed herself and Battle up against one of the still-standing buildings left on the block, taking care to hunch into a dark corner untouched by the bright moonlight. They waited. And waited.

And nothing happened. Battle cleared his throat.

"What are we—"

"Shh!"

"Nothing seems—"

"Mr. Battle, if my brother wants to be an idiot, that's fine, but you are too important."

Mikael removed his helm and spread his gauntleted arms.

"Nothing! They're gone!"

"They're not gone, Mikael!"

The ground began to shake, lightly at first, but growing in intensity.

"Mikael, get over here now!"

He was frozen in the middle of the street, hands out for balance. Blocks and bricks from the buildings around them fell from the sky. One landed right in front of Tidsnär, sending her leaping backwards. Another struck Battle's shoulder and knocked him to the ground. The shaking grew more violent. Wood creaked and cracked, metal moaned. It sounded like a dying leviathan. He saw a flitting image of Tidsnär leaping out into the street, then more debris fell from the sky. The earthquake reached its peak and then, just as fast as it started, it was over.

Battle struggled to get up. His shoulder felt like it was dislocated, and then he realized that it really was dislocated, and then he enjoyed the wonderful sensation of it slipping back into its socket all on its own accord with no consideration of his preference.

"Mikael!" he called, stumbling out into the street. "Tidsnär!"

The dust and dirt clouded the air making it nearly impossible to see where he was going. Then the building against which he had taken cover, a narrow, two-level townhouse, shifted and moaned and fell into the empty lot next to it, and the force created by the fall blew the dust and dirt momentarily clear of his path, and he saw, if only for a second, that he was standing on the brink of a massive canyon. A hole had opened up in the earth at his feet, and it was hundreds of feet deep. He saw no sign or trace of the siblings. That wasn't what disturbed him the most, however. What disturbed him the most was the howling blue glow pulsing at the bottom of whatever abyss they had fallen into.

The walk to Han's den was fraught with anxiety. Battle expected to be attacked at every intersection and every dark corner. The closer he got, the more impassable the streets became. First it was deep cracks in the road, then fallen buildings and their associated debris, and finally blockades—some professionally constructed (he'd built them himself during the war), some thrown desperately together.

The most curious thing Battle noticed was the lack of bodies. War, at least war as he knew it, was notorious for its contempt of the living, and it was even more contemptuous for the leftover vessels it so casually destroyed. Philadelphia. Wilderness. Spotsylvania. Washington. He remembered the stench as his brothers rotted (sometimes dead, sometimes alive), the cries, the moans, the pitiful whimpers. He remembered his wound, his belly covered with blood.

Before Tidsnär and Mikael brought him to this place, rescued him from a certain (and certainly painful) death at the dastardly hands of Clyde Barley, the lack of all of that would have puzzled and concerned him to no end. But now that he'd seen what he'd seen, knew what he knew, well, he might still have been concerned, but his puzzlement had dissipated into the boundless chasm.

Han's den stood alone, a true bastion amongst the rubble, exactly has Tidsnär described it. He had to wrench the old door open, and the frame cracked and dust and dirt sifted down from the awning above. He half-expected Ushi to come babbling out of the back, yelling at him as she usually did, disturbing the addicts in their daily repose, but he was only met with complete and utter darkness. It was so complete that the farther in he crept, the more he felt as though he was floating in a void. Until he barked his shin on something heavy and sharp and wood and cried out and fell to the floor, writhing.

"Confounded mess!"

Shin wounds were the worst. How had his maker felt it so necessary to bundle the most sensitive nerves in the body around such an unprotected bone? He'd seen men's shins explode before, shattered by Minié balls, fractured by bullets, and though he knew what had just happened to him was in no way similar, he couldn't help but make the connection. Still, his leg hurt. Hurt bad. His pant leg was already wet with blood, and when he stood up, he could barely put any weight on it. A rumble in the distance shook the building, and glass and crystals tinkled overhead. Hinges from some dark recess of the den whined and Battle, before he could catch himself, said, "Hello?" He clapped his hand over his mouth.

It was as if his voice had unleashed a caged beast, which, in a way, it had. He heard grunts and heavy breaths and the sounds of furniture —the addicts' chaise lounges and reclining chairs—being thrown against the wall. Even more terrifying was the glow, the pale blue glow, that preceded the creature responsible for the destruction. Panicked, Battle lurched for the back, heading, he hoped for Han's office.

The monster must have heard him because it let out a terrifying screech, and then the noise of it busting its way through the den increased in volume and violence. It screeched again when it saw him, and he turned and saw a massive figure barreling for him. But where before he couldn't see where he was, how far or near to safety he stood, now the glow lit the den up enough so that he could make the door to Han's office only a few feet away. He hopped forward, vaulting along on one foot, wondering when he'd feel the thing's claws bite into his shoulder and rip his arm to shreds. But the door was right there, and it wasn't closed all the way, and Battle threw himself at it then spun and slammed it closed. The beast thundered into it seconds later, throwing him backwards and onto his rear, but the door held, mercifully. At least for the moment.

The window provided enough light for him to see Han's safe standing in its usual place behind his desk. It was still as massive as it always was, with its impressive complex of Chinese characters weaving their way through each other, and the gold inlay Tree of Life seemed to glow in the moonlight, little rills of electricity running along the edges of the design.

But the socket was gone.

The monster thundered away at the door behind him. He heard the wood crack.

How? How was he supposed to open it? He shook his head, at a complete loss of what to do next, and, partly out of desperation, partly out of frustration, he put his hand on the Tree of Life icon and sighed.

Something thunked deep in the bass heart of the safe, and then ticking noises came, and the icon separated and a black hole formed beneath his now shaking hand.

The monster was now halfway through the door, its fists bloodied, its skin hanging off it in strips. Battle took a deep breath and let it out. Then he plunged his arm into the socket. It kept going and going until he'd placed his arm in up to his shoulder so that his cheek rested against the cold metal of the safe.

Nothing happened.

The monster kicked the last of the door away.

Battle closed his eyes.

"Please, please, please," he whispered.

Then he felt the grip and closed his hand around it. The machinery inside the safe thunked again and his arm was squeezed by something thick and terrible. Thousands of teeth bit into his flesh and he felt them pumping liquid into his body. He started to scream, and then he was consumed by a hot light that ate him from the inside out, and he disappeared into a deep, dark, terrible place.

GOD'S BONES
An Assemblage of Heroes

The dream started as it always did. He was lying on the battlefield, wounded and sick with it. He knew there was something wrong with his stomach. It felt loose, jumbled. But he didn't want to look down. He couldn't look down. All around him he heard the moans of the dying as the sun slowly lowered over the horizon. The sound of the flies buzzing drove him mad. He could feel them crawling around on him, flitting on his skin, tickling his insides. Then came the glow. The strange, blue glow . . .

And for the first time, the dream shifted, changed. He was no longer a dead man on the battlefield. He was standing in a room, a very important room (his dream logic told him that). Men with grim faces stood around a desk at which sat the tallest, gangliest person he'd ever seen. He recognized the gaunt features, the nearly concave cheeks, the hollow eyes weary with the burden of the

431

nation. He pinpointed one of the other men with them.

"I don't understand what you're saying, William. That we could . . . weaponize this?"

The man to whom he spoke, William, stood with his back to Battle so that he couldn't see his face. He was short in stature but stood tall and confident before his peers and his superior.

"That's exactly what I'm saying, sir. Those men, you didn't see them. I did. They were . . . there was no hope left for them. Some we could save, but there were just too many. If they weren't going to die from their injuries, they were going to die of infection."

"I saw the battlefield, son. I toured it myself. I know what those poor boys suffered."

"Not before it happened. You only saw the half of it. They lived! They lived, sir! We left them there to die because there wasn't anything we could do, but they didn't die. The next morning . . . we found them alive. Alive and well. Some even stood up and walked themselves to the surgery . . . but there was nothing to be done."

The gaunt man rubbed his eyes, beyond weariness.

"Yes, yes. The legend of God's Bones. God's mercy."

"Lee is coming. And Cambridge. They're coming to take the capital."

"And we'll be waiting for them."

"With what? An army of untrained slaves? They hardly stand a chance. Let me give it to them. It will make them invincible. I promise you this."

The gaunt man sat for a long time, pondering his options. Eventually, he sighed and said, "Desperation calls for desperation."

"Does . . . does that mean you approve?"

The question was confirmed with a barely perceptible nod.

"Thank you, sir. Thank you. You will not be displeased. I promise you that."

The dream changed again, and somehow Battle knew it was sometime after The Battle of Washington. The gaunt man looked as tired and wasted as ever, but now he was standing and his eyes blazed with fury. He leaned forward on his desk, planting both fists on the surface, looking like he was about to devour William who trembled on the opposite side.

"How dare you make me an accomplice to this horror, this abomination, this obscenity!"

"Mr. President, sir, I-I-I—"

"You what? Don't tell me you didn't know! You promised me! Invincible soldiers, you said. Not monsters!"

"There must have been a glitch in the formula, sir. The early tests—"

"Early tests be damned! As are all of you. All of us, myself included. We have conspired against God to create these vulgar things, and mark my words, there will be retribution."

"Pardon me, Mr. President," a different man said. He was tall and well-built, an aging man be still fit and in his prime. By the stripes on his uniform, Battle took him to be one of the more important generals in the room. The president glared at him, but seeing who spoke up, stopped his rage and conceded the floor.

"You are right about these . . . things. They are an imprecation in the face of our creator. But William does have a point. We beat them. We flattened their forces into the earth, sent the rest running for old Dixie. I hear Cambridge is licking his wounds in Norfolk. Lee is holding the line in Fredericksburg, but just barely. If we—"

"No."

"But, sir—"

"No! I will not hear it! I will not loose such profanity upon the world again. This Union will hold by the strength of its people, its *living* people, or it does not deserve to hold at all. Have I made myself clear?"

The general, clearly angered, biting back his retort, nodded once, a short, clipped affair.

The president straightened. Now that he had won the argument, all of the weariness seemed to seep back into his body. His shoulders stooped. His dark eyes grew even darker. He sat down, heavy and sad, in his chair.

"I would have a few moments, gentlemen," he said.

"Of course, sir."

The other men, generals, advisors, and other statesmen, murmured their farewells as they left, but one stayed behind. The short man, William. The president pressed his lips together.

"What more do you want, William?"

"Nothing, sir. I don't mean to bother you anymore, but . . ."

"Yes?"

"What will you have us do with the rest?"

"There are more!"

"Why, yes, sir. Those that didn't perish in the battle. A-and, of course, the reinforcements."

"Reinforcements!"

For a moment, it seemed as though the president was about to leap across his desk and throttle his tormentor right then and there. Then he calmed himself, swallowed the anger.

"Destroy them," he said.

"Destroy them? But, sir—"

"Try my patience no longer, William."

"Of course, but you see . . ."

"I said no more!"

"Yes. Yes. My apologies. It's just . . . how would you have me do it, sir?"

"Do I need to spell out every detail? Blast them, shoot them, burn them to crisps for all I care!"

"Burn them? I'm afraid that won't—"

"You created the blasted things, didn't you?"

"Yes, sir."

"Then find a way! Now get out!"

"But—"

"Out!"

Finally, William turned to leave, exposing his face to Battle . . .

. . . who found himself floating again inside a blinding white light, formless, voiceless. It was warm in the void, and though he was naked and his arms outstretched, the light caressed him, blanketed him. He felt no shame or fear, just peace. All around him thrummed rhythm of life, a muted heartbeat, bum bum, bum bum, bum bum, bum bum, the wash and hush of the ocean, and above that, the low notes of a piano, sad, slow, sonorous. He felt all things and nothing. He was conscious of only his body, but his body was no more than light, warm and ensconced in the womb.

Pearled ether floated around him like clear globs of mercury, mutating, shifting, crashing into one another to form new shapes before splitting in two and rolling off away from one another. Flaxen haired angels sang in the heavens above, their faces haloed by the purest of light, sending balls of electric blue energy into the air to cascade down onto Battle's body, and they burned and blackened his skin, and he screamed as they burrowed through the scars on his belly, eating away at the tissue until his organs were exposed, and the blue turned into a glowing, carpet of moss that covered him and burned and healed, healed and melted, until the light began to fade and the pain radiated up through his torso and into his arm, the arm he'd left in Han's vault in that cursed city of the future, and his veins were filled with fire and his mouth opened wide in a terrified scream and then he was in Han's office and Han was standing with his back to him playing with chemicals at his work station and Ushi by the door watching as Sebastian Battle, Civil War veteran, hero of the Battle of Washington cum private detective, apparated before her eyes, his arm jammed into the bio-lock apparatus one of her husband's most precious experimental vaults. Han turned as if his sudden appearance were a normal thing.

"Ah, Mr. Battle. So good of you to come. Come. Come here. Let me show you my latest discovery."

Ushi, cognizant, perhaps, of the tremendous pain Battle must have been in, bustled over.

"Quiet your babbling, Han. Mr. Battle needs help."

Han seemed to see his friend's predicament for the first time and joined his wife as she fussed around the vault.

"Turn it off, turn it off!" he yelled at her.

"I am turning it off!"

"If you had turned it off, it would be off now."

"Stop saying stupid things, Han, and help me with the leaver."

"It's stuck."

"I know it's stuck! The lock is made for your arm, not his!"

"I don't see how that matters."

"Your arm is skinny. Mr. Battle's, not so much."

Han began to protest but then something thunked heavily in the guts of the safe and Ushi gave a cry of triumph. Air hissed as if a pressure valve had been released, and more mechanical sounds cranked and turned and sang, and then Battle was free and his arm fell out of the socket and he slumped to the ground. His shirt sleeve was shredded, his arm covered in blood. Bruises and puncture wounds wound around it from his finger-tips to his shoulder, like a twisting cascade of screws had been turned into his meat and bones. He held his hand up before him and inspected the holes in his body, surprised he could even lift his arm.

"What is that godforsaken thing?"

Both Chens cried out in dismay, as if he'd insulted their grandparents.

"You watch your mouth, Mr. Battle," Ushi snapped. "The very fact that you arrived here the way you did means this 'Godforsaken thing' saved your life, eh?"

Battle rubbed his wrist. The wounds itched, but now that his arm was no longer in the

439

lock-trap, the pain had lessened significantly. His arm no longer hurt at all. The vault door stood open a crack, and he thought he saw several glass vials sitting on the shelf inside. He got to his feet and pointed at them.

"What are those?"

"Ah! It's done! My special formula, I think, yes?"

This was Han. Ushi tsked and opened the door all the way.

"Your formula, your formula."

Han ignored her as she took one of the vials out.

"Look, Han," She held it up to him. "It's *your* formula."

"That's not what I meant and you know it."

"I do all the work and you get all the credit."

"That's not true!"

"Oh? 'My formula. My formula.' Isn't that what you just said?"

"What would you like me to say, dear? 'I worked on the formula but my wife provided some of the ancient molds'?"

"It's a start."

"You know where I was," Battle said. "Don't you?"

"Where you were?"

"Before I appeared here."

"Mr. Battle, I can assure you—"

"You can assure me? What exactly can you assure me? That you didn't seem surprised at all when I materialized of nowhere?"

Han tried to maintain eye contact, but he shook a glance at his wife again.

"They took me there," Battle said.

"Who took you where?"

"Mikael and Tidsnär. They took me to the future."

"Future? Oh, Mr. Battle, surely you're telling stories."

Battle grabbed Han by the shirt and yanked him closer.

"I am not telling stories. I saw those . . . things. They told me you had the cure, that it was in that safe. That safe right there."

Han looked at his wife again, a hard look this time. He rolled his eyes from her to Battle.

"Okay, fine," she said. "We know."

Han seemed to relax and inflate at the same time.

"Oh, thank goodness. I thought I was going to have to play this silly game forever." Gone was his accent, his sheepishness. Yes, Mr. Battle. We know about the future. We know about what the horrible mold does to people."

"Mikael and Tidsär," Ushi asked. "They are okay?"

"Wait . . . so, you're both from the future, too?"

Han exchanged another look with his wife.

"Why, yes. Didn't Tidsnär or Mikael . . ."

"She mentioned you."

"Mentioned me?" He snorted. "Mentioned me. Of course they 'mentioned' me."

He went over to his worktable and started to aggressively reorganize things.

"Nothing's ever good enough for those two. Him with his jumper and her with that silly outfit. Who developed the formula? Who spent years in this place, waiting for the proper vessel to—"

"Han!" Ushi snapped.

He fell silent, leaning heavily on the edge of the desk.

"Please, Mr. Battle. Sebastian. Are they okay? Is Mikael . . ."

"I don't know."

She looked stricken.

"What does that mean? What happened?"

"We were heading here, to unlock that vault. Mikael . . . I don't know what he was doing. Showing off? He was in the street, yelling for those things to come get him. Maybe he was just blowing off steam. There were rumbles, an earthquake, I think. Tidsnär ran for him. And then . . . they were gone. I came here and found the safe in the ruins."

Battle watched as several emotions ran through Ushi's face. Then, wiping away a tear, she said, "was the plan to bring the cure back?"

"I don't know. They said it contains the weapons that will stop the creatures, but all you have are those vials."

"But if they say the weapons are in there, the weapons are in there."

Han recovered from his muttering enough to face the other two again.

"Then the vials are the weapon. My formula—"

"Your formula. Your formula."

". . . *our* formula is the weapon."

They paused as they let it sink in. Ushi rolled the vial between her fingers.

"Han, it's no good without the accelerant."

"I told you, we don't need it."

"Yes, we do. Every test—"

"Just let me see it."

She tossed it to him.

"Are you going to add the accelerant?"

"Let's see if we need to."

Han gestured for them to come over to his work station. There, lying on a wooden cutting board, lay two rodents. One had been gutted, its innards turned to outards as it were, barbarically achieved, as well, as if he'd repeatedly plunged a knife into the poor thing. The other had suffered the same fate; however, rather than leave it to its peace, he had dissected it, pinned its legs back to expose its sliced open belly, laying bare its mysterious inner-workings, its lungs and liver, stomach and spleen. And covering it was a substance with which Battle should have been familiar. He'd seen it in the horror of the future, seen it on the field at Washington, seen it populating his guts. A blue, mossy substance, nearly carpeting the entire cavity. Indeed, it had attached itself to organ and vein, whatever tissue it could find, sprouting up through the disaster, not so much healing as patching, binding ragged edge to ragged edge, bridging the multiple sliced tubes and tunnels of the body, the fleshy globs that gave life, even, Battle noticed, wrapping itself around and piercing through those parts that had not been cut or bashed or squashed. It spread from the torso, up its esophagus and into, he imagined, its jaw, mouth, sinuses, and finally, its brain. The poor creature smelled terrible, too—not just because of the exposed innards, but because of the blue stuff.

All of it, the science project, the guts, the invasive vegetation, the smell, all of it would have been perfectly scientific were it not for the fact that the poor thing's heart was still beating.

"God's Bones, Han," Battle said.

"Yes, Mr. Battle. Exactly."

Battle inspected the rodent closer. Its eyes had rolled back in its head, exposing the whites, and it twitched its whiskers, feeling the air. He ran his fingers past them and it lunged for them, trying to bite him. Not an entirely odd reaction considering its restrained state, but the aggression unnerved him.

"Here is the most miraculous thing of all," Han said.

He pulled out another rodent out of a nearby box, holding it around the neck so it couldn't bite him. It was whole and alive, and it squeaked and peddled its feet in the air, mouth working. Han nodded at the two creatures on the board. "Step one and step two," he said. Then he held the third rat up at them. "Step three. Now, observe."

And with one quick motion, he broke the third rodent's neck. It squeaked in pain and shock and fell limp in his hands. Han set it on the work station next to its brothers where it lay inert.

"Was that entirely—"

"Shh! Watch."

Battle did. The rodent lay still for some time, seconds probably, but what seemed longer. Then its neck spasmed, once, twice, and he heard the little bones of its spine crack and pop as it realigned and straightened. Its legs twitched, its lungs filled, and it was on its feet again in seconds, whiskers twitching. Han reached for it but it evaded his grasp, darting this way and that on the work station. This, to Battle, was not unusual. Rodents often fled the clutches of a superior predator. What was unusual, however, was the fact that once it reached the end of the table, it didn't jump and continue to run. It turned, faced its attacker, and leaped for him.

It must have surprised Han as much as it did Battle because he cried out and swatted the thing with the back of his hand. It flew through the air, hitting the wall with a thud and a squeak, and fell to the floor.

"The serum!" Han cried.

Ushi was there. She uncorked one of the vault vials and poured it over the creature, which was still lying stunned on the floor. It began to smoke and sizzle, but that was about it. It leaped for Ushi, who dodged it, then floundered under the work station and fell over onto its side, lungs pumping like a piston. It's breathing slowed, then hitched, then stopped altogether. Ushi shot Han a look.

"You're right," Han said. "Maybe I should . . ."

". . . get the accelerant."

He busied himself at his desk, first completing some equations, then searching for specific ingredients from a locker filled with vials.

"That was one angry rat," Battle said, still shocked at what he'd seen.

"Oh, yes. Oh, yes," Ushi replied. "It's because of the worms."

"The worms?"

He looked down at his own body, terrified.

"Nematodes, to be exact. They're microscopic. They vomit a bioluminescent bacteria that—" She saw him thinking, his wide eyes betraying understanding and terror, and placed a comforting hand on his arm. "Don't worry, Mr. Battle. They cannot survive above 96 degrees. Whatever bacteria you had inside you died a long, long time ago."

On the list of the many unexpected things Battle experienced in his life, his escape to freedom, his recovery from the wounds that should have killed him, a visit to the future only to find it a nightmare of destruction and horror, the house in which Jeremiah Kelly lived was not even close to the top.

Located on the upper south side of the city, Kelly lived in a five-story brownstone with a bay window on the third floor, a private garden on the ground level, and probably at least ten thousand square feet of finished living space. A low fence, maybe four feet tall, iron, spike topped, ran along the width of the sidewalk. Nominally a sweatshop owner, the house belied a different level of financial success altogether.

Ushi and Battle stood at the gate that separated master and mistress from peasant and rabble and looked up at the dark windows. In their hands, they each held more common defensive measures: a revolver for the detective, a short sword for Ushi. But they also each held a satchel filled with little vials of formula. Battle had yet to get over the change in her demeanor. The cantankerous wife had been replaced by a level-headed leader who appeared to have more power and intelligence than the man he'd considered for years to be a brilliant scientist.

"We will go in together, Mr. Battle," she said.

"He'll have guards, you know. Those things."

She held up her bag of serum, and the vials clinked inside.

"That is what the formula is for."

"Very well. If you're ready?"

Ushi took a deep breath and focused on the door. She looked like she was about to charge into the house.

"Ready."

Battle cast a confused look at her, then turned, grabbed the knocker, and knocked three times.

"Oh," Ushi said, feeling foolish.

They waited a while, and when it was clear that nobody was coming, Battle knocked again, harder this time, so hard, in fact, that the door slowly opened, the hinges whining. It was dark inside. All they could see was the hallway that led farther back, the staircase on the left, and the opening to the parlor on the right. Battle cocked his gun and gripped his back of serum.

"Should we go in?" Ushi asked.

"Shh!"

He'd tilted his head, listening to something.

"What is it?"

"You can't hear it?"

"No."

"It sounds like . . . breathing. Heavy breathing."

They peered into the darkness. Seconds ticked by. Battle closed out the world, dampened every noise, focused his hearing, pinpointed, narrowed.

Two eyes lit up in the dark hall. Bright blue, glowing and luminescent. Then the monster they were attached to sprinted into the daylight. It was a woman, or it had been. It was pale as death, its hollow cheeks and emaciated frame riddled with sores and ulcers. It screeched as it ran for them.

Battle fired and missed, fired again and hit its leg. It should have knocked the thing down but all it did was knock it sideways. It kept coming for them. It lunged forward. And now it was five feet from the open door. Three feet. Battle closed one eye and aimed. This was it. This one had to count. The creature leaped for him. He exhaled. Pulled the trigger.

It collapsed into him, hitting with full force, and they flew backwards, airborne, where his shoulder thudded onto one of the spiked rungs of the iron fence, and the rung exited out through the back of the beast that attacked him. Even that didn't stop its jaws from snapping, its claws from carving and Battle, with his last ounce of strength, pressed the thing off him and held it at arm's length. Then, using his right foot, he pushed himself off the iron rung. It made a sucking sound and the two of them, man and monster, tumbled forward. Battle hit his head on the ground and collapsed onto the twisting thing, the vials in his satchel cracking open and spilling out into its open guts.

Ushi grabbed him by the shoulder rolled him off as the creature jerked and shuddered. It was melting. Its face and exposed skin bubbled and smoked as serum worked through tissue. Soon it was nothing more than a puddle of guts and melted goo on the walk. Battle lay still on his back, unconscious, his gun resting in his open fingers.

"Well, well, well," someone said. "Looks like we got here just in time."

Ushi looked up.

Clyde Barley and his two goons, Bruiser and Buster, were standing there, looking with disgust that the bubbling mass of skin and bone and brain at their feet. Barley's face still bore the swelling and bruises from the beating Tidsnär delivered him.

"Hey, Mr. Clyde," Buster said. "What happened that lady?" Buster said.

"Looks like she got herself melted."

"Yeah, but how?"

"I got here same time as you, didn't I?"

"Oh, yeah. Smells bad, Mr. Clyde."

"It sure does."

Ushi stood up and reached for her weapon, but Barley had already drawn his own: a snub-nosed revolver that seemed to appear out of nowhere.

"Uh, uh, uh," he said.

"What do you want, Barley?"

"You the one who did this to my face? Gave me a goose egg on my head?"

"I don't know what you're talking about."

"You got a goose egg on your head, Mr. Clyde?"

"Shut up, Buster."

"But—"

"Bruiser!"

"It's a figure of speech, Buster," Bruiser said. "It means he's got a big bruise."

"Oh. Oh, I get it!"

Barley addressed Ushi.

"You're Han's slat, ain't you? I thought all you goo goos only spoke Mongoloid."

"You were mistaken."

"I bet." He gestured to the rapidly deflating mass of smoking tissue that used to be a woman. "That stuff gonna melt us, too?"

"Try it and see," Ushi replied.

"No thanks." He raised the gun and cocked it. "You do it."

She sneered at him, then leaned over and flattened her palm on the remains. Nothing happened.

"Good," Barley said. "Buster, Bruiser, pick him up." When they didn't immediately move, he turned around and said, "Get to it, numbskulls!"

Buster pointed.

"Uh, Mr. Clyde?"

He turned around, and Ushi was already running in the opposite direction. He fired a few shots at her, and then she ducked around the corner.

"Want us to get her, Mr. Clyde?" Bruiser asked.

"Nah." He fixed his attention back on Battle. "We got what we wanted."

Bruiser stepped around the boiling mass that used to be a human being, scooped Battle off the ground and threw him over his shoulder.

"You want I should pick up his bag?"

Barley thought for a second. He looked at the bubbling goo.

"Couldn't hurt."

The voices came to Battle out of the fog of his unconsciousness.

"Hey, wake up!"

"Maybe you should hit him, Bruiser."

"That'll just knock him out again."

"He's already knocked out, Bruiser."

"That's my point."

"I don't get it."

"Christ Jesus, Bruiser." This was Barley. "Just wake him up already."

"I'm trying, Mr. Clyde, but he's out cold."

"Well, warm him up then."

"I'm not sure that'll work, Mr. Clyde." (Buster). "I get sleepy when I'm warm."

"That's not what I meant."

"Huh?"

"Bruiser!"

"It's another figure of speech, Buster."

"Oh. Oh, I get it."

He didn't.

Battle took a deep breath and let his eyes flutter open.

"Hey, look at that," Buster said. "He's all warmed up now!"

Battle's head felt like it had been bashed into the ground, which, of course, it had. His shoulder was sore and throbbing, and he felt an itch deep in his bones and muscles that was somehow worse than the pain. He flexed his hands against the restraints—they'd tied him to a chair. Again. He was in the middle of a cavernous warehouse. Again. Kelly's sweatshop. All of the tables had been cleared out along with everything else. A pile of lumber sat near the exit.

Bruiser was kneeling in front of him, Barley and Buster standing a few feet behind. Battle thought he saw pity in the first goon's eyes, pity and concern.

"Got himself a head injury, Mr. Clyde."

"Oh, good. Then we're almost even." Clyde brushed his heavy aside and backhanded Battle, rocking his head in a semicircle. "That's for what that freak friend of yours did to my face." He made a fist and punched him in the eye. "That, too."

Battle let his head hang to the right. He spit blood. His eye had already begun to swell, he could feel it.

"I take it this isn't about the money?"

"Oh, we're long past the money. Like, Timbuktu past it."

"Where's that, Mr. Clyde?"

"I dunno, China or someplace."

"That's far away, Mr. Clyde."

"That's the point, Buster."

"So this is it, then?" Battle said. "You're going to kill me?"

"I was. I was. But then I sold you to someone who wanted it more."

"Sold me? I thought you said this wasn't about money."

"Everything's about money, even when it isn't."

Buster frowned at that one.

"You'll never get me past the Line."

"Past the Line? You're not even getting past the line that marks the exits, stupid."

"Who did you sell me to?"

As if to answer, Barley looked past his head.

"Me, Mr. Battle."

Battle turned around as far as he could. It was Jeremiah Kelly, of course.

"Surprised?"

Battle was not, but that wasn't what he was thinking about. He was thinking about his wounds. He'd expected the pain in his shoulder to flare up, but it didn't. He didn't feel any pain there at all. And other than the recent face-pummeling Clyde Barley delivered him, his head didn't seem to hurt anymore either.

"No. Not at all. I was hoping to find you."

Kelly appeared momentarily disappointed then quashed it. He held out his arms.

"Ta-da," he sang. Buster smiled, eyes alight. When Kelly didn't get the reaction he'd hoped for from Battle, he frowned. Then he removed a pouch from his jacket pocket and approached Barley. "For your effort, sir."

Barley nodded at Bruiser, who took it.

"You got a table around here we can use?"

"I assure you, Mr. Barley, I've included the full amount."

"All the same."

For a moment, Kelly's confident demeanor fell. Then he bowed.

"Very well then." He gestured. "I have no tables. The floor will have to suffice."

Barley, irritated, pressed his lips together. Then he shrugged.

"Okay. Buster. Bruiser. Chop chop."

Kelly turned his attention to Battle.

"I must admit, Mr. Battle, I'm rather impressed with your sleuthing. You made it much further than I anticipated."

"I take it you're getting out of the sweatshop business. Tired of taking advantage of poor immigrants?"

"Getting out of the . . . oh, sir. I'm not getting out of anything. Moving, yes, but never stopping."

"I know what you did to us."

"To whom?"

"Us. Lincoln's Boys. You poisoned us all."

Kelly's mouth opened in surprise before he resolutely closed it—a small gesture, no doubt, but enough to satisfy Battle.

"He was right not to let you do it."

"Who was right?"

"Lincoln."

Now Kelly couldn't contain his surprise. He stared, dumbfounded, at Battle. Then he laughed.

"My goodness, you are good. Very good. Let me ask you this, Mr. Battle. If our dear, failure of a president was so right, then why are we still a nation divided? Had he listened to me, he would have preserved the Union. But alas, his racism and outsized ego, or as he politically put it, his 'morality,' got in the way. And where is he now? Licking his wounds in Canada."

"Better that than to be held responsible for the destruction of the human race."

Kelly's anger suddenly rose up inside him.

"There were fail safes in place! I made sure of it! He was just too stubborn to understand!" He stopped himself and chuckled. "Dear me. You're just like him, aren't you? Him and his advisors. They always were able to tease out the worst in me. Oh well, it doesn't matter anymore. Quite done yet, Mr. Barley?"

"Give us a minute."

Kelly checked his pocket watch.

"I'm afraid I only have five."

"Is a one more than five?"

"The way you're counting, it is."

"This guy," Barley muttered. "Alright, you two. Hurry it up."

"Yes, sir, Mr. Clyde."

Kelly replaced his pocket watch and scanned the rafters, a slight look of discomfort passing over his face.

"I was once a patriot, Mr. Battle, yes. Now that I've gotten older, I see how foolish I was. Union. Confederacy. They're just excuses for the powerful to manipulate the poor, and that's who I fight for. The poor."

"By turning them into monsters?"

"A small price to pay to get rid of the oppressors. God's Bones might be a particularly brutal way to end it, but they'll thank me in the long run."

"They'll all be dead."

"The fail safes—"

"The fail safes don't work."

"How could you possibly know that?"

"I traveled to the future. I've seen it."

Kelly looked at him for a moment, and then he burst out laughing.

"Forgive me, Mr. Battle, but you almost had me believing for a second. I admit my creatures are marvels of science, but science is fact. Time travel is fiction. Now if you'll excuse me—" A gun was pressed against his temple. Clyde Barley's gun. "I'm not sure what you're doing, Mr. Barley. The money's all there."

"Yeah, it is."

"Do you mean to renege on our deal? That won't work out for you in the end."

"Shut up." Then, to Battle. "I don't like the sound of what he's talking about. What's he talking about?"

"It's too much to sum up."

"I ain't stupid. Try me."

"He's talking about End Times."

"End Times?" Barley gave Kelly a disgusted look. "This prick?"

In one swift gesture, Kelly ducked and grabbed Barley's wrist. Barley's finger squeezed the trigger, and the gun went off. Buster grunted. Kelly delivered a chop to Barley's throat and Barley dropped his weapon.

"Sorry to have to leave you boys," Kelly said, holding the gun level as he backed away.

"But my girls will be here soon, and I don't want to be here when they arrive." He kicked the exit door open with his foot. "And neither will you."

Then he popped out and slammed the door shut behind him. Battle heard the lock click, followed by a rumbling and tumbling that could only be the sound of whatever heavy items, furniture, shelves, other gear Kelly had pulled down to block the way.

Barely cleared his throat. His breathing was raspy and harsh, and his voice when he spoke was hoarse. "What's that supposed to mean?"

A metallic crash came from the dark half of the warehouse floor, like a half dozen iron doors had just been thrown open.

"Clyde," Battle said. "Get me out of this."

"What is that?" Barley asked. He got up and moved toward the source of the sound. Battle started to hop around, hoping to break the chair legs.

"Clyde, don't . . . dammit. Bruiser. Help me."

But Bruiser ignored him. He was busily wrapping a tourniquet around Buster's arm.

"What is it, Mr. Clyde?"

Barley shook his head. He jogged over to the exit and rammed his shoulder into it. The door opened a crack but no farther. And as

Battle struggled against his restraints, and as Barley struggled against the door, and as Buster tried to process the pain of his wound, a dozen blue eyes lit up in the ebon darkness of the warehouse. Battle saw it. So did Bruiser.

"Uh, Mr. Clyde?"

"What?"

A feral screaming as if straight from hell itself supplied the answer. Barley snapped his head around in time to see the floating eyes bouncing toward them.

"Bruiser, untie me," Battle said.

Bruiser paused.

"Strength in numbers. Come on, Bruiser."

The big man capitulated. He hopped over to Battle and started fussing with the binds.

"Where's my sack?" Battle asked.

"Your what?"

"My sack. Did you take it?"

With a grunt, Bruiser broke the knot. Then he turned his attention to the rope around his ankles.

"Bruiser!"

"Yeah, yeah. Buster's got it."

Streaks of light from the windows strobed the beasts as they ran forward. Shop girls. All of them. The torn dresses, the scuffed shoes, the scabs on their exposed arms and legs, the open sores on their face, the open wounds in their bellies, all told the story of the horror Kelly had visited upon each one.

And they were almost on him.

"Bruiser!"

He finally loosened the knot on one leg, but it was too late. The first monster leaped, arms pinwheeling, mouth wide open. Bruiser stood to face his attacker, balled his fist and braced his body and then, a foot from his farthest reach, a two by four cut the air in front of him and smashed the monster in the face. Its head exploded like a squash, and its body flipped backwards and took out the next two creatures.

It was Barley.

"Don't just stand there, you idiots," he rasped. Three more attacked, and he pounded each one.

Bruiser, still stunned, watched, while Battle, one leg still tied to the chair, lurched for Buster and his sack of serum.

"You gonna help or what?" Barley snapped.

Bruiser looked at the door his boss had been trying to break down and saw the piles of lumber lying against the wall. He ran for it. Barley did his best against the onslaught. He bashed and pounded, he clobbered and walloped, and blood and brains splattered and spewed, but without help, they quickly overwhelmed him. He went down in a heap, screaming as they bit and clawed.

And then Bruiser was there. He was a large man. That much has been established. He was surprised at how light the monsters were. Nothing more than sacks of bones. He yanked them off, tossing them behind him in a flurry of torn cloth and bruised and broken limbs. But for every one he threw, two more appeared out of the gloom, and even though Barley, now covered in bites and gouges, regained his footing, they found themselves backing away toward the front of the building where a set of huge windows lined the wall.

Battle had finally liberated his sack of serum from Buster's prone form and he joined them, hopping over on the chair. Most of the vials had broken, but there were still plenty left. He had no time to think of how to use them before the monsters pushed forward. Wielding the sack like a cudgel, he smashed head after head after head. The vials broke, saturating the sack and flying into the eyes and mouths and open wounds of the beasts. Barley and Bruiser joined the fray, and before long they'd created a stack of bodies, some with their heads bashed in, some melting.

But the beasts just kept coming. Wave after wave poured out of the open gates in the back. The trio swung and beat and bashed, but no amount of killing would stop them. A beast leaped and tackled Barley. Another hit Bruiser. And another, and another, and another. Battle swung his sack over his head, but the serum had run out, and the bottles were all broken into little shards and bits of glass, and one of the things rushed him from the right and he punched it in the face and its skull cracked but it didn't let go and another one came at him from the left and he saw its teeth aiming for his eyes and he screamed and then he was on the sidewalk in front of the warehouse.

Ushi grabbed the monster and smashed a vial of serum into its chest. It fell to the ground, shaking and jerking.

Mikael stood next to him.

He was alive.

"But—" Battle began.

"Now is not the time, Mr. Battle," Mikael snapped. He disappeared, reappearing seconds later holding Buster. Then Bruiser. Then Barley.

The top level of the sweatshop exploded, and the beasts flew out into the air, some already burned to blackened husks, some on

465

fire. Many smashed headfirst into the ground, but some landed perfectly well, and the attack renewed.

And then Han was there, leading a carriage with a water tank on its back, pulled by a team of horses.

"Move!" he screamed.

They all scattered and he loosed the hose on the monsters. They went down en masse, shaking and jittering. Soon the streets were awash in piles of melting flesh. Battle, the chair still tied to his ankle, limped over to Han.

"Han. We've got to stop Kelly. He's going to sell—"

But Han ignored him and retreated to the carriage. He reached in and pulled something out that had been lying at his feet. It was Jeremiah Kelly. He'd been bound and gagged, and his eye blacked and his lips swollen.

"You mean this Kelly?"

The relief Battle felt was countered by his irritation with his friend.

"God's Bones, Han. Your timing is far too dramatic."

The ocean did not abide by unnatural laws. Time meant as much to the tides as politics did to the clouds. While there might be creatures who preferred to conduct their daily business with the cycle of the sun, the law of the seas was no law at all. Where man saw chaos, the anglers and the eels, the whales and sharks, the night grubbers and lantern maws, the vipers and the fangfish found comfort.

The people who lived and worked at City Harbor knew this. They accommodated the ocean. They had to. Adapt or don't. See how the former worked out. So when a ship arrived, no matter what the size and no matter what the hour, the harbor was ready to serve its captains and crew.

And the ships did come.

Some sailed in on sweet breezes. Some pounded in on the cusp of a cyclone. Some limped in, battered and broken. Early. Late.

The ships did come.

One such ship, a clipper hailing from Halifax, arrived late on the night of the day Battle and his friends (and enemies) narrowly escaped Kelly's monsters. Its flag, a white fleur-de-lisé on a blue field. Its crew, the common Canadian mix of white and brown, all speaking a strange patois.

After a brief dialog with the harbormaster, the captain returned to the ship to wait, not allowing any of the crew to disembark for any reason. They were there to receive a shipment from one Jeremiah Kelly. No, they did not require any services as they were to leave once the cargo was loaded and secured.

Night gave way to dawn, and soon it became apparent to the captain that their cargo was not going to arrive. They'd been jilted. Angry and cursing, he ordered the clipper to leave as the sun rose over the horizon, heading east for the second leg of its journey, first to Lisbon, then Tangier, and finally Marseille-Fos.

But twenty nautical miles after they cleared the blockade, the men forgot their french, and the Fleurdeliesé came down, readily replaced by the stars and bars. They would bribe the mercs holding the weakest part of the barricade south of Corpus Christi and return home without Kelly's weapon, what he promised would "turn the failing fortunes of the Confederacy irreversibly in the direction of victory." Once the captains reported on Kelly's treachery, a price was put on his head. Ten thousand graybacks for the man who brought him to justice alive. Five thousand for anyone who brought him in dead.

And the cargo itself? It was never discovered.

But somewhere out in the country, fifteen miles outside the city, the basement of a farmhouse had been packed with crate after crate of a very singular substance. The freight had been paid, the boxes stamped, the crates loaded onto pallets. But nobody ever came, so there they sat.

Years passed and yet they remained unclaimed. And the rain fell, and the snow fell. Little by little, the farmhouse succumbed to the elements. The roof crumbled and rotted and finally collapsed. Next came the floors, then the walls, and then the whole thing fell in, covering the crates in the basement with bricks and flooring and all manner of detritus. Eventually, the house became nothing more than a weedy depression in the ground. Nature prevailed, and the once tamed forest that surrounded the property approached and encroached and finally, definitively, took over.

Nearly one century later, a man in a big truck drove through a path cleared by bulldozers close to the site where the house once stood. Behind him, workers dug and graded and burrowed into the earth, creating a creek bed where one had not existed before.

At the end of the day, the man removed a wooden sign from his truck bed and set about driving it into the ground. When he was done, when it was firmly in place, he stood back to examine his work.

"Future site of Hollow Hills Creek," it read. "A Primary Feature of Hollow Hills, America's First Planned Community."

Satisfied, the man clapped his hands and went back to his truck and got in and drove away.

POP!

It was one of Bennet's favorite memories. His honeymoon. He and his wife, Melanie, twenty-three years old, fit and attractive, took a cruise, the first and only cruise of Bennet's life. Fifteen days, ocean to ocean, from Los Angeles to Miami. The ship would have been enough for him. They lounged by the pool, drank mixed drinks in the hot tub, made love in their cabin. Then there was the sport fishing in Cabo San Lucas, the open-air markets of Puerto Vallarta, the beaches of Acapulco, the marvel of the Panama Canal. To say it was an enchanting way to start their life together would be an understatement. Melanie was the love of his life. He'd never known a more intelligent woman. That she was funny and beautiful didn't hurt either. What did hurt was the fact that she was dead now five years. Breast cancer. It hollowed her out. Broke her down. Took her from him.

A poster had reminded him of their honeymoon. A simple scene of a couple riding a horse on the beach at sunset. He could smell the sunscreen, taste the coconut flavored rum, hear the pop! of the campaign bot—

"Can you roll up your sleeve, Mr. Gold?"

Bennet popped out of his memory with a dazed "huh?"

Oh, yeah. The doctor's office. Mary Washington Hospital. His hip. A nurse smiled at him.

"Your arm? I'd like to take your blood."

"Oh, right."

He rolled up his sleeve and turned his head. It was strange, he knew, for a man who served two tours in Afghanistan and another thirty years on the force to be squeamish around blood, but he was.

"Just a pinch here."

Bennet took a deep breath and closed his eyes, tried not to think about the needle.

"All done," the nurse said.

The door opened, and Doctor Wang bustled into the room. She used a tablet to bring the x-rays of his hip up on the monitor hanging on the wall.

"Well, Bennet, I'm afraid we have some bad news."

"I figured as much."

She pointed at the monitor.

"I put two x-rays up. This one is a normal hip. This one is yours. As you can see right

here, the normal space between the joints is . .
."

Bennet zoned out. He knew where this was going. He was forty-nine and he needed a hip replacement. Hip replacement! At seventy, maybe, but forty-nine? How could this be?

He already knew the answer.

First, it was in his family history. His father. His grandfather. Even his childhood dog, Ringo. That should have been enough to make him careful, but like anyone else his age, when the pain started two years before, the popping joints, the aching bones, first after he exercised, then while he exercised, then waking him up in the middle of the night, then pretty much every waking moment of the day, he ignored it.

He wasn't an old man! He was still virile! He played rec-league flag football for Christ's sake! Well, not anymore, not since last year. The day he quit playing he should have gone right to the doctor. If Melanie was still alive, she would have made him go well before that. But she wasn't alive, and instead of going to the doctor, he started self-medicating, first with booze, then with pain pills. And now here he was.

". . . can't rule out the probability of a second replacement down the line."

Bennet gradually came around to what Doctor Wang just said.

"Excuse me?"

She relaxed a little bit, a soft expression crossing her face. She opened her mouth to try and calm him down when something caught her attention at the set of double windows that overlooked the parking lot.

"What is that?" she said, and she stepped over to it. "Oh my god."

The room was filled with a blinding white light. Dr. Wang held her hands up and grimaced, as if doing so would somehow block it. The light consumed her, swallowed her up, and then all of the oxygen was sucked out of the air. Bennet's ears felt like they were filled with putty, the pressure in his head was unbearable, and then it released with a POP! and the window exploded, showering the room with shards of brick and wood and glass.

Bennet had been sitting on the examination table, which was against the wall and partially blocked from the windows by a storage unit. It saved his life. Though his head was pounding and his jeans were shredded at the ankles, he was otherwise okay. A howling wind swirled outside, as if the blast had been created by an army of banshees. Dr. Wang was on her back near the door. Straddling her was a clown.

Bennet blinked hard.

Yes.

A clown.

A clown had blasted through the windows. And it was . . . eating Dr. Wang's neck. Her eyes fixed on his, her mouth working, blood trickling out of one corner. All too late, Bennet remembered his gun. He was a detective, after all. His .9mm was in its holster on his hip. He unsnapped the strap, took it out, and yelled, "Hey!"

The clown whipped around, its face covered in blood. Other than that, it looked like a regular old clown. Bright, white makeup, red, rubber nose, orange, curly wig. Its jumper was dotted in primary colors, and it wore stupid, green, oversized shoes. But its teeth. He'd never seen so many in a human mouth before. And so sharp. Maybe that's what made him pause. Maybe it was the explosions still going off outside. Maybe it was the screams, the sirens, the crunching cars. Whatever the case, it gave the clown enough time to leap for him. Bennet pulled the trigger, aiming for the thing's face. He had no idea how many times he hit it, only that at one point its head exploded with a POP!, and its body fell flat at his feet. He grimaced as he stepped over it, holstering his gun.

"Dr. Wang!"

She was gurgling, blood pouring out of the wound on her neck. Bennet was about to struggle to his knees when she convulsed three times and went still.

"Damn," he muttered.

Something caught his attention from the direction of the window, and he limped over, careful not to get too close. Dr. Wang's examination room was on the top floor of the hospital, which itself was located on a hill to the north of the city. He could see all the way downtown from that vantage. And what he saw terrified him.

It was a brain.

A huge brain.

The mother of all brains.

Pink and fleshy and pulsating and sitting square in the middle of the city. Princess Anne Street, it looked like. It had taken out Foode and half the block around it, burrowing into the ground like a meteor. As he watched, the top of the brain dappled, seemed to suck into itself, and then it expelled three black pods, pop! pop! pop! They shot into the sky in three different directions. One headed for the college, another for Mayfield, and the third landed right in the hospital parking lot below, destroying whatever cars or trees or people happened to be in its path. It cracked open, black goo oozing, and six clowns jumped out, cackling and screaming and honking antique bicycle horns. A man ran by and one of the clowns took him down and attacked his neck.

"Jesus," Bennet said.

He turned around, and there stood Dr. Wang. Only she wasn't Dr. Wang anymore. She was a clown version of her old self. Bright white makeup. Orange wig. Red nose. She screamed and ran for him, revealing rows of sharp teeth and Bennet, who didn't have time to draw his gun, did the only thing he could think to do. He stepped aside and stuck out his foot. The Dr. Wang clown, whose feet were now large and green and silly looking, tripped and tumbled out of the window. He leaned over the edge to watch as it fell four stories and landed on an ambulance, crushing the roof.

Clowns crashed through the windshields of the cars trying to escape, ran down old ladies on walkers, tackled orderlies, security guards, ambulance drivers, women on crutches. And whoever they attacked, whoever's throats they tore out or eyes they gouged or stomachs they dismembered, turned into clowns, too.

Zombie clowns.

And they were fast.

Bennet drew his gun and checked the clip. He only had nine bullets left, maybe less. He jammed it back in and snapped up his cane. Judging from the chaos he heard on the other side of the examination room, he'd need all nine and more if he was going to make it out alive.

He closed his eyes.

Took a deep breath.

Come on, Bennet. On the count of three.

One.

Two.

Three.

The next ten minutes were a riot of terror. Bennet lurched out of the examination room, squinting in the smoke and flickering hallway lights. Doctors, patients, nurses, orderlies created an almost impenetrable stream. He stepped into a break and was carried swiftly forward, faster and faster, too fast for him to be able to keep up for long. The rooms he passed were no more than empty holes. He saw a clown crash through a window and land on a doctor. He saw a clown tearing out the stomach of an old man. The stream turned into a flood, and someone kicked his cane out from under him. His leg buckled and he fell flat on his face. Feet stepped on his head, his neck, kicked him in the ribs. He tried to push himself up off the ground, but every time he tried, he was just trampled back down again. A boot to the head made his vision go dark and then he was on his feet. A woman in a hospital gown stood in front of him, yelling, "Let's go!"

Another explosion rocked the building. Screams from all around. Bennet turned to see nothing but open space behind him and the jagged frame of rebar and lumber, sparking wires hanging like vines. The woman yanked on his arm and dragged him away. He tried to follow the crowd to the nearest exit but she yelled "No!" and jerked him down a different hallway. They passed a child crouched on the floor, covering her ears. Bennet scooped her up, crying out against the pain in his hip. They reached an intersection and the woman turned to say something to him when another explosion hit and the space where she was disappeared. Bennet turned and staggered away.

He hit hallways at random, left and right, right and left, looking for an exit, finally finding one at the end of a long passage. He hobbled forward, holding the weeping girl against his chest. A security guard backed into view at an intersection, firing his weapon. Two clowns jumped on him and took him down. Bennet paused, and when they didn't reappear, he pushed on. All he could see as he backed into the door were smears of blood on the tiles.

Another guard was just inside.

"Get out of here! Go! Go!"

Bennet hopped down as best as he could, trying to avoid using his right leg. He made it down to the third floor.

Subhuman cries.

Gunfire from above.

The stairs on the second landing had been blown away. He backed onto the second floor where a man yelled, "Tina!" and ripped the little girl out of his arms.

A crazed woman, mouth red with blood, hair frizzed out in an orange wig, jumped for him and he stopped short and she flew by and landed on a man wielding a scalpel. She bit his face. The man dropped the blade. Bennet scooped it up and stabbed her in the neck but it did nothing but spurt blood, so he grabbed the fire extinguisher off the wall and smashed her in the back of the skull. She hit the ground, and he bashed her head again and again until it exploded with a POP!

The man she attacked was convulsing. His face went bright white, his nose turned into a red circle, and he sat straight up and lunged for Bennet's bad leg. Bennet fell on his rear and it pulled itself onto him, gnashing its teeth. He hit it in the forehead with the fire extinguisher, but it kept coming. He hit it again, but it swatted the extinguisher away like it was nothing. It pulled itself up to his face, and Bennet grabbed it by the shoulders, straining, straining to push it off of him. He held its chin in his hand like a tee, like he was setting up a golf ball, and then someone actually hit the back of its head like it was a golf ball.

The monster grunted and reeled.

"Hold it higher!"

Bennet pressed up.

Another hit. Half the thing's head disappeared.

"One more!"

The final blow took the rest of the skull off, and the beast collapsed to one side, where its face hit the floor, and when it did, its head exploded with a pop! Bennet looked up to see who had helped him.

It was another clown.

A golf clown. It twirled its club, a sand wedge, and rested it on its shoulder.

"Don't worry, brother," it said. "Name's Zeek. I'm one of the good ones."

Those two tours in Afghanistan taught Bennet this about fear: it was not an elective. Not in war. He had suffered mortar attacks, IEDs, and all-out firefights, and those were frightening enough. But he'd also reconnoitered narrow alleys where the heads of the enemy (or was it just children?) popped over the rooftop ledges to throw rocks or water or grenades. He led patrols down open streets where every movement could be a sniper, or a suicide bomber, or a child playing with a ball.

He learned early on that bombs and explosions and gunfire were scary, but silence was worse. Silence slithered and sneaked, played with his senses. He'd seen men go mad with silence. When he got back from his second tour, he found his anxiety ramped up not during the action movies he and Melanie went to or even when a firetruck blared its horn as it sped past their rental on Stafford Avenue, but when he was alone on a quiet Sunday, sitting out on the screened-in back deck, reading a book, sipping coffee, a cool breeze rushing through the fall leaves. It welled up in him like a burst pipe, and suddenly he knew that someone was watching him through a scope, the reticle resting on his forehead, or that someone else was going to sprint around the corner screaming "Allahu Akbar," or that a child holding a cellphone was standing under his deck, thumb about to depress the call button.

That kind of fear, the fear of imminent death, was exactly what he felt sitting on the roof of the Rt. 1 Taco Bell. Because it was quiet. Nearly completely quiet. No sirens. No fighter jets. No helicopters. No gunfire. Not even a scream. Just the hollow emptiness of the wind, the stillness of death.

Zeek sat next to him, swinging his legs over the edge and eating a bean burrito. An entire feast sat next to him: chalupas, enchiladas, nachos, churros, tacos, taco salads.

"You hungry?"

"Not really."

"Listen, man. You need fuel. After a trauma like that, your body is drained."

"That's not food. It's salt and carbs."

"Beans aren't bad for you."

"Everything else in there is."

"C'mon, man. Just one taco."

"Why do you care so much?"

"Because I want to live, and if I'm going to live, I need help. You, too."

On the horizon, the Mother Brain belched out three more pods: Pop! Pop! Pop!

"What do you think that is, anyway?" Zeek asked.

"The pods hold the clowns."

"Yeah, but why?"

"It's the end of the world."

Zeek put his burrito on his lap and thought. A couple of stray clowns wandering around below noticed them sitting on the roof and ran for the building.

"Zeek's an interesting name."

"What? You were expecting D'Shawn or Malik?"

Bennet shrugged.

"Zeek's an interesting name for anybody."

"Alright. What's your name?"

"D'shawn," Bennet said. "No, Malik."

They looked at each other, wondering if they should laugh or fight. They chose the former.

"It's Bennet," Bennet said. He held out his hand and they shook. "And we're not going to just survive. We're going to kill that thing."

"The Mother Brain? How?"

"Help me up."

Zeek stood and offered his hand. Bennet swallowed a groan as he got to his feet. He pointed east toward the river.

"See that?"

"See what?"

"At the gas station."

A tanker was parked in the Valero lot, its doors open. Even from that distance, they could see the blood smears.

"A gas tanker?"

"Yep. We're going to run it into the Mother Brain."

"*Into* the Mother Brain?"

"We'll jump out before it hits."

"How do you know it's even full?"

"I don't. But I want to live, too, and the only way that's going to happen is if we kill the Mother Brain."

"You know this for sure?"

"No. But it's better than waiting to die on top of a Taco Bell."

A few more zombie clowns erupted out of the woods on the other side of the road, chasing a man in his boxers and wearing shirt with the words "Gas, Grass, or Ass: Nobody Rides For Free" on it. He fired a handgun wildly. None of the clowns were hit, but one of the windows of the Taco Bell shattered. The clowns jumped on him.

"Look, man," Zeek said. "That's the kind of thing that only happens in movies."

"Maybe. But I've seen a tanker explode before. It'll do the job."

"When?"

"I'm a cop. Twenty years."

"Oh. So you've seen all kinds of things blow up."

"In Afghanistan, yeah. But as a cop, just a gas tanker. Once."

"Huh."

Zeek looked across the lot at the tanker. He looked back at Bennet.

"Can you make that run with your bad hip?"

"Nope. But you can."

"Bullshit."

More zombie clowns, drawn by the gunfire, ran down Route 1.

"Zeek, my hip is a jigsaw puzzle right now. Even if the tanker was an automatic, I couldn't drive it."

"You want me to drive a gas tanker into the Mother Brain and hope it blows up."

"I said we'll jump."

"How do you know I can even drive stick?"

"Can you?"

"Yeah."

Pause.

The Mother Brain pulsed again, pop! pop! pop! The pods shot into the sky, north this time. Zeek marveled at them. He pondered the ocean of zombie clowns that had gathered beneath them. He finished his burrito, balled up the wrapper, and threw it at them.

"What you do say, Zeek?" Bennet asked.

SCENES FROM BUDDY COPS II: THE BUDDY COPENING. STARRING OLD MAN AND GOLF CLOWN
Scene 1: Titles Exist For A Reason

A Middle-Aged Detective jumps down off the roof of a Taco Bell onto the hood of a gas tanker. He cries out in pain, holding his hip. This is OLD MAN Zombie clowns surround the tanker. Some of them have been crushed against the building. Many more are still alive and active. They reach for OLD MAN. Sitting in the driver's seat of the cab is a man in clown makeup. He is wearing a Scottish golf outfit. His Scottish golf outfit is covered in blood. This is GOLF CLOWN.

GOLF CLOWN
Get in, man! Get in!

OLD MAN
(grimacing as he stands)
How!

GOLF CLOWN
(scoots across the cab and cranks the
window down.)
Hurry!

OLD MAN manages to climb onto the roof
of the cab, scoots around on his belly, and,
with quite a bit of pain, swings his legs in and
lands safely on the passenger seat.

OLD MAN
(grabbing GOLF CLOWN'S ARM)
Did they bite you!

GOLF CLOWN
We gotta get out of here!

OLD MAN
(not letting go)
I saw them take you down! Show me
your arm!

Golf Clown shows him his arm.

> OLD MAN
> And everything else!

> GOLF CLOWN
> No way, old man—

> OLD MAN
> Show me!

> GOLF CLOWN
> It's been over ten minutes. If I
> got bitten, I'd have changed by now.

OLD MAN holds a gun to GOLF CLOWN'S
HEAD.

> GOLF CLOWN
> Their noses!

> OLD MAN
> What?

> GOLF CLOWN
> I said their noses.

> OLD MAN

What are you talking about?

GOLF CLOWN
Put the gun down, and I'll tell you.

MOMENTS BEFORE . . .

Zeek ran track in college, but college was over twenty years before the end of the world. But form and muscle memory die hard, and from the beginning of his sprint from behind the cleaners to the tanker in the Valero lot, he is able to widen the distance between him and the pack twofold. But twenty years is twenty years, and those years, filled with parenthood and lack of sleep and poor eating and sodas and alcohol, not to mention a complete absence of dedicated athletic training, catches up with him almost immediately, and with only a fifth of a mile left to go, his lungs feel like they're going to burst, and his legs feel like rubber. He makes a mental note to do more cardio when he gets out of this. IF he gets out of this.

Behind him rages a pack of clowns. Zombie clowns. He'd hoped that maybe his outfit would have tricked them, but apparently they could tell the difference. Being chased by a pack of anything is terrifying enough.

Wolves. Bears. Spiders. Maybe not kittens. Or puppies. Or meerkats. Or bunnies. Or babies. Or guppies. Or guidance counselors. Or kittens.

But zombie clowns?

Yes. Terrifying.

The pure variety of clown in the pack behind him is impressive, if unnecessarily thorough: Whiteface, Auguste, Auguste Lite, Tramp, Rodeo, Ice Skating (those are the least effective, on land, at least), Magic, Juggling, Mimes (the worst), Cop, Baseball, Doctor, Nurse, Boxer (singing and dancing), Astronaut, Admiral, President, Dictator, Rodeo (barrel and bullfighter), Mudhead, Shriner, Grimaldi, Harlequin, Bozo, Dodo, Literary, Drunk, Meth-head. If there were such a thing as clown watchers in the way there are bird watchers nearby, they might have collectively, and simultaneously, orgasmed. But no matter the variety, their feet, rather than feet, are large, red, rubber appendages. It is just such an appendage that trips Zeek as he is about to turn on his final burst of speed, sending him flying face-first to the road. Before he can do more than roll over onto his back, they are upon him.

Their teeth are brown and sharp and plentiful, their claws black and mossy and . . .

also plentiful. A dozen mouths lower for the feeding, those stupid, red, bulbous noses shining on their ugly, pale faces, and Zeek, in a moment of levity, cannot help himself. He means only to rip the nose off the closest one, but in doing so, he squishes it in his hand and . . .

POP!

The thing's head explodes in a gush of blood.

The other clowns pause, suddenly uncertain. They share awkward looks. Zeek wastes no time. He strikes out with both hands, grabbing noses and squeezing.

POP! POP!

One lurches for his belly. He grabs its nose.

POP!

Two more go for his legs.

He kicks them in the face.

POP! POP!

When it is over, twelve headless clowns have collapsed on him. The thirteenth has stood up, horrified at the slaughter of his fellows at the hands of this supposedly weaker prey, and it turns to run away when, throwing a paranoid glance over its shoulder, it trips over its own gigantic feet and smashes face-first onto the ground.

POP!

                    OLD MAN
Seriously?

                    GOLF CLOWN
Straight up, man.

OLD MAN looks out the window. Zombie
clowns have begun to encircle the cab.

                    OLD MAN
I want to try it.

He looks at GOLF CLOWN

        You in?

                    GOLF CLOWN
Hell no!

OLD MAN throws the door open directly
into the face of an oncoming Auguste Lite,
hitting it in the nose.

POP!

He carefully lowers himself down. A Rodeo
Clown lurches for him from the right. He
grabs its nose and squeezes.

POP!

A Harlequin comes from the left. OLD MAN spins and his hip gives out. The Harlequin trips over his good leg and falls to its knees. OLD MAN grabs it by the nose.

POP!

One Minute Later . . .

OLD MAN struggles back into the cab. He is covered in gore.

>   OLD MAN
> That was fun. Horrifying, but fun.

>   GOLF CLOWN
> Whatever you say, man.

Scene Two: Shooting The Gauntlet

The tanker hops the curb onto Route 1, squashing a White Face and a Juggler. Over a dozen jump on the back as it hits the median and heads north for Princess Anne. The tanker muscles through cars stalled in the middle of the road.

OLD MAN
Careful!

GOLF CLOWN
How else am I supposed to do this?

The tanker careens right onto Princess Anne, shaking a few zombie clowns off like bugs. They pass Captain D's. A zombie clown smashes the passenger side window with its fist. It is fat and wearing a bloodied tuxedo. It breaks out into an aria.

OLD MAN
We got an Opera Clown!

He grabs its nose.

POP!

Another clown smashes into the windshield from above. It is wearing a beret and a neckerchief, a black and white, striped shirt, and black tights.

GOLF CLOWN

Mime!

The mime mimics drawing a large knife from an imaginary sheath and acts as if it as about to stab him. GOLF CLOWN squeezes its nose.

POP!

A shirtless clown wearing a full, white beard fires a Manlicher in the passenger side window. The driver's side window explodes in a hail of glass.

> OLD MAN
> Hemingway clown!

> HEMINGWAY CLOWN
> The tanker crashed down Princess Anne Street. Its sides were scraped, its wheels humming with smoke, and its headlights alive with hatred and power. The tanker did not know fear. The tanker did not know pain. It only knew piston and fury. It would not be stopped.

> OLD MAN
> Ugh.

He grabs its nose.

POP!

The Mother Brain looms closer, its fleshy folds glistening in the sun. The top dimples, its muscles contract, and then, in a squirt of fluid and gas, it belches more pods into the sky.
They pass Carls.
They pass Jack Brown's.
They pass Red Dragon.
The tanker is now carpeted in zombie clowns.
GOLF CLOWN veers left, scraping several off on Happy Endings. He smiles a crooked smile and jerks it back to the right.
But the tanker is unbalanced. It leans heavily as they go up the hill past Smythe's Cottage. It crashes into the porch of The Kenmore Inn, bounces back and screeches across the intersection, smashing into the iron fence of Fredericksburg Baptist.

OLD MAN & GOLF CLOWN
AAAAAAAAAAHHHHHHHH!

The Mother Brain pulses one block away.

Zombie clowns swarm the intersection at William St. A hipster zombie clown looks at its phone while smoking a clove cigarette outside Hyperion.

HIPSTER CLOWN

This is such a rip-off.
#everyzombiemovieever.

A horrible stench fills the cabin. They are fifty feet away. A wave of zombie clowns washes over the tanker. The cab uncouples from the payload. The payload strikes St. George's Episcopal and explodes in a ball of fire. The Mother Brain shrieks, its flesh browning. The cab, sliding on its side, crashes into the meat and disappears into its pulsing, pink folds.

~

Here are the three worst memories of Bennet's childhood:

1. When he was eight years old, he suffered a series of panic attacks. They always occurred at night, and because of this, he and his parents assumed they were night terrors. He would awake from a deep slumber, or half-wake, and run screaming through the house, flipping on lights, turning on appliances,

trampling across furniture, certain that something was chasing him, about to catch him, that imminent death was upon him. For two weeks this went on, and rather than abate, they grew in intensity. He began to hallucinate. Faces breathed out of the walls.

2. When he was ten, he and his friends made a ramp out of bricks and boards and set it up in the middle of the street to use as a bike jump. Each successful jump, successful being defined as "not crashing," compounded his bravado. With each pass, they peddled harder. With each pass, they shot higher and farther. Bennet hit his last jump with the speed, he felt, of a Valkyrie. The ER doctor said he'd never used so many staples on a single skull that wasn't the result of a TBI.

3. When he was twelve, his two best friends, brothers born twelve months apart, barricaded him in a room in their basement. There were no lights, no windows. The room was empty, and, in the dark, it felt cavernous. Bennet yelled at them to let him out, that it wasn't funny, but they only laughed. Then he heard that laughter recede as they retreated up the stairs. Then he heard the front door open and close. Then he didn't hear anything at all.

One hour later, their mother happened to come down into the basement and saw the couches, the chairs, and the shelves stacked up against the door. She heard his whimpering.

These memories and many more swirled around in Bennet's mind on an endless feedback loop. He felt the smack of the pavement on the back of his head. He screamed and ran, chased by invisible terrors. He wept, blind and senseless, in a vast, open void. It reduced him to nothing but the sum total of a lifetime of fear and bitterness. After what seemed to be an eternity, a voice shattered the trauma. It was pure and dreadful, beautiful and foul.

"Hello, my pet."

Bennet wanted to scream. The voice infiltrated every aspect of his consciousness. It was there at the moment he became aware. It was there in his childhood. It was there when he fell in love. It was there for the birth of his children. It knew him. Then it became him.

Through clenched teeth, he managed to say, "What are you?"

And the voice replied.

"What is the moon to the ocean? What is the sun to the earth? What is the wind to the lake? I. Am. Mother."

"What do you want? Why are you doing this?"

"Shh. Shh. Hush, my pet."

"I'm not your anything."

"But you can be. I will soothe your pain. I will sing to you. Feed you. Nourish you. You will be mine. You will live in paradise. See?"

Bennet's mind filled with images. The best moments of his life, the joy and elation distilled and flushed into his veins. They hit his belly, his bowels. It was like mainlining bliss.

A scene opened up before him. A valley teeming with life. Antelope ran in packs across grassy plains. Streams sparkled in the sunlight. Sheep grazed on hillsides. Buffalo roamed. A lake shone in the distance. And wandering throughout the valley was everyone he'd ever known and loved. His grandparents. His beloved Uncle Henry. His sister. His childhood friends. His high school classmates, girlfriends, lovers, college roommates. Some lounged by the stream or swam in the lake. Some stood around a barbecue eating burgers. Some played volleyball in the grass or stretched as a woman in leotards led them through a yoga class. "Bennet!" they cried. They turned and waved at him. "Bennet! Bennet's here!"

Paradise.

Then his wife was in front of him. Melanie. Lovely as ever, her long brown hair, her blue eyes. His heart. Oh, his heart.

"We love you, Bennet," she said. She reached for his hands, held them in her own. "I love you."

"I love you, too. I miss you."

"I'm here, my love. Now."

"I-I don't know—"

"Shh. Don't think. Look. Look at us. We're all here for you. This can be yours. Forever."

"It can?"

"All you have to do is let go. Let it all go."

"But how?"

"Surrender. Surrender to me."

He wanted to. He wanted to give up. It would be easier. The sun was so warm. The water so inviting. He could live here for eternity, playing with his friends, making love to his wife, sleeping under the perfect dome of the universe. And his hip! His hip no longer hurt! Astonished, he lifted his leg up and down, up and down. He laughed out loud. Melanie laughed with him.

"It doesn't hurt," he said.

"No. And it never will. You will never feel anything bad again."

She smiled, radiant, inviting, filled with the promise of love and sex, and he basked in it, taking in the lips he thought he'd never kiss again, the hair he'd never feel again, the nose he'd never . . . wait a minute.

Bennet frowned.

Her nose.

It looked . . . strange. Strangely shaped.

Melanie had a cute little turned-up nose. Delicate and beautiful. But now it was oddly rounded. Just at the tip. It hadn't been like that a few seconds before. The sky rippled and turned to static, like a bad signal on an old television. His friends froze in place. Juddered. And Melanie's nose it—

What!

Her left nostril popped out. Like, really popped out, and now that whole side of her nose was round and . . . and—

It did it again! Her right nostril this time! Now her nose was perfectly round.

Her smile turned into a leer, and she stood there staring at him like he was prey.

"Your nose," he said.

"Yes, my love?"

"Are you sick?"

"No. Of course not."

"But—"

"But what?"

"It's not skin-colored. It's—"

Oh. My. God. Ohmygod.

It was red. Her nose was red. Melanie wasn't Melanie. She was one of those things.

"Bennet?" she said.

It was not her voice. It was the voice of the Mother Brain.

A feral cocktail of fear and revulsion, sadness and confusion, surprise and rage, filled his belly. It made him sick. Because in that moment, he knew exactly what he had to do. Faster than he thought he was capable, Bennet reached out, grabbed his wife's increasingly bulbous nose, and squeezed.

Zeek bounced into Bennet's hospital room two months later. He had, wisely, chosen not to wear his clown outfit.

"Detective Gold! How's that new hip?"

Bennet was sitting up in bed, reading a novel one of the orderlies had given him. *Under the Skin*, by Michel Faber. He put it down on his lap, leaving it open to hold his place.

"Hurts less and less every day."

"Stand up yet?"

"Got rid of my bedpan yesterday. How did you get my room number?"

Though the Mother Brain had been destroyed and all of the zombie clowns with it, there were people in the world who, unlike Bennet, had succumbed to the Mother Brain's lies. They did not take kindly to the man who facilitated her end. Bennet found that he had to take precautions similar to celebrities and mob informants in order to stay safe.

"Man. I've been working at this place for years. I've got connections."

"I see you're not clowning for a living anymore."

"Uh-uh. Not for me. Not anymore. Not for anybody anymore. Besides, thanks to what we did, I've got some better offers."

"Oh, really?" Bennet said it with a drawl.

"Got myself a book deal."

"I didn't know you knew how to read."

"Haha, Detective. I'm serious. Six figures and a movie option. I'm going to meet Beyonce."

"Be-who?"

"Never mind. What about you, man? How's it feel?"

"How does what feel? My hip?"

"No. You're the Hero of Fredericksburg."

Bennet waved it off. He'd read the papers. He'd turned down every request for an interview, had no interest in playing a role. Still, the story of what he did got out.

"It's all over the internet. Bennet Gold Saved The World."

"Oh."

"Oh? That's it. You realize they're going to give you anything you want, right?"

"How do you think I got his hip?"

"No, I mean more than that. You're never going to have to worry about anything again. Any house you want. Any car. Any t.v. Any woman. It's awesome, isn't it?"

Bennet thought about the valley. He saw his friends laughing and playing in the grass. He saw the perfect blue sky. He saw his wife's beautiful face. All gone. All gone.

"Yeah," he said. "Awesome."

BONUS MATERIAL

BEST DOG I EVER HAD
Chapter 1 of *The Hive*

When most people think of an alien invasion, they think of the dumb movies Hollywood pumps out every summer. Robots and spacesuits. Lasers and spaceships. What they don't think of is the thing that dropped onto our neighbor Mr. Gomez's farm and smashed his barn to smithereens, along with his horses, his pigs, his goats, and probably about a zillion rats. We didn't see it happen, Daddy and me, but we felt it. It was seven o'clock on a Wednesday morning, and I was laid up with a broken leg on the couch, dozing in and out while I watched sitcom reruns on the TV. *Hogan's Heroes. Gilligan's Island. The Love Boat.*

The broken leg came courtesy of Ruth Grace Hogg, starting fullback for the Caroline Cavaliers' Varsity Girl's Field Hockey team. I played forward for the Spotsylvania Knights, and for good reason, too. I lived in Spotsy, for one, and I was fleet and fast and good with my stick. Unfortunately, I didn't weigh much more than a hundred pounds. Ruth Grace

Hogg tipped the scales at about a buck ninety. I had legs like a colt. She had arms like a gorilla's.

When she saw little old me cutting up her team, she knew what she was about. She ran up to me, cocked them big hairy arms of hers, and whacked my leg like it was a piñata. Two hours later I was laid up at home on the couch, two pins in my femur and forty mgs of Vicodin in my head.

"Ain't you going to do something about it, Daddy?"

Daddy was in the kitchen, sipping a cup of coffee.

"Like what?"

"I don't know. Complain to the school board. Call the president."

"I'll get on my personal line to him directly."

"It's rude to tease an invalid. Can't you talk to her parents?"

Daddy looked like someone had just asked him to solve a calculus problem with a fish.

"Why'd I want to do something like that?"

"Because I'm your daughter. And she broke my leg. On purpose."

Daddy chuckled and shook his head.

"'Manda, you know I love you, right?"

"I'm starting to question the depths of that love."

"Well I do. But let me ask you something. You do know how much Ruth Grace Hogg weighs, right?"

"Who don't? The whole county shakes when she gets out of bed in the morning."

"And you know how much you weigh, right?"

I waited a long time before I answered.

"Yeah."

"I couldn't be more proud of you. You had you a job and you didn't let nothing back you down. But you did try to run down someone nearly twice your size, and you lost. So let that be a lesson to you."

"I thought you said you were proud of me?"

"I am."

"So why're you telling me to back off the next time?"

"I didn't say that."

I ever tell you Daddy could be infuriating? I sighed, took a deep breath, and said, "You mind telling me what you are telling me, then?"

"Next time," he said. "Run faster."

So anyway, the invasion.

It was late summer, and school hadn't even started yet. The August heat and humidity weighed down on everything like a wet blanket. Our house was built in 1921, as

511

Daddy was fond of telling just about everybody who cared to listen. To him, that was an accomplishment. To me, it meant that nearly everything was broken or breaking down. The pipes froze every winter, the windows were like sieves, and in the summer we didn't have air conditioning. Oh, Daddy did his best. He planted a couple of recycled wheezing window units in the windows, kept them alive with a healthy application of duct tape and freon, but all they did was make a racket while blowing not-really-cold air a few feet into the house.

Daddy'd just come in from loading Sparkles up into his truck, Sparkles being an old dog of his he'd gotten stuffed. It was a sad day for the old girl. The years had been unkind, and she'd started to smell. Daddy brought her to his regular taxidermist to fix the issue, but she gave him some sorry news: old Sparkles was rotting.

"Well no shit, she's rotting," Daddy said. "She's been dead fifteen years."

Apparently pointing out the obvious didn't improve Sparkles' condition. It was finally time to lay her to rest, and Daddy was going to do it Spotsy style. He got himself ahold of a remote-controlled detonator and some explosives—cherry bombs and fertilizer and the like—and stuffed her full to the brim. The plan was simple. He and his friends were going to drive Sparkles out to the country, set her up in a field, get drunk, and blow her up.

Daddy showed me the detonator as if seeing it would make me want to go.

"You sure you don't want to come?"

"No thanks."

"Alright then."

He put it in his back pocket and went over to fill his thermos up with coffee. That's when I felt this horrible pressure build in the air. It pushed down on me, like the atmosphere itself had gone feral and decided to attack. I held my hands to my ears, but the pressure kept building and building. I opened my mouth to scream but couldn't hear anything at all. Then it released and I could hear again. A sonic boom thundered in the distance, and the house shook and rattled and nearly jumped off the foundation. I thought it was an earthquake. Or maybe Ruth Grace Hogg having a fit. I almost fell off the couch. Plates and cups clattered in the cabinets, and Daddy's ham radio fell over and cracked on the floor. Then it fell quiet and still. I pulled myself into sitting position.

"What the hell was that?"

Daddy was kind of squatting down, hands out, looking like he was waiting for another blast. His overalls were covered in coffee.

"I dunno. And don't say hell."

"You say it all the time."

The phone rang and I gasped. I could tell he wanted to chew me out, but something big had just happened, and when the phone rang after something big had just happened, you answer it.

"Aw hell," he said and snatched it off its cradle. "Yeah? Yeah, Gomez, I felt it."

He covered the mouthpiece and mouthed "It's Gomez" to me like I couldn't hear. Gomer Gomez. Our next-door neighbor. (Out here a next-door neighbor could live ten miles away.) I turned my attention back to the TV. We didn't have a remote. Not that I minded. We was lucky to even get a signal at all. I struggled off the couch and hopped over to change the channels. I was looking to see if any of the local news stations were making a special broadcast. Channel 4, nothing. Channel 7, nothing. Channel 9, nothing. Daddy kept jawing away in the kitchen.

"Calm down, Gomez. I can't understand a word you're . . . Uh-huh. Your whole barn? Uh-huh. You get a look at . . . no, I wouldn't go out there. It'd be best if you didn't. I can't,

I got 'Manda here and she's got a—" Gomez screamed something and Daddy pulled the phone away from his ear with a grimace. "Gomez? You there? Damn." And he hung up the phone.

"What's wrong with Mr. Gomez?"

"Says a spaceship landed on his barn."

Daddy went over to his gun safe and started dialing in the combination.

"Spaceship?"

"Uh-huh."

"Out here?"

"Uh-huh."

"Damn."

"Dammit, 'Manda."

"He say what it looks like?"

"Uh-huh."

"You mind telling me?"

"Said it looked like a big wasp's nest."

The gun safe unlocked with a click, and he pulled it open and started grabbing boxes of ammo. Then he took out his favorite Remington .30 .06 and slung it over his shoulder and put a couple of .357's in a bag.

"You gonna kill it?"

"Gonna try."

"Can I come?"

"You're gonna stay right here, young lady."

"Why?"

"Because you're all busted up. And if there really is a spaceship out there that looks like a wasp's nest, there ain't much you'll be able to do."

"I can shoot one of them .357's."

"I know."

"Aren't you the one who always said it's better to have a man on your six?"

"Yeah, I did say that."

Daddy was already putting on his jacket and hat. He was halfway out the door.

"You really think Mr. Gomez's gonna have yours?"

That made him stop. Daddy wasn't that much of a thinker. I don't mean he was dumb because he wasn't. I mean that when a decision needed to be made, he liked to make it fast. Just like that, he said, "If you can get out to the car before I leave, you can come with me."

Mr. Gomez's farm was down Brock Road a stretch, just past Todd's Tavern. Take a few turns back toward Locust Grove, a few back roads, and there it was. Fifty acres smack dab in the middle of Spotsylvania County Virginia, the northernmost southern county in the whole damn state.

Daddy turned up the long gravel drive that led to the house, sending rocks clattering in the wheel wells and dust clouding in our wake. I bounced around in the front seat like a baby in a bucket, hoping the rifle on the rack didn't accidentally go off. Or the .357's in the bag, for that matter.

"Slow down, Daddy! You wanna break my other leg?"

He didn't reply. He had a way about him when he got set on something. He called it 'Enthusiastic Designation.' I called it 'Acting Like A Jerk'. I knew better than to bring it up. He just got cranky if I did.

He ganked the wheel and skidded to the right, steering around the side of Gomez's worn out farmhouse. Gomez was the type who liked to keep all sorts of things in his yard. Old tires. Rusted out tractors. Landscape drags and farming tillers. Daddy slalomed through it all like he was an expert, tearing up the grass, finally slowing down when he made it to the pond a few hundred yards behind the house.

Mr. Gomez's barn was just off to the side. Or it used to be. Now it was scattered all over the field like it'd been blown to bits from the inside out. In its place was something that I don't even know how to begin to describe, but

I'll say this: Either Mr. Gomez'd never seen a wasp's nest in his life, or he was the stupidest man on God's green earth. The thing that landed on his barn was round and greenish-brown with spikes sticking out all over the surface. Looked more like a sweet-gum ball than a wasp's nest.

Steam or smoke or something poured off the top, and there was a crack at the bottom—an opening or a door or something—with a warm, orange light pulsing from deep inside and green stuff oozing out. And boy did it stink. Hit us full on even with the windows rolled up. I couldn't think of anything worse I'd ever smelled.

Daddy, in his usual way, summed it up nicely.

"Smells like roasted goat shit."

Mr. Gomez's neighbors were already standing in the field between the barn and the house. Mr. Sokolov and his boy, Vlad, and old Mrs. Freeman, who looked as spry as ever in her work jeans and red flannel. Mr. Gomez's sons, Gomez and Gomer, Jr, were in the middle of trying to restrain their mother who kept pulling away from them. Daddy pulled up to Mr. Sokolov's truck and put it in park.

"You stay here and watch Sparkles."

"Seriously?"

He got out without another word, leaving

his door open and the keys in the ignition. I ain't one for whining, and I'm sure he was just trying to protect me, but the day I'm compared to a stuffed dog and come out equal will be the day I can fly and shoot bullets out of my nose. I wrenched the passenger side door open, hopped out, and grabbed my crutches. It was hard going, but Daddy didn't raise no bleater, and I caught him just as he tipped his hat at Mr. Sokolov.

"Hey, Skip." (Mr. Sokolov's name was Viktor). "What's going on?"

"That thing lands on Gomez barn. Gomez, he's sucked inside."

"Sucked inside?"

"Sucked inside."

Mrs. Gomez, or should I say the Widow Mrs. Gomez, seen us, pulled herself free of her sons, and came galloping over.

"Bill! Bill, please! You've got to do something! That thing has my Gomez!"

She collapsed into Daddy's arms sobbing and carrying on, and I never saw Daddy so uncomfortable. He was not a man to show his emotions. I think they embarrassed him. And if he wasn't already embarrassed enough by his own emotions, he was damn well mortified by other people's. He patted Mrs.

Gomez on the back a few times and then peeled her off and held her at arm's length.

"Okay, Mrs. Gomez. I need to you calm down and tell me what happened."

She nodded and tried to get herself together, and after a few deep breaths, she was finally able to talk.

"Gomez went about bonkers when that thing fell on our barn. After he made a couple of phone calls, he jumped in his truck and went speeding on down here, tearing up the lawn and my peonies."

Her eyes wandered back to the house.

"I told him not to go, that this was an issue for the president, but he wouldn't listen. You know how crazy he gets about the government."

"Yes, ma'am, I do.""

"He wouldn't let me go with him, neither. Me or the boys. So we watched from the kitchen window. He drove his truck right up to that thing, got out with his hunting rifle, and started shooting."

"Don't look like he did much damage."

"None at all. And then as God as my witness, when he started to reload, that crack opened up, and a tentacle slithered out, wrapped him up, and dragged him in. I don't remember what happened after that. I was too busy screaming."

Daddy looked around at everyone, seeing if he could muster them up to do something, but they toed the ground and refused to meet his gaze. Mrs. Gomez worried the front of her dress, her face reddening when she realized that nobody was going to do anything.

"If you all ain't man enough to anything, I am!"

And she marched off across the field, her sons right behind her, calling out "Momma! Momma, wait!" I tell you what, Mrs. Gomez'd worked herself up into a state. She was screaming and yelling (what exactly she was saying, I couldn't tell) tearing at her hair, jamming her finger into the air. None of us moved a muscle. She was going to do what she was going to do, whether it was good for her or not.

Daddy said, "Y'all think we should call the president?"

Mrs. Freeman spat on the ground.

"I ain't too sure what Slick Willie'll be able to do about this."

The Gomez boys did their best to stop her. Gomer jumped on his momma's back and Gomez, Jr. latched onto her legs, and they all got to screaming and yelling and clapperclawing. It might've gone on like that forever, but I guess that spiky ball'd had enough because three tentacles shot out of it, wrapped around each of the surviving members of the Family Gomez, and started reeling them in. That seemed to be enough for Daddy.

"Aw hell," he said and marched right back to the truck. He grabbed the .30 .06 off the rack and the .357's out of his bag and started loading them. "Y'all bring yours?"

He need't have asked. Mrs. Freeman already had her shotgun out, Mr. Sokolov had a .30 .30, and Vlad'd gotten himself a machete for some reason.

Daddy, Mr. Sokolov, and Mrs. Freeman positioned themselves in a line facing the thing and started shooting. Bam! Bam! Bam! Bam! Round after round. Bullets thunked into the thing's meat, but other than a little more smoke and what looked like green syrup pouring out of its side, they did about as much harm as a squirrel chewing on an elephant.

When they were done, the air smelled like goat shit and gunpowder, but it didn't do a thing to stop the tentacles. All we could do was watch as Mrs. Gomez and her boys were sucked inside with a syrupy slurp. Daddy waited a tic before he made his final assessment of their work.

"Well, crap."

And that's when the tentacles shot out again. Four this time.

The first one grabbed Mr. Sokolov and heaved him off his feet. Another one grabbed Mrs. Freeman. The third whipped out and snatched Daddy around the waist. The last one tried to get Vlad, but he sliced it off at the tip with his machete. The tentacle went wild, spraying purple gunk all over him that burned and sizzled. Vlad fell to the ground, screaming. Daddy fixed his eyes on mine.

"'Manda," he said. "Sparkles."

Oh yeah.

Sparkles the stuffed dog. Stuffed with explosives.

I don't know if any of you ever tried to run on crutches, but it ain't like pulling a string out of a cat's ass. Hurts your armpits, too. So I dropped one and hopped back to the truck, jumped in, and turned the key. The old thing cranked to life and I slammed it into gear and stepped on the gas, aiming straight for the hive.

That old hive must've known something was up because it shot three more tentacles at me as I sped toward it. One crashed through the windshield. Another hit the grill. The third missed entirely, but swung back around and grabbed the truck by the rear bumper. It yanked sideways, and I realized I didn't even need to drive no more. The only thing I had to concentrate on was getting out before it pulled me into them slimy green and yellow guts.

I forced the driver's side door open, but one of the tentacles slammed it closed again. Another swung at me through the busted windshield and I threw myself onto the bench seat. It smashed the driver's side window and wrapped around the frame, breaking off hunks of metal. Purple ooze splattered onto the dashboard and started to eat through it. I scrambled across the seat for the passenger side door and managed to get it open, and right when I was going to dive out, praying I didn't break my neck when I landed, my broken leg exploded with pain.

It was another one of them tentacles. Damn thing'd wrapped itself around my cast and got to squeezing.

If breaking my leg was the most excruciating thing I'd ever felt, squeezing it when it was already broke ran a close second. The vision in the corners of my eyes went black and I felt like I was going to vomit. The thing yanked again, and I felt something give in my knee. I was in so much agony that I couldn't even think straight. Another squeeze, another yank. I slapped around for something, anything I could use as a weapon, and happened upon a nice, long, hunk of the metal frame.

My body was halfway out the door, and I could see the opening of the hive, pulsing and squelching as we drew near. With a scream, I sat up and stabbed that tentacle with that hunk of metal. It pulled back, ripping my cast off and sending me tumbling ass over elbows out of the truck. I flipped once and landed strange, and then I was laying on my back in Gomez's field. Next thing I heard was an explosion, and a ball of fire filled the air.

One week later, both me and Daddy were sitting on the couch eating ice cream and watching *M*A*S*H* reruns. His arm was wrapped tight to his chest and he was wearing a neck brace. He didn't like it very much, and I didn't blame him. August in Virginia was hot enough in shorts and a t-shirt without adding a neck brace. I kept catching him in the middle of taking it off, saying it "cramped his style."

"Daddy, you try to take that thing off again, I'm going to sprain your other neck."

"I don't know what that means, but message received."

My new cast was even bigger and thicker than the one before, and the itching drove me nuts, and since I wasn't allowed to take a shower, and since Daddy told me that under no circumstances was he going to give me a sponge bath, I was starting to get a little ripe. He would, though, spring for ice cream.

"I personally like me some praline myself," he said, scooping a spoonful into his mouth.

"Yuck."

I took a bite of mine, trusty, dusty Neapolitan, and watched the TV. Hawkeye and Trapper John was in the middle of fixing a prank on that old stick-in-the-mud Frank Burns again.

"Well, one thing's for certain," I said. "I'm glad that old stuffed dog's finally out of the house."

Daddy gave me a playful slap.

"Don't you talk about Sparkles like that. Sparkles saved the world. Best dog I ever had."

Thank you for reading Chapter One of *The Hive*.

THE HIVE

JAMES NOLL

When an alien hive lands in Spotsylvania County, VA, Amanda Jett and her daddy are thrust into a nightmare landscape filled with body snatchers, brain-cracking fungi, crypto-monsters, melonhead children, mad scientists, and the tentacle-wielding Hive itself.

The Jetts have their own allies to help them, though, including Dr. Huntington, a brilliant inventor with the tools and technology they need to fight back, and the mysterious Girl, whose powers may be what they require to defeat the invaders.

But the Hive is changing the climate to suit its needs, and time is running out, forcing Amanda and her friends to make one last desperate attempt to stop the hive forever.

Get your signed copy at jamesnoll.net

THE RABBIT

Chapter 1 of
The Rabbit, The Jaguar, & The Snake

Hey, how's it going?

Lemme tell you the story about the time I saved the world.

Looking around right now at the burned out buildings and the churned up streets and the bodies in the gutters, I know what you're thinking: "This is how you save the world?" So I guess my answer is that I don't really know. And I don't really care. I kind of look at it as something that happened to me, like jury duty or a colonoscopy. But hey, that's jumping ahead now, ain't it? Let's start from the start. And there ain't no better place to start with than my Ma and Pop.

Pop came to America from the old world before the Model T, if you can believe it. Met my dear old Ma on the boat on the way over, and even though I knew it wasn't the truth, I like to think that the whole thing was a whirlwind romance. Love on the high seas. A jealous suitor. Fist fight in first class, a triumphant right hook followed by a wedding on the main deck, with the ship's captain and the clear blue skies and the icebergs floating by. In reality, pop was a penniless Jew from Minsk, and ma, she wasn't no better off. Their getting together was probably more like a scrum and a moan behind a crate in steerage, a pauper's union at the neighborhood temple, and nine months later, me.

I grew up in the slums of the Bottom with about five million other street rats. Living in a place called the Bottom was exactly like what you'd think it'd be like living in a place called "the Bottom." The one room tenements, the baking hot summers, the midnight bum-rolls, the cholera, the TB, the dysentery. Ah, the golden years. Ma toiled long hours as a seamstress in a heat box deathtrap, and Pop worked a whole bunch of miserable jobs. He was a fish monger, a ditch digger, a stone-cutter. He buried gas lines. Dug subway tunnels. I don't know how he did it, but eventually the old codger saved enough money to buy his own business. A newsstand. Established himself as a true entrepreneur.

Me, however, I was free as a bird. Lived like a king. I hung out the usual gang of gutter punks. Skinny Pete. Squinty. Slappy. The Mangler and the Jew. We got up to all kinds of hi-jinx, me and them. Alley smokes. Heel hacks. Knife fights. But then Ma died in a factory fire, and Pop didn't know how to put up with me. Granted, I was a bit out of control, and short of drowning me in the river, there wasn't nothing he could do to keep me in check. Plus, he'd just got that newsstand off the ground, and he couldn't have a liability running around, that liability being me, so his only option was that free school them papists run.

And by that I mean Catholic School.

And Catholic School was Catholic School.

I know what you're thinking. You're thinking, "ain't you a Jew? Them papists don't let no Jews in Catholic School."

Well, you're right, you're right. But pop, he wasn't no dummy. About three months before he signed me up, we started attending mass. Every Sunday morning, every Sunday night. Pop got himself in thick with the priests, told them that he wasn't no religious type, that it was too late for him but that he didn't want his only son to go to Hell. Next thing I knew, they're swinging that censer all over the place and tracing the sign of the cross on my forehead with water. And just like that, I was a mackerel snapper, with all the privileges and blessings and hope of heaven.

He packed me off to Our Lady of the Bleeding Hands and Slit Throat that very fall, and then my education began in earnest. And boy oh boy did it suck. Sure I got me a nifty uniform and three squares a day, and oh yeah, they taught me how to read, rite, and rhythmatic, but I also got myself a hefty backhand whenever I done anything to offend anybody, which, given my natural constitution, equated to a considerable amount of backhanding. I'd always thought I was pretty clever, a real yuk yuk guy, you know? I even got The Mangler to laugh on occasion. In my opinion, my mouth was the best part about me, but them priests didn't seem to share my sentiments. (Well, they did and they didn't, but more on that in a sec.) They hit me so much their knuckles'd swell up just looking at me. Unfortunately the kind of behavior in which I specialized also drew a different kind of attention, the kind ain't nobody want, and from there my story went from pitch black to pitch blacker.

Satan black.

Ninth bolgia of Hell stuff.

I don't feel like going into all the details cause there ain't no point in grossing nobody out. The only thing you need to know is this: all the things that happened to poor kids with no resources in Catholic School happened to me. Pretty unconceivable a century later; run of the mill back then.

I got my revenge, though, right? Not after they fucked me up permanent, and not until I was much older, old enough for everybody who hurt me to forget about who I was and what they done, but revenge was got. I won't go into the particulars. That story's been told already anyhow. Some jerk wrote it up in some dumb book he published. *A Stick in the Eye* or . . . what's that? Oh, yeah. *A Knife in the* Back. Anyway, it's a good read. A real pot boiler. Seven short stories and a novel. You should check it out. Especially the one about me.

Go ahead.

I'll wait.

Okay, maybe we ain't got the time for that kind of thing right now. For those of you who don't want to, or who ain't got the time or the patience, or who can't read, think of it this way: That priest's head looked good up there on my wall, didn't it? Not as good as them two goombahs, dumbass Basilio and fat little Arko, but good enough for government work.

So look, enough with the exposition. Here's where the story really begins.

About a year after that, I was killing time at Pop's newsstand, selling the typical newsstand type stuff, like newspapers, and magazines, and chocolates, when The Widow Mrs. Feldman stuck her head out her window.

"Howzit," she said.

It was a slow day. The war'd been over for three years, and the twenties was roaring like a lion. After the morning rush, ain't nobody was interested in the good news, so I sat back and put my feet up on a stack of City Sentinels to read the science section.

"Fuck you, you old witch."

"Hey, language, language. Is that any way to talk to your elders?"

"No. But it's the way I talk to you."

She laughed that chuffy laugh of hers. Half phlegm, half soot: "Huh huh huh. Huh huh huh."

"Jesus," I said. "You inhale a smoke stack or something? You gonna be alright?"

"You're a funny one," she said. "Real wiseass. You get that from your pop or your ma?"

Ma'd been dead for centuries, but Pop, he kicked it only a few months before. Lasted pretty long, him. Ninety-five years. Not bad for a time when most people died at half that age. It's fantastic, actually, unless you consider how he died, because he died kind of shitty, if you ask me, with the cancer eating away at his lungs until there wasn't no lungs left. I was already irritated before she reminded me of all that, but now I was irritated considerable more. I took my feet off the papers and plonked them on the sidewalk.

"You need your attitude adjusted?"

She waved me off.

"You don't scare me. Mr. Feldman was the last one who tried and look at what happened to him. Plus," she nudged her chin at the old abandoned townhouse. "I know what you done over there. And I like it."

I gave the old place a glance. It was all blackened at the base from when them two idiots tried to burn it down, and the windows was still cracked and grinning at me, but it was still standing, proud and unbeaten. I returned my attention to the article I was reading.

"Oh yeah?"

"Yeah. You got style, kid. And I know you been thinking about expanding your services."

Now that one shocked me a little. How the fuck she did know about that? She wasn't wrong, but, well, after I finished "The Unholy Triumvirate," I ain't had no inclinations to carry on. I felt I'd done my duty, purged my demons. Lived along with the knowledge them fucks who did what they done to me and mine would never be able to do it to somebody else and theirs. Until recently.

I'd heard things about what was still going on at that school. Good old Ronnie Resnick told me about it, and let me tell you something, I was none too pleased. In fact, I was so unhappy that I was actually thinking about giving them a little taste of my scalpel and bonesaw, add a few more trophies to my wall. But that was as far as I got, just the thinking about it, and as far as I knew, thinking about a crime wasn't a crime. That wasn't the problem, though. The problem was that The Widow Mrs. Feldman knew about the crime I was only thinking about.

"You know fuck all about it," I said.

"About what?"

I stared at her over the top of my paper. She wouldn't look me in the eye. Looked everywhere but, mumbling and muttering to herself. Dead giveaway. Finally, I said, "You know fuck all about fuck all."

"You're a laugh riot. A gaggle of giggles. I don't know fuck all? You just told me everything I needed to know."

"Ah you're a crazy bitch," I said.

But she wouldn't let it go. Kept laughing that hoarse laugh. I won't lie to you. It pissed me off.

"The fuck you laughing at?" I snapped. She laughed harder. A little ball of energy swirled up in my chest. I tried to keep reading, but it wasn't no use, so I folded the paper and slapped it down on the stand. "Can I help you with something?"

"No, but I can help you with something."

"Not interested."

"No, really. Listen. You look in the mirror lately? You look good for a guy your age."

"Watch it, you old hag. I might be horny, but I ain't desperate."

"What are you? Thirty-three? Thirty-four? You don't look a day over twenty."

"Sorry, you're not my type."

"I heard that about you."

Sometimes a body just got to absorb the insult. That was one of them times.

She said, "I know you know what I'm talking about. I know you seen it, too. You're in your prime. You'll never look better. I'm just trying to help you out a little. Give you a boost." I pretended to read again. "Look. I'm on your side here. You wanna stop them fucks from doing what they do?"

Fine. Fuck it. She knew. How she knew what she knew, I don't know. But she knew. I put the paper down.

"Yeah," I said. "I do. I'm gonna kill every last one."

The Widow Mrs. Feldman nodded.

"That's what I thought. C'mere a second."

"Fuck that. I ain't going nowhere. You come here."

"Got a bad hip." Her cat jumped up on the sill next to her and arched its back against her shoulder. She pet it. "Hey there, Demon. You come out to say hello?" Demon meowed. The Widow Mrs. Feldman reached behind her and put a glass of something on her sill. "Demon made you something to drink."

I looked at it. It was tall and skinny and filled up with something green and goopy looking.

"I ain't drinking that."

"It's cool and fresh, and it's a hot day, no?"

"Yeah, but I ain't drinking that."

She seemed to take that in, studying me, reading me, but she finally shut up so I was able to get back to the news. Whoo boy, the world was in a ton of shit. The Great War really fucked things up good. Unemployment rising in Germany. Some asshole in Italy and his black shirts. The old lady started to hum a tune. I didn't notice it at first cause she sung it under her breath, but then it seeped into my head, into my bones. I'd heard me a lot of music in at that point in time. "I Ain't Got

Nobody." "Ain't We Got Fun?" "I Ain't Nobody's Darling." Streets was positively filled with that new jungle bunny shit. But this was something different, eerie and earthy, like the trees and the rocks and the wind all got together to start a band. It was the most beautiful thing I ever heard, and I felt transported by it back to a time when there wasn't no bricks or buildings, no assholes or asphalt, just the sky and the ground and the oceans and the rivers, and the next thing I knew, I felt something rub my calf, and when I looked down I seen Demon winding his way around my ankles. I got dizzy. And out of the haze came The Widow Mrs. Feldman's voice.

"You sure you don't want that drink?" she said.

And you know what? I did get a thirsty right then. Parched, even.

Years passed, and it was around that time that I started noticing something different about me. My old friends, Slappy and the like, they got older. Fatter. Sicker. Slappy caught a case of the Nationalism, enlisted in the Army, and ended up a corpsesickle when he tried to fight the Bolsheviks in Siberia during the Russian Civil War. The Mangler was too smart to sign up for any government sham but dumb enough to get himself killed in a drunken pub brawl. I heard Squinty went blind, which anybody with half a brain could of predicted, and then I never seen him again. The Jew was the only one who made it out somewhat prosperous. Owned himself a pawn shop near the Industrial District. I seen him every now and then, always alone, muttering to himself, stooped over and worn, like the trials of life weighed on his shoulders so heavy that he couldn't take it no more.

But me?

I stayed the same. Like my body got to the ripe old age of twenty two and said, "Fuck it. I'm done." And that's when I knew. I knew what I was going to do. I was going to follow through on all them thoughts I'd been thinking.

Look, I got a lot of regrets in my life. Who don't? I regret not running away from them fucks at the Our Lady of the Bleeding Hands and Slit Throat before they got to me. I regret not taking on extra work somewhere so Ma didn't have to work in that heat box deathtrap. But one thing I don't regret is drinking the potion old Mrs. Feldman made me that afternoon. Changed my life, it did. Or at least I think it did. Who knows? All I know is that once I realized what was what, all them ideas that'd been swirling around in my head solidified, and the guy I was after wasn't the guy I was before, and everything I'd ever known, the fear, the pain, the helplessness, vanished, replaced forever with an anger that nearly consumed me.

So I expanded my services. And by that I mean killing any fucks what fucked with the well-being of a helpless kid. This took some creativity. You know, before you start in on the judging, you should remember who I was going after. I wasn't duping no co-eds into helping me carry my groceries up a flight of steps. I wasn't leaping out at grandma from alley corners. I went after the kiddie diddlers, the pedo-pokers. Remember what I told that priest?

"I wish I had someone like me around when I was a kid."

Well, I took that serious, and for a while, it worked out pretty well. I find you been diddling kiddies, I hunted you down and slit your throat. Worked out well for about five or six years, but unfortunately, no matter how skilled or careful or sneaky or creepy, there comes a time in every great killer's career when he ends up caught. Well, not every one, because has anybody ever heard of Jack the Ripper?

So, yeah, this was some time around '51? '52? I got wind of a local cop whose tastes ran unconscionable. First some kids started spreading rumors. Scumbag took Jerry Blumczech for a ride in his cruiser. Gave Arnold Gold an option in an alley. Then this new cop showed up, lo and behold, fresh out of nowhere, young guy, slicked-back hair, square jaw, and a bit swarthy in the palms if you know what I mean. I seen him talking with the kids on my street, and then he's walking them to school, buying them ice creams. Classic profile. I also noticed that little Robby Resnick—Ronnie Resnick's grandson—wouldn't go near the guy, avoided him at all costs, ran across the street when he offered him a chocolate, took the long way to school. Once I seen that . . . there ain't no words for it. I felt an anger I ain't never felt before, and not for me, but for that poor kid. I didn't save Ronnie Resnick's ass from a priest way back when just to have his grandson get his plowed by no cop.

If only I'd known.

Them kids was paid to spread them rumors.

Robby was paid to act like he was afraid of the jerk.

Blumczech never took no cop car pleasure

cruise.

Gold remained just as pure as his name.

And I fell into it like the sucker I was.

One night, returning home drunk from a date with one of The Widow Mrs. Feldman's bottles, an opportunity presented itself. I seen that sonofabitch pedophile cop walking across the street a block in front of me, and the dark twirlies descended. I didn't normally snatch nobody on the spur of the moment, and I definitely didn't do it when I'd been drinking, but up until that point I'd enjoyed a string of successes and I let it go to my head. Isn't that always the case with people like me? They call it a cycle or something; we plan and we stalk and we kill and we drink to forget it, even if we're not supposed to be bothered by it, and then we plan and we stalk and we kill again, a little sloppier this time, and a lot sloppier the next time, and worse and worse and then you're spiraling out of control like an idiot. So yeah. Pedocop spotted. Dark twirlies descended. I don't remember what happened after that. One second I was walking behind the guy, the next I'm surrounded by a bunch of dicks screaming at me to hold up my hands, goddammit or they'll shoot.

"Alright, alright," I said, and did what I was told.

Unfortunately for me, my hands was covered with gore. So was my face. And my chest. And them cops is shining the lights in my eyes and I can't tell if it's real or fake, can't see nothing, really, except them lights, and suddenly I realized I was straddling somebody, and when I looked down I seen a busted open chest cavity between my legs.

"Oh shit," I said.

"Oh shit's right," someone said, and slugged me solid right in the temple.

What'd they do? What do you think they done? They dragged my ass to the station and worked me over with a rubber hose. Ripped out my adenoids. Showered me with the old lead sprinkler. They could have saved their breath. I had no intention of lying. I wanted them fuckers to know what I done. Maybe they'd see the light. Maybe they'd understand that I was actually trying to help them out. So that's why when the beatings stopped and my face had time to unswell, and they hauled me into a little room with a bright light overhead and a two-way mirror (you seen TV), and the one cop was breathing down my neck and the other acting all official and polite, and they asked me "Did you fucking do this shit?" I said, "Yeah, I fucking did that shit" and that was that.

I don't think the cops expected me to do that, kill their boy so soon. I think they thought they were going to do some serious investigating, whip up the media, maybe fabricate an event, something they could use during an election year. They certainly didn't think any of theirs was going to die, and if they did, they didn't think it'd be as unpleasant as the way I made it. The guilt must have been phenomenal. The one I killed was fresh out of the academy. Top of his class. Asshole tighter than a corncob. True blue, him, and his dumbass superiors set him up to be gutted like an animal.

I seen the realization dawn on them right then and there in the interrogation room. Their eyes went dead, and they broke out another round of rubber hoses and wooden clubs and brass knuckles and beat the ever-loving shit out of me, punched my half-swole eyes until they was fully swole, pummeled my bread-basket until it was mush. When it was all done and I wasn't nothing more than a bloody pulp, they drug me down to the deepest, darkest, dankest part of the jailhouse, threw me in the moldiest cell, slammed the door, cut out the lights, and marched off, slapping each other on the back and giving each other hand jobs. Okay, maybe they wasn't giving each other hand jobs, but they was jerking each other off. I'd like to say I took it all professional, but I was scared out of my mind. I soiled myself silly. Them fuckers threw away the key. I was gonna die down there. I curled up on the thin mattress in the corner and cried myself to sleep.

The main think I had was "what happened?" Why didn't they parade me around in shackles? Publish my picture in the newspapers? Slap me in the chair and let me do the electric jiggle on live television? I'll tell you why. Because things didn't turn out the way they planned. Because I didn't do it the way they wanted me to. Because I didn't follow the rules, didn't fit into a box, and that makes normals itch, and no matter what anybody tells you, no matter how many times they say "live your dreams and be an original," they don't mean it true. Sure, live your dreams. Sure, be an original. But don't do nothing too dreamy or original or you'll freak us the fuck out and we'll throw you in the dungeon.

And that's all it was, them sticking me in that cell. Fear. Pure fear. I educated them on the limits of all that freedom they said they loved so much, and all the sudden they started to think maybe too much of it wasn't such a good idea, that were was people like me who took them serious, took them at their word, who didn't give a fuck. That scared the crap out of them more than anything else, because where there was one dumb enough or sloppy enough to get caught doing the kinds of things I done, there were probably a hundred more waiting in the wings, just itching to cut and slash and slaughter, and once they seen what the people in charge had in store for them, who do you think they'd be coming for?

Well that wouldn't do.

That wouldn't do at all.

Fortunately, there was another group of people that'd took notice of my talents. Powerful people. People like me. Violent, ageless. Better than that, they were from the Neighborhood. Not the neighborhood, the Neighborhood. There's a difference. What's the differ . . . ? Just give me a minute. You'll see.

One morning after breakfast (a rotten orange and moldy bread) I got a knock on my cell all polite like, like I had a choice not to answer.

"Yeah?" I croaked.

The voice on the other side sounded like the streets. Asphalt and brick. Dumpsters in alleys.

"That you?"

I worked my jaw and it clicked.

"Yeah it's me."

"Lemme in."

"What do you mean, 'lemme in'? I'm in here. You're out there."

"No. You're in there, and I'm out here."

"Six to one and go fuck yourself." A pause. "Please."

Another pause. Then the guy said, "You gonna let me in or what?"

Seeing as I'd just spent the last few weeks getting my adenoids ripped out, I really didn't feel like screwing around, you know?

"Remember what I said before about 'go fuck yourself'?"

He laughed. Can you believe that shit? Laughed.

"That's a good one," he said. "Good to maintain a sense of humor. But you know what? You ain't got no manners."

"I got plenty manners. For example, I said, 'Go fuck yourself,' then I added 'please'."

The silence on the other side of the door hung thick in the air. A mausoleum at midnight.

He said, "Maybe I'll come back another time."

His footsteps clopped away down the hall.

"Hey, I can be good!" I cried. "You come in here and I'll give you a shot of my bologna, how about that!" I couldn't stop laughing. "Oh sure, I got some cheese to go with it, too. And a little grease for extra flavor!"

After that, nobody came to visit no more. They stopped everything, the beatings, the food, everything. The former was a relief, the latter, a problem. I got creative. You ever eat a spider? It's not as traumatic as people think. I mean, sure, you gotta, you know, actually eat a spider, but then the stomach acid burns it to bits and you're ready for more. I became quite the arachnid connoisseur. Never reached Renfield status, but after ten days, twelve days, thirty days—who the fuck knew—I decided that, yeah, there really wasn't going to be a trial, and, sure, there really wasn't going to be no electric chair, neither, but the cell? The cell was my sentence. Twelve feet by twelve feet of eternal punishment. Four water-stained walls, a gray, concrete slab, a metal bed bolted into the wall, and that slate iron door.

So I ate spiders.

And flies. And silverfish. And cockroaches. And ants. And anything else that showed up. Catching a rat was like Christmas dinner.

Years passed, I guess. I stopped keeping track. Toward the end there, though, I couldn't really tell what was what no more. I can't remember when I started seeing things, but I started seeing things. Entire cities demolished by a ball of fire. Houses swallowed by earthquakes. Children snatched from porches. At first, I knew it wasn't real, then I thought it might be real, then I wasn't sure no more, and at a certain point, it didn't matter. There it was, and I was seeing it, so it was real.

And then one day the guy came back.

I was standing on my bed trying to coax a roach into my cupped hand when the knock came at the door again. I eyeballed it. Thought for a second. Almost had the fucker. Just. One. More. Second.

Another knock came and I said, "Just a minute."

The third knock came harder, and my hand shifted and the roach scurried up and away into a crack in the mortar and I pounded the cinderblock with my fist, crying "Motherfucker!" I turned my anger at the door. "You sonofabitch! You just cost me my lunch!"

"Tsk tsk," the guy said. "I see we haven't learned our manners yet, have we?"

I stared at that friggin door a long, long time. Sometimes when things started talking to me, if I stared at them long enough without saying nothing, they went away. So I stood there kind of hunched, my hands held up like I was about to pounce, my stringy hair covering my eyes. What was left of my prison uniform hung in tatters off my shoulders, and I didn't have no hips left, so I had to make a belt out of a strip of one of the pant legs to keep them from falling off. Not that it mattered. When the guy didn't speak again, I relaxed.

Phew, I thought. *He wasn't rea—*

"Hello?" he called. "You still there?"

"Oh," I said. "It's you."

He snickered.

"Yeah. It's me. You want to let me in now?"

"We gonna have this conversation again?" I sat down on my metal bed.

"I guess we are. So what's it gonna be?"

"Let's see. How's it go again? You want me to let you in, but you're out there and I'm in here."

"Noooo . . ."

"Yeah, yeah, I know. I'm in here and you're out there. Still don't change nothing."

"I don't begrudge you your bitterness."

"Bitterness? Bitterness? You got any idea how long I been down here? Because I don't.

You should get a look at me. I'm a ghost. A fucking wraith. And all for what? Getting rid of the scum who did what they done to them poor kids? I was helping them out! And they locked me away!"

There was a long pause after that, and ice started to form in my belly. Did I scare him off? Right when I was about to plead with whoever it was not to go, he said, "You mind I can ask you a question?"

Oh thank fuck.

"Go ahead."

"You ever wonder if there was other people out there like you?"

I thought for a minute.

"Like scraggly macs who's been thrown in a hole until the sun explodes?"

"I think you know what I mean."

I took a deep breath.

"Yeah," I said. "The thought did cross my mind from time to time."

"That's good. That's real good. So you wanna let me in or what?"

"I can't," I whispered.

"What's that?"

"I said I can't!"

"Oh yes you can. Yes you can. All you go to do is stand up and open the door."

"But it's locked! They locked me up! They threw me down here and melted the key!"

"So you won't do it?"

"The door. Is. LOCKED!"

"Is it? You ever try opening it?"

The fuck was he talking about? Of course I'd tried opening it. I hung on the handle until my fingers broke, kicked it until my toes bled. Or maybe not. Who knew. One second oozed into the next down there. I could cup my hands against the wall for hours, waiting for a beetle to crawl into it, or lick at the water trail until my jaw ached, and I wouldn't know if it was the next day or the next week.

"I dunno," I said. "Maybe I haven't."

"Well, why don't you give it a shot? If it opens, great. If it don't, well, I ain't like you'd be any more disappointed than you already is."

That was some hot logic right there. Couldn't even start to think of an argument against it, so I said, "Okay."

I stood up shaky and shuffled toward it, and the whole time I'm thinking, "It's a joke. The fucking fuck is fucking with me." I knew that when I grabbed it, I'd feel the metal in my fingers, the same icy handle that I'd been yanking on for years (or hadn't been), and once again I'd push on it, and once again it'd

555

creak and whine, and once again it wouldn't open. And then that son of a bitch on the other side would laugh and laugh, and I'd scream until my voice gave out.

Well. No time like the present, right?

I put my hand on the handle.

I pushed down.

You can imagine my surprise when, with a rusty squeal, the frigging door swung in at me.

Thank you for reading Chapter One of *The Rabbit, The Jaguar, & The Snake.*

An epic tale of adventure and survival, *The Rabbit, The Jaguar, & The Snake* follows the story of Bonesaw, a hood from the early 20th Century, Wheeler, a city detective from 2021, and Coatl, the last remaining general of a primitive, jungle empire.

Bonesaw is kidnapped by the Brotherhood, a mysterious clan whose members never age and never get sick. They give him a choice: either compete in The Gauntlet (Golgotha, Hell, and The Battle Royale), or they'll kill him. Unfortunately, the contest is designed to produce maximum body count, and even if he can make it out alive, he might not like what they have in store for him afterward.

After surviving an attack from an otherworldly beast, Detective Katherine Wheeler investigates a string of murders with similar, horrifying details: each victim was killed by something that erupted from inside their bodies. As the corpses pile up, she realizes that an invasion is underway, one that could wipe out mankind.

Finally, Coatl faces his most dangerous foe yet: the monstrous tecuani. When they overrun the last stronghold in the empire, he realizes the world has one last hope for survival: Ka-Bata and his army. To reach him, Coatl must travel hundreds of miles through the jungle, a journey treacherous enough without the tecuani larva growing in his leg.

Separated by time and space, these three unlikely allies, The Rabbit, The Jaguar, and The Snake, must find a way to join forces. If they can, the human race has a chance to survive. If they can't, it is doomed.

Get your signed copy at jamesnoll.net

A NOTE FROM MILO

Hey, uh, hi. Milo here.

I'm not really sure why the author asked me to do this, but, uh, well, so he kinda needs reviews of his work? And he'd, like, really appreciate it if you left an honest review on wherever you leave reviews or whatever. Even if you don't like it.

So, like, yeah. That'd be great, I guess. For him. Uh, thanks.

ABOUT THE AUTHOR

James Noll is a freelance writer, an educator, a musician, and a novelist from Fredericksburg, VA. He's published five other books: The Mad Tales Trilogy: *A Knife in the Back, You Will Be Safe Here,* and *Burn All The Bodies,* the first book in The Bonesaw Trilogy: *The Rabbit, The Jaguar, & The Snake,* and *The Hive,* a serialized novel. *The Wounded, The Sick, and The Dead* is his second collection of short stories. It consists of the stories and two novellettes published with Seasons 1-3 of *The Hive* plus three new short stories and a novella.

Check out his work at www.jamesnoll.net

www.ingramcontent.com/pod-product-compliance
Lightning Source LLC
Chambersburg PA
CBHW020243030726
47499CB00001B/36